P9-CCJ-959

BALL PEEN HAMMER

USA Today and International bestselling author

Lauren Rowe

Ball Peen Hammer Copyright © 2016 by Lauren Rowe

Published by SoCoRo Publishing
Layout by www.formatting4U.com
Photography: Blue Photo NYC.
Cover model: Bryan Benisvy.
Cover design © Sarah Hansen, Okay Creations LLC

All rights reserved. No part of this book may be reproduced or transmitted in any form without written permission from the publisher, except by reviewers who may quote brief excerpts in connection with a review.

Prologue

He bends over the woman's back, grabs a fistful of her dark hair, and thrusts into her one last time, his eyes searing holes into my flesh.

And that's it. I'm gone. Put a fork in me. I'm done.

I've got to have him.

I don't care what I said last night. And I certainly don't care about his stupid brother. In fact, I don't care about anything or anyone except *me* and what I want.

And what I want is him.

I want to kiss him. And have sex with him. And then do it again. I want to touch and kiss and lick and suck every inch of that insane body of his, and then do it again. And I want him to touch me, every inch of me, inside and out, all the way inside the deepest, most secret places of my body, and make me come again and again.

No matter what we said to each other last night, or how my heart's inevitably going to shatter when the pleasure's all gone and there's nothing left but pain, in this moment, I want him like I've never wanted another man.

And, by God, I'm going to get him.

Right freakin' now.

Chapter 1
Maddy

My phone buzzes with an incoming call and I peel my eyes off the video I'm editing to see who's calling. It's my big sister, Hannah—the one person in the world I'll always pick up for, no matter what I'm doing.

"Hey, Banana," I say, answering the call.

"Hey, hon. Whatcha doin'?"

"Nothing much—just, you know, smokin' crack, having sex with an underwear model—the usual Friday night stuff. And that's just a warm-up for tomorrow night when I'll be mainlining black tar heroin and hosting a gangbang."

"You're editing another wedding video, I presume?"

"Yeah. The bride from last weekend was hoping to show her grandma the finished video at Granny's Ninetieth Birthday Bash on Sunday. Apparently, her grandmother was too frail to travel to Seattle for the wedding, so I've been working 'round the clock to get it done in time for her."

"You're such a sweetheart, Maddy."

"Not at all. Rush-editing a wedding video on a Friday night is my idea of fun, believe it or not. Maybe not *quite* as thrilling as hosting a gangbang, but it's a close second."

"Meh. Gangbangs are totally overrated. After a couple dozen of 'em, the novelty wears off."

"Good to know."

"So, hey, procrastinator, I'm calling to find out if you bought your plane ticket yet?"

"Nope, still holding out hope you'll be able to snag me a parking spot in your building. Wishful thinking, I know."

3

"Or maybe *not* wishful thinking..." Hannah says, her tone spiking with excitement. "Get your oil changed and your tires rotated, sissy—you're gonna be driving your car to L.A., after all."

I let out an excited howl. "Really? Oh my God!" This news is a godsend. It means I'll be able to shoot weddings on weekends during the upcoming school year and make some much-needed extra cash. "Thank you so much, Hannah!"

"You're welcome."

"How the heck did you do it?"

"Sister magic."

"But wait, Hannah." My stomach clenches with sudden wariness. Hannah once told me people were renting out spots in her building for, like, four hundred bucks a month, thanks to the proximity of her building to campus. "If this spot is gonna cost me more than, say, fifty bucks a month, I can't swing it," I say. "Tuition for the first trimester wiped me out, and I still gotta buy books when I get to school."

"No, no, no. This parking spot don't cost a thing, baby, just like J.Lo and her love." Hannah belts out the chorus of Jennifer Lopez's song "Love Don't Cost a Thing" at the top of her lungs, replacing the word "love" with "parking spot."

"Yeow," I say, pulling the phone from my ear. "You almost burst my eardrum there, babe. Warn me next time before you break into spontaneous J.Lo, please."

"Okay, warning: I'm about to burst into spontaneous J.Lo again." She promptly bursts into an enthusiastic mash-up of "Jenny on the Block," "Let's Get Loud," and "Waiting for Tonight."

I can't help but giggle. There's no one like my sister.

"Okay, I'm done J.Lo-ing for now," Hannah says, exhaling. "You were saying?"

"Be serious for a minute, Banana. How much is this spot gonna set me back? We both know, thanks to observing our dear, hapless mother our entire lives, absolutely *nothing* comes for free, not even J.Lo's love. Actually, come to think of it, Ben Affleck has gone on record to say the 'Bennifer' era was the lowest point of his life, so I'm sure he'd say quite emphatically that Jenny's love does, in fact, cost 'a thing.' He might even say it cost him his very soul."

Hannah scoffs. "Screw Ben. He can't blame his tortured soul on

Jenny from the Block. If the mighty Jennifer Garner couldn't fix that broken-ass man, then he's obviously not fixable."

"Hannah, *please* be serious. If you're planning to pay for the spot, I can't let you do that—you're already gonna let me live with you rent-free."

"I'm not paying for the spot."

"Well, then, did Henn finagle some kind of favor from Reed? Because I don't feel comfortable letting Henn—"

"*Listen to me, Linda*," Hannah says, cutting me off. It's a reference to a viral video Hannah's become obsessed with recently in which a precocious little boy repeatedly calls his mother by her first name (Linda) and commands her to "listen to him." "This parking spot is a gift from the universe, simple as that—completely free. Well, it won't cost you any *money*, that is—nothing's ever *completely* free."

"Ha! I knew it. You sold your little sister into sexual slavery, didn't you?"

"Well, of course. How else could I get you a parking spot mere blocks from campus for nothing out of pocket? Besides, you won't mind your sexual servitude when you see the guy who's giving you his spot—in fact, I'm pretty sure you'll thank me."

"Ooooooh. You've got my attention, Linda. Is he hot?"

"As *hell*."

"But is he *my* idea of hot or yours? Because your idea of hot is some dork in a black cape, playing Magic, The Gathering."

"Not Magic, The Gathering. I'm all about World of Warcraft these days."

"Oh my God, Hannah. You're hopeless."

My sister giggles. "Trust me, Mr. Parking Spot is *everyone's* idea of hot. Mine, yours, J.Lo's, Mom's—well, okay, not Mom's. He's not a total *loser*."

We both snicker.

"Tell me more about Mr. Parking Spot," I say. "I must admit, I'm skeptical of his hotness."

My skepticism is well grounded, by the way. My sister's idea of hotness rarely overlaps with mine. While Hannah's always had a thing for quirky hipster-nerdy-gamer types like her adorable boyfriend, Henn, I've always had a near-fatal weakness for artsy-

5

musician James Dean types (guys who, unfortunately, always seem to hand me a one-way ticket to the friend-zone before I've managed to string two coherent words together in their presence).

"Well, gosh, lemme think," Hannah says in a teasing voice. "Well, first off, Mr. Parking Spot is in a *band*."

"Bah-*wooh*?" I blurt, doing my best Scooby-Doo-smelling-a-Scooby-snack impression.

Hannah chuckles. "Yeah, I thought that'd get a Scooby-Doo-*bawooh* out of you."

"What instrument does he play?"

"Guitar. Oh, and he's the lead singer, too."

"Santa Maria!"

"And he writes all his band's lyrics."

"Oh my."

"And the lyrics he writes are *deep* and *profound*."

I gasp. "Santa Madonna!"

"But, wait, there's more. Guess why he doesn't need his parking spot?"

"Oh, dear God, no," I whisper.

"*'Cause he rides a motorcycle*," Hannah says, confirming my hunch.

"Sweet Sassy Molassey!"

Hannah laughs.

"Okay, it's official," I say. "Fire up the engines of unrequited love to full-throttle, Johnny. I'm goin' in."

"And, to top it all off, he lives right across the hall from me, so you two will practically be roomies."

I clutch my heart, anxiety gripping me. "Shit just got real—and very precarious."

Hannah laughs again.

"Hannah, all joking aside, this is gonna end *really* badly for me," I say, my voice tight. "I'm so sad for what's about to happen to me."

Hannah scoffs. "Why do you *always* think that way? You have to think *positively*—envision what you want and then make it a reality."

"Banana, I'm an extremely positive person and you know it. I just don't happen to be *delusional*."

"Come on, Linda, listen to me," Hannah says. "How many times have I told you? New city, new school, new Maddy. That's your mantra now. You're not shy and introverted anymore; you're a man-eater, baby."

I let out a loud exhale. My sister can give me as many pep talks about manifesting my reality and transforming myself into some kind of *femme fatale* as she wants, but we both know what's gonna happen here: I'm gonna fall for this rock-star guy and he's going to pat me on the head, feed me some kibble, and say, "Hey there, little buddy. Let's be friends!" It's just the way it always goes with me when it comes to me and the guys I find sexually attractive.

Now don't get me wrong: hot guys have liked me—the same way they like kittens and Homer Simpson and waffle cones. "You're awesome, Maddy!" they've said, if we happen to be in a class together and they've had the chance to get to know me over time. But for some reason, no matter how much the hotties come to like me once they've gotten to know me, they're never inspired to jump my bones.

Of course, boys have shown interest in being more than friends with me throughout the years, many of them making it clear they wanted to do the horizontal tango with me (and I've quite pleasantly done exactly that with three of them, including my first long-term boyfriend, Justin); but, if I'm being honest, other than Justin, the guys I've dated (and eventually slept with) haven't included anyone who's particularly turned me on.

"Come on," Hannah says. "Say it for me: 'new city, new school, new Maddy.'"

I roll my eyes, but begrudgingly repeat after my big sister.

"Excellent, Linda," Hannah replies after I've given her what she wants. "You're not Madelyn the sweet, shy, rule-following good girl anymore. Starting now, you're Madelyn the Badasselyn every minute of every day, not just when you're kicking ass and taking names behind the lens of a camera."

"Yeah, right. I'm Madelyn the Badasselyn." I snort. "You know what I was envisioning when you said Mr. Hottie lives across the hall? I had a premonition of me knocking on his door at three in the morning in my 'Adventure Time' pajamas, holding a basket full of baked goods, saying, 'Hey there, neighbor! I heard you playing your guitar in there and thought you might like some baked goods to fuel your creativity?'"

Hannah giggles.

"Please, Hannah, for the love of God, don't let me bring this über-cool-rock-star-motorcycle-dude baked goods at three in the morning. Chain me up or threaten to show him one of my dance-recital videos if I so much as mix sugar, flour, and eggs."

"Aw, come on, your tap-dancing videos are adorable."

"The ones when I'm *six* are adorable, maybe; the ones when I'm thirteen with buck teeth and frizzy hair? Not so much."

"They're *all* adorable, Maddy. You were always a cutie—just a little bug in a rug."

"Mmm hmm. Remember the one where I tap-danced to 'Born in the USA'?" I ask.

"Is that the one when you're wearing that red-white-and-blue top hat?"

"That's the one."

Hannah giggles for a good long minute. "Okay, yeah, you looked kinda like the Cat in the Hat on meth in that one, I must admit."

I laugh despite myself. She's right. I totally did.

"Oh my God, Maddy—I love you so much," Hannah says, exhaling. "Okay, fine, if you're ever on the verge of going full-on Martha Stewart on Dax's ass, I'll take drastic measures."

"His name is *Dax*?"

"Yeah, Dax Morgan. He's Kat Morgan's little brother—er, Kat *Faraday's* little brother. I keep forgetting to call her that."

"Ah," I say, the situation suddenly making a whole lot more sense. "Why didn't you say he's Kat's little brother? Now it makes total sense why he'd donate his parking spot to our cause."

Hannah met her dear friend Kat Morgan a few years ago when they started working together at a PR firm here in Seattle, and Hannah hasn't stopped telling outrageous and hilarious Kat-stories ever since. Hannah wound up quitting her job and moving to L.A. to be with her boyfriend, Henn (right before Kat got married and had a baby), but the pair has nonetheless stayed super close, especially since Kat's husband, Josh, is besties with Hannah's boyfriend, Henn.

"Wow," I say. "If Dax is half as attractive as his sister, then he must be drop-dead gorgeous."

"He's absolutely hideous."

I laugh.

"Actually, Dax and Kat look like male-female versions of each other. Their family calls them The Wonder Twins."

"Ah, jeez, there are *two* of them? Well, that's just God showing off."

"No, there are *five* of them. Kat has four brothers—I met the whole Morgan clan at Kat's wedding in Hawaii—and every single one of them is a freak of nature. But Dax is the one who looks like Kat's cookie-cutter twin."

"Holy hell. My left ovary just started vibrating."

Hannah giggles.

"So does Dax go to UCLA?" I ask. "Did Reed cut him a deal on an apartment, too?"

It's a fair question. Hannah's building is mere blocks from UCLA's campus (hence, the reason I'm moving in with her next week), and almost every resident in her building is a student. And since Henn and Josh's third musketeer from their days at UCLA (a music mogul named Reed Rivers) owns Hannah's apartment building, it seems likely to me he would have given Kat's brother a deal on an apartment the same way he gave one to his best friend's girlfriend.

"No, Dax isn't a student," Hannah says. "He moved to L.A. because his band got signed by River Records."

"Oh my God. Wow. Good for them."

"I know. It's huge. So, anyway, I'm told Reed likes to put his new bands up in his apartment building while they're recording their debut album."

"Wowza. Dax must be ecstatic."

"Well, yeah, but I think he's also kinda stressed out, from what I can tell."

"I can only imagine. Must be a lot of pressure. So did Dax give you a hint about what he wants for the parking spot—other than my sexual servitude, of course?"

"He said maybe you could do some sort of promo video for his band?"

"Oh my God," I breathe. "That's what he wants as *payment*?"

"So he says."

"I'd *love* to do that." I place my fingertips on my laptop

keyboard, poised to run a search. "Okay, I'm in Google-mode, babe. Is his name spelled D-A-X?"

"Yeah. Dax Morgan—and his band is called 22 Goats."

"22 Goats? What the heck?"

"Don't ask—I have no idea."

I input the search and a whole bunch of photos, videos, and links pop up on my screen. "*Oh, hello*," I say, beholding the glorious visions of gorgeousness gracing my computer. "Wow, Dax really *is* the male version of Kat."

"Like I said."

"And the entire universe's idea of hot," I add.

"Told you so. He's a freak, just like all the Morgan siblings. Freaks, freaks, freaks, all of 'em. Disgusting. Hideous. Grotesque."

"Jee-*zus*, he's easy on the eyes." I click on one of the videos in which Dax and his band are performing an edgy but soulful rock ballad in a crowded club. "Wow, he's so *passionate* when he performs," I whisper as I watch, my skin electrifying. "Oh my God, Banana, my left ovary just popped out an egg, and I'm not even mid-cycle."

"Yeah, well, get in line. Every co-ed in my building has been hurling her eggs at Dax since he moved in. The guy gets assaulted with teeny-tiny yolks every time he leaves his apartment."

We both laugh.

"I'm suddenly picturing Dax covered in tiny splotches of yellow goo," I say. "The same way women in fur coats get doused with red paint."

"Totally," Hannah says, laughing.

"How old is he?" I ask.

"Twenty-one, I think? He said he'd be a junior at Seattle U this year if he hadn't dropped out to pursue his music."

I watch Dax and his band some more, utterly drawn to his undeniable charisma and talent, and finally take a deep, self-controlling breath. "Okay, enough stalking and fangirling for one night. I've gotta get this dang wedding video edited for Grandma Tilly's Ninetieth Birthday Bash. Thanks again for arranging the parking spot for me, Hannah—you're the best sister in the world."

"Anything for you, lil sissy—you know that. But, hey, honestly, now that you're driving here, I gotta admit I'm worried about you making the drive all by yourself."

I scoff. "There's nothing to worry about."

"Is there someone who could make the drive with you? If you can find someone to road trip it with you, I'll buy them a one-way flight back to Seattle, on me."

"Oh my gosh, Banana. You're so sweet. But I'll be fine."

"Seriously. Is there anyone you could ask? I'd feel a lot better about it if you weren't alone."

I twist my mouth, considering potential co-pilots, but I can't think of anyone. "Washington schools have already started up again," I say. "Everyone I know started classes last week."

"Well, how about Mom, then?"

"No, she's visiting her new boyfriend in Louisville next week."

"Mom's got a new boyfriend in Louisville?"

"Smith."

"*Smith*? Is that his first or last name?"

"First name, I think. Actually, I'm not sure. That's all she's ever called him: Smith."

"Whatever happened to that guy Brook?"

"Brooks. With an 's.' He's kaput."

"I thought Brooks was supposed to be Mom's 'Prince Charming'?"

"Yeah, well, it turns out Prince Charming has gambling and porn addictions."

"Next, please!" Hannah shouts, and we both laugh—but it's "humor borne of pain," as Hannah's boyfriend Henn is fond of saying.

"If you wanna worry about someone taking a trip alone, worry about Mom," I say. "She's meeting this Smith guy in person for the first time after a solid month of 'I love you' emails and phone calls."

"Love-at-first email again?" Hannah asks.

"Of course."

"We ought to teach Mom about this newfangled thing called FaceTime," Hannah says. "I think it'd change her life." She lets out a long sigh. "Well, hopefully, this Smith guy is The One."

"Fingers crossed," I say.

"If not, she'll figure it out," Hannah says. "Mom's a big girl."

"Well, so am I," I say. "You don't have to worry about me driving alone."

"No, you're not a big girl. You're my sweet little Madelyn the Badelyn and you always will be. Hey, why don't I fly up there and drive down with you? We can play license-plate bingo like we used to do when we were kids."

"Hann, you were just telling me yesterday how swamped you are at work. You can't take time off from a brand new job to babysit me. You're still trying to make everyone at your new job love you, remember?"

Hannah exhales a long breath, wordlessly confirming just how much she's yearning to succeed at this new PR job of hers. Working in the publicity department of a major movie studio is my sister's dream job, after all, and now she's living her dream.

"If I feel even remotely drowsy while driving," I assure her, "I'll stop at the first motel I come across. In fact, right after we hang up, I'll go online and chart out my pit stops. And I'll put my phone in the glove box whenever I'm driving, just like I always do. There'll be no distractions."

"I'm not only worried about the driving part, I'm worried you'll be a twenty-one-year-old woman traveling alone for twelve hundred miles. Who knows what sicko might see you at a gas station and attack you?"

"Jeez, Hannah."

"Just saying. You can never be too careful."

"I know, but... jeez."

Hannah exhales again, clearly ill at ease.

This is nothing new, of course. My sweet sister's always been my fierce protector, ever since we were little, and that protectiveness only intensified three years ago when the car I was riding in as a passenger was T-boned at an intersection. I got carted away from the wreckage with a broken collarbone and wrist, a severe concussion, a collapsed lung, and some bone-deep bruises to my body, heart, and soul; but both drivers—my boyfriend, Justin, and a father of four in the other car who'd apparently looked down to reply to a text as he approached our intersection—died at the scene.

"So, hey, I gotta go," I say. "Be sure to send me Dax's phone number. I'll call him to work out the terms of my sexual servitude."

"Will do. I love you lots and lots, Tootsie Pop."

"I love you, too, Banana Cream Pie. Thanks again."

Chapter 2
Maddy

"Dax," a male voice answers.

Oh, jeez. His voice is as sexy as the rest of him. Or maybe I'm just *projecting* extreme vocal sexiness onto him, based on the seven YouTube videos of him I just watched, one after the other, immediately before placing this call.

"Uh, hi, Dax?" I say. "This is Madelyn Milliken?" Oh man, my voice is betraying the racing of my heart. "Hannah's sister?" I continue.

"Oh, yeah, hey."

"My sister told me to give you a call about the parking spot?" Shoot. I'm finishing every sentence with a question mark. I hate it when I do that. I take a deep breath. "My sister told me to call you?" Shoot. I did it again. Gah.

"Yeah, Hannah said you need to have your car during the school year so you can work on weekends."

"Yeah, tuition and books is kind of wiping me out?" Shit. Another question mark.

"Well, you can totally use my parking spot," Dax says. "I've got a motorcycle, so I don't need the second spot assigned to our apartment."

"Thank you?" Goddammit. "Thank you?" *Goddammit! "Thank you!"*

"You're welcome!" Dax shouts, mimicking the exuberant tone of my last offering. "Glad to help out. Kat's always talking about how much she loves Hannah Banana Montana Milliken, so I figure any sister of Hannah's is a sister of mine."

Well, damn, that's gotta be a new record for me. "Thank you so much, Dax!" I sing out, trying my damnedest not to sound the least bit crestfallen that I've just been dropkicked into the frickin' *sister* zone.

"So you're transferring to UCLA?" Dax says, apparently unaware of my current state of disappointment.

"Yeah?" I reply.

"Where from?"

"U Dub?"

"I was studying music at Seattle U until last year."

"Yeah?"

"Dropped out when the band got signed."

"Congratulations on that, by the way." Phew, no question mark that time.

"Thanks. So Hannah said you're going to film school—that you won the top prize at some film festival last year?"

"Yeah?" I say. Fuck a duck—the question mark is back! "*Yes*," I correct myself. "*I did.*"

Dax pauses, apparently waiting for me to elaborate on that statement, but he's gonna have to wait all day. I feel like my tongue is tied into knots along with my stomach.

"Okay, well, that's cool," Dax finally says. "So, hey, I'm thinking, if it's cool with you, my band could use a promo video—you know, something to kind of introduce us to the world when the album comes out. I'm thinking maybe some performance stuff, maybe some behind the scene stuff? Nothing too long or fancy, pretty basic. I'm hoping the label's gonna do some stuff at release time, but I don't wanna count on it, you know? And, even so, every little bit helps to break a new band these days, even if you're signed to a badass label." Dax exhales a deep breath that speaks volumes about the pressure he must be feeling.

"I'd be thrilled to help you, Dax," I chirp. "I absolutely love music and musicians." Oh my God. I can't believe I just said that. I clear my throat. "I'd be happy to do whatever I can to help you. Like you said, we're practically family, right?" Oh, God. Someone muzzle me.

"Cool," Dax says, sounding genuinely thrilled. "So why don't we plan to chat about the video when you get down here?"

"Sure thing."

"So when are you coming to town?"

"Um. I'll probably leave in four or five days—I still need to pack and finish up a few things here. And then it should take me two or three days to do the drive, depending on weather and traffic." I clear my throat. "But, um, yeah, once I get down there, whatever you need, I'll be happy to supply it." Oh my effing God. Did I just say, "I'll be happy to '*supply*' it'?" What am I—a customer service rep for a lumberyard? "Uh, I should have about a week before classes start once I get down there, so maybe we can shoot the video then?"

"Great."

"The editing might take a little while for me to finish, to be honest—I'll have a full load of classes and weddings to shoot on weekends, thanks to your parking spot."

"No worries. We've got six months 'til the album release."

"Oh, okay. Great."

"I'm super excited about this, Maddy. Thanks. Hannah said you're, like, a genius filmmaker."

"She did? Well, I dunno about *that*. I just love visual storytelling. I think maybe I see connections and themes where other people don't?"

"That's exactly how I think about songwriting: connections, themes, stories. Same-same."

"Wow. Cool." I want to say more but my tongue is too tied up. I can feel my cheeks flushing.

"So, okay, Maddy," Dax says breezily. "I gotta get my ass to the studio."

"Right on," I say, but then I cringe at myself. I never say that. "Thank you so much for the parking spot, Dax. It's a life-saver."

"Glad to do it. Well, okay. Catch ya later, Madelyn the Badelyn."

Oh my God. Hannah told him about that? I'm gonna kill her.

"Catch ya later, Dax... the... ," I reply. Battle Axe? Frickity Fracks? Crap, I can't think of anything even remotely clever to say.

Oh, he's already hung up. Thank God.

I put my phone down and slap my forehead with my palm. Why do I always crumble like feta cheese around guys I'm attracted to? How the heck do other girls manage to come off as smooth and flirtatious and snarky in these situations? *I'll be happy to supply it*, I said to him. Good lord.

Like a turtle crawling into her shell, I return to doing the one thing that always transports me to my happy place: editing video.

Twenty minutes later, my phone buzzes with an incoming call. Oh my God. That's Dax's number on the display screen.

"Hello?" I say, my heart racing.

"Hey," Dax says. "It's Dax—Dax Morgan."

I smile to myself. As if I know another Dax? "Hi?" I say.

"So, hey, I just went across the hall and told Hannah about our conversation and, um, it turns out I've got one more favor besides the video to ask in exchange for the parking spot. Sorry."

"Oh. Okay. Sure." My skin pricks with anticipation. "What do you need?"

Dax exhales. "Um, so I've got this *brother*. Keane."

"Keane?"

"K-e-a-n-e. He's been wanting to visit me here in L.A.—I guess he's been invited by some huge talent agency to audition for them. So, anyway, would you be willing to give Keane a ride? I know it's a huge favor, but he'd pay for half your gas."

"Sure," I say without hesitation, and instantly make a face at myself. What the hell am I doing? I don't want to drive over a thousand miles with a complete stranger in my cramped hatchback. "Sounds great," I add brightly, yet again pissing myself off.

Dax lets out a little puff of air, obviously relieved. "Great. I'll let him know what's up and text you his number so you two can work out the timing."

"Great."

"Okay, well," Dax says, "I'd better get myself something to eat before I head to the studio."

"Okay. Thanks again for the parking spot."

"Sure thing. Catch ya later. Bye."

The minute I hang up, I flap my lips together, annoyed with myself for saying yes so easily. I have no desire to drive for two solid days with some dude I don't know. I'm terrible with new people. And, damn it, I was looking forward to having some uninterrupted solitude to mentally prepare for the major life changes ahead of me.

I sigh audibly and put my face in my hands.

Shit.

Chapter 3
Keane

Friday. 10:07 p.m.

I pull my car in front of a large home in Bellevue and glance at my watch. I've somehow managed to make it to this gig with twenty minutes to spare—pretty impressive, considering I was a human pile of rubble a mere ten hours ago.

I check my phone to make sure I've got the right address, and I'm assaulted with an onslaught of unread texts and Instagram notifications, all apparently sent to me earlier today while I've been sleeping off last night's rager. Shit. I must have traded contact info with more people than I realized at my booking agent's birthday party last night.

I scroll through the barrage of unread texts and notifications, not particularly interested in any of them, until my eyes land on a text from my younger brother, Dax: "Yo, Peen Star. Call me ASAP. I need a favor from you, dude. It's important. Thx."

I tap out a quick reply: "Yo, Rock Star. I'm heading into a job right now, about to make some lucky ladies' fantasies come true (as usual). Tonight BPH is Johnny Law with a Big Ol' Dong and the bachelorette is America's Most Wanted." I attach a police officer emoji, a bride, and a crying-happy-tears emoji. "I'll call u tomorrow. Maybe Sunday. Monday at latest, brah. (Because, ya kna, it's hard work being EVERY WOMAN'S FUCKING FANTASY). Peace out."

Actually, despite what I just wrote, I'm not in any rush to call my little brother back, though I love the guy to pieces. Here's a tip: If you want Keane Morgan to hit you back any time soon, don't send him a text that says, "I need a favor from you, dude." Just sayin'.

I look at my watch. Eighteen minutes to showtime.

17

I continue scrolling through my texts and discover two from my older brother Ryan, both from yesterday: "Hey, Peen. I've got 2 tix to the Mariners game on Thurs night if you and the Mrs. want em? I'm thinking maybe you and your lovely wife could use a romantic night out at the ballpark? Turns out I'll be seeing Muse Thurs night with Kum Shot and the entire Faraday crew. Lambo scored us backstage passes (because he's the wise and powerful Joshua Fucking Faraday, baby!). Confession? I love my brother-in-law more than I love any of my actual blood brothers, including you. Sorry, Peenie, but it can't be helped. P.S. Don't shake your ass too hard, Magic Mike. Wouldn't want something to shake loose and detach."

Now, that's how you do it, brah. You want another tip about getting Keane Morgan to hit you back? Offer him free baseball tix. (Daxy really should take notes.) But before tapping out my "Hell yeah, I want the tix!" reply to my older brother, I quickly read his second text, which is time-stamped thirty minutes after his first:

"Hey, PEENelope Cruz!" Ryan writes. "Mom says to call her. She left you a vm 2 days ago, telling you she has extras for you (lasagna, you fuckwit!) and you never called her back. Bwahahahaaaa! Looks like your loss is my gain, sucka! Nom nom nom. Best lasagna ever!"

And just like that, all the goodwill inspired by Ryan's first text about the baseball tix vanishes. I tap out a reply with angry fingers, gritting my teeth as I do:

"FUCK U, you extras-stealing, Viking-ass, pillaging motherfucker! Z and I are growing boys! We needed that lasagna, man! U shoulda had my back and texted me about Mom making me some grub, not swooped in to steal my extras, u twat head! Oh well, haha, joke's on u, Pretty Boy! I'll just sweet-talk Mom into making me an ENTIRE PAN of lasagna and probs a pot of chili, too. Ka-BAM, son! It shouldn't be too hard to do, since Mom loves me the most." I attach a middle-finger emoji to the end of my text and press send.

Goddammit! I live for Mom's extras and Ryan knows it. For fuck's sake, I'm the only one of the five of us who can't boil water. I need Mom's home cookin' to survive and thrive, man. *Fucker.*

I quickly tap out a second message to Ryan: "It's now abundantly clear ur the enemy, brah, so I suggest u watch your back-stabbing back." I attach a dagger-emoji and a pair of eyes. "BTW, would u PLEASE tell Mom to quit calling me all the time and TEXT me, for fuck's sake? I've told her a thousand times I never check my VMs since nobody ever calls me except Mom and my fucking landlord. And, hey, tell Jizz I'm deeply offended she didn't invite me to see Muse with all u cool kids. What's the point of having a sister who's married to a kazillionaire with famous friends if she doesn't use her newfound wealth and connections to finagle her FAVORITE brother backstage tix to Muse? Tell Kat I am NOT pleased with her. In fact, tell her she's officially on my shit list and she's gonna have to work REALLY hard to make me love her again. Peace out." I attach a microphone-emoji—the Morgan siblings' universal method for declaring "I just dropped the mic on your punk ass, you little bitch."

"Oh, shit," I say out loud, suddenly remembering the baseball tickets.

I tap out a third text to Ryan:

"Oh, yeah! Almost forgot. Hell yes, I want ur baseball tix, brah! Thx, Captain! U da best!!! (Except for the fact that ur an extras-stealing, backstabbing fuckface.) Leave the tix on ur kitchen counter and I'll swing by and grab 'em some time this week. Oh, yeah, um... Confession? I still have ur house key. I totally lied when I said I put it back in the drawer last time. Aw, come on, Pretty Boy—don't be mad at ur favorite bro. We both know when I see ya next time I'm just gonna flash my dimples and make u forget u were ever pissed at me, so why bother being mad at me in the first place? Thx again! I love u da most, Rum Cake!" Heart emoji.

After I send my final text to Ryan, I shoot a quick text to my sister, Kat: "Hey, Kum Shot. Thanks so much for inviting me to see Muse on Thurs nite with ur crew! Gonna be a blast! Oh, wait, no... that's right: U DIDN'T FUCKING INVITE ME! Because u SUCK!" I attach a middle-finger emoji. "Say hi to Lambo and give Little G a big hug from her favorite uncle. Love u guys so much (even though u suck ass like a Dyson)." Heart emoji.

I glance at my watch. Still about ten minutes before Ball Peen Hammer reports for duty. Damn it. Why'd I get here so fucking early? I hate waiting.

I continue scrolling through the endless messages and notifications on my phone. Oh, there's a text from my oldest brother, Colby: "Hey, fuckwad. Call me. I left you a vm three days ago and you never called me back."

I ignore this one. Colby knows better than to leave me a goddamned voicemail—which means it's his own damned fault if I didn't call him back. That's shame on him, not me. *Delete.*

Oh, hey, there's a text from my booking agent, Melissa, someone I'll always hit back, no matter what:

"Hey, Keane!" Melissa's text says. "Thanks for coming to my birthday party last night! I LOOOOOOVED the show you and the boys put on for me!" She attaches a blushing-face emoji. "So, hey, hot stuff, a new client has specifically requested BPH for a private show tomorrow night. She saw you perform at Hot Spot last month and it seems you made quite the impression. Apparently, it's a 'divorce finalization celebration,' so it's probs gonna get pretty wild. I told her you're booked at HS this Sat night, but she said she'd pay 2x what you make at the club. I told her, no, she's gotta pay 3x + $100 as your guaranteed tip (my 20% to be taken off the top) and she said ok. (Damn, I'm good.) If u want the gig, I'll send Brent or Felipe to take your place at HS—but you gotta lemme know ASAP. If I don't hear from you before midnight tonight, I'm gonna have to confirm Brent for the horny divorcée. LMK."

I scoff loudly, even as I'm sitting alone in my car, and tap out a rapid-fire reply: "Oh, sure, Mel, you're gonna send BRENT to the horny divorcée. Riiiiight. The woman asks for BPH specifically and ur gonna send her the Cowboy Kid? For fuck's sake, the poor woman's lady-boner would go completely soft! Just do me a favor and make sure this one knows she's getting the legendary BALL PEEN HAMMER and not my actual balls, peen, and hammer. Mmmmmkay? BTW, I shouldn't have to be the one to tell clients I'm not slangin' dang, Mel. It's awkward, to say the least, for me to do it in the moment. So do your job for once and tell the clients I'm not a paid cock when you book the gig. Don't be a greedy little bitch, M. If a potential client doesn't want me cuz I'm a pro, then five more clients WILL for that exact same reason. So, yeah, if this client wants someone with actual talent and a body like a god who's gonna give her a happy memory to fall back on every time she's fucking some old bald guy with a beer belly, back hair, and tragically low testosterone levels, then hellz yeah, book the fuck out of it. BPH will be there with donkey balls on, baby. But if this divorcée is looking to sow her newfound wild oats with a cabana boy who's got a plug-and-play pecker, then by all means send Brent. Peace out." I attach a heart emoji, making sure Melissa knows I love her, even when I'm busting her balls.

I look at my watch. Five minutes until showtime. Jesus God. Is time standing still? I continue scrolling through my texts, looking for anything to pass the time, and a text from a number I don't recognize catches my eye:

"Hey, Keane! This is Jade from Melissa's party? I got your number from Samantha. Was thinking we could hang out some time. Call me!" She attaches a winking emoji and a pair of lips.

Well, first of all, I don't remember a chick named Jade from last night's party. And, second of all, I don't even like Samantha. She's always a total bitch to Z. Bros before hoes, babe. *Delete.*

I keep scrolling through several more texts until another message catches my eye: "Hi there! This is Madelyn Milliken, Hannah's sister? Please call or text me whenever it's convenient, so we can make arrangements for next week. I'm pretty flexible regarding timing! Looking forward to taking this trip with you!"

I stare at the incomprehensible message for a long beat, trying to understand its meaning. Who the fuck is Madelyn Milliken? And what the fuck is she talking about? What *trip*? Is that, like, some kind of coded drug reference? 'Cause I might like to party on occasion, for sure, but I'm not some kind of junkie or drug dealer, for fuck's sake. Or is she assuming I'm gonna physically *go* somewhere with her? Ha! What the fuck? And why the hell should I care if she's got a sister named Hannah?

Wait.

A thought is suddenly rapping at the back door of my brain. *Hannah Milliken.* That name does sound vaguely familiar, actually. I look up at the ceiling of my car for a beat, racking my brain. Nooooooope. False alarm. I got nothing. Sorry, Madelyn Milliken, whoever the fuck you are: there shall be no Peen for you. *Delete.*

I glance at the time. *Yee-boy!* It's showtime, baby.

I grab my hat off the passenger seat of my car, slide a pair of mirrored-sunglasses onto my face, and survey my reflection in my rearview mirror. Hot damn, I'm a handsome-and-happy motherfucker. And, good God, I look like such a prick in this get-up. *Awesome.*

Chapter 4
Keane

I pull out my portable speaker with built-in disco lights from the trunk of my car and stride purposefully toward the large house, the handcuffs attached to my belt jangling softly as I go, a smile dancing on my lips. Oh man, I love my life.

"Well, *hello*," a thirty-something-year-old brunette says when she opens the front door, her eyes devouring me. Behind her from inside the house, female voices are shrieking and laughing with what sounds to my expert ear like drunken revelry, while loud music blares. The song playing is "Crash" by hip-hop mega-star 2Real, who just so happens to be the biggest star on my baby brother's new record label. (Hot *damn*, I'm proud of my rock-star baby brother!)

"Ma'am," I say to the brunette at the door, spreading my legs a bit and subtly tilting my package toward her.

Okay, that dick-tilting thing I just did? *Totally on purpose.*

Hey. Quit rolling your eyes at me, baby doll. It's not a good look on you.

It's my *job* to make women want me, sweetheart—and I'm damned good at my job. I may not be in the business of professionally fucking women, but I sure as hell *am* in the business of making women *want* to fuck me. Which means that, right from the word go of every job, through everything I do—including that subtle dick-tilt maneuver I just did—I'm serving up what women want most from their walking fantasy: an alpha male. That's right, baby, with every little thing I do, I make sure the horny ladies know I'm a guy who'd dominantly lead their naturally submissive asses to the Promised Land, if ever they were lucky enough to get a piece of me.

Whoa, whoa, whoa. Don't get your panties in a twist, babe. When I say women are naturally *submissive*, I'm talking about sex,

22

okay? Obviously, I know women run countries and corporations and kick ass and take names every which way. Have you met my mother and sister? Dude. *I know*. What I'm saying is that, when it comes to *sex*, women are wired through biology and physiology and probs a bunch of other -ologies to crave total domination. I'm not talking about dom/sub shit like doggie collars, whips, and chains here—though I've got no objection to any of that shit, if that's your bag—I'm talking about something way, *way* more fundamental than any of that. I'm talking about the basic fact that virtually every red-blooded woman, whether she admits it or not, no matter how independent and ass-kicking she might be *outside* the bedroom, secretly wants a man to own her ass *inside* it.

Oh, you wanna fight me on this? Okay, sure. Can't wait to hear your analysis on the subject, perhaps over tea and crumpets. I tell you what, sweetheart. What say we schedule a time to chat about the issue right after I count the five hundred or so bucks the horny women at this bachelorette party are gonna stuff into my crotch, two inches from my dipstick?

Yeah, that's right. I make about five hundred C-notes per night in tips, when every other chump in the biz makes two-fifty tops, if he's lucky. How can this be, you wonder? Is it 'cause I'm so fucking pretty? Well, yeah, I am, actually—way prettier than your sister. But that's a given in this biz. You gotta be pretty to get a decent agent and book the jobs. Is it 'cause my dance moves are extra filthy? 'Cause they are. And it certainly doesn't hurt my cause that I genuinely love making horny women scream. *I love it*. But none of that stuff is my secret sauce—that one special ingredient that gets me twice the tips as any other guy.

So what's my secret? Okay, I'll tell you, but only 'cause you're so pretty and sweet: *I'm awesome at sex and women can smell it on me*.

You know how dogs can sense an earthquake just before it happens? Yeah, well, this confidence-thing with me and my sexual prowess is just like that. My dominance in the bedroom (and wherever else the mood happens to strike me) is an earthquake and women are my horny little bitches.

Hey. Ho. Whoa. Calm down.

Quit with the eye-rolling thing again, babe.

23

I'm using the word "bitches" to mean "female dogs" 'cause I'm making a clever pun here. I didn't just call women "bitches" in a hip-hop kind of way. Calm your tits.

But anyway, what I'm telling you is the God's truth—no bluffing or exaggeration, whatsoever. Just good old fashioned *verisimilitude*. (Oh, dude, if Z were here, he'd fist-bump me for that one.) Bottom line? I fuck like a motherfucking god.

You doubt me?

Well, don't.

I might be just a baby at twenty-three, but I'm also a Morgan brother—and, trust me, we Morgans know how to bang. My whole life, my older brothers have shared information with me, telling me what they've figured out firsthand, sending me links to the best blogs to read and the best instructional videos to watch. My older brother Ryan in particular is our fearless leader in this arena, a fucking sex-guru that guy, I swear to God—though my oldest bro, Colby, the Grand Cheese of the Morgan siblings, is no slouch, either, when it comes to ringing the bell.

Now don't get me wrong. My brothers don't send me videos of themselves mid-bang or anything like that, and we don't, you know, lure women into some kind of depraved Morgan-brother igloo. We're just normal guys who like to bang well and often. Nothing too kinky, as far as I know. All I'm saying is that we Morgan brothers share information with each other—hell yeah, we do—lots of it—all in the name of 'helping a brother out.' Literally. Which is why, at the tender age of twenty-three, I've already perfected all sorts of pretty nifty tricks to get women off, not the least of which is a little maneuver we Morgan boys like to call "The Sure Thing."

Still rolling your eyes at me, baby doll? Yeah. Didn't think so.

What's The Sure Thing, you're dying to know? Well, it sucks to be you, I guess. Maybe you won't roll your eyes at me so much next time and then I'll tell you. All you need to know right now is that it's next level, baby, the kind of thing that makes a woman addicted to it and gives a guy the kind of swagger women can *smell*—which, in my line of work, translates into dollar bills for me and wet panties for the horny ladies.

Speaking of which, the curvy brunette at the door is looking at me like she's already thinking about tackling me.

"Is there a problem, Officer?" the brunette says coyly, jutting her ample chest toward me and flashing a huge smile.

"Yes, ma'am," I say, smiling back at her. "A *big* problem." I motion vaguely to my crotch when I say "big."

My new friend lets out a sexy little giggle and leans her shoulder against the doorjamb. "Oh my God. Wow."

"Is there an Allison Mendocino inside the residence, ma'am?" I run my free hand across my chest, right over my fake badge, across my pecs, and widen my stance a bit more, letting my bulge take center stage.

"Yeah, Allison's inside. Oh my God, she's gonna lose her mind when she sees you. You're absolutely..." The woman bites her lower lip, apparently considering her next word. "*Scrumptious.*"

Oh, that's a new one. I like that. "Thank you," I say smoothly. "That's sweet of you to say."

"Not being sweet—you're man-candy at its finest, Officer..." The woman leans forward and squints at my badge. "*Hammer.*" She giggles. "Officer Hammer? Oh my God."

"My full name is Officer *Ball Peen* Hammer," I say, flashing her a huge smile—the one that unleashes my dimples with extra sauce. "What's your name, sweetheart?"

"Francesca."

"Oh, pretty name. Hi, *Francesca.*" I shake her hand. "It's a *pleasure* to meet you."

See what I did there? How I used the words "pleasure" and "Francesca" in close proximity to each other? Yeah, that was on purpose. You want a little tip? When first meeting a woman you want to fuck (or, if you happen to be in my line of work, when first meeting a woman you're trying to make *want* to fuck *you*), use her name early and often in a confident, masculine voice. Why? Because when a woman hears you say her name, it subliminally makes her feel like you're staking a claim over her—you know, displaying your sexual dominance. And then, if you double down and explicitly link her name to the concept of *pleasure*, well, then, at that point you're sending a coded message straight to the pleasure-center in her brain— which means you've got a horny fish on your line. You're welcome.

Francesca makes a little noise of excitement and grips my hand tightly. "The pleasure's all mine."

"Aw, you're a sweetheart, Francesca. It's such a *pleasure* to meet you. It really is, *Francesca*—a huge *pleasure*."

Francesca looks ready to jump my bones right here and now on the porch. "I'm sorry to go on and on complimenting you," she breathes, still holding my hand. She takes a step forward, pulling our bodies together. "Forgive me. I'll stop in just a second, I swear. But you're perfect. I mean, *literally*. I can't stop staring."

I smile. "Aw, Frankie. Can I call you Frankie? Thank you. Such a *pleasure*."

Look, I never say this out loud because women dig a guy who at least *pretends* to be somewhat humble (outside the bedroom, anyway), but the truth is I know I'm most women's idea of physical perfection. If I had a dollar bill for every time a woman has hit on me, totally out of the blue—and I'm talking about my buddies' moms and women standing in grocery-store lines, not just women at bars or my shows—or, shit, if I had a *nickel* for every time a woman's told me she'd do just about anything to experience one night of pleasure with me—then I'd be a millionaire by now. No, actually, a *billionaire*—not even exaggerating. Probs even a *trillionaire*. No lie.

My new admirer leans forward, giving me a nice view of her curves. "Hey, would you take off your glasses for a sec?" she asks. She glances behind her, toward the raucous sounds of the party inside the house. "I just want a quick peek at your eyes before I take you in there and throw you to the she-wolves." She bites her finger, and her massive wedding ring sparkles in the dim light of the porch.

"My pleasure, Francesca." I lower my sunglasses and level her with my best smolder—and she gasps. I wink, smile, and slide my mirrored glasses back over my eyes.

"Wow. Your eyes are *gorgeous*," she breathes. "I think you might be the most attractive man I've ever met."

Cha-*ching*. Add another nickel to my trillion-dollar bank account in the sky, baby. "Thank you," I say. "So, hey, will you do me a favor when we get in there, Frankie? Will you cut the music and lights?" I motion to my speaker. "I've got my show all cued up for you pretty ladies."

"Sure thing," Francesca says. "You ready to head in there now... Officer *Hammer*?"

"I sure am. And so is my hammer." Another wink.

She bursts out laughing. "Oh my God. Follow me, sweetie."

"My pleasure, Frankie."

I follow her through the entryway of the large house, admiring her round ass as she leads the way.

We turn a corner and I'm met with a familiar and awesome sight: a group of women, all of them obviously buzzed and chomping at the bit to let their freak flags fly. One of the women (clearly, tonight's bachelorette) is sitting in the middle of a couch, wearing a sparkling tiara and beauty-queen sash that proclaims in large, glittering letters, "I LOVE COCK!"

I can't help but smile at that. From what I've seen over the past year and change of doing this awesome job, bachelorette sashes usually say "FUTURE MRS. SO-AND-SO" or "BRIDE TO BE." Looks like this is gonna be a particularly rowdy group.

"Oh, laaaaadies!" the Gatekeeper calls out to her friends, prompting them to look our way—and, just like that, the room bursts into a gigantic Molotov cocktail of estrogen. *Awesome*.

Chapter 5
Keane

"Allison Mendocino?" I bark in my best cop-voice.

"Oh my God!" the bachelorette shrieks, putting her hand over her heart.

"There's been a criminal complaint filed against you, Allison. It seems you've been a very bad girl."

The overhead music cuts off and the lights in the room go dim. Quickly, I flip on the swirling, multicolored lights attached to my portable speaker, press "play" on the song I've cued up—"Candy Shop" by 50 Cent—and strike an athletic stance a few feet from the couch.

"Allison Mendocino, you're under arrest," I say.

Every woman in the room goes ballistic.

"You have the right to remain silent," I say, colorful lights skimming over my body. I flash a wicked grin and run my hands over my chest and straight down my torso toward my package. "Anything you say can and will be used against you in a court of law." The women are already squealing with glee. "Or, fuck it, baby, scream your motherfucking head off. It's just you and me, after all."

Everyone shrieks with delight.

"Oh my God," the bachelorette says again, this time putting her hands on her blushing cheeks.

I let my gaze drift across every single enraptured face in the room. "I'm Officer Ball Peen Hammer, beautiful ladies." My hips have begun gyrating to the beat of the music and a huge smile has spread across my face. "You ready to let loose and have some fun with Officer Hammer tonight?"

Every woman in the room screams her affirmative reply.

"I can't hear you, ladies!" I bellow.

28

They scream even louder, throwing up their hands. A blonde on the end of the couch throws a crumpled bill in my direction, bless her heart, and I blow her a kiss.

I stride toward the bachelorette on the couch, the handcuffs attached to my belt jangling, and come to a stop directly over her, my crotch in her face, my body gyrating into her personal space. "You ready to have some fun tonight, sweetheart?"

Allison the Bachelorette makes a face like she's trying to contain an internal meltdown. She nods.

I take my sunglasses off and, with my eyes locked onto hers, begin grinding my hips to the beat of the sexy song. "You gonna let your hair down for me, Alley Cat?" I coo, touching her hair. "Get a little wild for me?"

Bachelorette Allison sighs loudly.

I touch Allison's cheek gently, moving my hips exactly the way I do when I'm culling a body-quaking orgasm from deep inside a woman, and she makes a sexual sound. "You want it mild or wild tonight, *Allison*?" I ask. "What's your *pleasure*, sweetheart?"

My entire body is moving without reservation now. I'm in the zone.

"Wild!" the ladies around us shriek in unison.

Another woman throws a bill at me. And then another.

"Mild or wild, *Allison*? What's your *pleasure*?" I ask, pulling the bachelorette up to standing, pressing my body into hers. I grind myself into her crotch, exactly the way I'd do it if she were my woman and I was fucking her nice and slow, and she gasps. "I'll take it as slow as you need, sweetheart," I whisper into her ear, my lips grazing her skin. "It's all about you tonight."

"Oh my *gawd*," the bachelorette breathes, her pelvis moving rhythmically with mine, despite the shy blush in her cheeks. "Wild?" she chokes out.

I run my hands down the bachelorette's arms and brush my lips against her cheek. "Right answer, baby." Without warning, I cuff her wrists and the entire room, including the bachelorette, goes batshit crazy.

I pull the bachelorette to an empty chair in the middle of the room, guide her trembling body to sitting, and straddle the chair with her in it, just as the song switches to... "Pony" by Ginuwine.

Whoa, whoa, whoa.

I saw that, baby doll—another eye-roll.

You better check yourself before you wreck yourself, sweetheart.

Yeah, okay, I've lifted this song straight from *Magic Mike*, along with over half the dance moves I'm about to do. But so what? I'm not in the wheel-reinvention business. I'm in the bid-nass of giving ladies exactly what they want—and that's this song coupled with Channing Tatum's *smoove mooves*.

I begin moving my hips to the cadence of the song, grinding and thrusting my hips into the bachelorette's lap, and when I'm sure every woman in the room is clenching her thighs and whimpering, I slide back up to standing, rip my hat off and throw it onto the couch—a move that provokes catcalls and several more bills thrown my way.

When the song reaches its chorus, I begin slowly unbuttoning my shirt, much to the howling delight of the room. With each movement of my fingers down the buttons of my shirt, I stare more and more intensely at the bachelorette, doing my damnedest to make her feel like it's just her and me in the room.

"You've been a bad girl, Allison," I say, opening my unbuttoned shirt to reveal the chiseled chest and abs I've worked my ass off to get. "A very, very bad girl." A huge smile spreads across my face. *"And now it's time for justice to get served."*

Chapter 6
Keane

Sunday 4:38 p.m.

I summon every last drop of strength in my tired body and grit out one more chest press, grunting as I do.

"You feeling okay, baby doll?" my big, black mountain of a roommate and best friend, Zander, asks as he guides the barbell onto the rack above my head. "My little sister could kick your ass today."

I sit up on the bench, sweat pouring down my back. "Yeah, well, your little sister could kick my ass every day, so that's not saying much."

Zander flashes a huge smile, showcasing straight, white teeth. "True."

"My ass is dragging from sheer over-use," I say. "Mel's party on Thursday night almost killed me, then I did this insane bachelorette party on Friday, and, last night, a pack of cougars tried their mighty best to rip me limb from limb. I'm a slab of pummeled man-meat today, baby doll—a human Fruit Roll-Up."

"Oh, cry me a river," Zander says. He begins loading additional weights onto the barbell for his set. "You've got the best job in the world, Peenie. You're not gonna get any sympathy from me."

"Well, I didn't say I'm expecting your *sympathy*, just saying BPH needs a little R&R, that's all. When we get home, how 'bout you make me some chamomile tea and rub my feet while we watch the game?"

Zander chuckles. "Oh yeah, I'll get right on that, buttercup." He swats at my leg with one of his muscled arms. "Get up. I've got a client coming in for training at five thirty and we've still gotta do battle ropes and sled runs after this."

31

"Battle ropes and sled runs? Fuck no. Have mercy on me, drill sergeant."

"Man at night, man in the morning."

"Is this how you treat your paying clients when their asses are dragging—or am I getting special asshole-treatment just 'cause I pay you with dimples?" I flash him a broad smile that's sure to make my dimples pop.

"This is how I treat everyone, tired or not, dimples or not—although, I must admit I smile a bit more enthusiastically when someone's paying me to kick their ass in actual dollars. Now come on, sweet meat, quit whining and get the fuck off the bench."

I drag my sorry ass off the bench and Zander takes my spot.

"So," Zander says, readying his grip on the barbell. "Did BPH break his cardinal rule and bang the bachelorette this weekend?"

"Brah, I've told you a hundred times—BPH don't bang the clients. You know how that shit turned out for me back in my little-dab'll-doo-ya phase at the beginning. And, anyway, women gettin' ready to say 'I do' are never the ones sniffing around for some side peen—trust me—it's always the bachelorette's horny friends who are the sniffers."

"Really? I woulda guessed at least half the bachelorettes are looking for one last hurrah, especially when they see the legendary Ball Peen Hammer in action."

"Come on, do your set, Z. I don't wanna stand here yapping all day about the poontang I'm not tapping. Our couch and that foot rub are calling my name."

Zander chuckles. "A foot rub's not gonna happen, P."

"Oh, I think it will."

Zander lifts the barbell off the rack and all conversation ceases until he's completed his set and the barbell has been safely returned to the rack.

"If it were me," Zander says, sitting up on the bench, sweat dripping down his face, "I'd consider it a point of pride to give a chick her last bang as a free woman, before she's shackled to one man for eternity."

"Oh, hey, speaking of being shackled to one man for eternity, Ry has Mariners' tix for us for Thursday night."

"Cool. Who are they playing?"

My phone buzzes with a text and I pull it from my pocket.

"Hey, no phone during workouts," Z says. "You know the rules."

I ignore him and look at my phone.

"Hi there!" the text says. "This is Maddy Milliken, Hannah's sister? I sent you a text on Friday. Maybe you didn't get it? I'm hoping to coordinate with you about our trip. Please give me a call as soon as you can so we can work out the details. Thanks so much!"

I grunt loudly. "I feel like I've got amnesia or something."

"What?"

"This chick's been texting me and I have no idea who she is."

"Well, that's nothing new."

"No, no, I mean—this one's different. She's not, you know, throwing herself at me—she just keeps talking about us taking some trip together."

"And that's not throwing herself at you?"

I hand Zander the phone and he reads the message.

"Where does she think you're gonna take her?" he asks.

"I have no fucking idea."

"Who's Hannah?"

"I don't fucking know—that's what I'm saying. Dude, did I bump my head recently?"

"Okay, well, text the girl back and say 'Who the fuck are you and what the fuck are you talking about?'"

I twist my mouth, thinking. "It's just so weird. What am I missing?"

"Was Hannah Milliken that crazy but exceedingly hot chick you hooked up with in the bathroom at Nico's a couple weeks ago?"

"No, that chick's name was Lindsey Meineken, I'm pretty sure. Or Merkel? Maybe Meister. Whatever. But she definitely wasn't a Hannah."

"Did you ever call her again?"

"Nah. Boring as hell. Like talking to a brick wall."

Z hands my phone back to me and shrugs. "Hit this girl back and ask her what the fuck she's talking about and then put your phone the fuck away. No phones during workouts."

I stuff my phone in my pocket. "Eh, I'll figure it out later—let's keep going." I lie down on the bench and get myself into position. "Okay, Z," I say, grasping the barbell. "Quit yapping and do the job I pay you in dimples to do. Kick my ass as hard as you kick your badass sister's."

Chapter 7
Keane

Monday 1:22 p.m.

My phone rings with an incoming call, but I'm in the middle of deep-fucking a MILF I met at the grocery store earlier today (to Akon's "Smack That," of course), so I don't answer the call. It's okay, though. No one but my landlord or my mom ever calls me—oh shit, I just thought of my mom while fucking a woman who's almost twice my age.

Gross.

But kinda hot in a fucked up way.

Chapter 8
Keane

Tuesday 10:04 p.m.

I'm lying on the couch with my beloved wife, watching *The Matrix* on TV, scarfin' white-cheddar-flavored popcorn outta bag, drinkin' beer outta bottle, and getting stoned outta my mind. I don't smoke all that often, actually, but when I do, I like to get so high I can't remember how to work the TV remote.

"Keanu is such a badass," Zander says as Keanu Reeves dodges a bullet in warped time.

"Dude," I say, shoving a handful of popcorn into my mouth. "Was that shit in slow-mo or am I really, really stoned?"

"That shit was in slo-mo—*and* you're really, really stoned."

"That's one handsome and happy motherfucker right there," I say, nodding at the TV and shoving another handful of popcorn into my mouth.

"Yup," Zander says. "Keanu's a handsome and happy motherfucker all the livelong day."

"Yee-*boy*."

"Heeeeeey," Zander says slowly, clearly having some sort of epiphany.

"What?"

"Keeee-aaaah-nuuuuuuuuuuuuu," Zander replies. He looks at me like he's expecting a response.

"Yeah?"

"Keanu. *Keane*. Keanu. *Keane*. There's only one letter difference."

"Whoa. Keanu. *Keane*. You're totally right, brah."

"And yet that one little letter makes all the difference," Zander adds.

35

"Now see? That's why I love you so much, Z. You're a deep thinker and shit."

"I love you, too," Z says. "Couldn't have asked for a better wife."

"Aw, thanks," I reply. "But I'm the husband."

"Naw, we're both the wife. Hey, you know who should be our sister-wife?" Zander says. He motions to the TV. "Keanu."

"Oh, yeah. Now *that's* an episode of *Sister Wives* I'd totally watch. He's one pretty dude."

Zander hands me the joint and I take a long drag. "Thanks, baby doll."

"You bet. Okay. Hand it back over here, sweet thing."

I hand him the joint and he sucks on it.

For a long moment, we stare at the movie again.

"I'd do Keanu if he were a chick," Zander says. "Or, I guess, if *I* were a chick. Either way." He takes a sip of his beer and shoves his big hand into the popcorn bag.

"Fuck it," I reply, swigging my beer. "I'd do Keanu, as is. No sex-change required."

"Oh, so you're bi now? You're coming out to me right here and now? Cause if so, I support you one hundred percent, baby doll—it doesn't change a goddamned thing between us."

"Well, of course, it doesn't change a goddamned thing between us. Nothing ever could. But, no, I'm not bi—though I kinda wish I were. That'd be so awesome."

"Why would that be awesome?" Zander asks.

"Unlimited choices, brah."

"Ah."

"But, yeah," I continue, "I'm a pussy-man through and through. Pussy, pussy, pussy for Peenie, all the livelong day."

"All hail to the Pussy," Zander agrees.

We clink beer bottles.

"Shit. If I weren't so stoned right now," I say, "I woulda just given myself a raging boner with all this pussy-talk. *Pussyyyyyyyy.*" I sigh happily. "God, how I love me some pussy."

Zander sighs loudly. "Amen, brother."

My phone buzzes with an incoming text and my glazed eyes travel slowly to my display screen: "Hey DICKWEED. It's Maddy Milliken AGAIN. Hellooooooooo?!?!?!?! Anyone out there?? Are you getting any of my texts and calls? At this point, you're either dead—in which case may you rest in peace and I'm sorry for your family's loss—or you're the biggest flake the world has ever seen. Keane, I need to know if you still want a ride and, if so, how much space you need for your stuff in my car? I'm not freakin' Uber, you know. I made a promise and I'm trying to keep it, but this is RIDICULOUS. If you still need a ride, I gotta know how much stuff you're planning on bringing because I've got a little hatchback and I'm stuffing it to the gills with everything I own. This is last call, dude. I'm leaving tomorrow morning at 8, with or without you. If you're coming, then tell me where to pick you up and what you're packing. If you're not coming, then, hey, I tried my best to connect with you, so I don't think it would be fair for me not to get the parking spot, after all. Either way, SHOW SOME COMMON COURTESY AND REPLY TO THIS FUCKING TEXT!"

"Uh-oh," I say when I've finished reading the entire message.

"What?" Zander asks.

"Maddy Milliken's all-caps mad at me."

"Uh-oh. What'd you do to her, Peenie? Did you fuck her mother?"

I chuckle. "Naw, I didn't fuck her mother." I scratch my head. "I don't think? Unless Maddy Milliken is, like, eight years old and plays soccer?"

Zander laughs.

"Do eight-year-olds drive hatchbacks?" I add.

"Lemme see that," Z says, grabbing my phone. He reads the text. "Maybe you fucked her sister Hannah?"

"Haven't we already talked about this? To the best of my knowledge, I am not acquainted with nor have I fucked either of the Milliken sisters."

"Well, maybe you should rethink that. Every Hannah I've ever met is a cutie. If you're gonna fuck a Milliken sister, my vote is Hannah."

"Well, sure, I'd fuck *Hannah* over *Maddy*." I swig my beer. "That's a no-brainer. I wouldn't fuck *Maddy* if you paid me."

"That's not saying much. You won't fuck anyone if they paid you."

"True. But especially not Maddy Milliken. The chick doesn't even know how to give a guy a bit of *explanation* in a fucking text before hauling off and calling him a dickweed."

"Hell yeah. You should text this Maddy girl and say, 'Hey, baby doll, ever heard the word *exposition*? That's from English 101—look it up, hon.'"

"Wow, Z, look at you being all literary and shit."

"I'm smarter than I look," Zander says. "I've got brains *and* brawn, sweet-meat."

"You sure do," I say. "Show me them guns, sweetheart."

Zander flexes one of his mammoth arms for me.

"Yee-gads. You're a motherfucking monster, son."

"I really am," Zander replies, sinking back into the couch and spreading his muscular thighs. "You know what you should do? Just go straight for the jugular. Ask her, 'Who the fuck are you, Maddy Milliken, and what the fuck are you babbling about?' That ought to suss things out."

"*Suss*? What the fuck is 'suss'?"

"You know, *suss* things out," Z says. "Get to the bottom of things."

"Oh. Huh. Learn something new every day."

"Now use it in a sentence, Peenie. That's the best way to remember a new word."

I think for a moment. "The two handsome and happy lads were in a bit of a pickle, but they nonetheless had high hopes they would one day be able to suss things out."

Zander nods definitively. "*Excellent.*"

"Hey, that should be our band name," I say, referring to the imaginary band Zander and I have been naming for years. "*Sussing Maddy Milliken.*"

"Done."

We clink our beer bottles and take long swigs in celebration of our new band name.

"Well, whether I'm *sussing* Maddy Milliken or not," I say, "I can't send her a text that says, 'Who the fuck are you?'"

"Why not?"

"What if I fucked her? That'd be awkward, to say the least."

"Wait a minute—you *did* fuck Maddy Milliken? I thought you said you didn't. And here I was thinking I was a stud for merely *sussing* Maddy Milliken."

We both burst out laughing.

"Nah, actually," I say. "I really don't think I've fucked Maddy Milliken. *But what if I did?*"

"What the fuck does that mean? Did you or didn't you? Do you often fuck a woman and have no memory of doing it?"

"Well, no, of course, not—not to my knowledge, anyway. But that's my entire point. How do you know when you've forgotten something? See what I mean? If you've *forgotten* something, how would you know that?"

"That's fucked up. You're fucking with my head, Peen."

"Just sayin'."

"That's some serious *Matrix* shit right there, man." He swigs his beer. "Hey, maybe it's just a wrong number? You got your number changed 'cause of that stalker chick a while ago, right?"

"Oh, yeah." I point at Zander emphatically. "That's gotta be it."

"Yep, that's gotta be it," Zander agrees, clearly energized by the idea. "Maybe Maddy Milliken's trying to reach the dude who used to have your number?"

"Yee-boy, that's gotta be it." I re-read the message, but, immediately, even to my stoned brain, it's clear this new idea is a nonstarter. "Nope. She called me Keane. She knows my name."

"Oh. Shit. Not a wrong number, then."

"Fuck."

"You seriously think you fucked a chick and don't remember it?" Zander asks.

"Highly unlikely," I concede. "My dick's got the memory of an elephant."

"And that's not the only *elephant*-like thing about your dick, Peenie Weenie."

"Yee-boy!" I shout.

We high-five each other.

"Now, *my* dick?" Zander says. "No memory at all. In fact, I think my dick's got Alzheimer's, man."

We both burst out laughing.

"So what should I say to Maddy Milliken, then?" I ask. "Should I just say, 'Who the fuck are you and what the fuck are you talking about, sweetheart?'"

"Gimme your phone," Zander says, grabbing my phone out of my palm. "I gotta see her exact words to give you appropriate counsel."

"Holy guacamole, baby doll. You and your fancy words today."

39

"She called you 'dickweed,'" Zander says, looking at my phone. "Wow. I like this girl. If you haven't fucked Maddy Milliken yet, then I really think you should consider doing so."

"I'm never gonna fuck Maddy Milliken. She hates me."

"Yeah," Zander agrees. "Sure looks that way." He looks at my phone again and snickers. "Hey, she wants to know what you're *packing*, Peen Star."

"She does? Well, she should get in line—so do half the sexually active women in Seattle."

In one fluid motion, Zander pulls his big, black dick and balls out of his sweatpants, making me cringe at the horrific sight of them, snaps a photo, presses some buttons on my phone, and then shoves my phone back at me. "There you go, baby doll. Consider Maddy Milliken officially *sussed*. You're welcome."

"What the fuck?" I say. I look at my phone and, I'll be damned, Zander's replied to Maddy Milliken's text with a photo of his big ol' dong and balls, no caption or explanation included. I look up at Zander. "Dude. Maddy Milliken's not going to be pleased."

"Hey, she wanted to know what you're packing."

"Zander," I say. "You can't send an unsolicited dick-pic to a chick. Not cool."

Zander bursts out laughing.

"What?" I ask.

"'Dick-pick to a chick.'"

I join him in laughing. "Dick-pick to a chick," I say, and we laugh for a solid two minutes.

"It's the social-media edition of 'Old MacDonald Had a Farm,'" Zander finally says, wiping his eyes. "Dick-pick to a chick-chick, everywhere a dick-pic. Here a dick, there a pic, everywhere a dick-pick."

"E-i-e-i-o," I answer.

We both laugh hysterically again.

"Look, no worries," Zander says, swigging his beer. "If it turns out this Maddy girl actually knows you, then she'll know right away my chocolate Easter bunny's not yours, snowflake—and if she thinks my mocha-choca-latte-ya-ya is yours, then she clearly doesn't know you from Mr. T... in which case, why the fuck would you care if she's pissed at you?"

"Aaaaaah," I say.

"See what I did there?"

"You got brains for days, Wifey."

Z taps his temple, a big smile on his face. "And that, my beloved Peenie Weenie, is how the big boys *suss* a woman out." Zander brings his beer bottle to his lips again. "Stick with me, baby doll—I'll show you the world."

We drink our beers and watch the movie again for a long moment. After a while, I glance down at my phone and I'm assaulted with the image of Zander's dick and balls again.

"Jesus, Z."

"What?"

"Haven't you ever heard of man-scaping?"

"Huh?"

"Your balls look like the Cookie Monster eating a bratwurst."

Zander lifts the waistband of his sweats, reaches into his pants and takes a gander at his junk. "Yeah, huh. I guess it's been a while since I had a date with my electric razor, now that I think about it. Well, shit, now I feel kinda bad for that amazing girl from last night." He sighs happily. "*Daphne.*"

"You liked her, huh?"

"I think I'm in love. Hey, thanks for helping me out with her. You went above and beyond this time, wingman." He motions to my hair. "I owe you big."

"Any time."

My phone buzzes with an incoming text: "OH MY GOD!!!!! Real mature, you LITTLE PRICK! (Yeah, that's right, I'm calling you a LITTLE prick AFTER seeing your dick, Keane!) What the HELL is wrong with you? If you don't want a ride, just say so! I didn't want to drive you in the first place, jerksauce! LOSE MY NUMBER, YOU FLAMING ASSHOLE!!!!"

I stare at my phone, my eyes glazed over. "Maddy Milliken is not pleased," I say evenly.

"No?"

"Nope."

"Lemme see that." Zander grabs my phone from me. "Hey, Mr. Happy's not *little*, Maddy Milliken!" he shouts at my phone at full voice, but he's smiling. "Maddy Milliken's a cool chick. I really like her."

"Well, I don't like her. In fact, I actively *dislike* her."

Zander laughs. "Aw, come on, she's a cutie. 'Lose my number, you flaming asshole!' That was pretty cute. Plus, she called you 'jerksauce.' She's adorbsicles."

"She's not cute or adorbsicles. She's a tight-ass who sends incomprehensible text messages to poor, defenseless men. She should be ashamed of herself."

"Well, either way, Maddy Milliken's now officially *sussed*." He tosses my phone onto the coffee table. "She thinks you're a black man."

"With a little pecker and fuzzy balls."

We both laugh.

"So what the fuck did she mean she didn't want to give you a ride in the first place?" Z asks.

"I have no idea."

My phone buzzes with yet another incoming text on the coffee table and Zander picks up my phone.

"Uh- oh," Zander says, looking at the screen.

"Is Maddy Milliken all-caps screaming at me again?" I ask, shoving a huge handful of popcorn into my mouth. "This ought to be good."

"Um. Peen?"

"What?"

"Um."

"Spit it out, fucker." I take a swig of my beer. "Hit me with the Wrath of Maddy Milliken. I can take it."

"Were you planning to go to L.A.?"

I pause, taken aback by the question. "No. I mean, yeah, sort of. I was planning to hang out with Dax—watch him record his album for a couple days and then maybe audition for that fancy talent agency that contacted me last month—but I haven't set a date or anything." The hairs on my arms stand up. "*Why?*"

"Well, it seems Maddy Milliken thinks your plan to visit L.A. is a bit more *concrete* than that."

"Huh?"

Zander hands me the phone and I read the message on my screen: "And btw, asshole," the text says. "I only said yes to giving you a ride as a favor to Dax! When he said 'could you please give my brother a ride to L.A.,' I thought he was talking about his actual BROTHER, not some random 'bro' of his with the social skills of a pogo stick!!!! You know what? If your 'bro' won't give me the damned parking spot now that I'm not driving your disgusting ass to L.A., I don't give a crap anymore! I'd rather not have parking all school year than have to spend one freaking minute alone in a car with you, let alone three effing days! DON'T CONTACT ME EVER AGAIN, YOU SEX OFFENDER!!!!"

I finish reading the message and swallow hard. "Oh fucking shit."

"This is bad," Z says.

"Dax is gonna kill me," I say, my stomach clenching.

"Why? You couldn't have known. Dax didn't even bother to tell you."

"Oh my God." I slap my forehead. "Daxy asked me to call him the other day and I never did. He said it was important." I frantically scroll through my legions of unread texts until I get to a text-thread with Dax. Oh shit. Since that first text from Dax the other day, the one he sent to me right before I went into that rowdy bachelorette party on Friday night, there are now maybe eight unread texts from him. (Confession? Sometimes I don't read my texts in a timely manner.)

"PEEN!" Dax writes in one of his many texts. "CALL ME! I left you two VMs!!!"

And on and on.

"Peen, you asshole. CALL ME. Are you dead? There's this girl named Maddy Milliken. I stupidly gave her your number before I'd talked to you and now she's gonna be calling you. I want you to drive to L.A. with her. I'll explain everything when you call. It's too long to text. P.S. Lay off the weed."

"Peen, are you dead?" another text reads. "Did you guzzle your cologne, thinking it was tequila, you dumbfuck?"

And, finally, there's the last one of the bunch: "Peen, fuck you. I didn't wanna have to text about all this but you leave me no choice. Remember Kat's friend Hannah from the wedding? Well, she's got a little sister named Maddy. ARE YOU FOCUSING, PEEN? Hannah lives across the hall from me (because her boyfriend is Reed's best friend so Reed gave Hannah a smokin' deal on an apartment) and the other day Hannah was telling me her little sister's gonna be driving from Seattle to L.A. (cuz the sister's transferring to UCLA film school). FOCUS, PEEN! Hannah doesn't want Maddy making the drive alone (apparently, Maddy was in some horrible car crash a few years ago, and Hannah gets really worried about her baby sister driving long distances), so I volunteered you to make the drive with her. DO NOT FREAK OUT, PEEN! First off, you keep saying you wanna visit me in L.A., so now's your chance. Second off, Hannah's super nice so let's do her a favor just because Morgan boys are cool like that. And, third off, as I mentioned, Hannah's boyfriend is Reed's best friend, so I figure doing a solid for Reed's best friend's girlfriend just makes sense in the karmic scheme of things. In case you're not fully understanding the full picture here (which is highly likely), Reed's the guy who decides if my album gets rock star marketing or sits on a shelf collecting dust, so I wanna be Johnny on the Spot when it comes to him or anyone in his inner circle. Got it? So you're driving to L.A. with Maddy Milliken and you're going to be polite and nice and pretend to be normal at all times (as hard as that is for you). FOCUS, PEEN! You will be the best, most fictitiously admirable version of yourself the whole fucking road trip! Oh, yeah, and DO NOT FUCK HER! We both know that won't end well and I don't want you creating any kind of drama that could splash back on me. Like I say, Maddy's gonna live across the hall with her sister, so I don't want you pissing her off and leaving me to pick up the fucking pieces after you leave. I'm under a ton of pressure here, man, so don't add to it, fucker. Plus, don't tell anyone about this part, but I've heard some sketch stories about Reed and believe me he's not a guy I wanna piss off IN ANY WAY. So let's keep Reed and everyone in his universe happy while I'm recording my album, okay? CALL ME, FUCKER! Or at least reply to this text and tell me you understand the sitch. I love you, bro. CALL ME."

I look up from my phone, my eyes wide. "Shit," I say, frantically swiping into my missed-calls folder. Fuck. There are no less than four missed calls from Dax in the last few days. Plus, there are missed calls and texts from my brothers Ryan and Colby. And two voicemails from Maddy Milliken's number. And, worst of all, ho-lee shit, I'm a dead man—there's a text from my sister, Kat, telling me if I don't call Daxy right away, she's gonna make me wish I was never born. And, motherfucker, I totally believe her.

I open my mouth to tell Z I'm a dead man, but, before I can speak, there's a loud, emphatic pounding at my door.

"Keane!" a voice yells on the other side of the door.

"Oh, shit," Zander whispers. "Is that Ryan?"

I nod, my eyes wide.

"Keane!" Ryan's voice says.

"He never calls me Keane," I whisper. "Ever."

"Oh shit," Z says. "You're a dead man, Peenie."

"Oh shit," I agree. "Dude. I'm motherfucking toast."

Chapter 9
Keane

"Keane! You in there, man?" my older brother Ryan's voice bellows on the other side of the door. "Keaney? Are you okay?" He pounds on the door again. "Keane?"

"Fuck," I whisper.

Z and I stare at each other, two raccoons in headlights.

"Keane?" Ryan says on the other side of the door again.

"Get the door," Z whispers.

"No," I whisper back. "Let's hide and hope he goes away."

The lock on the door clicks open—hey, when the fuck did Ryan get a key to my apartment?—and I scramble up from the couch, looking for a place to hide.

The door swings open and Ryan bounds into the room, clearly frantic, but the minute he sees me, his face rapidly morphs from anxiety into an expression of relief and then shock—or is that last one rage?

"What the fuck?" Ryan bellows.

"Hi, Captain. Nice to see you."

Ryan stares at me for a beat, apparently thrown off his game. "Why the fuck is your hair blue?"

I touch my hair absently. Oh yeah. I totally forgot about that. I flash my brother a huge smile.

"You're *stoned*?" Ryan asks.

I nod.

"Out of your fucking mind?" Ryan asks.

I nod again. And then I shake my head. "Not out of my mind. Well, okay, yeah, out of my mind."

Ryan grits his teeth. "Dax made me rush over here to check on you; he's so worried about you. He says he's been trying to reach you for three days, you moron." Ryan nods at Z. "Hey, Zander."

46

"Hey, Captain."

"You stoned out of your mind, too?" Ryan asks.

"Yup. Out of my mind," Zander says, smiling. "I just sent a chick a photo of my big ol' cock and hairy balls."

"Well, good for you, Z. I'm sure she'll cherish it forever." Ryan returns his glare to me. "Dude. Seriously. Have you been high for three solid days?"

I shake my head. "Just tonight. I haven't smoked for a solid month before now. I've been really busy lately."

"Doing what?"

I shrug. "Being every woman's fantasy, you know." I flash Ryan another huge smile, but he's obviously not charmed. "Working out with ZZ Top every day." I flex my impressive tricep muscle for him. "I'm totally ripped these days, brah—best shape of my life."

"Congratulations."

"And, uh, I took some extra bartending shifts at Hot Spot on nights when I don't have a gig. Oh, and I fucked a MILF I met at the grocery story yesterday. Nice little marathon sesh—kinda lost track of time on that one."

Ryan raises his eyebrows. "You went to a grocery store?"

"I go to the grocery store all the time, Ry. I gotta eat."

Ryan stares me down.

"Okay. Fine. I was in the mood to fuck a MILF, so I went to find one in the produce section. MILFs like shopping organic."

"Whose mom was she?"

"I don't know. But her kid called while we were fucking and the MILF had to take the call. Turns out the kid forgot her shin guards for soccer practice." I snicker. "It was so rad."

Ryan can't help but smile. "That is kinda rad."

"You shoulda seen the MILF's shopping cart, man. It was full of little-kid food. You know, like Skippy and Fruit Roll-Ups and shit." I laugh. "We ate all of it right after we fucked. So awesome."

Ryan shakes his head, grinning. "I must admit, that's pretty fucking rad."

I smirk. "I had her going so good, she was speaking in tongues, man."

"Good boy."

"Always."

We share a smile.

"So why the fuck is your hair blue?" Ryan asks. "You look like a fucking Smurf."

Z raises his huge arm. "That shit's on me, Captain. This amazing girl I hooked up with last night was trying to decide which shade of blue to dye her hair—because, you know, she wasn't sure whether to go blue-blue or sky-blue or more like aqua-blue? So, since her hair's pretty much the same shade of dirty-ass-blonde as Peenie's here, I offered our boy up as her guinea pig."

Ryan can't help but chuckle at that.

"She was really grateful I'd offered him up," Z continues, snickering. "And you know what women do when they're grateful, don't you?"

Ryan grins. "Yeah, I sure do."

Zander's smile stretches across the full width of his handsome face. "Peenie was just being a good wingman, Captain, going the extra mile for his beloved wife." Z smiles at me lovingly. "Thanks again, Peenie. You da best. Best night of my life."

"Anything for you, Z. You know that."

Zander looks at Ryan again. "You wouldn't blame Peen for dying his hair blue if you saw this girl." He sighs reverently. "*Daphne*."

"Good times?" Ryan asks.

"I think I'm in love."

"So did this Daphne girl wind up dying her hair to match Peen's after she saw the color on him?"

Z motions to me like the answer's self-explanatory. "What do you think?"

Ryan and Zander burst out laughing.

"*Hey*," I say, but I'm smiling.

"You owe him one, Zander," Ryan says. "He looks fucking ridiculous."

"Oh, I know. Peenie fell hard on his sword for me this time."

Ryan glares at me. "Wipe that goofy grin off your face, Papa Smurf. I was really worried about you. And Dax is going out of his head. He thought maybe you fell off your balcony or something—which, knowing you, isn't outside the realm of possibility."

"Sorry," I mumble. "I just didn't check my phone for a few days, that's all. You know how I get sometimes. I hate being reachable every minute of every day—it stresses me out." I flash him my dimples, the ones the ladies can never resist, and Ryan returns my smile, which I take as a very good sign. "Sorry, Rum Cake," I continue. "I really am. I was just taking a technology-vacay for a bit, I guess—I wasn't avoiding anybody in particular. I was just..." I sigh. "You know how I get sometimes."

Ryan looks at me sympathetically. "Yeah, I know."

There's a long beat, during which all anger seems to evaporate from Ryan's body.

"So, you've got a thing for MILFs these days, huh?" Ryan asks.

"Divorced soccer moms." I wink. "The produce section during school hours is a MILF-y wonderland. Highly recommend. Five stars."

Ryan chuckles.

I shrug. "Nothing serious for me these days; you know how it is."

"Are all the MILFs divorced?"

"Mostly."

"If they're not, you're following the Ten Year Rule like a good boy, right?"

"Yes, Master Yoda."

"Good boy." Ryan exhales again and his eyes flash with unmistakable sympathy for a brief moment. "Keane, you can't go MIA like that on us, okay? If I didn't find you here today, we were gonna tell Mom and Dad."

I'm aghast. "No."

"Yes."

"You wouldn't do that to me. Not *Mom*."

"Well, answer your goddamned phone more than once a week and we won't have to resort to that."

"Shit. You're not serious, are you?"

"Yes, I am. Why the fuck didn't you at least answer Dax? You *always* answer Dax. He said he called and texted a bunch of times. He was really worried, Keane."

I shrug. "Dax said he wanted me to do him a favor so I didn't call him back right away. And then I just forgot. Sorry. I wasn't avoiding him on purpose. I was just busy, you know, being every woman's fantasy." I flash him my dimples again, but this time, Ryan shoots me a look of sheer annoyance.

"You know what, Keane? This is bullshit," Ryan says. "I know things haven't worked out the way you'd hoped, but that's life. It's time for you to move on and grow up. This stunted-teenager routine is getting old. Everyone faces disappointment in life. Pick yourself up and move on."

I'm shocked and I'm sure my face shows it. Why's he turning all parental on me all of a sudden?

Ryan's face turns sympathetic. "Keaney, you can't let one setback turn you into a complete loser for the rest of your life."

I press my lips together. "It wasn't just a setback, Ryan. It was everything."

Ryan exhales. "No, it wasn't. You think so, but you're wrong. Get up, wipe the dirt off your knees, and move the fuck on. Your dream didn't work out? So find a new dream."

I swallow hard, not knowing what to say.

"Well, glad to see you're all right," Ryan says after an awkward beat. "I want to get home to my hot wife. Call Dax." He turns to leave.

"Ry, wait."

But Ryan doesn't stop. He continues striding toward the front door, obviously done with me.

"Ryan, wait. *Ryan.*"

Ryan stops and looks at me.

"I've got a situation that can only be described as an emergency."

Ryan looks concerned. "What happened?"

I grimace, not wanting to tell him.

"What is it, Keane?"

"It's bad."

Ryan's eyes darken with anxiety. "Did you get some girl pregnant?"

I make a face. "No. I'm always really careful about that." I look at Z. "Unlike you, dumbshit."

"Hey, antibiotics cleared that right up."

We both laugh.

Ryan exhales. "What is it? You owe someone money? Is some guy named Johnny T-Bags threatening to break your legs?"

"No, I'm good on money. Tips have been really good."

"Then what?"

I pause.

Ryan throws his hands up in a gesture of impatience. "I don't have all day, fucker. Spit it the fuck out."

I slowly hand Ryan my phone, my head bowed. "Read all Daxy's texts in order, starting from the bottom, and then look at the string of texts with someone named Maddy Milliken."

"Maddy Milliken? Is she related to Kat's friend Hannah Banana Montana Milliken?"

I roll my eyes and slap my forehead. Jesus. Where the fuck was Ryan four days ago? "Just read everything," I say. "It's too much to explain."

Ryan grabs my phone and takes a seat on my couch, and for what seems like forever, he sits, his head lowered, his gaze concentrated on my phone. Occasionally, Ryan laughs or says, "Oh, Jesus," but, mostly, he remains very quiet.

Finally, Ryan looks up. "Peen, you're the biggest idiot I know, hands down."

"I know," I say.

Ryan whips his hard glare onto Z. "And you're a close fucking second."

"Sorry," Z says. "I was just trying to help."

"Help me, Ryan, please," I say. "I don't wanna fuck things up for Dax."

"What am I gonna do with you, Keaney?" Ryan says, rolling his eyes. "Shit."

"I don't mind fucking shit up for myself—obviously," I say, motioning to my blue hair. "But I don't wanna fuck things up for Dax. All his dreams are about to come true."

"Yeah, I know. *Shit*. Gimme a second." Ryan looks up again, biting the inside of his cheek.

"I must admit I can't understand how me driving with this chick is supposed to have anything to do with Dax's record label..." I begin.

"Shut up, Peen," Ryan barks. "I'm thinking."

I wait.

"Dax is being crazy about the record-label part, but it doesn't matter," Ryan finally concludes. "He's under pressure and we gotta

51

support him on this one, even if he's being paranoid. The main thing is he wants to keep everyone happy in Reed's inner circle, and I get that. Sort of. Regardless, if he promised to help Hannah, then we gotta help him deliver on his promise. We're not gonna let him look like an idiot with the people who hang out with his new boss."

I nod.

"Okay, here's what we're gonna do, shit-for-brains. I'll call this Maddy girl and pretend to be you."

I breathe a huge sigh of relief. Ryan's our family's fixer. If he's on the job, everything's gonna be fine.

"I know just what to say to her," Ryan continues.

"Thanks, Ry."

"Now go to your room and get your shit packed for L.A. and then get your sorry ass to bed."

"Wait, what? You're gonna make me drive to L.A. with this chick?"

"You got a better idea?"

"No," I admit. "But I can't go to L.A. *tomorrow*. I promised to take my wife to the Mariner's game on Thursday."

"Yeah, with my tickets, you twat-head."

"But we were gonna have a romantic night out."

Ryan looks at Z. "You got someone you can take to the game on Thursday night, Z?"

Zander smiles. "I sure do."

"Traitor," I say.

"Go get packed," Ryan commands, his patience clearly at its breaking point. "You're going to L.A."

"Seriously, man," I say. "Don't make me sit in a car with this Maddy chick for three fucking days—she hates my guts."

"No, she doesn't," Zander interjects. "She hates *my* guts—she's just severely *annoyed* with you. Once she finds out my dick's not yours, all will be forgiven. Right, Cap'n?"

Ryan sighs. "Hopefully. I'll do my best when I talk to her."

I let out a deep sigh of resignation. *Fuck*. I can't figure out a way to get myself out of this road-trip from hell.

"Come on, Peen," Ryan says. "Time to man up."

"Yeah, I know." I let out another long sigh. "Thanks for helping me, Ryan. I owe you one."

"Dude, you owe me, like, a *thousand*. You'd need seven lifetimes to pay me back for all the shit I've done for you."

"And that's why I love you the most."

"Yeah, yeah. Go pack a bag and get your ass to bed. You gotta be well rested if you're gonna have any chance of making this girl think you're a semi-normal human tomorrow."

"Will you call Daxy for me?"

"Yeah, I got it covered. I'll tell him to chill the fuck out and stop acting like a fucking lunatic."

"Thanks."

"But don't fuck this up for Daxy—I'm warning you. He's got a lot riding on this album. We all gotta support him however we can. This is big."

"I'll be on my best behavior—handsome and happy, all the livelong day." I wink at him. "'Night, brah." I turn and shuffle toward my bedroom.

"Hey," Ryan calls after me.

I stop and turn around.

"Whatever you do, don't fuck this girl, Keane. That won't end well and you know it, and we don't wanna create unnecessary drama for Dax, like he said. She's gonna live across the hall from him, remember? He's not acting crazy about that part. She's off-limits, Keane."

I throw up my hands like I'm offended at the suggestion. "Jesus Christ, Ryan, I'm not gonna fuck Maddy Milliken. I can already tell she's annoying as shit, a total tight-ass. *Definitely* not my type."

"Well, I think she's adorable," Z sniffs.

"If by 'adorable' you mean *annoying*," I say. "Don't worry, I'll treat her like a little sister—an *annoying* little sister who hauls off and calls people 'dickweed' before she's even bothered to provide a fuck's worth of *exposition* in her goddamned texts."

Zander laughs. "Don't forget 'flaming asshole.' She called you that, too."

"Yeah, well, that was only after she saw your baloney pony, you fucker."

"No way. She called you a 'flaming asshole' way before I sent her a smiling photo of Mr. Happy."

"No, she didn't."

"She sure as shit did."

"Shut the fuck up," Ryan says sharply, and we both stop and stare at him. "God, you're both such fucking idiots."

Z and I smile at each other.

"What the fuck were you two thinking, sending this poor girl an unsolicited photo of Z's junk?" Ryan says. "Not cool. You can't be doing that shit, guys."

"Hey, I had nothing to do with it," I say, holding up my hands.

"It's true," Z says. "That one's on me."

Ryan shakes his head. "Jesus, Z. You don't even know this girl. You gotta be careful with dick-pics, especially with a girl you don't know."

"Ah," Zander says. "But sometimes a dick-pic to a chick-chick isn't really a dick-pick to a chick-chick, son."

"E-i-e-i-o," I add, and Zander laughs.

Ryan looks up at the ceiling, apparently praying for patience. "Go pack your bag, Keane. You gotta be handsome and happy bright and early tomorrow."

"Aye, aye, Cap'n," I say, saluting him. "Don't worry, come tomorrow morning, Maddy Milliken won't be able to resist my *ebullient* charm."

"Ooooh, great word," Zander says.

"*No*," Ryan says emphatically. "Don't try to charm her, for the love of God. No Ball Peen Hammer shit, okay? Just pretend to be normal, for once in your life."

"Gotcha," I say, winking. "Normal shit, all the livelong day."

Zander chuckles. "Good luck with that."

"And don't try to get a rise out of her either, like you always do with people who annoy you," Ryan adds. "Just engage in pleasant conversation about the weather or, I dunno, ask her about her hobbies, hopes, and dreams."

"Of course," I say. "The ol' H, H, and Ds. I got this, baby doll. Ain't no thang."

"And don't start calling her by some weird nicknames within the first thirty seconds of meeting her, either," Ryan says. "Not every woman likes to be treated like your fraternity brother, Keane. You gotta feel her out before unleashing the Peen on her."

"I don't treat people like my fraternity brother," I say defensively. "I wasn't even in a fraternity."

"I mean don't start calling her Mad Dog or baby doll or sweet cheeks or some other shit like that within the first thirty seconds, okay? Go easy on her. Get a read on her first before you barrage her with your unbridled Peenie-ness."

"Save your breath, Rum Cake. Women love me."

"They do," Zander says. "Women love Peenie. And so do I, by the way." He winks.

"Thank you," I say. "I love you, too."

Ryan exhales. "You two are Tweedle-Dee and Tweedle-Dumbshit, I swear to fucking God."

Zander and I simultaneously reach out and high-five each other.

"Just pretend to be normal, that's all I'm saying," Ryan continues.

"You got it, baby," I say. "One order of Normal Dude coming right up—hold the mayo. So is that it? Are we done?"

"Yeah."

"Okeedoke. Thanks again for saving my bacon, brah." I turn around and shuffle toward my room. "Nighty night."

"Don't fuck this up," Ryan barks at me as I walk away.

"I heard you the seventh time," I call over my shoulder. "No fucking up will transpire."

I hear Zander chuckling behind me.

"I don't know why you're laughing," Ryan says. "You're as big an idiot as Peen. You can't send a dick-pic to a girl you don't even know, Z."

"It was a *strategy*, Captain," Zander replies. "I was *sussing* her."

"*What*?"

"I was *sussing* her," Z says slowly, emphasizing every sound. "I was sussing Maddy Milliken. Back me up on this, Wifey."

I stop and turn around, just before reaching the threshold of my bedroom. "Yup. Z was full-on sussing Maddy Milliken."

"What the fuck does that even mean?"

"Sussing," Zander says. "You know, like luring a gopher outta hole."

Ryan makes a face that communicates his disbelief. "Well, I'm sure this poor girl didn't feel *sussed* by your big, black cock, Zander—I'm pretty sure she felt more like *traumatized*. That's quite a dick you got there, son."

"And fuzzy balls," I add.

"Yee-boy!" Zander shouts, and I laugh.

"Go to your room, Keane," Ryan says, pointing sternly to my bedroom like he's ordering a misbehaving beagle into his doghouse.

"Okay, okay," I say. I turn around and stride purposefully into my bedroom, a huge smile on my face. But just as I turn to shut my door, I hear Ryan's scolding voice one last time:

"Jesus, Zander. Haven't you ever heard of man-scaping, for fuck's sake? *Fuck.*"

Chapter 10
Maddy

Wednesday, 8:02 a.m.

He's got blue hair.

"Hi," I say, shaking Keane's hand.

Keane Morgan's got blue hair? Well, that's an unexpected development. His hair is tousled and spikey at the same time—the kind of hairstyle a guy fusses over in the mirror for a solid twenty minutes in order to make it look like he's just rolled out of bed... and... it's... *blue*.

Huh.

I've seen plenty of *girls* with blue hair—and I typically think it's a super cute look for them—but I've never seen this look on a guy. And certainly not on a guy who looks like he just rolled in from playing beer pong at a frat party. Definitely not what I was expecting.

Other than his unexpectedly blue hair, however, I must admit Keane Morgan's an outrageously good-lookin' guy. Hannah warned me all Kat's brothers are as bizarrely attractive as their stupefying sister, of course, but I wasn't prepared for Keane to be *this* big a freak. I don't think I've ever seen eyes quite this blue in all my life. Is he wearing colored contact lenses? Or is the implausible color of his eyes some sort of optical illusion, a false suggestion subliminally implanted into my brain by his startling hair?

"Hey, *Maddy*," Keane says, shaking my hand and flashing a smile that reveals outlandish dimples and straight, white teeth. "It's a *pleasure* to meet you, *Maddy*."

"Uh, thanks?" I warble. Shoot! I'm doing that question-mark thing with my voice again. I pull my palm from his and cross my arms. "*Thanks*," I amend.

Holy bajeebus. Keane's body is crazy-fit. The way he's filling out his simple jeans and T-shirt is nothing short of insanity-sauce. Even his frickin' *forearms* are attractive, for the love of Adonis. His hands. His *ears*. Is there anything even remotely unattractive on this guy other than his blue hair?

I uncross my arms and immediately cross them again. He's... *wow*.

"Thanks for the ride," Keane says breezily. "It's gonna be a *pleasure* hanging out with you, *Maddy*."

"Thanks?" I say.

"And, hey, I'm sorry again about my laggery these past few days. I've been stretched like an Abba Zaba lately—ya know, work hard, play hard."

"Stretched like... huh?"

"Stretched like an Abba Zaba." He gesticulates like he's stretching something between his hands. "You know—taffy?"

"Oh."

"You've never had an Abba Zaba bar?"

I shake my head.

"Chewy taffy with a peanut butter center?"

"Nope."

"Oh, holy shit, Mad Dog. We gotta pop your Abba Zaba cherry as soon as humanly possible. Abba Zaba's one of life's simple"—he grins and winks again— *"pleasures."*

There's an awkward beat as I stare at Keane, dumbfounded. What the heck on a Ritz cracker is this strange creature standing before me who says the word "pleasure" every third word? This blue-haired, blue-eyed, dimpled, broad-shouldered creature who within the first thirty seconds of meeting me has already called me "Mad Dog" and said he wants to "pop my Abba Zaba cherry"? Did he talk like this during our brief phone call last night? I really don't think so. In fact, I'm pretty sure he talked like a regular human last night.

I point to the small duffel bag in Keane's hand. "Is that all you're bringing with you?"

"Yup, this is it, *Maddy*." He holds up the bag. "Everything I need to be handsome and happy all the livelong day, stuffed into one little bag." He winks at me for the third time in forty seconds. "I guess I'm just a man of simple *pleasures*, baby doll."

Aaaaaaaaaand I'm back.

Whatever hormone-induced spell has been threatening to overtake my body was just now broken—or dare I say *smashed*?—by that "wink + pleasure + baby doll" thing Keane Morgan just tried to pawn off on me as "charm." I feel like I've been smacked across the face with a "pull yourself together!" stick and, just that fast, I'm remembering this blue-haired Adonis is the very same jerk who didn't have the courtesy to reply to a single one of my messages for *days* and then, totally unprovoked, sent me an up-close-and-personal photo of his friend's Alabama black snake.

Honestly, I'm not buying the line of crap Keane tried to peddle me last night on the phone. Am I really supposed to believe that, after Keane's best friend's phone battery died, he drunkenly used *Keane's* phone to try to send a dick-and-balls photo to his girlfriend, but erroneously sent it to me? Please, child. Does he think I was born yesterday?

And on top of that, does Keane truly expect me to believe he missed *all* my calls and messages thanks to some sort of self-imposed "technology cleanse"? Seems pretty far-fetched to me, especially now that I'm meeting the guy. I mean, come on, Keane doesn't strike me as a devout practitioner of transcendental meditation. Pfft.

Okay, so the guy's physically gorgeous—so what? As far as I'm concerned, Keane is nothing but a big ol' bullshitter, and quite possibly even a douche. Yeah, I said it. I mean, seriously, who uses the term "baby doll" other than total douches? It's just plain rude. Not to mention completely sexist.

"So, are you ready to hit the road, then?" I ask, motioning to my car.

"Sure thing."

I open my car's hatchback, grab Keane's bag, and stuff it into a tiny crevice between my jam-packed stuff.

"So, hey, Maddy," Keane says behind me.

I turn around and look at him.

"So are you game to press the restart button here?" he asks. "I'm sorry we got off on the wrong foot. Totally my fault, of course." He flashes a crooked smile. "I'd be grateful if you could find it in your heart to forgive my idiocy and start over."

Gosh, that was a lovely speech. Perfect, really. He displayed just the right amount of humility and remorse—flashed just the right amount of dimples while maintaining earnest and direct eye contact at all times. Bravo. But, sorry, I'm not buying any of it. If he lied to me last night, then he's lying to me now.

"Sure, Keane, your idiocy is officially forgotten," I say (because, whether Keane Morgan is a liar or saint, he's still my one-way ticket to a free parking spot mere blocks from campus). "Water under the bridge."

Keane's smile lights up his entire face. "Awesome," he says, sounding relieved. He shifts his weight, spreads his legs slightly, and levels me with his astonishing eyes-that-match-his-hair. "Hearing you say that gives me extreme *pleasure*, Maddy." He grins and his dimples pop again. "Extreme *pleasure*, indeed."

Chapter 11
Keane

For the past forty minutes or so, Maddy and I have been silently driving south on I-5 out of Seattle, listening to a mutually agreed upon indie rock station on Pandora. I've tried to start conversations several times, believe me, but it turns out Maddy Milliken's not what I'd call "a natural conversationalist."

"Hey, bee tee dubs," I say after a long stretch of awkward silence. "I can drive whenever you want. Just lemme know if you need a break, baby doll."

"Thank you, but I prefer to drive," she replies, pursing her lips. "And please don't call me 'baby doll.'"

"I'm an excellent driver," I say.

"I'm sure you are," Maddy says, scrunching up her nose like she's smelling the underside of Zander's balls. "But I prefer to drive."

"No," I say, chuckling. "That's my *Rainman* impression, sweet cheeks. 'I'm an excellent driver.' You know, Dustin Hoffman in a gray suit?"

Maddy presses her lips together, clearly mustering all her energy to simply *tolerate* me. "I haven't seen that one," she says, her voice tight. "And please don't call me 'sweet cheeks.'"

"You haven't seen *Rainman*?" I bellow. "Dude. I thought you were going to film school."

"I am."

"Well, *Rainman* won Best Picture. Aren't film students supposed to be obsessed with watching all the Best Picture winners? You better get on that. It's a good one, babesicles."

Maddy lets out a long sigh and touches her forehead like I've just given her a migraine. "Thanks for the tip, *babesicles*," she says, her mouth tight. "But although *some* film students might be obsessed

61

with watching Oscar-winning dramas, I'm not one of them, *sweet cheeks*, because my personal dream is to make award-winning documentaries, *baby doll*." She glances away from the road to *glower* at me. "To each her own, right, *sugar lips*?"

Wow. That was more verbiage all at once from Maddy than she's unleashed during the entire past hour—not to mention the most sass she's displayed, too. Yee-boy! This is gonna be fun.

"Oh dear," Maddy says, putting her fingertips to her mouth. "I'm sorry. Does repeatedly being called insincere terms of endearment *bother* you, Keane? Does it perhaps make you feel like a slab of meat?"

"Hell, yes, it makes me feel like a slab of meat," I say, flashing her a wicked grin. "*And I love it.*"

Maddy twists her mouth, clearly trying not to smile.

"So you wanna make documentaries, huh?" I say.

"Yup."

"Like what?"

"Anything, really, as long as it's real and raw and thought-provoking." She bites her lower lip, apparently considering her next words. "My favorite thing in the world is finding quiet moments of magic other people maybe don't notice because they're too busy looking down at their phones."

"Well, shit, you're speaking my language now," I say. "*Not* looking down at my phone happens to be my superpower."

Maddy chuckles. "Yeah, I noticed, *dickweed*." She bursts out laughing at her own joke.

"I'm sorry about that again," I say.

She sighs. "Oh, don't worry about it. Water under the bridge, remember?" She glances away from the road to flash me a shy smile. "Honestly, we're good, honey nuggets."

Okay, that was awesome. I know Maddy said words similar to those this morning, but there's no comparing the genuine way she just delivered them to the tight-ass way she said them earlier this morning.

"Hey, excuse me real quick," I say, pulling my phone out of my pocket. I tap out a quick text to Zander: "Not even 9:00 yet and I do believe Maddy Milliken's been sussed."

"Niiiiiiiice," Zander replies. "How'd you do it?"

"Apology + dimples = Forgiven."

"Well don't stop now, baby. Suss the living hell outta her! Ask her about her H, H & Ds."

"Oooooh, yeah. Totes forgot all about that. Doing it now. Bye," I write.

I shove my phone into my pocket. "Sorry about that," I say to Maddy. "So, hey, I've got a couple questions for you..." I begin, and then I proceed to ask Maddy a shit-ton of questions about her hobbies, hopes, and dreams. And much to my surprise, Maddy's answers to all my questions are so fucking interesting and entertaining, I soon find myself asking more and more questions just for the fuck of it—not even for the purpose of sussing her—until, finally, I'm shocked to find myself balls-deep in the conversation and hanging on Maddy's every word.

When my stomach growls, I look down at my watch thinking we've probably been talking for about an hour, and I'm shocked outta my skull to discover we've been chatting nonstop for close to *three* solid hours.

"Ho-lee sussage," I say, looking up from my watch. "Is your hatchback a time machine?"

Maddy looks at the clock on her dashboard. "Oh my gosh," she says. "I've been talking your ear off forever. I'm so sorry. Wow. I never do that, I swear."

"Don't apologize. You made documentaries about spelling bees and wheelchair-rugby and gorillas sound cooler than *Iron Man*, dude."

She smiles shyly at me.

"So have you made any documentaries yet?"

"I've made mostly short films, other than this one full-length documentary I made last year. That film is what got me into UCLA, actually."

"What's it about?"

"The men's and women's basketball teams at U Dub."

"Wow. Not at all what I thought you'd say."

"What'd you think I'd say?"

"Global warming? Shining a spotlight on some sort of social injustice?"

Maddy smiles broadly. "Well, yeah, actually, it's about how the

63

men's team gets a shit-ton more support and adulation than the women's team, even though the women work just as hard."

I laugh. "Social injustice. Damn, I'm good."

She laughs and nods. "I know it might sound heavy-handed in the explaining of it, but the actual movie itself doesn't come across as preachy, I swear. It's thought provoking, for sure, but it's also thoroughly entertaining and touching and funny. One critic called it '*Hoop Dreams* with a gender twist.'"

"I'm assuming that's a huge compliment?"

"Huge."

"You know how I knew that, even though I've never heard of *Hoop Dreams*?"

"How?

"Because by the expression on your face, it's clear that other movie is your idea of porn."

Maddy belly laughs at that. "Yes, it is, actually."

I laugh with her. "What's your movie called?"

"*Shoot Like a Girl*."

"Ah. Very cool."

"Thank you."

"And, just so you know, when I said 'cool' just now? I was spelling that 'k-e-w-l.'"

"*Wow*. It must be *really* cool, then."

"It is."

We share another huge smile.

"So how'd you get the idea for your movie?" I ask.

"You sure you wanna hear this? It's kinda long."

I motion to the road ahead of us. "It appears I've got some free time."

Maddy takes a deep breath and launches into an explanation of how she was hired to film both teams' basketball games for the coaches to use the footage at practices. "And, right away," she says, "when I started attending both teams' games, it irked me how, at the men's games, the stands were always jam-packed with screaming fans, while at the women's games, the place was usually only a quarter-filled and as quiet as a morgue. And that gave me my idea. So I got all necessary approvals and was allowed to shoot more than just games—you know, interviews with players, practices, stuff like that.

And when I finally started editing all the footage I'd shot, I realized, 'Oh my effing God, I think I've captured lightning in a bottle here.' I just knew I had the makings of an edge-of-your-seat sports movie combined with thought-provoking social commentary. There was even a little side story of unrequited love, because this one guy on the men's team was obviously in love with one of the female players, and she had no idea about it. I kept showing footage of the guy sitting in the stands at the women's games, *yearning* for her. It was so sweet."

"Did the guy wind up getting the girl after she saw the movie?"

"No," Maddy says, clearly disappointed. "She saw the movie—but they didn't get together."

"What? How is that possible?"

Maddy makes an exaggerated sad face. "She told him she just wanted to be *friends*."

"What the fuck?" I say. "I'm so bummed. That's not the way that story's supposed to end."

"I know. The dreaded friend zone." She smiles ruefully. "Unfortunately, it's a permanent address for some of us."

"Damn. I was thinking you were gonna say she saw the movie and they lived happily ever after."

"That's definitely the ending I would have written if my film had been scripted."

"Shit, I feel like I wanna call that guy up and give him some lessons on slaying it with the ladies. There's absolutely no excuse for a guy to get friend-zoned, ever."

"Well, it's not his fault. If there's no chemistry, there's no chemistry. Some things can't be forced."

"It's not about *forcing* a goddamned thing. If a guy knows what he's doing, then chemistry with any girl he wants is a foregone conclusion."

Maddy glances away from the road to shoot me a snarky look. "You do realize you sounded like a serial-killer-psychopath just now, right?"

"I thought that guy was a baller?"

"Well, he plays *basketball*, yes, but he's really shy. Not everyone is like you, Keane."

"Shy or not, there's no excuse for a guy to get friend-zoned, especially a baller."

"So you're telling me you've *never* been friend-zoned?"

I scoff. "Of course not."

"Oh my God. I'm driving twelve hundred miles with a psychopath."

"It's never happened to me. How does that make me a psychopath?"

"It's awfully hard for me to believe you've *never* been rejected *once* in your whole life."

"Oh, I've been *rejected*—girls have broken up with me when I've acted like a dick. I've just never been 'friend-zoned' before. Every single time I've been sexually attracted to a woman and made a move, she's been sexually attracted to me in return. And then, just to be clear, that's the part of the story when we've had fucking awesome sex."

Maddy blushes.

"So, hey," I say. "We've gotten sidetracked *again*. Finish telling me about *Shoot Like a Girl*. You've got my full attention—although I should mention that's a lot like having the full attention of a gnat, so don't get too excited."

Maddy laughs. "How about this—given your gnat-like attention span, I'll try to make my movie sound as much like *Ironman* as humanly possible."

"Excellent plan."

Maddy proceeds to tell me a shit-ton more about her movie, throwing in the phrase "and then everyone put on an iron suit" at random intervals, and I must admit, her excitement for her movie is infectious. "My favorite part was the juxtaposition of the male experience with the female one. For example, I'd show a bunch of the guys talking about their dreams of going into the NBA and buying houses for their mothers, and then I'd immediately toggle to female athletes saying they knew their college careers wouldn't lead to fame or fortune, but they played for the love of the game and their teammates, or maybe I'd show them playing in an empty stadium."

"Very cool," I say.

"Is that k-e-w-l?" Maddy asks.

"Absolutely. Great word, bee tee dubs: *juxtaposition*." I stop and think for a beat. "'When an army of neuroscientists studied and compared the very large brain of Maddy Milliken with the pea-sized brain of Keane Morgan, they couldn't help noticing the *juxtaposition* was a stark one, indeed.'"

Maddy laughs.

"So, anyway," I say. "You were saying?"

"No, no, I'm done talking. You've now heard everything there is to hear about my movie. Sorry my explanation was so long. You must be pulling your hair out from boredom."

"Not at all," I say. "I feel like I just watched a TED talk. And, just so you know, even if you'd bored me to tears (which you didn't), I wouldn't pull out even a *strand* of my glorious blue mane. My azure locks are my crowning glory."

Maddy giggles. "You're so funny, Keane."

"I might be funny, but you're amazing. Seriously, Maddy, you're the Steve Jobs of documentaries."

"Oh my gosh, Keane, you're making me blush."

"I've noticed that's not a hard thing to do."

Maddy blushes again.

"So when can I see this masterpiece of yours, Scorsese? Gimme some popcorn and Milk Duds and sign me the fuck up."

Maddy's face lights up. "You'd watch my movie? Wow. Well, you can watch it tonight, if you want. It's on a hard drive in my bag."

"Hell yeah, I wanna watch it tonight. We'll do a basketball-documentary double-header: *Shoot Like a Girl* and that other basketball documentary, too—the porno you mentioned."

"*Hoop Dreams*?"

"That's the one. I should warn you, though: I've never watched a documentary before, other than at school and on ESPN. You'll be popping my documentary-cherry, so be gentle with me."

"Oh, don't you worry, baby doll," Maddy says, her eyes flitting from the road to me, a devious smile on her lips. "When I pop a guy's cherry, I *always* make sure the lucky guy experiences nothing but extreme and outrageous *pleasure*." She winks and then bursts out laughing at herself.

Chapter 12
Keane

Oh my God, I think Maddy Milliken just sent a subliminal message to the pleasure-center in my brain. Because, I swear to God, when she said the word "pleasure" and shot me that naughty look to go along with it, my dick kinda tingled a little bit.

I open my mouth to reply to her—intending to sling some sexual innuendo back at her to make those cheeks of hers burn extra hot— but I get thwarted by the song that comes on the radio: "Stressed Out" by Twenty One Pilots.

"Oh, I love this song!" Maddy chirps, turning up the volume. She begins dancing in her seat and singing along to the song, the unexpected heat between us from a moment ago instantly gone.

Or was I just imagining that heat?

The more likely scenario is that Maddy stumbled into sending a subliminal message to the pleasure-center in my brain the same way a broken clock is right twice a day. Because this girl ain't no seductress, I can tell you that right now.

I watch Maddy singing for a long beat, smirking at her unadulterated display of dorkiness. Huh. I didn't notice this 'til just now, but I think Maddy might be kinda cute. I mean, she's not *sexy* or *hot* or whatever—she's a total dork, but, yeah, she's most definitely *cute*. Really cute, actually. Adorable nose. Cute little freckles on it. Smooth, soft-looking skin. A glow in her cheeks. She looks like one of those girls you'd see on a commercial for facial cleanser. A pretty girl-next-door type. Yep. Definitely cute.

My gaze drifts down the length of Maddy's long brown hair— which I'm suddenly noticing is actually kinda pretty. I like the way it flutters around her shoulders and down the front of her blouse. Ho-lee shit. Speaking of her blouse, what the *fuck* is up with that billowing yellow monstrosity? How the hell is a guy supposed to assess a girl's merchandise when she's wearing a loose-fitting shirt that makes her boobs as hard to find as fucking Waldo? I scrutinize her chest for a beat, trying to make heads or tails of her topography, but that motherfucking shirt is too big a cock-blocker for me to gauge a damned thing. Now, if I were forced to venture a guess, I'd say Maddy's hiding some pretty nice boobs under there—maybe even spectacular ones—but, as good as I am, I just can't be sure.

I jerk my gaze away from Maddy and look out the passenger window, my pulse pounding in my ears. What the hell am I doing? I can't be thinking about Maddy's tits. She's my honorary little sister. Sisters don't have tits. They have *breasts*.

Shit.

Now I'm thinking about Kat breastfeeding Little G.

I cringe.

What the fuck am I doing?

I gotta stop this shit right now.

Maddy's off-limits. Plus, she's not even my type. *At all*. I like hot girls and they like me back. I don't go for sweet girl-next-door types. And I definitely don't go for smart girls. *Hell no*.

The song ends and Maddy turns down the radio. "So, hey, we've been talking about me this whole time. Tell me something about you."

I clear my throat and look at her. My cheeks feel hot. "Sure," I say. "Ask me anything."

"Dax said you've been invited to audition for some big talent agency in L.A.?" she says.

"Yep."

"That's exciting. Does that mean you're moving to L.A.?"

"I dunno. Maybe. Depends what opportunities come my way."

"So you're an actor? A model?"

One side of my mouth hitches up. Oh my shit. Dax didn't tell Maddy what I do for a living? Ha! This whole time I thought she knew. "Neither," I say evenly. "I'm a stripper."

Maddy's cheeks burst into flames. "*Oh*," she says.

"Actually, I'm one of the top male strippers in Seattle," I add, thoroughly enjoying the sudden bloom in Maddy's cheeks. "Been doing it for just over a year."

"Oh," Maddy says again. "Cool?"

"This agency I'm auditioning for reps models and commercial actors in one of their divisions—they're a huge agency—so if I could get on their roster for that stuff it'd be amazing. But the reason they contacted me is they also book male strippers for all sorts of high-end stuff—clubs, private events, movies, TV shows. Ever since *Magic Mike*, you wouldn't believe how much demand there is for male strippers, especially in L.A."

"Oh. Wow." Maddy shifts her hands on the steering wheel. "Cool?"

I can't stop smiling at how flustered Maddy seems all of a sudden.

"Yup," I say. "I'm a stripper, Maddy. A strip-per. I take my clothes off and shake my ass for a living." I laugh to myself. I only said that last part to see if I could get that last square inch of Maddy's face to turn bright red... which I did. "So, hey, you hungry, Mad Dog?" I ask. I clap my hands together and she flinches like I've just smacked her ass. "I could eat a horse. Whaddaya say we pull off the highway and grab some grub-a-dub-dub?"

Maddy clears her throat. "Cool?" she says, her voice tight. She clears her throat again. "*Cool*." She swallows hard. "Yeah. Um." She clears her throat again. "Cool?" She flashes a very awkward smile that makes me laugh out loud. "I'm pretty hungry, too," she says. "Cool."

Chapter 13
Maddy

I can't stop staring at Keane across the table. He's not doing anything in particular; he's just sitting there, quietly looking at his menu, the bicep on his left arm bulging every time he flips the page of his menu. But ever since he told me what he does for a living, I can't stop imagining him ripping off his clothes in front of a frenzied pack of screaming women. I already know Keane's got an insanely fit body—all I had to do was look at the guy for a half-second and that was abundantly clear—but now I can't stop thinking he must have a truly *mind-blowing* body underneath that T-shirt and jeans.

"Are we ready to order?" our waitress asks, sliding up to our table. She looks pointedly at me. "What can I get you, honey?"

"Hi. Um, yes." I clear my throat. "A turkey club and fries, please?"

"Sure thing. And what about you, honey?" the waitress asks Keane.

Keane smiles at the waitress, flashing his dimples, and she leans toward him like a sunflower straining toward the sun. I'd guess she's in her mid-forties or so, but the smile she's flashing Keane has instantly taken ten years off her face.

"Hi, Amy," Keane says, looking at the waitress's nametag. "Pleasure to meet you. How are you this fine day?"

"I'm great. And how are you, sweetie?"

"Handsome and happy all the livelong day."

The waitress laughs. "Great to hear. Love the hair, by the way."

Keane runs his hand through is tousled blue hair. "Thanks. I did it at the request of my better half."

My cheeks instantly burn with heat. Oh my God. Keane's got a *girlfriend*? Oh jeez, I feel like an idiot. For the past hour or so, I was

71

actually thinking Keane was *flirting* with me—not that I wanted him to do that, mind you, not even a little bit—but, *still*. Is my radar that defective?

"Sounds like an excellent reason to do it," the waitress says, shooting me a smile that tells me she thinks I'm the "better half" Keane just referenced.

"I'm just a natural-born giver, Amy," Keane says. "It's a blessing and a curse."

The waitress chuckles and smiles at me again, this time sending me a nonverbal message that clearly says, "You lucky bitch!"

Keane looks down at his menu again, pursing his lips. "Let's see. Decisions, decisions. I think I'll have a double cheeseburger with extra bacon, extra pickles, hold the onions." He looks at the waitress again, his blue eyes twinkling. "Never know when a spontaneous make-out sesh might suddenly break out—gotta be prepared for all eventualities."

The waitress *guffaws* at that, but I scowl like I've just bitten into a lemon. What the fuckity? Why is Keane talking about having a spontaneous "make-out sesh" when he's got a frickin' girlfriend back home? And, by the way, who does he presume his spontaneous "make-out sesh" partner would be in that scenario? Because if he thinks it would be me, he's sorely mistaken. Even if he didn't have a girlfriend, which it turns out he does (despite all the flirty signals I thought he was sending me in the car), Keane's soooo not my type. I'm not trying to be mean about it, but Keane's IQ would need a fifty-point boost before he'd even be within *spitting* distance of the type of guy I'd even *think* of going for.

"French fries with your burger?" the waitress asks Keane.

"Yeah, and a chocolate milkshake," he replies. "Extra whipped cream. Oh, and a side salad, too. Gotta get my veggies. You got any soup?"

"Beef chili or chicken noodle?"

"Chili. Thanks." He closes his menu and looks up at me. "I'm a growing boy, sweetheart." He pats his flat stomach. "It takes a village to keep this body looking like manna from heaven."

The waitress laughs for the millionth time, but I can't join her. I'm too distracted with a thousand thoughts, not the least of which is: "What kind of girl says 'hell yes' when asked to be the girlfriend of a baby-dolling stripper-man like Keane Morgan?" I'm betting Keane's girlfriend is gorgeous as hell but stupid as dirt. Whoever she is, I hope she's at least nice to Keane because, as quirky as he is, he doesn't seem like he has a mean bone in his body.

"Coming right up," the waitress says, drawing me out of my rambling thoughts. She stuffs her notepad into her black apron and grabs our menus off the table. "I'll be right back with a couple waters for you."

"Thank you," Keane and I say in unison as she departs.

"So...?" I say the minute the waitress is gone. "You've got a girlfriend, huh?" I'm trying my best to sound nonchalant, but I'm not sure I'm succeeding.

"Aw, hell no," Keane says, waving his hand. "I'm single and ready to mingle, baby."

I make a face of confusion. "So who's your better half, then?"

"Oh. My best friend and roommate, Zander."

Relief floods me, though I don't know why.

"Actually, I believe you're acquainted with my beloved Zander," Keane says. "Or, at least, with his dick and fuzzy balls."

"Ah, yes," I say, matching Keane's polite tone. "I do believe I am."

"I'm really sorry about that, bee tee dubs. I had absolutely nothing to do with Z sending you that photo, I swear, but Zander's my best friend and the whole fiasco happened 'cause I'm such a fuck-up when it comes to checking my phone, so it's on me."

"Apology accepted. And you can tell Zander I apologize for calling his dick 'little.' It really isn't all that little—well, at least, as far as I know from my limited experience."

Keane leans sharply forward, his face aglow. "Oh, now *this* is an interesting topic of conversation. Exactly how 'limited' is your 'limited experience,' Maddy Milliken?"

I make a face. "It's none of your business, Keane Morgan. It was a figure of speech."

Keane smirks. "Is 'limited' less than five?"

"It's none of your business."

"I'm guessing four or five guys, tops. How old are you?"

"Twenty-two next month."

"You gonna be a senior at UCLA?"

73

I've suddenly got a lump in my throat. I clear it. "No, a junior. I, uh, took a little time off." I hold my breath, hoping Keane doesn't ask me *why* I took time off—because talking about the year I took off from school after the car accident isn't something I'm even remotely willing to do. But, thankfully, Keane forges right ahead like a dog digging up a bone.

"Okay, then, my guess is five," Keane says. "That's my final answer."

"It's none of your business what my number is."

"Fine." He leans back in his chair. "I'll be sure to tell Zander he's not suffering from Little Dick Syndrome. He'll be relieved to hear it." He smirks. "Although, honestly, Z doesn't need anyone to tell him that. He's already well aware he's swinging a hefty bat."

I can't help but giggle. "Have you known Zander a long time?"

"Since eighth grade, which makes him the longest and most successful relationship of my life, other than my family. I always tell Z he's the great love of my life."

"*Oh*. Are you two friends or... ?"

Keane waits a beat, and when I don't finish my sentence, he grins. "Are we a couple? No. We're both straight. There ain't no hanky panky going on in the Morgan-Shaw household—well, I mean, not with each other, that is. There's *plenty* of hanky panky going on in the Morgan-Shaw household, if you know what I mean." He winks.

"Yeah, pretty sure I know what you mean."

"Now, if I were gay, believe me I'd put a ring on that motherfucker's finger so fast, it'd make his head spin. Which is why I'm totally in favor of gay rights, bee tee dubs. If there's a gay guy out there who's been lucky enough to find a boyfriend like Zander, then by all means, that dude should be able to lock that shit down. If I were lookin' to settle down, I couldn't do any better than Zander. Only glitch with that particular matrimonial plan is the fact that we're both totally and completely addicted to pussy."

"Here we go," the waitress says out of nowhere, appearing with two glasses of ice water and saving me from my complete speechlessness. "Your food should be up pretty quick. You want your chili and salad first, hon?"

"That'd be great," Keane says. "Thanks."

"So, um," I say after the waitress is gone, but then I stop, still trying to process everything Keane just said. "So. Um," I begin again. "Uh. Zander doesn't have a girlfriend?"

"Not at the moment, although Z tends to fall hard and fast. He's a 'love at first sight' kinda guy, big-time, unlike me. I'm sure by the time I get back to Seattle, Z will be married to this chick named Daphne he just met, with triplets on the way." He chuckles. "Actually, helping Z get laid by Daphne is the reason I dyed my hair."

"Huh?"

Keane leans his elbows on the table and his biceps bulge under the sleeves of his T-shirt. "So check it out. Z and I were at this bar by our house and this bombshell Daphne was telling us about how she's been thinking about dyeing her hair blue. So Z pulls me aside and he's like, 'You gotta help me with this goddess of a woman, Peenie. I think I'm in lurve.' So I'm like—"

"*Peenie?*" I ask, interrupting him.

"Yeah, that's my nickname: Peen, Peenie, Peenie Weenie. My stripper name is Ball Peen Hammer."

I burst out laughing. "Oh my God, Keane."

Keane flashes me a truly adorable smile.

"You named your stripper persona after a teeny tiny hammer?"

"*Hey*. It's *ironic*." He winks.

I'm laughing my ass off uncontrollably.

Keane flashes me an over-the-top smolder. "Ball. Peen. Hammer. *Baby*. Ka-bam, son!"

I laugh. "Oh my God."

"So, anyway, back to my hair," Keane continues, his eyes sparkling. "Zander was like, 'Peenie, you gotta help me get laid by this gorgeous, once-in-a-lifetime goddess. I gotta answer the call of my primordial destiny!'"

I laugh again. "*Primordial* destiny? What the hell does that mean?"

Keane pauses. "I dunno, actually. Z says it all the time and I've never asked him. But, anyway, Z figured since my hair's the exact same color as Daphne's—'"

"Hang on a sec," I say, holding up my hand. "Sorry to interrupt again. What color would that be?"

"Dark blonde." He pulls out his wallet and flips it open, and I lean forward and peer at Keane's driver's license photo.

"Wow," I say. "You look *that* amazing in a driver's license photo? You're insanely photogenic."

"As all psychopaths are, my dear." Keane flips his wallet closed and slides it toward the middle of the table. "Thanks for the compliment. So, anyway, Zander begged me to help him get laid by the girl of his dreams and the next thing I know"—he motions to his hair—"I look like a Smurf."

I burst out laughing at the dry expression on Keane's face. "Well, did it work, at least? Did Zander get the girl?"

"Yee-boy. Did he ever. Z said she was the best he's ever had."

"Was Daphne the girl Zander intended to send that dick-pic to?"

Keane looks confused.

"Because... last night on the phone you said your best friend mistakenly sent that dick-pic to me while drunkenly trying to send it to his 'girlfriend.'"

Keane presses his lips together but doesn't reply.

"Ha! I knew it," I say, instantly certain Keane was full of shit last night on the phone. "Zander *meant* to send that dick-pic to me, didn't he?"

Keane looks apologetic. "I didn't lie to you, Maddy. My older brother Ryan did." He looks sheepish. "It was my brother who called you last night, not me."

"I knew it!" I blurt loudly, this time slamming my palm onto the table and making our cutlery jump. "Within thirty seconds of meeting you this morning, I *knew* you weren't the same guy I talked to last night!"

"How'd you know?"

I roll my eyes. "Oh, come on, *Peen*. You were so normal and charming on the phone last night—smooth as frickin' silk—and today you're just"—I motion to his hair—"*you*."

"What the motherfuck?" he says, touching his hair. "I'm normal and charming all the livelong day."

I laugh. "No, Keane. Normal people don't say 'all the livelong day' or 'baby doll' or 'stretched like an Abba Zaba.' And they don't dye their hair blue to help their best friend get laid. Or call *Hoop Dreams* a porno. Or use the word 'pleasure' every five seconds. Or a thousand other things you've already done in my presence and I've only known you half a day. If you were normal, you'd know all that, *babesicles*." I lean back in my chair and cross my arms over my chest.

"Well, *fine*. Maybe I'm not *normal*, but I'm definitely charming as fuck. Way more charming than my fucking brother, that's for sure. I'd even go so far as to say I've got *ebullient* charm."

I chuckle. "Keep telling yourself that, *Peenie Weenie*."

"I don't need to tell myself that, sweet cheeks, because all the horny ladies tell it to me every day."

I roll my eyes. "Why the heck did your brother call me, instead of you? Were you too scared to talk to a girl who'd called you a 'flaming asshole'?" I mock shudder. "Oh, I'm so scary."

"Fuck no, I wasn't scared of you; I knew right from the start your bark is worse than your bite, Mad Dog. I was just too stoned to call you, that's all. I didn't wanna fuck things up even more than I already had. Plus, it's Ryan's job in life to fix my fuck-ups, and I didn't wanna take away his reason for being."

I don't want to do it, because I hate to encourage him, but I laugh out loud *again*. "Yeah, I know what you mean about older siblings," I say. "Hannah thinks it's her job in life to protect me. In fact, I'm guessing my sister's extreme protectiveness is the reason you're on this road trip with me."

"Yeah, so I've heard."

"I knew it!" I say, slamming my palm against the table again.

"Dude. Would you stop doing that? You're making me twitchy."

"You didn't really need to go to L.A., did you, Keane?"

Keane looks as guilty as sin. "Shit. Is that what I just said?"

"Pretty much."

"Shit."

"Were you planning to go to L.A. at all or is the whole thing a gigantic lie?" I ask. "Do you even have an audition with that talent agency?"

"Yeah, that's all real. It was an open-ended invitation, though. I'm not in any rush."

"I freaking knew it," I say, shaking my head. "*Hannah*."

"It's no big deal. I was planning to visit Dax and do the audition thing at some point."

"I'm so sorry you got forced into making this drive with me.

You must have been so freakin' annoyed with me. Here I thought I was doing you this huge favor, and all along you were doing my sister one."

"It's okay. I'm actually enjoying myself."

I feel my cheeks burst with color. "So am I," I say, my throat suddenly tight. I clear my throat. "Even though you're abnormal and lacking in charm, of course."

"Bullshit. I've got *ebullient* charm, baby. All the livelong day."

"Mmm hmm. So you keep informing me."

"I do."

"Okay. Sure. So tell me the story of how Zander sent me that disgusting dick pic. Walk me through the thought process that led you and Zander to think sending me a photo of Zander's dick and hairy balls was a splendid idea."

"'Thought process'? Uh, I wouldn't go quite that far. We were stoned outta our minds, watching *The Matrix*, and Z read your text where you said you wanted to know what I was 'packing.'"

"Ah. Now I see."

"Confession?" Keane leans forward like he's about to tell me a huge secret. "Zander and I are idiots."

I laugh.

"Well, that and I didn't bother checking my voicemails for days so I didn't understand your initial texts. And since chicks hit me up all the time, day and night, wanting to get a piece of me, or, actually, a piece of Ball Peen Hammer, Z and I thought you must have been one of my groupies."

"You have *groupies*?"

"Well, no. *Ball Peen Hammer* does. Hordes of 'em. And bee tee dubs, baby doll, I just said '*hordes*,' not '*whores*,' so don't get your panties in a twist, Miss Gender Equality."

I laugh. I can't help it. He's freakin' adorable.

The waitress returns to the table with Keane's chili and a small green salad and we both lean back from the table as she places Keane's food in front of him.

"The rest should be out soon," she assures us.

"Great, Amy," Keane says. "Thanks a bunch."

The minute the waitress leaves, Keane digs into his chili, scooping large spoonfuls into his mouth like he hasn't eaten for days.

"Good?" I ask.

"Great. You want some?"

"No, thanks."

"Lemme know if you change your mind."

I watch him eating for a moment, fascinated. I've never met anyone like Keane Morgan. He's Daffy Duck trapped inside Prince Charming's body. Quite an entertaining combination, I must admit. He's like watching my own private reality TV show.

"So do you and Zander regularly help each other with the ladies?" I ask.

"Well, yes and no," he says between bites of food. "I'm Z's wingman all the time, but he's never mine."

"Well, gosh. That doesn't seem fair."

"Oh, he'd totally lay down his sword for me if I needed him. But I never need him so it's a moot point." He scrapes the bottom of his chili bowl and moves enthusiastically onto his salad.

"Never? I thought every guy could use a wingman, at least once in a while."

Keane shrugs and takes a huge bite of his salad.

"So how do you do it without a wingman? Do women just fall at your feet because you're so normal and charming?"

"Well, yes, women fall at my feet—they fall outta the sky and land at my feet like raindrops on a stormy day—but not because I'm normal and charming." He snickers.

"Gosh, that must be awfully nice for you."

"It is."

"Any woman you want, huh?"

"Yup. On command." He snaps his fingers.

I snort. "Are we talking about women or dogs here?"

Keane levels me with his startling blue eyes. "Oh, we're talking about women. Beautiful, sexy, horny women."

I raise my eyebrows.

"As long as, you know, the woman in question is single and available—although I've certainly fucked my share of married and 'unavailable' women on the down low, don't get me wrong. I just mean, yeah, if she's single and available and I want to sleep with her, then I can pretty much have her. It's like picking chocolates outta box. Pickles from a jar."

"'Pickles from a jar?'" I say, laughing.

"Pickles from a jar." He winks.

"And you sometimes sleep with married pickles?" I say.

"Occasionally."

I crinkle my nose with distaste.

"It's not my preference, actually. That was mostly a while ago, when I was still drunk with my superpowers. I've learned to control myself better since then—figured out how to use my powers for good. Lately, I've been on a little trend of having sex with divorced women with small children, just for kicks. Sleeping with marrieds started to make me feel pretty gross about myself after a while, so I stopped cold turkey. Now, I only do it if the pickle's been married at least ten years, but those opps come few and far between, usually at weddings, so marrieds aren't really on the menu these days."

I'm utterly fascinated. What is this creature? I've never encountered anything like him. "But cheating is cheating," I say. "Whether it's at year one, ten, or twenty. Why the ten-year distinction?"

"Hey, I'm not the one cheating. I'm single. I'd never cheat."

I look at him with skepticism.

"Dude. I'm a Morgan. We don't cheat. Meet my mom and dad and you'll understand. Married thirty years, still in love. When Morgans commit, we commit. When Morgans are single, we play the field. It's how we roll."

"But what's the logic about the ten-year thing? If you're willing to sleep with a married woman, why care how long she's been married?"

"Okay, actually, this is kinda deep. So don't roll your eyes about this part or I'll be totally offended and I might even cry."

I chuckle. "Okay. I'll do my best not to make you cry, Keane."

Keane levels me with surprisingly earnest eyes. "I believe with all my heart women don't cheat unless they're not getting what they need at home. You keep a woman sexually satisfied, she's not going anywhere, ever, because women are biologically wired for monogamy. It's pure science, baby. So I figure before the ten-year mark, I gotta be a good karmic bro to all the husbands out there and cut them some slack. I mean, odds are high a couple's gonna pop out a couple kids during their first decade, right? Maybe they fucked like rabbits at first and then they hit the seven-year itch and the husband's doing his mighty best to get his mojo back in between diaper changes and breastfeeding. So I follow the Ten Year Rule and I figure that's more than a fair shake, from a karmic standpoint. Because, like I say, I believe in karma big-time and I wouldn't want some twenty-three-year-old punk layin' pipe with my future hot-as-fuck wife and mother of my four babies, you know? Bros before hoes on a cosmic scale. But I swear to God if I'm not still satisfying my future wife by the time our ten-year anniversary rolls around, if I'm not still making her speak in tongues every goddamned night of our marriage, then I'll be the first one to tell her to leave me or get her bell rung somewhere else."

I literally cannot form words.

"Ten Year Rule," Keane says. He claps his hands like a magician finished with a trick.

"How the hell did you come up with all that?"

Keane shrugs. "I dunno. It's just how my mind works. I talk about women and sex with Z and my brothers all the time. But since I'm the only one of us who's ever dabbled in marrieds, I'm pretty sure that one's mostly my concoction."

"Would you be willing to say all that stuff again on camera?"

"Which part?"

"The whole thing."

"Why?"

"Because you just blew my freakin' mind and I've got to document it. I'd never be able to describe what I just witnessed and do it justice."

"Who would you want to describe it to?"

"The entire world."

Keane laughs. "What would you do with the video?"

"I have no idea. Absolutely nothing unless I get your permission first, I promise. But I have to get all that on video before I let this moment pass. I just have to document this. *Please*, Keane, it's the way I am. *I. Must. Document.*"

"Oh my God." A huge smile spreads across Keane's handsome face. "Am I a 'quiet moment of magic,' Maddy Milliken? Admit it, I totally am."

I'm trying to keep from smiling, but I'm sure I'm not succeeding.

81

"Say it for me and then I'll do the video," he persists.

I twist my mouth. "You're a quiet moment of magic, Keane Morgan."

Keane nods emphatically. "Yee-boy." He shifts his weight in his chair like he's preparing himself for battle. "Okay, let 'er rip, you documentary filmmaker, you. I am now officially your muse."

"Thank you." I point my phone at him. "Okay. Action."

Chapter 14
Maddy

Keane places his forearms on the table and breezily goes through his explanation of The Ten Year Rule again for me, only this time, now that my camera's on him, he's even more charming than before, if that's even possible.

"You come alive for the camera," I say when he's done talking. "It's insane how much charisma you have."

"Thanks. Yeah, I'm a natural-born ham. My mom calls me a ham and cheese sandwich. The weird thing is, as a kid, I was actually really shy, believe it or not."

"I don't believe it."

"God's truth. When my mom used to drop me off for pre-school, I was the kid who clung to her skirt and then sat in the corner after she left, bawling my eyes out, saying, 'I want my mommy.'"

"Aw. Poor little Keaney."

"True story."

"How'd you get over your shyness?"

"Baseball at first. Being on a team. Being good at something. And then I met my beloved Wifey and he was the last piece of the puzzle. Zander unleashed my inner Peen and I just never stuffed that fucker back in again." Keane motions to my phone. "So you got what you need, baby doll?"

"Uh, yeah, I think I'm good, honey biscuit," I say. I take a quick peek at the footage we just shot and my heart skips a beat. "Keane, oh my God. You're crazy-photogenic. You absolutely light up the screen."

"Thanks."

"Have you ever done any acting or modeling?"

"Nah."

"You should."

"You think?"

"Absolutely. You're a natural."

"Hmm. Thanks. I'll take that under consideration."

"I bet if we loaded this video onto YouTube and seeded it the right way, it'd go viral. Hey, you could be a YouTuber. Some of those guys make a lot of money."

"Yeah, but then I'd have to post shit all the time. No thanks. I can't even answer all my texts. How would I remember to post shit on the daily?"

"Can I upload this video, just to see if I'm right? I can always take it down if you want."

"Knock yourself out."

"Can I go large?"

"I don't even know what the hell that would mean, but, sure, do whatever."

"Cool. I'm gonna style you." I quickly create Twitter and YouTube accounts for "Ball Peen Hammer" and upload the video. "How about an Instagram account?" I ask. "Do you have one for Ball Peen Hammer?"

Keane shrugs. "Not for Ball Peen Hammer, just for me, but I never check it."

"Say cheese," I say, holding up my camera. "Show me those dimples, honey nuggets." I snap a drop-dead gorgeous photo of Keane and upload it to his brand new Instagram account, and then I post links for all Keane's new accounts to some sites for lovers of "hot guys" and "cute boys" and "male strippers" and "man candy." "I'll upload a six-second edit of the video to Vine later," I say. "You're a natural for Vine. You're a walking GIF."

"Why are you doing all that?" Keane asks.

"It's fun," I say, shrugging. "This is my version of a video game. I just wanna see how many points I can rack up. When I decided to start doing wedding videos to earn money for school, I made a website and social media accounts for Wedding Videos by Maddy, threw some videos up there, seeded those suckers to social media sites for newly engaged couples, and within a matter of weeks I had every weekend of the summer booked with weddings. I'm a savage beast with social media marketing, believe me—this is totally my *thing*."

"I thought documentaries were totally your *thing*."

"This is my other *thing*. You can't really have one without the other these days. No sense making videos or films no one sees, right? You gotta be able to make 'em *and* market 'em."

Keane shrugs and takes a big bite of his food. "Whatever floats your boat, Madagascar. Go forth and conquer."

I squeal. "Awesome. God, I love doing this stuff." I put my phone down on the table. "So, back to your pickles. You said they fall at your feet like raindrops, but *not* because you're normal and charming?"

"Correct."

"So what is it that lures them? Do you simply flash your blue hair and killer dimples and the pickles leap out of their jars and hurl themselves at you like little pickle-missiles?"

Keane leans forward, grinning. "You think I've got 'killer' dimples?"

I can't stop myself from returning his huge smile. "I think you've got *dimples*. I can see them, plain as day." I point. "One. Two."

"Yeah, but you called them '*killer*.'" He flashes them at me again.

"I was speaking *sardonically*. I think *you* think your dimples are killer."

"Liar. You think they're killer and you know it." He flashes them at me again. "Great word, by the way. *Sardonically*. Please define."

"Done in a mocking, cynical, or sarcastic manner."

Keane purses his lips, considering something for a beat. "The handsome lad called the cute girl with the fancy vocabulary a liar, and he absolutely did *not* mean it *sardonically*."

I laugh.

"Come on, pickle," Keane says. "Admit my dimples make you wanna hurl yourself outta your jar and jump my bones."

I snort. "Not even a little bit."

"A *lot* bit, then."

"Nope."

"Liar."

"Not lying. Neither you nor your dimples have any effect on this

85

particular pickle. But, don't worry, *Ball Peen Hammer*, I don't happen to be one of the pickles in your target demographic. I've never even seen *Magic Mike*."

"*What?*"

"Actually, I've never witnessed a male stripper in any form."

"Not even in Vegas?"

"I've never been to Vegas."

"*What?* Good lord. Are you a monster?"

"I know. It's my cross to bear, unfortunately."

"Come on. You've at least seen a stripper at a bachelorette party."

"Dude. I'm twenty-one. I've never been to a bachelorette party. My best friends are still in college."

"What the *hell*? First Abba Zaba and *Rainman* and now *Magic Mike* and Las Vegas? Poor sheltered, cloistered, innocent little Maddy Milliken. The list of ways your cherry needs popping is longer than my... *arm*." He snickers and leans forward like he's telling a secret. "I normally woulda said a different part of my anatomy right then, but I'm keeping things super Disney for you 'cause you're my sweet and innocent little sister."

"Gosh, thanks a bunch. Phew."

"You've seriously *never* seen a male stripper in action?"

"I guess they're just not my thing."

"How do you know if you've never seen one in action?"

"If strippers were my thing, I'm sure I'd have managed to see one by now."

Keane twists his mouth, considering that bit of logic.

"But, hey, like I say, I'm not your target demographic, so your core belief that every woman wants you is still soundly intact."

Keane exhales and shakes his head. "This is such bullshit."

"What's such bullshit?"

"You *think* you're not my target demo, but you so are. You're a woman and you're single, so—wait, you're single, right?"

"Yeah, I'm very, very single." I snort. "Lately, I might as well be a nun."

Keane holds up his index finger. "Ah, now that's an interesting item for our '*juxtaposition* of the genders' file. A guy says he's 'very, very single,' he means he's playing the field, handsome and happy all the livelong day. A chick says it and she means she's not gettin' any. That's a kinda interesting *juxtaposition*, don't you think?"

I make a face that says, "You've made an interesting point."

"So is your nunnish-ness a religious thing, like a 'saving-yourself-for-marriage' thing—or more of a 'celibacy-because-I-can't-get-laid' thing?"

"Why are you so interested in my sex life?"

"I'm interested in everyone's sex life. I love sex. Doing it, talking about it, thinking about it, researching it, hunting for it. And did I mention 'doing it'?"

"*Hunting* for it?" I make a face of disgust.

Keane ignores my obvious distaste. "Hell yeah. My favorite things about sex are, in this order: doing it, hunting for it, and talking about it—and I *especially* love talking about it with someone like you."

I feel myself blush. "What's someone like me?"

"A celibate girl who blushes every time I say anything even remotely sexual."

My cheeks burn even hotter.

Keane points at my face. "Just like that."

"I'm not actually *celibate*," I say, my cheeks on fire. "I'm just in a bit of a dry spell lately. It's not a master plan, trust me."

"Ah. The ol' 'married to Jesus by default' thing."

"Something like that."

"You religious?"

"No."

"Me, neither. But I do believe in something bigger than myself."

"Same."

"Okay, well, then, cool. You're not actually *married* to Christ; you're just going steady with him. Plus, it *appears* you've got at least two out of three girl-parts, so that means you're one hundred percent my target demo, whether you like it or not, which therefore means you're most definitely swooning over my killer dimples right this very second and wanting to jump my bones like a lion on an alpaca." He flashes his dimples. "Or, I suppose, like a pickle hurling herself outta jar."

"I'm not swooning over your dimples and I don't want to jump your bones."

"Impossible. When it comes to women wanting me, women are my puppets and I'm their puppet master. It's as simple as that."

"Keane, I'm sorry if this disrupts your precarious grasp on reality, but—wait. Two out of three girl parts?"

He points at my chest. "One. Two. I can *sorta* see the general shape of your merchandise, but I gotta tell ya that blouse ain't doing you any favors, sweetheart."

I make a face reflecting my disdain.

"So, anyway, you were saying?" Keane says. "You're dying to jump my bones like a horny puppet and...?"

"Uh, *no*. I was saying I'm not the least bit attracted to you in a sexual way, especially now that I know you're a total and complete pig who '*hunts*' women and calls them 'puppets' and scopes out 'merchandise.'" I grimace. "And I was also saying you shouldn't get an inferiority complex over my lack of sexual interest in you because I'm most definitely not your target audience."

"Okay, first off, I'm not a pig. I'll have you know I have a deep and abiding respect for women—just ask my mom and sister and any girlfriend I've ever had—all of whom still love me, bee tee dubs, 'cause I've never cheated or had a messy or mean-spirited breakup in my entire life. I might be flakey and selfish, and sometimes I'm a dick, but I'm not a pig. And, yeah, I love sex. That doesn't make me a pig. It makes me a twenty-three-year-old dude with a dick and balls. So what if I like making a scavenger hunt outta getting laid sometimes? When you have women throwing themselves at you right and left, you gotta find ways to keep things interesting. Sometimes I'm like, 'Hey, I wonder if I can get laid today by a soccer mom with brown hair I meet in the produce section by the *tangerines*?' You try walking in Ball Peen Hammer's shoes and see if you don't start doing the same fucking thing." He runs his hand through his hair and his bicep bulges under his T-shirt sleeve as he does. "Now, as far as checking out the merchandise. So what? That doesn't make me a pig, either. That makes me a guy who loves women and everything about them, especially their gorgeous bodies. Okay, and the puppet thing? I stand by my statement. Women are my puppets. *In the sack*. I pull this string over here and they come for me. I pull that one over there and they do it again. It's my favorite game. And that makes me a pig in your eyes?" Wow, he's really working himself up over this. "No, it makes me *awesome in the sack*—every woman's fantasy. Believe me, no woman has ever called me a pig after sleeping with me. Quite the contrary." He takes a huge breath and leans back in his chair. "And second off, why the *fuck* do you think you're not my target audience, baby doll?"

I'm absolutely stunned into silence for a very long beat. "I... Wow." I shake my head like I'm erasing an Etch-a-Sketch board. "I..." But I still can't find words.

"Cat got your tongue, sweet thing?" He grins.

"That was quite a speech."

"I feel passionately about the topic."

"Obviously. Wow. I didn't mean to offend you."

"You did. I'm not a pig. Start that rumor and my mom and sister will string me up by my balls. And I very much like having my balls."

"Sorry. I take it back. You're not a pig. You're just a horny, delusional, psychopathic, arrogant, blue-haired puppet master who collects pickles."

"Thank you. Glad we cleared that up."

I chuckle. "You prefer to be called all those things to 'a pig'?"

"Fuck yeah." He puts his forearms on the table, his eyes sparkling. "So, let's talk about the more important issue: what the *fuck* makes you think you're not my target audience?"

I shrug. "It's not personal. You're just not my type."

Keane laughs. "I'm everyone's type."

"God, you're so freakin' cocky, it's scary."

"Does cocky connote a heightened but ultimately insupportable sense of confidence?"

"Yes, it does. Very well said."

"That's actually a Zander-ism. He says that line whenever a woman calls him cocky, which happens a lot. Zander's big on fancy words and definitions. You'd love him—he's super smart like you. But, regardless, the point is I'm not cocky because my heightened confidence is one hundred percent *supportable*." He beams a huge smile at me, his eyes twinkling, his dimples taunting me.

"Well, Keane, whether you believe it or not, I'm honestly not the least bit attracted to you."

"Say that again, please."

89

"I'm not the least bit attracted to you."

"One more time," Keane says.

"Gladly." I say it again.

"Hmm," he says. "I can't understand that strange jumble of vowels and consonants coming out of your mouth, Maddy Milliken. What do those funny sounds mean?"

"No one's ever said that to you before?"

"Never."

I roll my eyes.

"Maddy Milliken, Professional Eye-Roller."

I do it again.

"They're gonna get stuck like that, baby doll." He exhales with sudden frustration. "Why aren't you admitting you find me attractive? I'm willing to admit I find *you* attractive."

I raise my eyebrows in surprise. "You do?"

"Well, of course. I'm not *blind*." He motions to me like he's saying something self-explanatory.

I feel myself blushing, yet again. "Thank you."

"You're super cute—no, you're more than cute. You're *pretty*. In fact, I'd go so far as to say you're 'highly attractive.'" He leans forward on his elbows and clasps his hands. "I'm not personally *attracted* to you, mind you, but I most definitely find you objectively *attractive*."

I do a double take. "What the heck does that mean?"

"It means you're smart and funny and cool and pretty and if I were thinking about setting a bro up with someone—you know, a guy looking for an actual *girlfriend*, and not just a pretty girl to bang— then I'd be more than confident setting him up with you. It means I consider you my honorary little sister."

"Oh, Jesus Christ," I mutter, slapping my palm to my forehead.

"Hey, keep your boyfriend outta this, Maddy Milliken." Keane leans back into his chair, squinting at me. "You're really, truly not attracted to me?"

"Same as you. I find you *objectively* attractive, but I'm not *personally* attracted to you—at least, not sexually. But, I swear, if I knew a girl who was looking to have one night of meaningless fun with a horny Smurf or a psychopathic bobble-headed troll-doll, I'd totally hook you two up."

Keane purses his lips but doesn't say anything.

"All right, here we go," the waitress says, appearing out of nowhere to lay plates of food onto the table. "Ketchup's there. You need anything else, kids?"

Keane looks at me and I shrug.

"Nope. I think my honorary little sister and I are good," he says, his eyes burning.

"Great," the waitress says. "Enjoy."

Keane and I silently dig into our food for a very long while, not looking at each other, until Keane suddenly and emphatically puts down his burger and leans forward sharply.

"You're so full of shit," he says, scowling. "You totally wanna bone me."

I'm aghast. "Absolutely not," I breathe.

He narrows his eyes. "I don't believe it."

"Believe it."

"Liar."

"Oh my God. You really *are* a psychopath. No wonder you think you can have any woman you want—you've got delusions of grandeur."

Keane squints at me and slowly shoves a French fry into his mouth.

"I can prove I'm not sexually attracted to you," I say emphatically.

"Oh, really? Please do."

"If I wanted to 'bone' you, as you so artfully put it," I say, "then I wouldn't even be having this conversation with you. Because when I think a guy's hot—when I'm even the slightest bit sexually attracted to a guy—I become a babbling, pathetic pile of goo who can't string two coherent words together. Every freaking time."

"Well, clearly not 'every freakin' time,' seeing as how you've been talking my ear off without taking a breath for the past four fucking hours."

I gasp and put my palm on my chest. I feel like Keane's just slapped me across the face. "Gosh, I'm sorry I've bored you so horribly with my constant babbling," I grit out, but my haughtiness is an act. In truth, I feel like I'm on the verge of tearing up, just that fast. "Why the hell did you keep asking me questions if listening to me talk was so torturous for you?" I say, my voice straining. Oh my God. My eyes are burning. My throat feels tight.

"Maddy."

"For your information, I hardly ever talk the way I've been talking to you with anyone, other than my sister. Normally, when I'm talking to someone I've just met, male or female, whether they're rippling with muscles and dimples or not, I have to force myself to talk in complete sentences until I get really comfortable, which usually takes a stupidly long time." My words are coming out in a torrent of embarrassment and hurt.

"Maddy, you're—"

"It's just that you kept asking me so many questions and it seemed like you were genuinely interested in what I was saying and it was just so easy to talk to you and you have that stupid blue hair and those crazy dimples and for some reason I felt like I could let my guard down and—"

"*Maddy.*"

Keane's sharp tone has commanded my attention. I abruptly stop talking and bite my lip, trying to keep it together, my chest heaving.

"Calm your tits, dude," Keane says softly, his tone much kinder than his word choice. "If you've got 'em under that god-awful shirt, that is." He flashes me a kindhearted smile. "Tamp down the crazy just a notch, sweetheart."

I smash my lips together, trying to keep them from trembling.

"I asked you questions because I was interested in everything you were telling me," Keane continues in a calm, soothing voice. "Because talking to you is *awesome* and I've never met anyone like you, ever. I was simply making the point you're clearly capable of coherent conversation with a guy you want to bone, that's all. Don't get all wilty-flower-insecure on me, okay? You've totally misunderstood me."

My eyes are stinging, so I blink rapidly, trying to keep my threatening emotions at bay. Other than my first boyfriend, Justin, I honestly can't remember the last time I've warmed to someone so easily and quickly—but I'd certainly never tell Keane that. "I'm not normally so sensitive," I say, clearing my throat and sucking back my emotion. "I think you just hit the bull's-eye on a really big insecurity of mine."

"I get it," Keane says softly. "But, trust me, Maddy, you haven't bored me at all. Have I bored you?"

I roll my eyes like that's a ridiculous question. "I think *psychopathic* pigs would have to fly before you could ever bore me." I rub my face. "I'm sorry. I don't know why I reacted so strongly."

"You just misunderstood me, that's all."

"I'm not normally so sensitive," I assure him.

"So what if you are? Maybe I'm abnormal and un-charming, and you're sensitive. Maybe together, we're like peanut butter and chocolate."

A little smile overtakes my lips. "Which one am I?"

"Chocolate, of course. Someone needs to take Zander's place when he's not here."

I grin.

"Maddy, seriously. Even if I were being a prick to you, which I totally wasn't, why would you give a shit what I think? I'm an abnormal and charm-less idiot."

A full smile spreads across my face.

"Ah, there it is. Turn that frown upside down, choco-nana. Come on."

I chuckle. "Where do you get all the weird stuff you say?"

Keane shrugs. "God."

"*God* sent you 'choco-nana'?"

"Hey, God likes 'quiet moments of magic' as much as the next guy."

We share a beaming smile.

"You feeling better now, Mad Dog?"

I nod. "Sorry about that. I'm fine now."

"Cool." He looks at me for a long beat. "No more wilty-flower shit, okay? At least not with me. I love hanging with you. Swear to God."

"I love hanging with you, too."

"Cool. So now that catastrophe's been averted, I'm gonna ignore you and suck down this milkshake before it melts, okay?"

"Please do."

Keane takes a huge swig of his milkshake and his eyes practically pop out of his head. "Oh my fucking God!" he blurts. He shoves the milkshake across the table at me, his eyes on fire. "You gotta taste this, Madagascar. Best milkshake you'll ever taste."

93

I dutifully take a long sip and, oh my effing God, he's right: it's the best milkshake I've ever tasted.

"Insanity, right?" Keane says.

"Absolute psychosis."

Keane flags down the waitress and she comes over to the table. "Could you bring us another glass? I gotta share my *amazing* milkshake with my *amazing* little sister here. We're celebrating what an awesome, funny, smart, pretty and *amazing* little badass she is."

"Wow, that *is* cause to celebrate," the waitress says. "Coming right up."

"It's okay," I say to Keane. "I'm pretty stuffed from my sandwich."

"*Hey*," Keane says sharply, pointing his finger at me. "Life's short, baby doll. You gotta enjoy every 'quiet moment of magic' that comes your way—and I'm telling you sharing this milkshake with me is gonna top your list of quiet moments of magic."

"So that's your new catchphrase? 'Quiet moment of magic'?"

"Yeah, pretty cool, right? I figure if I say it enough times, I can trademark it and make a gazillion dollars."

I laugh for the millionth time today.

The waitress returns with an empty glass and a canister of whipped cream, and Keane takes great care pouring half his shake into the new glass. "You'll thank me profusely for this," he says, topping off my half with a mammoth pile of cream. "Which is what all the horny ladies do after I get through with 'em—they thank me profusely." He winks and pushes the glass toward me. "Here you go, sweet meat."

"Yeah, um. Back to that women-thanking-you-profusely thing." I wait for a young family to walk past our table before speaking again. "How exactly do you make women throw themselves at you again? Do you just show up and say, 'Here I am, baby doll,' and they tackle you?"

"Pretty much."

I make a face registering my disbelief.

"It's true. Women sniff me out like dogs sensing an earthquake. They just *know*."

"Oh my God, Keane. Don't compare women to dogs. Pickles were bad enough."

"Hey, at least I didn't call 'em horny bitches, which I usually do when I'm making my earthquake analogy."

I scowl. "Oh for the love of God. Please don't call women bitches."

Keane belly laughs. "I never do. My mom and sister would cut off my balls, trust me. I only do it when I'm making my earthquake analogy 'cause it's a clever *pun*. Get it? 'Cause bitches are dogs and dogs sense earthquakes?"

"Yeah, I get it." I push my plate aside and lean forward. "So, okay, I'll bite," I say. "What do women sense about you the same way *bitches* sense an impending earthquake?"

"You can't guess?"

"Hence the reason I'm asking the question."

"You sure you can handle it?" Keane says, his eyes darkening. "Because after I tell you, you're gonna be obsessed with the idea of sleeping with me."

I snort. "Lemme guess. You're gonna tell me you have a big ol' dong, right? Because according to studies, and as confirmed by my personal experience, that really doesn't matter."

"Oh, so we're back to talking about your experience, are we? *Excellent*. So, tell me—"

"Move along, Keane," I say, cutting him off.

Keane bites his lip. "You do realize you just implied you've only been with small-dicked men, right?"

"Move the *fuck* along, please."

"Whoa. An f-bomb from Maddy Milliken. You must be especially hot and bothered."

Oh, good lord, the expression on Keane's face is so freaking cocky, I wanna slap it right off him. "Are you gonna tell me or not?" I ask. "Because I'm rapidly losing interest in this topic." I put my hand to my mouth like I'm yawning.

"*Fine*. But first let me say, since you've asked me directly and you're obviously *dying* to know, yes, I've got a big ol' dong. Massive. A weapon of mass destruction. Puts Shamu's cock to shame. Women spontaneously orgasm when they see it. Men cower. Dogs scamper away whimpering and communist countries surrender their nukes. But, no, that's not what I was gonna say about what women sense about me." He's been slowly stirring his milkshake

95

with his straw as he speaks, and now he pushes his glass to the side. "Okay, sweet little innocent Maddy Milliken. Are you ready?"

"Yes."

"Because I'm now gonna tell you my deep, dark secret."

"Yay."

"Brace yourself."

"I'm braced."

"Don't say I didn't warn you."

"I won't."

"I think you should sign a waiver before I tell you."

"Consider it signed." I make a motion in the air like I'm signing a document.

"And a non-disclosure agreement."

I make another signing motion in the air.

Keane licks his lips. "Okay. Here it is." He pauses dramatically and says his next sentence slowly, his eyes boring holes into my face. "I'm diabolically talented in the sack."

I press my lips together and flare my nostrils, doing my mighty best not to laugh in his handsome face.

"You said making a video go viral is like racking up points on your own personal video game? Well, having fucking amazing sex is racking up points on mine."

I cringe. "And how exactly do you 'rack up points' in your game? Sheer numbers of partners or something else? Actually, wait—don't tell me. I don't wanna know."

"Nothing to be scared of." He smirks. "I rack up points by making the woman I'm with come as many times as possible in a sesh," he says, his eyes blazing like hot coals. "I make her my puppet. I pull her strings and her body does whatever I want it to do. *And it's awesome.*"

I raise an eyebrow at him, but, still, I don't reply.

"There's a shitload of ways to do it, depending on the woman. Everyone's different. But there's one thing that works like a charm pretty much every single time, and usually within a matter of minutes. My brothers and I call it 'The Sure Thing.'"

I bite my lower lip, my eyes locked with Keane's. "Well, good for you," I manage to squeak out, my throat tight.

"Good for both of us," he says, smirking. Keane levels me with a heart-stopping smolder. "*And that's what women can sniff on me.*"

I open my mouth to reply but nothing comes out.

Keane leans back in his chair, his eyes burning. "Uh-oh, Maddy Milliken. Have you suddenly lost the ability to string two coherent words together?" He pulls his milkshake toward him and takes a languid suck on his straw—a gesture that makes me think about those lips taking a languid suck on various parts of my anatomy. "You still think you're not my target demographic?" he asks. He bites his lower lip and smirks. "Because, if that's the case, baby doll, then I think you'd better check your neck for a fucking pulse."

Chapter 15
Keane

"You want me to drive now?" I ask as we walk toward Maddy's car in the restaurant parking lot.

"No, thanks. I prefer to drive."

Maddy's cheeks are still flushed from my "puppet master" speech inside the restaurant and she hasn't looked me in the eye since.

"I'm an excellent driver," I say, leaning against Maddy's car as I wait for her to unlock it from her side.

"So I've heard," she says, still not looking at me. "Hey, I should probably fill up my tank before we hit the road again," she adds, unlocking her door.

I look up the street. "There's a gas station," I say, indicating a station up the road.

"Perfect."

We pile into her car to make the short trip.

"Thanks for buying lunch," Maddy says. "I'll buy next time."

"Nah, we can go dutch from here on out. This time was on me 'cause we were celebrating your badassery. A girl can't pay for her own Celebration of Badassery."

"Thank you. That was really sweet of you."

"You're welcome."

Maddy starts the engine and backs her car out of the parking spot (so carefully, by the way, you'd think she was a little old lady with her ten beloved grandchildren in the backseat) and I look out the passenger window, my chest tight, my heart racing.

What the hell am I doing?

Fuck.

I'm under strict orders not to bang this chick and all I wanna do is bang this chick. And not because I actually *wanna* bang this chick, mind you, but because I'm not *allowed* to bang this chick. I know that's the psychological phenomenon going on here, and yet I can't stop myself from falling prey to it and at least trying to make her wanna fuck me—which is something I know for a fact is an ego thing and nothing more because I'll never, ever fuck her.

Shit. I've always been this way. Tell me I'm not allowed to have a cookie, and I sure as fuck wanna have a motherfucking cookie. Or two or three. (Just ask my siblings, whose many, many cookies I've stolen throughout the years.) But this time, shit, I gotta keep my hands outta the cookie jar and my pecker in my pants and stop trying to make this girl blush just for the sheer sport of it.

I don't even want Maddy. She's a sweet girl. Definitely not the kind of girl who sleeps around, which means she's not my type *at all*. Maddy's the kind of girl who places deep meaning on sex—the sort of girl who's probably never even had a one-night stand. I'm one hundred percent positive if I banged Maddy and opened her eyes and body to what she's been missing out on her whole life (with the three or four small-dicked, talentless dudes she's slept with), she'd get attached to me like a puppy adopted from a shelter. And just like Ryan said, that most certainly wouldn't end well.

I take a deep breath.

This is just a dastardly case of mind-fuckery, son. I just gotta get control of my mind.

Maddy turns into the gas station, pulls the car alongside a pump, and reaches for her purse from the backseat.

"It's okay," I say. "I got gas this time. You can pay next time."

"Okay," she says. "Thanks."

"Hey, while I pump the gas, why don't you go in there and see if they've got Abba Zabas?" I say, indicating the small minimart on the far end of the station. "We'll pop your Abba Zaba cherry tonight while popping my documentary cherry." Oh, fuck. I gotta stop this shit right now.

"Wow, sounds like we're gonna have ourselves a cherry-popping extravaganza—a virtual cherry orchard of poppery." She laughs and grabs her purse from the backseat.

"Oh, and grab a bag of popcorn, too, and Junior Mints and Milk Duds," I say as she shuts her car door.

"Roger," she says.

"Rabbit," I reply, and she giggles. Yeah, that one always slays. I woulda said that to anyone, right? That wasn't flirting. That's just what I always say when someone says "roger," right? Fuck, my head's a mess all of a sudden. "Did you know it's illegal under federal law to watch movies without consuming popcorn, Milk Duds and Junior Mints?" I call to her as she begins walking away.

Maddy turns to look at me and flashes a truly lovely smile. "No, I did not know that. Good law."

I shove the gas nozzle into the tank and watch Maddy walking away, her yellow hippie-blouse billowing around her frame in the slight breeze.

Maddy's actually got a nice ass on her. Round cheeks. I like round cheeks. Something to hold onto. But why the *fuck* is she wearing that goddamned shirt? Would it kill the girl to show off her curves the tiniest bit—give the teeniest peek of the merchandise?

Aw, shit. I'm doing it again. *Fuck.*

I top off the gas tank, take a seat in Maddy's car, and pull out my phone to distract myself from my racing thoughts of cookie thievery.

Well, let's see.

First things first, I've got a text from my wife, attaching a GIF of some weird guy making a ridiculous love-dovey face on a loop with the flashing caption, "I'm in luuuurve!" "Daphne's coming over tonight after work," Z writes in a text accompanying the GIF. "Don't ever come home, Peenie!"

I laugh. "You're welcome," I type in reply.

There's a text from Dax: "Hey, Peen Star. What's up? You on the road?"

"Hey, Rock Star," I reply. "Yep. All systems go. I'll deliver the package safe and sound in a couple days. I got this, Baby Bro."

I keep scrolling and stop at a text from the L.A. talent agency I've been in contact with. The message is from a guy named Adam: "Hey, Keane. We're thrilled you're coming to audition for us. Your timing is perfect. This Friday, we've got a showcase for our male talent at Giselle's on Hollywood Boulevard. We've invited a handful of casting directors and talent scouts to watch the show for their various projects. One of the casting directors is casting a reality TV show. Another one is casting talent for a feature film that takes place in a male strip club so they need lots of extras and maybe some speaking talent, as well. Could be a great opportunity for you. We'll reserve one of the slots for you in the showcase. The show is open to the public, but the industry folks will be seated in a VIP section by the stage. We'll use the slot as your audition for our agency, plus for the industry folks. Sound good? Lemme know. Your slot is 10:30. In the meantime, send me all your social media links, videos, etc. for me to check out and pass along to the VIPs attending."

I tap out a reply: "Hi, Adam. Yeah. Sounds great. Thanks for the opportunity. I'll plan to be at Giselle's by 9:30 on Friday to check out the stage, give the sound guy my music, etc. I didn't pack any of my costumes (didn't know I'd be performing while in L.A.), so I'll do something in my street clothes. I don't need a costume to stand out right now, anyway—I've got blue hair. (Long story that involves helping my best friend get laid). LOL. See you Friday." I attach the Ball Peen Hammer social media links Maddy made for me earlier today and press send.

I keep scrolling past a bunch of God knows what until I get to a text from Ryan: "Yo, Peeno Noir! Did you catch your ride to L.A. this morning like a good boy?"

"Yes, Captain My Captain. On the road with Maddy now. All systems go."

Ryan replies right away: "You being handsome and happy all the livelong day, son?"

"Yes, and so fucking normal it hurts," I reply. "Literally. My balls physically HURT from the forced normalcy."

"Your balls? WTF?"

"They're the most sensitive spot on my body, brah. They feel everything. They're like delicate little butterfly wings."

"LOL. Well, tell your butterfly-balls just a couple more days and then they can Peen out as much as they like."

"Roger," I write.

"Rabbit," he replies. "And remember: Do not fuck her!"

I grunt and tap out a hasty reply. "MOTHERFUCKER! U DON'T HAVE TO KEEP REMINDING ME NOT TO FUCK MADDY!" I attach a middle finger emoji.

"HEY!" Ryan replies, attaching his own middle finger. "WHY THE FUCK ARE YOU ALL-CAPS SCREAMING AT ME??!!! UNWARRANTED!"

"Because I heard u the 1st, 2nd, and 3rd times, mofo. Stop nagging me! I won't fuck Maddy. I'll be normal and charming. I won't call her weird nicknames. And, btw, I already asked her about her H, H, & Ds. I'm on it, baby doll! Ain't no thang, actually, because Maddy's super cool. Already feels like she's my little sister. I might even like her more than Jizz."

"Oh, speaking of which, did u see Jizz's video of Little G? So kayoot!"

"The one from a couple days ago?"

"No, group text about an hour ago. Check your goddamned phone once in a while, loser."

I scroll through my texts and, sure enough, there's a group text from my sister, sent to our whole family, attaching a video of my eight-month-old niece as she holds court in my sister's Jacuzzi bathtub like the little mermaid princess she is. I press play on the clip and my heart bursts at the sight of my favorite female splashing happily with her bath toys. I can see my sister's calves in the frame, straddling Gracie, her feet hidden under the tub water, her hand protectively grasping Gracie's wet shoulder.

"Hey, my little Scorpio," my brother-in-law Josh's voice says from behind the camera. "Say hi to everyone, baby."

"Heeeyahahiii!" Gracie shrieks happily.

"Watcha doin', Gracie-cakes?" Josh asks his baby girl.

"Babuh bada!" she replies, just before splashing the water with splayed fingers.

Josh and Kat laugh together and the camera pans slightly to the right to include Kat's full body in the frame, her blonde hair tied in a knot, her face aglow.

"Hey, fam," Kat says, waving. "Don't mind us; we're just livin' the dream." She breaks into a huge smile. "Actually, we are." She leans over and kisses the top of Gracie's fuzzy blonde head. "Say, 'Hi Gramma Lou and Grampa Tom Tom!' Wave hello to all your sweet uncles!"

Gracie waves and smiles and splashes again.

"Gaga bubbadoo!" Gracie shrieks, making Josh and Kat laugh hysterically.

"We love you all," Kat says. "Bye, bye!"

The video ends.

102

"Oh my *God*," I say out loud. "Ka-*yoot!*" I turn my phone on myself and shoot a video. "Hi, Little G!" I bellow. "It's your favorite uncle! Don't believe the hype about your other uncles, baby doll, because they're all wannabe Uncle Keaneys!" I point at my hair and make a funny face. "Would any of your other uncles do *this* to themselves just to amuse you? I think not! That's 'cause Uncle Keaney loves you the most!"

I post the video into the group and within a minute my oldest brother, Colby, replies.

"Hey, Gracie, look! It's an Oompa Loompa! Call me, Keane. I've called you twice." Middle finger emoji.

"I'll try to call u tonight," I type, although I've got no intention of calling my eldest brother tonight. First off, Colby more than anyone else in my family thinks I'm an idiot; second off, I'm pretty sure I still owe Colby some duckets from when we all chipped in to buy Josh some pricey bottle of tequila for his birthday a while ago. I tap out an additional reply to Colby: "Oh, and bee tee dubs, Oompa Loompas have GREEN hair, Cheese Head." Middle finger emoji.

"Oh my gosh, Keaney! Look at your hair!" my mom writes on the heels of my reply to Colby. "Good lord!" She attaches a microphone emoji and I laugh out loud.

"Mom," I write in reply, "I'm sorry to inform u, that's not an appropriate use of the microphone. U gotta write something a whole lot more badass than 'good lord' if ur gonna drop the mic on my punk-ass. Someone, please for the love of God, show our dearest mother how it's done, since Colby's obviously horrible at it. Love u, Momma." I attach a heart. "P.S. U clearly know how to text, woman, so how about u put ur mad texting skillz to use with me on occasion instead of calling so much? Explore the full functionality of your smartphone, Mom."

Barely thirty seconds after I've pressed send on my text to my mom, the group chat blows up with a slew of rapid-fire messages:

"Hey, look! It's Thing One! Where's Thing Two?" my sister writes, followed by a microphone emoji. "That's how it's done, Mother Dearest."

From my brother-in-law, Josh: "Oh no! The entire cast of My Little Pony took a giant crap on Peen's head!" Microphone emoji.

And then from Dax: "Yeah, right after Thing Two barfed on him." Microphone emoji.

"C is for cookie. That's good enough for me. Cookie, cookie, cookie starts with C," Ryan writes. Microphone emoji. "P.S. Good one, Lambo."

"Thanks, Captain," Josh writes. "Back at ya, bro. Hey, you and the missus still coming over for drinks tomorrow before Muse?"

"Yeah. We'll be there at 6."

"Cool. I got the good stuff for ya." Winking emoji.

"U understand how to use the microphone now, Momma Lou?" I write. "Let the masters of cruelty be ur guides."

"Oh, crap, that shoulda been my band name," Dax pipes in. "Masters of Cruelty. That would have been so kewl."

"Oh snap! Woulda been supes kewl," I write. "And, hey, all u cool older kids, stop talking about Muse right in front of me! Ur hurting my sensitive feelings, u fuckers!"

"Language!" Mom writes. "Good lord. You're all a bunch of sailors. Where did I go wrong? Okay, I think I understand the cruelty angle now, honey. How's this? Keaney, please call your mother, you big flake! I miss hearing your sweet voice!" Microphone emoji.

I laugh out loud again. "Yeah, that was pretty cruel, Mom. Good job."

"Come on, Louise," my dad pipes in. "You know guilt doesn't work on Keaney. He can only be lured by food. Hey, Colby, are you up for going fishing on Sunday? I got a new rod I want to try out. Love to all." Heart emoji. "P.S. Keaney, you look like a human blueberry." Microphone emoji.

Mom quickly replies: "I tried to lure Keaney with food all last week, but he didn't answer any of my calls! Oh, Kitty and Josh, I forgot to tell you I've got bunco tomorrow night, so Grampa Tom Tom is gonna babysit Gracie all by himself." Microphone emoji.

"OMG! Someone delete the microphone emoji off Mom's phone!" Kat writes. "Mom, you're officially in microphone-emoji lockdown. Dad, you sure you can handle Little G by yourself? I can get a sitter if you'd rather. Gracie's been doing this horrible cranky thing at bedtime lately. I think she's teething."

"Oh, I'll be fine," Dad writes. "I handled you as a baby, didn't I, and she can't be any crankier than you were. Hey, now that I think about it, you're still pretty damned cranky. Are you teething, Kitty?" Microphone emoji.

"Hardy har, Dad," Kat writes. Cat emoji. Heart emoji.

"Hey, I'll help babysit Gracie," Colby pipes in. "I could use some Little G time. Nom nom nom. Tell her she'd better keep her thighs hidden or they're getting chomped with some BBQ sauce."

"Awesome!! Thanks, gentlemen," Kat writes. "Wow, my baby's such a lucky girl." Heart emoji. Four-leaf clover. "See you handsome guys tomorrow at 6ish? May God be with you both!"

"I'm so jealous!" I write. "Save me a couple big bites of Little G's left thigh for next time, dudes. Hey, Mom, TEXT me about food and I promise I'll come running. And don't listen to Pops, btw. I TOTALLY respond to guilt (as long as there's food involved, preferably lasagna or chili). Love to all except the FUCKERS going to Muse without me. (Sorry, Momma Lou, no other word would do.) Gotta go be handsome and happy all the livelong day now, folks. Peace out." Heart emoji.

I go back to the one-on-one thread with Ryan. "Little G looks so much like Jizz, it's insanity-sauce," I write.

"I know," Ryan writes. "For Lambo's sake, I hope that kid got her mommy's looks and her daddy's personality, or else he's FUCKED."

I laugh out loud. "Totesburgers," I write. I look up from my phone, suddenly wondering what the hell's taking Maddy so damned long. How long can it possibly take for a girl to buy some candy? "Hey, I gotta go," I write to Ryan. "Don't worry about a thang, sugar nuts. Everything's good on my end."

"Cool. Stay good, Peenie Baby."

"Will do. I love u da most, Cap'n. Oh, bee tee dubs, I already outed u as the voice on the phone. Maddy said ur way more charming than me, so she already knew it wasn't me."

"Bwahahahaaaaaaaa!!!!!!!" Ryan writes. He attaches a microphone emoji followed by a middle finger.

A new series of texts pops up in the group chat, all of them talking about how cute Gracie is, but I don't got time to participate in a family lovefest, son—I got shit to do—so I mute all notifications. But just as I'm about to shove my phone in my pocket, I check the one-on-one thread with Daxy one last time, just in case. And, good thing I did, because he's replied to my earlier text.

"I owe you, Peen! You da best!" Dax writes. "P.S. I kinda like

105

the blue hair, actually. You know what a gigantic boner I've always had for Marge Simpson."

"Hey, dumbshit, u just indirectly said you've got a boner for ur big brother," I write. "We all know I'm a giver, but surely that crosses a line. Hey, no worries on the road trip. It's turning out to be kinda fun. Maddy's cool."

"Awwwwwwww, SHIT! DO NOT FUCK THIS GIRL, PEENIE!" Dax writes.

I scoff. Why does everyone feel the need to say that to me? "I'm not gonna fuck her!" I write. "Can't I think a chick's cool without wanting to bang her?"

"NO, YOU CANNOT."

"U can stop with the all-caps shit, dude. I'm not gonna fuck Maddy Milliken."

"PROMISE ME."

"I promise. Jazeebabeebus."

"Thx. Be good."

"Love u da most, Rock Star."

"Back at u, Peen Star."

I stuff my phone in my pocket and look up, peering toward the minimart. Seriously, how long does it take a girl to buy some fucking candy?

All of a sudden, a tidal wave of anxiety crashes into me.

Shit.

I had one job on this motherfucking road trip: protect Maddy Milliken from harm, big or small, and deliver her safely to her big sister in L.A. *Fuck.*

I leap out of the car and sprint toward the minimart at the far end of the gas station, muttering "fuck, fuck, fuck" under my breath as I go.

Chapter 16
Keane

As I swing open the glass door of the minimart, I hear the distinctive sound of Maddy giggling, and when I take two steps into the store, there she is—the giggler herself—standing in one of the far aisles, her back to me, talking to (and giggling with) some dude. And by the full smile on the dude's face and the sparkle in his eyes, it seems his conversation with Maddy is going extremely well.

"That's so cool," the guy says, chuckling. "Me, too."

"Really?" Maddy says, her back still to me. "That's hilarious. I never thought anyone would agree with me on that."

"I guess we're both just a little bit *nuts*, huh?"

They both laugh.

I walk slowly toward them in the next aisle over, pretending to look at bottles of motor oil while sizing up the dude. Not a bad-looking guy. He looks to be about my age, maybe a little bit older. Football physique. Probs played in high school would be my guess. O-line, if I had to assign him a position. Light brown hair. Big hands. Broad shoulders. Baby face. I know his type. Jock. Mr. Personality. Maybe even a Big Man on Campus. Pretends to be sweet and sensitive with the ladies when in reality he's nothing but a brazen hunter. Motherfucker.

"Did your brother say if he's ever taken a class up at North Campus?" Maddy asks.

Now that I'm standing a few feet behind Maddy, peering at her and Baby Face from the next aisle over, I notice they're having their giggle-filled conversation alongside the candy rack—and right in front of a big ol' box of Milk Duds.

I pick up a rearview-mirror car freshener and pretend to look at it with deep interest.

107

"Is North Campus where most of your classes will be?" the guy asks.

"Yeah, that's where all the artsy stuff is—theatre, film, television, dance. The science classes are way down in South Campus. I guess they don't want the left- and right-brainers to mingle—probably worried we'd riot. Or maybe just *literally* bore each other to death."

Baby Face laughs like Maddy's just said something insanely hilarious and I roll my eyes. What a kiss-ass. Maddy's funny, sure, and super clever and smart, but that wasn't even close to one of her best zingers. At best, that was hilare-y-ish. At any rate, it certainly wasn't deserving of the gigantic laugh this guy threw at it.

"My brother gave me a tour of campus once and I'm pretty sure we went through North Campus," Baby Face says. "Is that where the sculpture garden is?"

"Yeah. That's it."

"Oh, that place was really cool."

I'm no longer even pretending to look at the car freshener in my hands.

"Yeah, I love it," Maddy says effusively. "I can totally picture myself grabbing a coffee, sitting on a bench in the sculpture garden, and working on my laptop in the California sunshine. I'm so excited."

"Totally. I'd *live* in that sculpture garden if I went to school there." The guy's gaze shifts from Maddy straight to my hair and then lands on my eyes. "You're gonna love the weather..." he begins, his eyes locked with mine, but he doesn't continue.

Maddy turns to follow the guy's line of sight and her face lights up. "Keane!" she blurts. She looks at her watch. "Oh my gosh. I had no idea I'd kept you waiting so long. I'm so sorry—I just lost track of time. This is Brian. Brian, this is Keane."

Brian lifts his large hand in a half-hearted wave. "Hey."

"I'm giving Keane a ride to L.A. to visit his brother."

The dude's face becomes visibly friendlier toward me. "Oh, hey. Great to meet you, man." I feel his eyes flicker over my body, sizing me up.

I don't mean to do it, but I flex my arm muscles under his gaze.

"Brian's brother goes to UCLA, majoring in mechanical engineering," Maddy says. "What are the odds, right? We were both looking at the candy and Brian asked me my favorite and within three seconds, we'd already put it together that I'm driving to UCLA and his brother goes there. He was just telling me a whole bunch of stuff about campus and Westwood—places to eat, you know."

"Cool," I say, my eyes not leaving Brian's.

Maddy looks at Brian. "Well, that, and Brian was trying to convince me he's the world's biggest authority on candy bars."

Baby Face smiles at her. "I am."

"What-*ever*." She puts up her hand like she's so done with him and they both laugh.

I feel my jaw tighten and my arm muscles tense again.

"I'm so sorry to have kept you waiting," Maddy says to me.

"No problem."

"So, hey," the dude says. "I know you've got a long drive ahead of you. I'll let you two get back on the road. Drive safe, okay? It was great talking to you."

"Oh my gosh, it was so nice to meet you, Brian. Thanks for all the info."

Baby Face flashes what he undoubtedly thinks is a panty-melting smile. "My *pleasure*, Maddy."

Whoa, whoa, whoa! Did this douche just try to subliminally infiltrate the pleasure-center in Maddy Milliken's brain—and right in front of *me*? Motherfucker!

Baby Face goes in for a brief hug and, to my surprise, Maddy seems more than happy to return his gesture.

The second they break apart, the dude's eyes flicker over to me again. "So you two are just driving together or... ?"

"Yeah, we just met today," Maddy says breezily. "Keane got emotionally blackmailed into making the drive with me, poor thing." She laughs. "My big sister was worried about me making the drive all by myself so Keane's brother, who lives across the hall from my sister, inexplicably offered Keane up as my personal bodyguard." Maddy rolls her eyes and grins at me. "Keane's racking up big-time karma points for sure."

I try to return Maddy's grin, but my mouth feels tight.

"Cool," Brian says. "So, hey, I visit my brother all the time. We should exchange numbers so we can grab a coffee or drink next time I'm down there."

"Or, hey, maybe a Tommy-burger, right?" Maddy chirps, pulling out her phone.

"Absolutely. You'll see. They're an institution."

"I can't wait. What's your last name?" Maddy asks, her fingers poised over her phone.

As they exchange information, I make my way to the end of my aisle and loop into theirs, not taking my eyes off Baby Face the whole time. Shit. This dude's hunting Maddy so hard, it's making my blood boil. Jesus, he's going full-throttle *rifle* on Maddy's ass right now, completely foregoing his crossbow altogether.

When I reach the two of them in the middle of their aisle, I shuffle past the dude and stand next to Maddy, shoulder to shoulder, and then, on a sudden impulse, put my arm around her shoulders and squeeze her tight, making her wobble in place at the unexpected jolt to her balance. "Hey, sis," I say, squeezing her like a rag doll. "You totally fell down on your candy-acquiring duties."

"I know. I'm sorry." She subtly wiggles out of my grasp. "Brian and I got into this hilarious argument about the best candy bar of all-time, and—"

"And I'm totally right," Brian says, cutting her off, and they both chuckle at some inside joke.

"No, *I'm* totally right," Maddy corrects.

Brian smiles at her. "I'll actually be down in L.A. in a month. How 'bout I call you then?"

"Great."

"Nice to meet you, man," Brian says, looking at me. He nods but doesn't put out his hand.

I nod back.

Brian strolls away, buys a Snickers bar and a can of Red Bull, and leaves with a little wave to Maddy.

The minute he's out the door, Maddy takes a giant step away from me, her face etched with annoyance. "What was *that*?" she asks.

"What?"

"That weird *thing* you just did?"

"I don't know what you're talking about."

Maddy puts on an exaggerated scowl, like she's Hulk Hogan eying an opponent. "'Hey, Brian,'" she says in a low voice, clearly intending to imitate me but sounding more like Arnold

110

Schwarzenegger imitating Maddy imitating me. "'I'm Maddy Milliken's bodyguard and I'm going to beat you the hell up now,'" she adds.

"What are you talking about?" I say, chuckling.

Maddy pauses, assessing me, and finally shrugs. "Nothing. I guess I imagined it."

"Imaged *what*?"

"Your weird... I dunno... *vibe*."

"Oh, well, yeah. I was worried about you."

"Worried about me? I was standing in a minimart, buying candy. Pretty low-risk activity, I'd say."

"Uh, you absolutely were *not* standing in a minimart, buying candy—you totally fell down on that job, dude. You were standing in a minimart, getting picked up by a douche. And second of all—"

"*What?*"

Shit. What the fuck am I doing? I've got to stop this shit right now. "Don't get riled up, baby doll," I say in my most soothing voice. "All I'm saying is you took so damned long in here, I started thinking maybe the store was getting robbed or you'd fallen into the toilet or something."

Maddy twists her mouth. "Brian didn't seem the least bit douchey to me."

I shrug.

"What gave you the impression he's a douche?"

"Just a figure of speech. So are you gonna do the job I hired you to do or not?" I motion to the candy rack. "'Cause based on your performance thus far, you're totally fired."

"And I wasn't getting 'picked up,'" Maddy says, her tone full of indignation. "Brian's brother goes to UCLA. Can't I talk to a helpful, nice guy without it being some sort of a sleazy pick-up?"

"Sure you can. However, in this instance, you were talking to a helpful, nice guy who was picking you up so he can bone the living fuck outta ya."

"*Keane.*" Maddy's cheeks burst with color. "Don't say that. Oh my god. You're insane. Brian was just being helpful, that's all."

"Yeah, so he can bone the living fuck outta ya."

"Stop saying that. Please. It's offensive and absolutely not true. This topic of conversation is officially over." She makes a weird hand gesture like she's a magician making me disappear and then turns her attention to the candy rack, her cheeks on fire. "I don't see Abba Zaba bars. Do you?"

"Maddy, that dude couldn't have been any clearer about his intentions. I mean, come on, you're funny but you're not *that* funny."

Maddy's face falls. "What do you mean?"

"No, I mean, you're funny. Really funny. I just meant he was laying it on awfully thick, that's all. Going a bit overboard with the yucks."

Maddy clenches her jaw and turns toward the candy rack again. "Wow, you sure know how to make a girl feel fantastic." She purses her lips. "Okay, I don't see Junior Mints, either." Her voice is tight. "I guess Milk Duds will have to work extra hard for us 'til we can get to a supermarket." She grabs a box of Milk Duds off the shelf.

"You seriously don't think that guy was interested in bonin' the fuck outta ya?"

"Would you stop saying that? Please, Keane. It's gross."

"What's gross? Those particular words or the act of someone bonin' the fuck outta ya?"

"Both."

"Getting boned is gross? Oh, shit, no wonder you've been going steady with Jesus lately."

"Keane! Stop it. That's not what I meant. Sex isn't gross to me. Not at all. I meant the idea of sex with *Brian* is gross because I wasn't attracted to him in that way and I need to feel both an emotional *and* physical connection to a guy to even think about letting him 'bone the fuck outta me.'" She makes a weird face.

"First time you've ever said those words in your entire life, huh?"

"And, regardless, Brian *definitely* wasn't attracted to me—he was just being helpful and nice—so whether he wanted to 'bone the fuck outta me' or not is a moot point, anyway." She makes that same weird face again.

"It was no easier saying it the second time around, was it?"

She scowls at me.

"Okay, now I totally understand the source of your wicked dry spell, honey muffin. You're deaf, dumb and blind when it comes to reading a guy's signals."

"No, I'm not. I have zero trouble reading a guy's signals—and in this instance, the signal Brian was sending me loud and cuh-lear was 'fuh-riend zone.'"

"No way. That dude was sending you a 'buh-hone zone' signal all the way to Pompei, Beyoncé."

"No freakin' way to Bombay, Pelé."

I chuckle. "So why'd you give him your number, then?"

"Because I know all of two people in L.A.—my sister and her boyfriend, Henn—and I'm probably gonna be, you know, a little lonely at school until I can make some friends. At least this way, I'll have some social interaction to look forward to in a few weeks, just in case I haven't made any friends by then."

"Well, of course, you'll have friends in a whole *month*, Mad Dog. Oh my God, you'll have more friends than you could shake a stick at."

Maddy's eyes flicker with obvious anxiety. "Not necessarily," she says softly. "Not everyone's like you, Keane."

My chest suddenly feels tight. "Hey, don't sell yourself short, sweetheart," I say. I take a step toward her and push a stray hair away from her pretty face. "Trust me, your dance card's gonna be completely filled within a week, I guarantee it." I look into Maddy's brown eyes for a beat, and then let my gaze take in the entirety of her pretty face. Wow, I hadn't noticed until just now how beautiful Maddy's lips are.

Oh, fuck.

I abruptly lower my hand from Maddy's hair and jerk my body away from hers, clearing my throat. "And, hey, if not, then, great job, Helen Keller: you just made yourself a burger-date with a guy who wants to bone the livin' fuck outta ya."

Maddy socks me in the shoulder. "Stop it."

"Ow." I rub my shoulder. "You're mean."

"Well, you're annoying." She socks me again. "And you're a *dickweed*."

I rub my shoulder again. "Hey, I strongly prefer to be called 'flaming asshole,' please."

"Oh, I'm saving that one for the next time you say something that forces me to punch you." She lets out a grunt. "Please stop needling me about Brian, okay? It was nice talking to him, that's all—he helped calm my jangly nerves about school. I'm excited about starting a brand new school, for sure, but I'm nervous as hell about it, too."

"Aw, don't be nervous, sweet thing. You're gonna do great. You're the Steve Jobs of documentary filmmaking, remember?"

Maddy twists her mouth adorably. "Look, the bottom line about Brian is that, even if he were into me, which he's *not*, he won't be 'bonin' the fuck outta me' because *I'm* not into *him*." She makes another weird hand gesture, like she's banishing me to the hinterlands of hell. "And that's the last thing I'm gonna say on the topic of Brian or 'bonin'.'" She abruptly walks away from me to the end of the aisle, and I follow her. "Do you see popcorn?" she asks, looking at a shelf filled with bags of potato chips and pretzels. "Oh, here it is. You like it plain or flavored, baby doll? What's your *pleasure?*"

I grab a bag of white-cheddar popcorn off the shelf. "In honor of my beloved wife. Zander and I have made some beautiful memories together while eating this stuff."

"Great," Maddy says, grabbing another bag of popcorn off the shelf. "I'm all in favor of honoring your beloved wife any chance we get." She looks at the items in her hands. "So are we good with popcorn and Milk Duds, or will we be breaking the law if we don't have Junior Mints, too?"

"Are we in Oregon yet?" I ask.

"We crossed the border an hour ago."

"Okay, then we're good," I say, loping back down the aisle toward the candy. "There's a little-known *exception* to the law requiring the consumption of popcorn, Milk Duds, and Junior Mints while watching a movie, applicable only in the state of Oregon, that says chocolate peanut butter cups can be substituted for Junior Mints in a verified emergency." I hold up a bright orange package of chocolate peanut butter cups. "But *only* when the chocolate peanut butter cups are consumed by a sensitive, pretty girl with a boner for gender equality and an intense sexual attraction to Jesus, and only while she watches a kick-ass documentary about basketball, unrequited love, and gender inequality with a dude with blue hair, ebullient charm, and killer dimples." I flash her my dimples.

"Wowza," Maddy says, laughing. "That's a *really* specific law."

"Yeah," I say. "We got lucky this time. If we were still in Washington, they'd probably lock us up and throw away the key."

"Well, then, we shouldn't tempt fate," Maddy says. "First chance we get, let's stop at a grocery store and stock up on all necessary supplies. God only knows what the law will be once we cross into California tomorrow."

"Good idea," I say.

Maddy's mouth twists, just for a beat, like she's trying her damnedest not to smile. "You're annoying, you know that?" she says.

"I've heard that a time or two. So you ready to buy this grub-a-dub-dub and hit the road, sweet thing?" I ask. "Or are we gonna spend our whole vacation standing in this godforsaken minimart?"

A beaming smile spreads across the full width of Maddy's pretty face. "Hell no, we're not gonna spend our whole *vacation* standing in this godforsaken minimart, sugar lips," she says. "Let's roll."

Chapter 17
Keane

"So why aren't you into Brian?" I ask, propping the minimart door open for Maddy with one arm while holding our bags of popcorn and candy in the other.

"Aw, come on!" Maddy throws up her hands and quickens her pace toward her car. "Obsess much?"

"I'm just curious," I say, following closely behind her. "Brian was a handsome enough dude; you said yourself he was 'nice and helpful'; and he was clearly sportin' major wood for you. So why wouldn't you at least give him a shot? Not everyone can be as perfect as your boyfriend Jesus, you know."

"Yeah, Keane, I require guys to emulate the son of God to get a burger date with me," she says, rolling her eyes. We've reached her car and she digs into her purse for her keys. "I'm pretty sure I've mentioned that my recent foray into abstinence hasn't been intentional."

"So why not give this Brian dude a shot?"

"Because I either feel physical chemistry with a guy or I don't. And I didn't feel it with him."

Maddy unlocks her car and we pile inside.

"Yeah, but maybe physical chemistry can develop over time," I say, stowing the bag of junk food on the floor next to my feet.

"I don't think so."

"No?"

"Not in my experience. Hang on." She holds up her hand. "Silence while I back out, please."

I bite my lip and remain quiet as Maddy slowly backs her car out of its parking spot, furrowing her brow as she does.

"Thank you," she says when she's got her car free and clear of the gas station and we're headed down the road toward the freeway on-ramp.

"You're an excellent driver, Rainman," I say.

"Why, thank you. Okay, on further reflection, I'd like to amend my last statement. I *do* think physical chemistry can increase or decrease the more you get to know someone, but what I'm looking for is something different than gambling on there being a gradual increase of attraction. I want that smacks-you-in-the-face, undeniable, heart-racing, all-consuming *heat* with someone, you know? And I don't think that kind of attraction develops over time. Do you?"

I consider my answer for a moment. "No. Or, at least, it's never happened to me. That kind of thing is pretty much instantaneous—you either got it with someone or you don't."

"Exactly."

"So what's missing with Brian, you think?" I open one of the three bags of popcorn we bought at the minimart.

"You're *hungry*?" Maddy asks, incredulous.

"Snacky."

"But you just ate enough food to feed a small army."

"That's because *I'm* a small army, sweetheart." I flex my arm. "Ka-bam, son! It takes a lot to keep this body looking like manna from heaven."

"So you keep telling me."

I hold the bag of popcorn out to her. "You want some, honey biscuits? It's delish."

"No, thanks, sugar booty. I'm still stuffed from lunch like any normal person would be."

"Suit yourself. So, what's wrong with Brian, you think? Why no fireworks?"

"Nothing's *wrong* with him. Wait, yeah, I changed my mind. Send that bag over here, hot stuff." She motions to the popcorn bag and I hand it to her. "It's not something that can be explained logically," she says, chomping a handful of popcorn. "He's cute. Nice. Funny. On paper, he seems like the perfect guy for me to pursue. I just don't go for jock types, I guess. I dunno. Who the frickity-frack knows why anyone feels attraction to one person and not another?" She dives into the bag again.

"Good stuff, huh?"

"Dangerously addicting."

"It's Z's favorite." I take another huge handful. "Yeah, Brian's definitely a jock type. I'm guessing O-line."

117

"*O-line*? Is that a some sort of sexual reference?"

"Oh, for the love of God, woman. Have you never watched a football game in your life? *Offensive line*, babe. You know, the guys who protect the quarterback?"

"Ooooooh." Maddy snorts. "That's funny. I thought it was some slang I'm too dorky to know about. Okay. Well, whatever. The point is Brian was sweet and nice but, for whatever reason, he didn't make my pulse race. And I've recently decided I'm not interested in any guy who can't make my pulse race right off the bat."

"A guy has to make your pulse *race* right from the get-go or he's shit out of luck with you? Dude, that's a pretty tall order, don't you think? Can't a guy be kinda nice and moderately good-looking and then, if things seem to be going well, you jump into the sack with him to see where things might lead?"

Maddy scoffs. "Do *you* sleep with girls who are 'kinda nice' and 'moderately good-looking', just to 'see where things might lead'?"

I consider that briefly. "No. Never."

"Of course, not. Because you want to feel intense physical chemistry, right away. Why bother otherwise?"

"Well, yeah, but I've got my pick of all the pickles in the world. Why should I settle for a pickle who doesn't give me a raging woody from minute one?"

"So you're implying *I* don't have my pick of pickles the way you do?"

I laugh. "Pick of pickles."

"Pick of pickles," she repeats, and we both laugh. "Peter Piper picked a peck of pickled pickles because he had his pick of pickled pickles to prick with his pickled pecker," she adds.

I laugh my ass off. "Say that again."

She does.

"Oh my God, Maddy. I gotta get that on video. I'd never be able to describe that to Z." I pull out my phone.

"No, Keane." She puts her hand up. "I don't like being on camera."

"Come on, baby doll. For me and Z. I won't post it or anything like that, I promise. That was just too cute not to *document*."

She puts down her hand. "Fine. For you and Z only. I hate being on camera."

"Thank you. It's just how I am, baby. *I. Must. Document.*" I press the button to record. "Okay, action."

Maddy repeats her pickled tongue twister and I laugh just as hard again.

"Got it. Thank you."

"You're welcome."

"You know what that reminds me of? When Z sent you that dick-pick, I said, 'Hey, Z, you can't send a dick-pick to a *chick*,' and then we both lost our minds because we thought 'dick-pick to a chick' was so fucking funny. Z called it the social-media edition of 'Old MacDonald Had a Farm': 'Dick-pick to a chick-chick, everywhere a dick-pic—"

"E-i-e-i-o," Maddy sings, and we both burst out laughing.

"Oh man, it's still funny as hell to me and I'm not even stoned."

"I think it's hilarious."

"My brother Ryan didn't think it was funny *at all*."

"Sounds like Ryan wouldn't know funny if it bit him in the ass, son." She throws up her hand to me without taking her eyes off the road and I side-high-five her.

"See? That's why I love you the most, Maddy Milliken— because you're funny as hell."

Maddy blushes.

"Now don't get all obsessed with me 'cause I said that, okay, baby doll? It's just a figure of speech. It's what I say to all the cool kids." I wink.

"I will refrain from getting obsessed with you," she says. "I promise."

We both chomp some more popcorn.

"So do you?" I ask after a long moment.

"Do I what?"

"Have your pick of pickles?"

"Oh." Maddy snorts. "I forgot all about that." She pops a piece of popcorn into her mouth. "Absolutely, positively *not*." She laughs. "But so what? Does that mean I should settle for pickles who don't get my motor running *at all*? Is that your implication? Because I really don't think so. I used to settle—in fact, I've made a romantic career out of it—but I've recently decided that, since I'm going to a brand new school and starting a new life in a new city, I'm a man-eater now, baby. Ka-bam, son!" She flexes her arm.

I laugh. God, she's so cute, I can't stand it.

"From here on out," Maddy continues, apparently oblivious to the wide smile I'm flashing her, "I'm not settling, even if that means I'm gonna be alone 'til the day I die. I'm no longer going steady with *Jesus*—I'm going steady with *me*."

"Holy fuck, brah. You're Kelly on *90210*."

"Oh my God, I love that show!" She furrows her brow with mock solemnity. "'I. Choose. Me.'"

"Yes!" I say, chuckling. "I was so pissed about that."

"Me, too! I was like, 'Aw, come on, Kelly! Just frickin' *choose!*'"

We both laugh.

"Oh, and we can't forget the best episode *ever*," Maddy says.

"'Donna Martin graduates!'" we both shout at the same time and then burst into laughter.

Another side-high-five ensues.

"Dang it," Maddy says after our laughter has died down. "I can't think of another *90210* quote to save my life. You got another one for me, sugar lips?"

"Hmm. Well, there's a pretty good one where Brandon says if Steve Sanders were any stupider, he'd have to feed him fertilizer.'"

Maddy bursts out laughing. "That's *90210*? I don't remember that one."

"Yeah, it was in one of the later seasons after they'd gone away to college. I don't remember what Steve Sanders did, but it was something really boneheaded. Z uses that one on me a lot. Sometimes, he just calls me Steve Sanders if I've been particularly stupid."

Maddy chuckles. "I gotta meet Z."

"You'd love him. And he'd love you. Actually, he already does. He liked you at 'jerksauce' and fell deeply in love with you at 'dickweed.'"

Maddy makes an adorable face.

"Okay, then, enough *90210*. Back to you and your sex life, dude," I say.

"Oh, yes, please." She rolls her eyes.

"Maddy Milliken, Professional Eye-Roller."

She does it again.

"I'm surprised you still have full range of motion of dem eyeballs, sweet cheeks. Okay, tell me this: how many guys have made your pulse race like you're talking about?"

Maddy daintily places a single kernel of popcorn into her mouth. "One. My first boyfriend, Justin. Every other boyfriend since him has been a nice guy, but the physical sparks just weren't there."

"*One*? Jesus, Maddy."

"Such is life for us mere mortals, Keane."

"How many guys you been with all together?"

She presses her lips together.

"Aw, come on," I say. "I won't tell anybody. I gotta know what I'm working with here."

"Three."

I'm flabbergasted. "Your number's *three*?"

She nods, blushing.

"Oh, for the love of all things holy, woman."

"I'm a boyfriend-type of girl." She shrugs. "So now you see why I've decided to do things differently from here on out. From now on, a guy being 'nice' isn't good enough. I want it all—emotional *and* physical sparks." She makes a face reflecting extreme distaste. "Honestly, without a strong physical connection, sex can actually be kind of... *icky*. Oh, shoot," she says suddenly, her gaze trained on the road ahead of us. "We got traffic, son."

As Maddy applies the brakes, I peer out the windshield, and sure enough, we're coming up on a shit-ton of brake lights.

I look at my watch. "Rush hour, you think?"

"It's still a bit early for that, isn't it? Maybe there's been an accident?"

"You want me to drive for a bit?" I ask.

"No, it's okay."

"Okay. Just lemme know if you change your mind, Mario Andretti. But just so you know, I got my one and only speeding ticket at age seventeen; if you let me drive, I'll put my phone in the glove box while driving, the same way you do, and I'll keep both hands at ten and two at all times, never taking my eyes off the road except to *occasionally* flash you my killer dimples when you say something especially cute. I'm not sure if I've mentioned this to you yet, but I'm an excellent driver."

121

"Yeah, I think I heard that somewhere. Thanks. I'll keep your offer in mind. So do you agree with me or not?"

"About what—that I've got killer dimples?" I flash my dimples. "Yes, I do."

Maddy's unfazed, which is becoming par for the course with us. "No, you narcissist, do you agree with me I should hold out for *both* emotional *and* physical attraction from here on out or do you stand by your advice that I should start jumping into bed with guys who do absolutely nothing for me physically and see where it leads?"

"Oh, *that*. Well, no, now that you put it that way, I'm not standing by that advice. Actually, I'm gonna pull a one-eighty here because I think you're looking at this whole thing completely backwards."

"How so?"

"Your assumption is you'll find emotional attraction *first* and then have to figure out whether there's enough of a physical spark, too. But why the hell wouldn't you turn things around? I mean, yeah, if you're looking for an actual *relationship*, then, sure, you gotta find the whole package. But why the fuck are you looking for a boyfriend at all? Fuck it. You're young and single, about to start a new school. If I were you, I'd start this new-school-new-city thing off with a *bang*—pun intended—and have yourself some good old-fashioned chitty-chitty-bang-bang. Forget about the emotional-and-physical-connection thing for a while and get yourself laid by some guy who really gets your motor running full-throttle."

Maddy chuckles. "Oh my God, Keane."

"Seriously, Maddy. Why not go for it once in a while and have some fun? Ain't no shame in that. In fact, the whole thing would be an act of protest against gender inequality."

"How on earth would jumping into the sack with every hottie I meet, no matter how big a jerk he is or how stupid, be an act of protest against gender inequality?"

"Why should men be the only ones in our society who get to sleep around with *impunity*?"

"Big word, son."

"Zander."

"Ah."

"Why is sleeping around perfectly fine for men but women are slut-shamed? Hey, that's an interesting *juxtaposition*, wouldn't you say? That could be your next documentary right there—*juxtaposing* the male and female sexual experience—and sleeping around could be your *research*." Oh man. The look on Maddy's face is too much fun not to keep hurtling ahead. "Yep, that's exactly what you should do," I continue. "Find yourself a dude who makes your pulse race and let him bone the livin' fuck outta ya 'til you're screaming your own name 'cause you don't even know his."

Maddy bursts out laughing at that one.

I laugh with her. It's hard not to do—the girl's got an infectious laugh. "Think about it," I continue. "It's the perfect antidote for all that ails you." Oh man, I'm a runaway locomotive now, feeding off the sparkle in Maddy's eyes and the bloom in her cheeks. "First off, you'll have fun, which is reason enough. But, second off, it'll get your confidence going, which, in turn, will attract even more alpha-type hotties, which will create a viciously *awesome* cycle of *awesomeness*, until one fine day, when you least expect it, Mr. Emotional-and-Physical-Connection will waltz straight into your life unannounced, behold your newfound swagger, and say, 'Oh, hey there, baby doll. Sorry I kept you waiting—I was outside, parking my white horse.'"

Maddy shakes her head. "Maybe that's the way the world works for *you*, Ball Peen Hammer, but it's not quite like that for the rest of us. We mere mortals can't all jump in the sack willy-nilly with our pick of pickles."

"You don't think you can bag any hot guy you want?"

The look on Maddy's face tells me she doesn't.

"Bullshit. Look at yourself. You're gorgeous. Smokin' hot. You could get any guy you wanted—you just have to believe in yourself a bit more. Although it certainly wouldn't hurt if you'd show off your merchandise a bit, for fuck's sake."

Maddy's eyes dart from the road just long enough to glare at me. "And here I was about to say 'thank you for calling me gorgeous.'"

"Aw, come on, Madagascar," I say. "You must know you look like the fucking sun in that billowy yellow shirt—and I'm not saying that in reference to your bright and sparkling personality. What the fuck are you doing wearing a flowing yellow shirt that makes it impossible for any guy to figure out what you've got going on under there? Dude, I'd bet dollars to doughnuts you've got a slammin' hot bod under there and guys can't make out hide nor hair of it 'cause your shirt's so damned *billowy*."

"Keane, I know you don't like this word, but you really are a pig."

"I'm just saying what everyone orbiting the sun is thinking— and, bee tee dubs, when I said 'the sun' in that sentence, that means you."

"*Pig*."

"Would you rather I think it and not say it?"

"Yes. Most definitely. *Pig*."

"Bah. Honesty's a good thing. It's how we learn and grow, sweetheart."

"Well, guess what? I don't need to 'learn and grow' because I don't dress to give guys a peep show. I dress for *me*." She glances down at her shirt. "And I happen to like this shirt. *A lot*."

"Well, great. Glad you like looking like a fucking planet."

"The sun's not a *planet*, Steve Sanders. It's a *star*."

"Oh, well, aren't you a fancy-pants college student. You think that little lesson in astronomy makes your shirt any more attractive? Because it doesn't. Okay, fine. Good for you, Galileo, you've made yourself look like a giant ball of gases. Happy?"

Maddy can't resist chuckling. "You're so *mean*. Your momma should have named you *Mean* Morgan instead of Keane Morgan."

"I'm not mean—I'm honest. But, hey, if I'm mean, then I'm cruel to be kind. You wanna become a man-eater who gets boned by guys who get your motor running from the get-go? Then ditch that fucking horrible shirt and show off what God gave you."

Maddy sighs. "I can't believe I've agreed to be stuck in a car for two solid days with the most unenlightened human on planet earth." She motions to the popcorn bag in my lap. "Gimme some of that popcorn, you pig. I need to self-medicate."

"Knock yourself out, *Sunshine*."

Maddy's mouth is scowling at me as she plunges her hand into the popcorn bag—but her eyes are most definitely smiling. "For your information, I have no desire to waggle my boobs at guys to make them want to sleep with me. All that would do is attract a bunch of *pigs* like you."

"'*Waggle* your boobs'?"

Maddy scowls at me.

"Okay, fine, Sunshine. Stick with attracting 'nice' guys who don't get your motor running *at all*. Enjoy your 'icky' bonin' all the livelong day. I was just trying to be helpful."

"Hmmph."

"Hmmph yourself. And, bee tee dubs, I'd love a demonstration of how you 'waggle your boobs' some time. How else are we gonna know for sure whether it would, indeed, attract pigs like me or make them run away squealing with terror?"

"Ha! In your dreams." She scowls at me again, but she can't hide the smile in her eyes.

There's a long beat as we both chomp some more popcorn and watch the slow-moving traffic ahead of us.

"God, we're moving at a snail's pace," Maddy says after a while. "I wonder what's going on up there? Do you see ambulances or sirens or anything?"

We both peer ahead of us as best we can, but there's no way to see what lies ahead beyond the long line of jam-packed cars.

"Naw, I can't see a thing," I say.

"God, I hope it's not an accident," Maddy says, her voice laced with anxiety.

The anxious tone in Maddy's voice suddenly makes me remember something Dax mentioned in one of his texts: *Hannah's extra protective of Maddy because Maddy was in a horrible car crash a few years ago.*

The hairs on the back of my neck stand on end at the thought. Was Maddy hurt badly? Was she terrified? Shit. I hate thinking of anything bad happening to her. I study Maddy's profile for a moment as she scrutinizes the traffic in front of us, her face scrunched with concern.

"Hey, baby doll," I say. I touch her shoulder gently. "What do you say we get off this parking lot and look for a quiet place to chill for a bit? Have ourselves a little rest-and-relaxation sesh while we let this traffic jam sort itself out?"

"It might clear up quickly, you never know," she says. "If you want, I can try to find an alternate route on side roads for a bit, if you're in a hurry to get to L.A.?"

"Meh. I'm in no rush. I gotta be there by Friday night at nine, but 'til then, I'm free as a bird. What's your timing like?"

"My first class is a week from Monday."

"Well, all right, then. Sounds like we got some green grass, tall trees, and puffy clouds in our very near future."

Chapter 18
Keane

"Can I ask you a personal question?" Maddy asks.

We're lying underneath a large tree in a grassy park we located courtesy of Google maps, sprawled on top of a blanket we retrieved from the back of Maddy's car, gazing up at the late-afternoon clouds in the sky. A cool breeze occasionally rustles the tree above us, making its leaves shimmer lazily against the backdrop of the clouded sky.

I'm on my back and Maddy's lying alongside me on her belly, her chin propped up by her hands; and without meaning to do it, I keep finding myself absently running my fingertips up and down Maddy's back as we talk.

"Ask me anything you like," I say. "Personal questions are my favorite kind."

Maddy shivers as a cool breeze wafts over us.

"Scoot closer," I say. "I'll be your pillow and blanket, baby."

She snuggles into me and I throw my arm across her back.

"Better?"

She nods.

"What's your question, boob-waggler?" She swats at my shoulder and I laugh. "Your term, not mine," I say.

Maddy rolls her eyes.

"What's your question?" I ask.

"Have you ever slept with a pickle you felt *zero* emotional connection with?" she asks. Her tone is earnest, but the moment she sees the smile unfurling across my lips, she rolls her eyes again.

"What?" I ask, still smiling.

127

"That," she says, indicating my mouth. "You just answered my question loud and cuh-lear." She scoffs. "I can't believe I just asked *you* of all people that question in all seriousness."

"Why 'me of all people'? What kind of 'people' am I?"

She pokes my shoulder. "The muscular and highly narcissistic kind."

"Oh, really?" I put my free arm behind my head, still smirking at her. "You assume because I work out and don't pretend to be humble about what I see in the mirror, I must be a manwhore?"

"Well, aren't you?"

"Yes, but that's beside the point. You shouldn't assume it. I know *plenty* of guys at the gym who are way more buff than I am and they don't sleep around. One guy I know is a twenty-five-year-old virgin, believe it or not. Liam. He's waiting for marriage."

"Really?"

I nod. "And Liam's way more ripped than I am, by far. Dude looks like a god."

"Huh. Well, good for him. But just to be clear, you're nothing like Liam, right? Because you, unlike our ripped and virginal Liam, are a total and complete manwhore?"

"Well, *yeah*." I grin broadly. "And thank God for that, baby." I move onto my side and so does Maddy, until we're facing each other, our bodies stretched out on the blanket, goose bumps erupting on our skin in the cool breeze. "I'm just saying you can't *assume* a guy's a manwhore based solely on appearance."

"Okay, well, good to know. But, just so you know, every freakin' thing about you screams 'manwhore!', so if you don't want people thinking that about you, then maybe you should tone down the 'I'm a total and complete manwhore!' vibe you're giving off. Just sayin'."

I grin at her. The way the late-afternoon sun is hitting Maddy's hair, it's this crazy, shimmering shade of auburn, kinda like dark cinnamon (a hair color I've always had a bit of a weakness for ever since I made out with Sophie Broughton in seventh grade). "Well, see," I say. "I don't give a shit what anyone thinks about me, so I'm good."

"Yeah, well, I guess a guy can't call himself 'Ball Peen Hammer' and then turn around and give a crap if everyone thinks he's 'bonin' the fuck outta women right and left,' huh?"

We're practically lying nose to nose—and up close like this, I'm noticing for the first time Maddy's eyes are the exact color of Tootsie Pops.

"Okay, first off, sweetheart," I say, "you can't get away with saying the phrase 'bonin' the fuck outta women right and left.' You sound like Laura Ingalls Wilder trying to say that. Second off, lemme be crystal clear about something: even though I might 'bone the fuck outta' women now and again, I ain't no fuckboy. My momma raised me better than that. And, third off, you got me all wrong. Ball Peen Hammer doesn't bone the fuck outta women; *Keane Morgan* does. In point of fact, being a stripper has cut into my random acts of bonery, big-time."

Maddy smirks and a lock of her auburn hair tumbles into her face.

Oh man, I shouldn't do it, but I can't resist. I reach out and push her hair off her face, and damned if her hair against my fingertips isn't softer than I expected it to be. "Don't flash me that snarky look," I say. "Your face is gonna freeze that way and then where will you be?"

"It can't be helped," Maddy says. "You just said being a male stripper has 'cut into your random acts of bonery' with a straight face."

"Hey, I'm speaking the God's truth. I got laid way more *before* I became Ball Peen Hammer."

Maddy rolls her eyes. "Well, first off, sweetheart," she says, adopting my exact tone from a moment ago. "I think you should leave God out of any conversation about how much you get *laid*. Second off, I don't believe you for a New York minute. And, third off, I can't think of a third off."

"Oh my God." I prop myself onto my elbow in sudden indignation. "You think I'm nothing but a paid cock, don't you?"

Maddy props herself up, too, matching my body's position, her facial expression quite clearly communicating, "If the shoe fits..."

"You know what, Maddy Milliken? I'm deeply offended. I'll have you know I'm good at my job—a true *professional*. Probs the top male exotic dancer in Seattle. Most guys make half of what I do on a good night."

Maddy snickers. "Yeah, based on everything you've told me, I'm sure you're *extremely* good at your job."

129

"Oh my fucking God. You've got it all wrong. Contrary to what you're obviously thinking, I don't fuck clients. *Ever*." My heart is racing. Has Maddy been assuming I fuck for a living this whole time?

"Really?" she asks, her eyes wide.

"Absolutely. I peddle the *fantasy* of getting to sleep with me, baby, not my actual *cock*."

"Wow. I'm sorry. I didn't realize—wait, oh." She grins. "You're totally pulling my leg, aren't you?" She snorts. "Oh, you're good."

"Maddy, stop it. I'm serious. I don't sleep with clients. It's a firm rule and I never break it."

Maddy sits all the way up, color rising in her cheeks. "Oh. Wow. I'm sorry. I truly thought... *Oh*."

I sit up, too. "Well, you thought wrong. I don't fuck clients. And, like I said, stripping has cut into my sex life, big-time. Really, it's a wonder I get any no-strings sex at all these days, given my schedule."

Maddy looks at me quizzically.

I exhale with frustration. "Think about it. I'm always working on weekend nights, which is when ninety-nine percent of all casual hook-ups in the universe take place. That's my first major hurdle right there, since, like I say, I don't fuck clients. And then, on top of that, whenever I'm not working, where am I? At the gym with Z. And since I don't sleep with women at the gym, either, I'm pretty much screwed when it comes to getting screwed. The fact that I still get laid at all is a testament to just how irresistible to women I really am."

"Why don't you sleep with women at the gym? I'd think the gym would be the perfect place to find women to 'bone the fuck outta.'"

"Dude, you gotta stop saying that. You seriously cannot pull that off."

"No?"

"No."

"Bone the fuck outta," Maddy says, a twinkle in her brown eyes.

"Still no."

"Hmmph. Well, okay. Regardless, I'm just saying it seems like the gym would be an extremely fertile ground for finding yourself some willing fuck-buddies. Everyone's in great shape and wearing skimpy little workout clothes and—"

130

"Dude. 'Fuck-buddies' doesn't trip off your tongue any more convincingly than 'bone the fuck outta.' Sorry, Laura Ingalls Wilder. Try again."

"No? Jeez. Okay, well, hmm. How about this: I'd think the gym would be the ideal place for you to find willing and highly attractive *playmates*."

"Much better. And, yes, to your point, one would think the gym would be an ideal playground for a guy like me. But, trust me, when you're not looking for a girlfriend and you start hunting in the same place where you hang out every day of your life, it becomes really messy, really fast. Just trust me on that. Yeesh."

Maddy makes a face. "It creeps me out when you refer to picking up women as 'hunting.' It makes you seem like a serial killer."

"It's slang, baby doll—I slanghai'd it from this hilarious dude at the gym. Don't get yourself all riled up about it. It's how boys talk when girls aren't around."

"I've never heard a boy say that before."

"I just said it's how boys talk *when girls aren't around*, Steve Sanders. If you're around, then boys aren't sayin' it."

"But *you* just said it and I'm sitting right here—and last time I checked, I'm still a girl."

"Maddy, doy-burgers. When you're with me, you're not a *girl*. You're *Maddy*."

Maddy makes a face like she's not sure she understands the distinction.

"That was a compliment, bee tee dubs," I say.

"Oh. Well, thanks?" She lowers herself onto her back on the blanket, her arms behind her head. "So has Ball Peen Hammer *ever* slept with a client, or have you always followed your no-sex rule from day one?"

"Oh, hell yes, Ball Peen Hammer's slept with clients—by the truckloads in the beginning." I shake my head, remembering myself practically overdosing on pussy for the first thirty days of my new career. "For, like, the first month I was a kid in a candy shop. But it didn't take long for me to figure out banging clients, or their friends, or *anyone* I met within fifty yards of a gig, was a very, very, *veeeeeeeeeeeery* bad idea if I wanted to earn an actual living in the game."

131

"What happened?" Maddy asks.

A cool breeze wafts over us and we both shiver.

"Are you cold?" I ask.

"A little," she replies.

"You want me to get your sweatshirt from the car?"

"No, just put your arm around me again and I'll be fine."

"Sure thing." I lie on my back and she scoots extra close, pressing her body into my side and placing her cheek on my shoulder. I wrap my arm around her and hold her close, and, instantly, my body warms against hers.

"So tell me what happened when you had sex with all those truckloads of clients," she says, draping her arm over my torso. "Tell me the whole salacious story."

"Oh, you want the whole *salacious* story, huh? Good word. That's like X-rated, right?"

"Correct."

"Okay, I'll tell you, but don't judge."

"No judgment."

"Promise?"

"I thought you don't care what anyone thinks of you."

"Yeah, but you're not *anyone*. You're *Maddy*."

She pushes her body into mine in reply and I squeeze her shoulders.

"Okay. Where to begin?" I take a deep breath. "When I started out, I couldn't believe how women threw themselves at me. It was like I was some kind of sultan or sheik. All I had to do was *point* at a woman and she was grabbing my hand and unzipping my fly before we were even in a back room. Now, don't get me wrong, before then, women had always hit on me. I'm talking about friends' moms, women at grocery stores or gas stations, women standing in line at the ATM, but nothing like that. I guess when you're a stripper, women feel like you're not an actual person anymore, you're just this service animal. A pork chop they're ordering at the butcher shop."

Maddy laughs.

"It's no exaggeration. You'd be shocked how aggressive women can be when they feel like you're for sale. So, anyway, I partook in the spoils of strippery all the time with no regard for consequences for about a month. But then, all of a sudden, things went to shit so fast, my head was spinning. A woman I'd fucked after a bachelorette party called my agency, asking for my cell number—not to hire me again, but to *fuck* me again. Another one wanted to invite me for a weekend in Cabo—like I was gonna be her boy toy for the weekend. Then another and another, none of them actually wanting to hire me for my actual job. So my agent was like, 'What the fuck are you doing to these women, dude? We've never seen anything like this before. We're not your pimp, man.' It sucked. No one wanted to hire me for my actual job again, or if they did, it was for a one-on-one lap dance in a hotel room, if you catch my drift. You see what I mean? They all thought I was nothing but a whore, literally. But these women didn't realize two things. First off, I didn't need stripping as a way to find women to fuck—I could do that on my own, thank you very much. What I needed was a *job*. My prior job had just ended and I had rent to pay. And second off, even when I fucked a client, I wasn't doing it for cash, despite appearances. I was there to do the job and if, while there, someone *happened* to catch my eye at a gig— someone I woulda fucked regardless, then I'd go right ahead and partake. Why not, I figured? You know how lawyers or accountants get cocktails after work? It was like that for me. I was just winding down after my shift, having fun, you know? But I never viewed fucking as *part* of the job or as part of my payday. So, then, all of a sudden, I started getting a reputation, just that fast. Women told their friends and word spread like lightning—because, of course, when I fuck a woman, I do it well. And now I'm being called to show up for a gig at a hotel room, thinking I'm doing a legit party, and it turns out there's only one woman in the room and she's holding up a C-note and pulling off my pants as I walk through the door. And the second that was the sitch—the minute I realized I'd become nothing but a paid cock, that these women thought I'd fuck *anyone* holding a C-note, literally, no matter who she was or what she looked like, I was totally skeeved out. But there's no way to say 'no thanks' to a woman in the heat of the moment without her getting her ego bruised like yesterday's banana. So now I've got women saying they're gonna rat me out to the agency and post all kinds of shit about me on Yelp unless I refund their booking fees, which I did. So now I'm wasting Saturday nights on this shit, my highest paid night of the week, when I coulda been at a legit gig, making good money." I sigh. "So that's how it all went to Shit Town, USA on a bullet train. In less than a month, I'd had more sex than I'd ever had in my entire life, but I was outta cash, my rep in the biz was shit, and I'd made an army of horny women very, very angry with me. Not good."

"Wow. That sounds... horrible."

For the first time in as long as I can remember, I'm feeling insecure with a girl, anxious Maddy's thinking less of me because of everything I just confessed to her. I clear my throat. "But, hey, at least the whole experience taught me something important about myself, right? The Talented Mr. Ripley don't get hard for cash, baby."

"The Talented Mr. Ripley? That's what you call your penis?"

"Yup."

"Did you name him or was he christened by someone else?"

"I named him. He's mine, after all. I got naming rights."

Maddy giggles.

"What? You haven't named your wahoo?"

"*No.*" She giggles again.

"Well, maybe you should. Start calling your bat-cave She-Ra Princess of Power and you'll jumpstart that motor of yours in record speed. Or maybe Hello Kitty? Delilah? *Jaws*? Any of those speak to you?" Maddy bites her lip, drawing my attention to her mouth—her beautiful, kissable mouth—and, out of nowhere, my cock tingles something fierce. Oh my shit. I gotta get my hand outta this cookie jar right fucking now. "Whatever floats your boat," I add quickly, taking a deep breath, forcing myself to think about starving children in Africa. I clear my throat. "So, anyway, what I've come to realize about myself the hard way—sarcastic pun intended—is that I not only don't *want* to fuck for cash, I *can't* fuck for cash. It's *physically* impossible for me, if you know what I mean." I grimace. "Call me old fashioned, but it's just the way it is with me. The Talented Mr. Ripley's gotta want it or he'd rather roll over and go night-night. So, anyway, the last straw was this one older woman I *really* didn't wanna fuck a second time around. She was objectively hot, though it's hard for me to think of her that way now; probably almost twice my age, some fancy attorney; and, as I learned the first time I fucked her, she was super aggressive in the sack, but not in a fun, sexy way—in this, like, weird *angry* way. Kind of freaky-creepy. So, anyhoo, this woman threatened to say I'd forced her the first time around if I didn't get my ass down to her hotel room and give it to her again, only this time using whips and chains or some shit like that."

"Oh my God, Keane."

"Yeah. So that's when I knew I'd gotten myself into some pretty deep shit. Here I was twenty-two years old, nothing but a horny young lad looking for a little fun and some extra cash, you know? Brand new to the game, not taking it seriously whatsoever, and now I had this wacko attorney-bitch threatening to say I'd *raped* her if I didn't fuck her again and whip her ass with a cat o' nine tails while I did it? Horrible. I didn't know what the fuck to do. I mean, the easy answer was to go down there and give her what she wanted—but then what? Was there gonna be a third, fourth, and fifth time, too? Was this woman gonna own my ass—or, rather, my dick and balls—'til the end of time?"

Maddy looks stricken. "What'd you do?"

"Well, first things first, I called the Morgan family's fixer—my older brother Ryan. And, thank God, as usual, he knew exactly what to do. He called our brother-in-law, Josh—although this was right before the wedding so he was just Kat's fiancé at the time. But, anyway, talk about a fixer, holy fuck—Josh Faraday is a fixer-next-lev, son. So Josh brought in some hacker dude he went to college with and—"

"Henn!"

"What?"

"The hacker-dude Josh brought in had to be my sister's boyfriend, Henn. Josh and Henn have been friends since college and Henn's a world-class hacker."

"*Henn?*"

"Peter Hennessey, but he goes by Henn."

"Hey, I think I partied with that guy at Josh and Kat's wedding. Funny guy? Kinda nerdy?"

"That's him."

"Wow. He never said a word about helping me. I woulda thanked him."

"Well, that's Henn for you. My sister says he's a locked vault when it comes to his work. Totally discreet."

"Wow. That guy really saved my bacon. I'm gonna have to thank him if I see him in L.A. Buy him a drink."

"Oh, I'm sure you'll see him," Maddy says. "Hannah and Henn are joined at the hip whenever he's in town. But, anyway, I got you off track. Finish your story."

"Oh. Yeah. Where was I?"

"Josh brought in a hacker."

"Oh yeah. So Ryan and Josh told me to go down to the crazy bitch's hotel and get her to say or do something she wouldn't want the world to see or hear—whatever I could stomach getting her to do—and to make a video or audio recording of it on the sly. So that's what I did."

Maddy sits up on the blanket, her hand on her heart. "Did you have sex with her like she wanted? With whips and chains?"

I laugh. "No. I met her in her hotel room with my phone in my jacket pocket, set to record audio. I told her I wouldn't do exactly what she wanted—that this was gonna go down my way. She was pissed and started threatening me, so I said, 'Okay. Here's the deal, sweetheart: I'm gonna make you come at least three times in the space of thirty minutes doing things my way. And if I don't, then we'll do things your way.' She lit up like a Christmas tree, so I was like, 'And, bee tee dubs, I want a hundred bucks per orgasm.' So she goes, 'Oooooh, yeah, baby. You're on.'" I exhale, suddenly realizing I've never told anyone this story besides Ryan, Josh, and Z. "How the fuck am I telling you this story after knowing you for one day, Maddy Milliken?"

"Because we knew each other in a past life. Come on, Keane. There's no judgment here, I swear. I'm dying."

I exhale and then just blurt it out. "So I finger-fucked her for exactly twenty-three minutes, walked away with four hundred bucks in my pocket and an audio recording she'd never want to see the light of day. The hacker used the recording to scare the shit out of her and I never heard from her again, thank God. The End."

Maddy looks flabbergasted.

"Too *salacious* for you? I thought you said no judgment."

"I'm not judging. I'm just... blown away." She cringes. "And skeeved out."

"It was totally gross, not gonna lie. But I recorded her saying all kinds of crazy shit.'" I cringe. "So that night, Josh's hacker sent her a beefcake photo of me to entice her to open his email, and when she did, it gave her some kind of virus that gave him access to her computer. So he let her know he was in her system and one button-push away from emailing that audio recording to every person on her contacts list—which included every judge, attorney, and client she'd ever worked with, not to mention her Husband the Federal Judge."

Maddy puts her hand over her mouth.

"So that was it for me. Lesson learned. I figured I'd spent twenty-three minutes in hell to narrowly escape disaster and I might not get so lucky next time. And that was the last time my alter ego has laid so much as a pinky on a paying pussy or let a client lay a fucking pinky on me where the sun don't shine. The very next day, I switched to a much better agency, changed my name to Ball Peen Hammer, and never looked back."

"Wow, Keane."

"Meh. Live and learn, right? Now I know, if I wanna survive in the industry and not get caught up in some crazy-ass shit, I gotta deliver the *fantasy* of my cock to the horny pickles and never, ever my actual cock."

"What was your stripper name before Ball Peen Hammer?"

"Peen Star."

Maddy laughs. "Oh, Keane." She grins at me with such genuine warmth, all anxiety I'd been feeling a moment ago melts away. "God, I have a thousand questions," she says.

"Shoot. Ask me anything you want, Sunshine. And just to be clear, when I call you that, I'm talking about your god-awful shirt."

Maddy ignores my jab. "How do you know she had *four* orgasms in such a short amount of time? That's pretty hard to believe. Maybe she knew down deep she was being a monster but she didn't know how to get herself out of her predicament so she..."

I scoff, making her stop talking.

"What?" Maddy asks.

"Women can't actually *fake* an orgasm, contrary to popular belief."

Maddy returns my scoff. "Sure they can. I've done it myself. Many times."

"What? *Why?*"

"To end a particularly prolonged sexual experience that was doing nothing for me."

137

I make a face like she's just said something truly tragic. "Wow. That sucks."

"Ask any woman. We've all done it. I'm not alone."

I shake my head. "That's really, really sad."

Maddy shrugs. "Such is life for us mere mortal women. Sadly, there's billions of us and only one of you."

"Well, if whatever guy you were bonin' didn't realize you were faking it, then he's a fucking idiot. And a horrible lay."

"It's not always a guy's fault if a woman doesn't reach orgasm. Women are complicated. And, likewise, it's not a guy's fault if he can't tell the real thing from a simulation, either. Women can be convincing—or, at least, I can."

"Okay, first off, women are not complicated, at least not when a guy's got the owner's manual, like I do. And second off, no woman can successfully fake it with a guy who knows what the hell he's doing."

"That's just not true. I bet you'd be surprised at how many women have faked it with you."

"Not a one. Because I know exactly what to look for to confirm the real McCoy."

"What? Rosy cheeks? I get those when I'm even *thinking* about sex. That doesn't mean a damned thing."

I shake my head.

"Moaning?" Without warning, Maddy lets out a sexual moan like she's in the midst of an epic orgasm and my cock jolts in response. Maddy smirks at me like she's awfully proud of herself. "That was very *When Harry Met Sally* of me, wasn't it?" she says.

I shake my head. "It's not moaning that's the tip-off, although thanks for that demonstration. Highly arousing."

"It's not moaning?"

"You're so far off-base, it's ridiculous."

"What, then? Heavy breathing?" She breathes in and out noisily for a long moment like she's Darth Vader. "Luke, I am your father," she says.

I laugh. "No. You're so cold, you're standing in a blizzard."

"What then? What's this magic 'tell' that makes it so obvious a woman's having an actual orgasm?"

Out of nowhere, my stomach tightens with unease. "Maybe we shouldn't be talking about this stuff," I say softly.

"Why not?"

"Because it's really, you know, personal."

"Oh my God. After everything we've talked about today, *now* you're feeling shy?" She hoots with laughter.

"No, I mean, for you. You're not used to talking this way, and I don't want to, you know, make you think I'm trying to... get something going here."

Maddy scoffs. "Get something going? Keane. Oh my God. You think you're in danger of 'making my motor run'?" She laughs like the mere thought is ridiculous. "This is the most comfortable I've ever been with a guy. I've never been friend-zoned so hard in all my freaking life. I promise there's absolutely no sexual attraction here on my end, any more than there is on yours. I'm just having fun talking so freely about all this stuff with a guy for the first time in my life. Please, I beg you, don't censor yourself."

Maddy feels *that* confident we're in the friend zone? Well, shit. She's not having *any* confusion on that point *whatsoever*?

"Come on, Keane. Please?" Maddy says. "I won't think you're leading me on or flirting with me or trying to get into my pants. I swear to God, cross my heart, hope to die."

Well, shit, I feel like she just went a little overboard with the assurances. Because even if I'm not trying to get into her pants (which I'm not because she's my honorary little sister), I'm pretty sure I've been trying to make *her* want to get into *mine*. Is that a prick-move? So sue me. It's how I'm wired. It's just what I do, especially with someone who's forbidden fruit. And she hasn't felt that vibe from me *at all*?

"Keane," Maddy says sharply. "For God's sake. Tell me the secret. How do you know for sure when a woman's having an orgasm? *Spill*."

I exhale.

"Dude. Come on. You're killing me here."

I make a "you asked for it" face and let out a long, audible exhale. "Okay, Curious George," I say. "Here it is. While a woman's *actually* having an orgasm, no matter what kind it is, her asshole ripples along with everything else, contracting and releasing along with her climax. It's not something she can fake. And she can't consciously move those muscles like that, either, even if she wanted

139

to. So when I know a woman's really close, I press my fingertip gently against her asshole, or inside it if she's into ass-play, and when I feel her muscles tighten and ripple in the right way, I know for a fact she's reached the finish line. No faking even remotely possible."

Maddy's cheeks are absolutely blazing. She shifts her weight on the blanket next to me. And then she shifts again. She opens her mouth and closes it. "Oh," she finally says. She swallows hard and clears her throat. "*Cool.*"

Chapter 19
Keane

"So you really made that woman have *four* orgasms in a half hour?" Maddy asks after she's composed herself somewhat, her cheeks still bright red.

"I coulda squeezed more outta her," I say, "but I was so fucking skeeved out, I decided to take my four hundred bucks and run."

"And you did that to her with your fingers or...?" She grimaces.

God, Maddy's so cute, I can't stand it. Obviously, this poor girl's never had a guy touch her the right way, not even once.

"Yeah. Just fingers," I say. "That's the easiest way to make a woman have multiple orgasms in one sesh, actually. Nothing to it at all." I snap. "That's all The Sure Thing is—a fingering technique. But then once you get a woman going really well with your fingers, you can train 'em over time to respond the same way to your cock. For some women that takes some time for their bodies to start responding the right way, though—and time is something I don't normally have, since I'm not in the market for a relationship."

"Why aren't you in the market for a relationship, by the way?"

I shrug. "Just not. I'm having too much fun to be tied down. Can't figure out how to be Ball Peen Hammer to the best of my ability while I've got some girl sitting at home, pissed at me for not calling her back."

Maddy looks deep in thought.

"You still sure you're okay talking about this stuff?" I ask.

"Yeah, I'm fine. Um. How exactly do you do this 'Sure Thing' technique? Is it complicated?"

I lick my lips and take a deep breath. Fuck. Telling Maddy all about this is gonna lead to nothing good, and I know it. No doubt about it, if I tell Maddy how I do this, she's gonna ask me to do it to her before this road trip is through—and, God help me, when she asks me, I'm gonna say yes because I won't be able to resist. Which means, of course, I'll fuck her, too—because no woman can come over and over and then not beg for cock at some point. Which, of course, means telling Maddy about this will ultimately lead to me fucking Maddy (because I'm only human and when a woman begs for cock, I'm gonna give it to her). And, of course, when all this goes down, Maddy's gonna love it and get attached to me and think there's something between us I can't deliver on—which will lead to her being pissed as hell and maybe even hurt afterwards. Which means Dax will string me up by my dick and balls because he's a fucking psycho these days and I'll rue the day I ever told Maddy the ins and outs of The Sure Thing in the first place.

I look at my watch. "Hey, maybe we should get back on the road, huh?"

Maddy sits up onto her elbow on the blanket and gazes down at me with blazing eyes. "Will you tell me how you do it?"

I take a long, steadying breath, my eyes locked on hers. "How about I tell you another time, Sunshine?" I whisper.

"When?"

"Another time." My heart is pulsing in my ears. Motherfucker. Why am I doing this? If it weren't for the fact that Maddy's forbidden fruit, I wouldn't even be talking about this shit with her. We'd be talking about the weather or her hobbies, hopes and dreams. Right?

"I want to know how you do it," Maddy says softly. "No one's ever done anything like that to me before." She blushes.

Oh man. Here we go. She's a kitten's breath away from begging me to do it to her right here and now.

"I'll tell you another time," I say, my eyes still locked on hers, my pulse pounding in my ears.

"Why not now?"

"Because I... don't... think it's a good idea."

Maddy blinks rapidly, breaking eye contact with me, and then takes a deep breath. "Okay," she says, like she's just come out of a trance.

There's a long silence between us.

"Let's hang here a little bit longer, just to be sure there's no more traffic," she says.

"Okay."

We lie back down on the blanket and she puts her cheek on my shoulder again.

After a moment, she says something, pointing to the sky, but I'm too busy battling internal demons—forbidden-fruit-demons—to hear what she's said.

Fuck. The truth is I want to tell Maddy about The Sure Thing because, yes, I want her to beg me to do it to her. I want to make her come over and over 'til she's speaking in tongues; I wanna see her pretty brown eyes roll back into her head and feel her asshole clenching and releasing against my fingertip; I want her to beg me to fuck her. *And then, by God, I wanna fuck her.*

But, honestly, I'm not sure any of those impulses are real. I think it's highly likely I'm just responding to the idea of stealing cookies outta the cookie jar.

"Um," I say. I swallow hard. "What did you just say?"

"I said that one looks like a turtle," she says, pointing at a distant cloud.

Oh man, now I can't get the idea outta my head: *I want to fuck her.*

Shit. I gotta stop this. I'm doing this because Dax declared her 'off-limits' and she's forbidden fruit.

"Yeah, a turtle with a raging hard-on," I manage to say.

Maddy laughs. "He doesn't have a hard-on; he's just carrying a hoe because he's on his way to his turtle garden."

"A *hoe*?"

"Yeah. He's gonna plant some sunflower seeds in his garden and he needs a hoe."

"Only you would see a turtle with a *hoe*," I say. "Are you insane, by any chance?"

"Only you would see a turtle with a hard-on," she replies. "Are you Keane Morgan, by any chance?"

I shrug.

This is crazy. I don't want Maddy, specifically. I just want what I can't have. And that's not fair to her. In fact, fucking Maddy when I know I just want to fuck the cookie I'm not allowed to have would be a supremely dickish thing to do.

And being a dick to Maddy isn't on the menu. No fucking way.

"That's what I don't get," Maddy says.

Oh, apparently, she's been talking. "Huh?" I ask. "Sorry. I got distracted."

"I asked how you protect yourself nowadays so you don't get trapped by another nut job like that attorney-lady?" Maddy says.

"Oh. Um. Yeah. Well, like I say, first off, I don't fuck clients. Ever. That's the biggest thing. And second off, I'm with a really good agency now, so it doesn't come up nearly as much. I make sure my agent tells every potential client the deal right up front if there's even a *whiff* the client thinks she's paying for laying." I clear my throat. "And, um, third off, when I give lap dances at a private show, I have a firm 'no touch' rule. They can touch the abs and ass or whatever, but nothing that jiggles or hardens."

Maddy's eyes are locked with mine. Her expression is unreadable to me.

"What are you thinking?" I ask, pushing her hair away from her face.

If she were to lean forward ever so slightly, even an inch, I just might kiss her. But she doesn't move forward, which is probably a good thing. In fact, she leans slightly back.

"I'm thinking you must have a lot of self-control," she says.

My heart lurches into my throat. Is she reading my mind? "In what way?" I ask.

"Well, I'm sure you've met some attractive women at gigs, women you've wanted to have sex with."

"Not anyone who was worth going back to Shit Town, USA for. If there's a hot chick at a gig I have to forego, then I just tell myself there'll be another hot chick tomorrow at a bar who's fair game."

"But don't you sometimes get, you know, sexually aroused by the women you dance for?"

"No," I say without hesitation.

"*No?*" She seems shocked. "Even if there's a really attractive woman and you're, I dunno, rubbing your crotch against her?"

I smirk. "I don't know what you're imagining I do during performances, but I don't rub my dick against women like a cat rubbing against a scratching pole."

"Well, jeez. I dunno. How the hell would I know that? I told you I've never seen a stripper in action."

"I never even pop a woody when I'm working."

"You don't?"

"I'm not a dog. As hard as it might be to detect, I've got a brain. And when I'm working, I'm actually thinking about shit. Now don't get me wrong—I have a total blast when I perform—I'm pumped up and turned on like crazy, just not in the way you're thinking. I'm focused on delivering the fantasy, reading the room, making sure I'm pushing all the right buttons. I'm feeding off energy and getting jacked up by how much fun the women are having. Not to mention I've grown up a bit since the early days. Now, it's not very often there's a single woman at a gig I'd want to have sex with, anyway. I'm pretty selective about my fuckery nowadays. The Talented Mr. Ripley demands filet mignon."

"I can't even formulate a reply to that," Maddy says.

A cool breeze kicks in and she snuggles her body closer to mine.

"It's pretty simple," I say. "I view my job as making every woman *wanna* fuck me—not actually fucking 'em. Plus, even if I were to meet a really fuckable woman at a gig these days, even if I were tempted to break my rule, I still wouldn't do it because I promised my momma."

Maddy sits up and looks down at my face, her features contorted with surprise. "You promised your *mom* you wouldn't fuck women at gigs? Holy hell, Keane. That had to be an interesting conversation."

I chuckle. "Well, no, not in those exact words, for fuck's sake. I believe the actual promise I made was: 'I swear I'm not a gigolo, Mom.'"

"How in the heck did that conversation come about?"

"Oh man, it was horrible. About three months after I'd started stripping, my mom and dad found out what I'd been doing. So my mom sat me down and asked me point-blank, 'Keaney, tell me the truth—are you a gigolo?' Luckily, by the time she asked me that question, I hadn't fucked anyone at a gig for quite some time, so I was able to look her square in the eye and swear on my life the job was legit and that I was good at it and making an okay living. So now I've gotta live up to my word."

"You're close with your mom?"

"Oh, yeah. With the whole fam. Four brothers and a sister, my brother-in-law, my baby niece—we're all tight as ticks."

"I met Kat and Josh at my sister's birthday party. They're both hysterically funny and shockingly gorgeous, just like you."

I smirk to myself. "Maddy Milliken just told me I'm 'shockingly gorgeous.'"

Maddy blushes.

I rub Maddy's back for a moment, hugging her to me, smelling her hair, enjoying the warmth of her body against mine. Damn, Maddy's hair smells good—like a garden of flowers. "Yeah, Josh fits right in with our family's sense of humor," I say. "Thank God Kat married a guy who can keep up, or else he woulda been eaten alive at Thanksgiving along with the turkey and mashed potatoes."

"Do you wear cologne?" Maddy asks, out of nowhere.

"Just a splash. Enough to make every woman within spitting distance of me start sniffing, not enough to make 'em fling themselves at me uncontrollably. A guy's gotta be able to walk down the sidewalk, you know."

Maddy chuckles. "It's nice."

"You're not alone in thinking that, baby doll. But thank you."

Maddy stretches out like a cat and her entire body stiffens, and then softens, against mine. And, motherfucker, out of nowhere, my cock tingles. *Again.* Fuck. I gotta stop this shit. Why the hell am I toying with Maddy? Teasing her, tempting her, making her want me? *I don't want Maddy.* I'm sure of it. I just want *her* to want me—that's got to be it. But she's not a woman at a job. She's a sweet, adorable girl who isn't used to guys like me—a girl I wouldn't normally give a second glance to if she weren't off-limits. Right? Hell, I don't even know anymore. I'm all fucked up in the head, not knowing which way's up or down.

"I'm surprised you never get a hard-on when you strip," Maddy says. "I thought men get hard whether they want to or not, as long as they get certain kinds of stimulation. You rub it, it gets hard."

"Well, shit, Maddy, no one is giving me a hand job while I perform, if that's what you think."

We both laugh.

"Okay, yeah, I get hard when I'm getting a hand job," I say. "And, yes, I get hard when I'm thinking about fucking a woman I actually wanna fuck. But I don't get hard when I'm thinking about getting paid, son."

146

"Well, what the hell do I know?" Maddy says. "I told you I've never seen a stripper."

"Dude, I *dance*. Shake my ass. Give lap dances. Do some *smoove mooves*. I'm not standing there rubbing against anyone's thigh for long enough to give myself an *involuntary* hard-on." She's still chuckling and I join her. "I suppose in theory I could give myself a woody if I rubbed up against the trunk of a *tree* for long enough, but that's not at all what I do when I perform. It's a *show*. Actually, some of my moves take a lot of concentration and skill."

"Well, gosh, I didn't mean to *offend* you," she says.

"Well, you did. I'm horribly offended. Ain't no time for popping woodies when you're doing a handstand, baby."

Maddy looks up from my shoulder, obviously surprised. "You do *handstands*?"

"Hell yeah. I do all kinds of cool stuff."

"Would that be 'cool' as in k-e-w-l?"

"Heck yeah."

"Show me." She sits up, a look of pure excitement on her face.

"Here?" I look at around at the park. "I can't do my smoove stripper mooves for you at a park. There's a kid right over there flying a kite."

"Well, then, do one of your G-rated smoove mooves. You got any of those?"

I look into her big, brown eyes and, goddammit, I can't resist her.

"Fine. I'll show you a little something-something. But be warned, you're gonna become completely obsessed with me after I do it."

"Waiver signed." She makes a motion in the sky like she's signing something.

"Okay." I leap up onto the grass next to our blanket, rub my hands together, and go into a full handstand, eliciting whoops and wild applause from Maddy. And then, just because I'm a total show-off and can't help myself, I walk on my hands for a bit like a circus performer until I feel a cool breeze wafting across my abs—which, of course, tells me my shirt has ridden up toward my chin.

"Whoa, I'm getting the full show here, Ball Peen Hammer," Maddy yells. "Take it off, baby!"

"Don't make me laugh," I breathe, my muscles straining. Damn, this is already making my left elbow hurt. This used to be a whole lot easier before my surgery a year and a half ago.

"Sorry," Maddy says. *"Take it off, baby,"* she whispers, obviously intending to toss me a toned-down version of her prior catcall—but she's only made me laugh even more.

I walk on my hands for a few more seconds, and once I'm sure I've given Maddy another long gander at my abs, I become completely still atop my hands, slowly shift my body weight above my right arm, and lift my left arm off the ground a few inches.

"Oh my effing God!" Maddy shouts. She claps uproariously. *"Amazing."*

I lower my left arm back to the ground, center my body weight again, and easily pop back up to my feet.

"Incredible," Maddy says, applauding, her face on fire. "You're... seriously... wow. You're *amazing*, Keane. If stripping doesn't work out for you, you should join the circus."

I shrug like it ain't no thang and flash her my dimples.

Maddy's face is glowing. Oh man, I betcha if I stuck my fingers deep inside her and touched that magic spot just right, she'd go off against my fingers like a bottle rocket. Not that I'd ever do that, seeing as how she's nothing but my honorary little sister and I've promised I won't fuck her. But, still—I bet she would. Oh, shit. I gotta stop this. Sisters don't have tits. And I certainly don't stick my fingers deep inside them. I feel like slapping the shit out of myself. *Stop this shit right now, Peen.*

"You're insanely fit," Maddy chirps, obviously oblivious to the tug-of-war happening inside my head. "The balance that must take— the strength. Wow, wow, wow. You're a monkey."

"Thanks," I say smoothly. "Sweet of you to say." I level her with my best smolder and place my palm on my stomach and run my hand over my abs, subtly lifting my T-shirt as I do. "This little R&R sesh has been a real *pleasure*, hasn't it, Maddy?"

"Absolutely," Maddy chirps out, her Disney-princess tone not even in the ballpark with mine. "So glad we weren't sitting in traffic this whole time. That was a grand stroke of genius, Mr. Monkey Man. So, you ready to hit the road again? I bet that traffic jam is *finito* by now."

What. The. Fuck? Is she even human? I was doing my best smolder just now. I was lifting up my shirt and giving her another peek at my abs—and *touching* them suggestively, too. And doing all that while sending a subliminal message to the pleasure-center in Maddy's brain via Federal Express. And she's acting like we've been talking about the weather?

"Sure," I say. "Let's get going."

"Cool," Maddy says brightly. She hops off the blanket, grabs it off the ground, and begins shaking it with gusto to get leaves and grass off its underside.

I stand, rooted to my spot, watching her, dumbfounded.

"Wow, if those are your G-rated smoove mooves, I can only imagine how *smoove* your R-rated mooves are," she says. "No wonder the pickles hurl themselves at you."

Did I just fall into some sort of psychedelic rabbit hole? Why isn't Maddy falling all over me? She should be doing that thing she supposedly does with guys she wants to bone—that thing she told me about where she can't string two coherent words together when she sees a hot guy. Where the fuck is *that* Maddy?

Maddy snorts again as she folds up the blanket. "And here I thought that hot bod of yours was only good for bonin' the fuck outta pickles and puppets," she says. "Looks like you're multi-talented after all, Ball Peen Hammer." She looks at me and smiles. "You ready to roll, sugar lips? I saw a restroom on the far end of the park. I'm just gonna hit that before we go."

"Uh. Great."

"Coolio," Maddy chirps happily. "Let's roll."

Chapter 20
Maddy

I turn up the radio as I drive at full speed down the freeway, the traffic from earlier in the day all cleared up. I look over at Keane. He's looking out the passenger window, quiet as a mouse. In fact, he's been unusually quiet since we left the park.

I turn up the music, intending to signal to Keane it's fine with me if we don't talk for a bit. I could be wrong, but I'm guessing Keane needs more quiet time than the average person. From my experience, it always seems like people with the most charisma are the ones who, on the flipside, need the most downtime. At least, that's the way it was with my first boyfriend, Justin. He had the biggest personality of anyone, and always needed the most downtime, too.

The song on the radio ends and a new song—"Trip Switch" by Nothing But Thieves— begins, immediately snapping Keane out of his quiet mood.

"Oh my shitake mushrooms," Keane says, sitting up in his car seat and turning up the volume on the radio to full-blast. "I *love* this song." He begins singing along and, instantly, his high-powered charisma re-enters his body.

When the song ends and is followed by a mellow love song— "Like Real People Do," by Hozier—Keane turns the radio down and settles into his seat again.

"Six months from now, 22 Goats will be the band we're jamming to on the radio," he says.

I smile at him. "For sure."

"Dax's music is incredible. You're gonna flip out when you hear it."

I'm about to say, "Oh, I've heard every single one of Dax's

150

songs, thanks to the full hour I spent stalking him on YouTube—and, yes, he's fantastic." But, for some reason, I don't want to admit that to Keane. So I keep my mouth shut.

"Daxy's gonna be a huge star," Keane continues. "When the world discovers him, they're gonna go nuts for him."

Aaaaand that's it for now, apparently. Keane leans back in his seat again and looks out the passenger window, becoming oddly quiet again.

So I remain quiet, too, letting Keane do his thing while I listen to Hozier's beautiful love song on low-volume.

But when the next song begins and it's one of my all-time favorites—"Blue Jeans" by Lana Del Rey—all bets are off. I gotta sing my girl's praises.

"Oh my shitake mushrooms," I begin, blaring the song, but when I glance over at Keane, he's fast asleep.

I smile to myself, turn the volume on the radio back down, and steal a long glance at Keane's sleeping face.

Good lord, he's handsome. His features are so darned symmetrical and smooth. It's like he's the masculine version of Marilyn Monroe. Just sort of... objectively perfect. No bad angle.

Or, hell, maybe it's just the gorgeous song that's getting to me. Because this song is oh-my-effing-God.

I focus on the road again for a long moment, listening to Lana Del Rey's haunting voice singing about eternal love and brutal heartbreak, willing myself not to look at Keane again. But before long, I can't resist stealing another teeny glance at his gorgeous features.

Yep, he's still perfect. Same as the last time I looked.

It's funny, when Keane's awake, it's his eyes that grab my attention so much, I forget to look at anything else. But now that he's asleep and inanimate, it's his lips that are taking center stage. And his chiseled jawline. That little indentation in Keane's chin makes him look like a cartoon action-hero—a blue-haired, re-imagined Captain America.

I smile to myself again.

Keane makes absolutely no sense in a logical world. He's got superhero-looks with a sidekick personality. He's Batman and Robin all rolled into one. To say the boy marches to the beat of his own drum is like saying Tiger Woods sometimes likes to hit little white balls with a stick.

I steal yet another glance at Keane's sleeping face and take in the shocking mess of his tousled hair. I can't believe I'm thinking this, but I think I actually *like* Keane's blue hair now. It suits him. Especially now that I know *why* he dyed it. Sure, maybe he's impulsive and crazy, but, still, he did it to help a brother out. And I think that's sweet.

I sigh.

That's Keane Morgan in a nutshell. He's the sweetest asshole-pig-narcissist I've ever met. Adorable. Gentle. Silly. Easy to talk to. When we were lying together on that blanket in the park, I felt so comfortable, I could have fallen asleep in his arms, right then and there, my cheek resting on his shoulder, my body warmed by his. To think I didn't even know him twenty-four hours ago boggles my mind. I feel like I've known Keane my whole life.

And, whoa, I've *never* talked to a guy about sex the way I do with Keane.

I grip the steering wheel and fix my eyes on the road.

Can Keane really do all that stuff he claims? He says he gave that horrible blackmailer *four* orgasms in less than half an hour? Is that even physically *possible*? It sometimes takes me twenty minutes to give myself *one* with a freakin' vibrator. No guy I've been with, even Justin, has even come close to being able to do what Keane says he can do as easily as snapping his fingers.

I shift my hands on the steering wheel again.

Keane's gotta be full of shit, right? There's no other explanation. If "The Sure Thing," whatever it is, actually makes women come over and over on command in rapid succession, then surely I would have experienced it by now, right? Because, especially in the age of the Internet, why wouldn't all guys learn that trick and do it every time? He's gotta be exaggerating. I bet if Keane went fishing in a puddle and caught a goldfish, he'd come back bragging about how he'd harpooned a great white shark on the stormy seas.

I look at Keane yet again.

God, he's just so gorgeous, especially when he sleeps. When he's sleeping, he almost looks... *humble*.

The thought makes me snort to myself.

I look at Keane yet again, unable to resist, and it suddenly occurs to me I'll probably never witness this sight again—the simple sight of Keane sleeping, the light of the late-afternoon sun casting a golden hue over his perfectly formed features.

Shoot.

I shouldn't do it—I *know* I shouldn't. It's reckless. Risky. *Wrong*. Plus, I promised my sister I'd keep my phone in the glove box at all times while driving.

And yet...

This is one quiet moment of magic I simply can't resist documenting.

Still keeping my eyes on the road ahead of me, I reach across Keane's sleeping body to my glove box and slowly pull out my phone. And then, ever so carefully, my eyes shifting between the road ahead of me and my phone, I swipe into my camera, set it to 'video mode,' and oh so quickly capture a short clip of Keane's gorgeous, sleeping face illuminated by the late-afternoon light.

Chapter 21
Maddy

Wednesday, 7:04 p.m.

"Whoa," Keane says, stirring from his nap and sitting up in his seat, his tousled blue hair a complete disaster. "I fell asleep?"

"For almost an hour."

Keane looks at the clock on my dashboard. "Wow." He looks outside his window at the setting sun. "Sorry."

"Did you sleep well?" I ask softly. "Looked like you were sleeping like a big ol' blue-haired baby."

"Yeah. Like a rock." He wipes his eyes. "Do you want me to drive for a bit, Mario Andretti?"

"Nope, I got it. I'm gonna pull off to a motel soon, if that's okay with you."

"Yeah, sure. I'm dying to watch your movie." Keane runs his hand through his hair, pats it down and smooths it, and just like that, he magically looks like a (blue-haired) Abercrombie & Fitch model again. "Sorry I deserted you, Mad Dog," he says. "Won't happen again. Co-pilot reporting for duty." He salutes me.

"It was fine. Gave me a chance to think and recharge for a bit."

"Yeah, I try not to do that."

"Recharge?"

"Think." He grins.

"Are you a big napper?" I ask.

"Totally," he says. "I don't usually get a full night's sleep 'cause of my job. Weird hours. Plus, when I get home from a gig, I can't fall asleep right away—I'm just too amped—so I'm pretty much always playing catch-up on sleep."

"Yeah, and besides your schedule, I'm sure it takes regular

154

recharging to keep that 'ebullient charm' of yours at full wattage," I say.

Keane looks surprised, but he doesn't say anything.

"I wasn't being snarky," I say quickly. "I'm just saying being the life of the party all the time, both in your personal *and* professional lives, must take its toll, especially given your natural tendencies."

Keane looks at me like he's expecting me to elaborate further.

"I mean, you know, since you're a natural introvert," I add.

Keane looks surprised. "Why do you think I'm a natural introvert?"

"You said you were shy when you were little. That's what that tells me. It doesn't mean you can't be extroverted in certain situations; obviously you are, quite successfully. It just means you need to take quiet time to recharge on a regular basis to keep yourself running on all cylinders."

Keane looks thoughtful for a moment. "No one ever sees that about me," he says. "Everyone always thinks I'm Ball Peen Hammer, twenty-four-seven."

"Nobody can be Ball Peen Hammer, twenty-four-seven," I say. "Not even Ball Peen Hammer."

"That's why I don't answer my phone sometimes. I get this weird, I dunno, *overwhelmed* feeling, like I gotta shut it down or my circuits are gonna overload."

"I'd imagine that's pretty common for people with 'ebullient charm.'" I grin at him.

Keane looks earnest. "You think?"

"Sure," I say softly, taken aback by the sincerity on Keane's face. "Nothing comes for free. Not even J.Lo's love."

"Um. Actually, I think you've got that one wrong, baby doll. J.Lo's love 'don't cost a thing.'"

"Nah, even J.Lo's love costs *something*. It's just the way the universe works. If you're Ball Peen Hammer day and night with the horny pickles, or puppets, or earthquake-sensing dogs, or whatever the hell they are—"

Keane laughs.

"Then at some point you've gotta pay the ferryman and revert back to being shy little Keaney Morgan, at least briefly, just long enough to refuel the tanks. You gotta pay for your sparkling personality somehow."

I glance at Keane and, oh my God, the sweet look on his face is light years away from the cocky peacock I've come to know.

I focus back on the road, my heart squeezing.

"Honestly, I know we joke about it, but sometimes I think I'm, I dunno, seriously abnormal," Keane says, his tone earnest. "I don't mean abnormal like, you know, wearing an aluminum hat so I can talk to Martians, or collecting tiny figurines for an elaborate dollhouse in my cellar."

I laugh. "Did you just pull those two examples out of thin air or is there something you'd like to tell me?"

Keane laughs. "I think I just get abnormally *overwhelmed* sometimes. So that's when I shut down and check out."

"We all need time to ourselves," I say. "That's not abnormal at all." I look away from the road, briefly, just long enough to wink at him and he bites his beautifully shaped lower lip. "Have you always felt that way—like you get abnormally overwhelmed?" I ask.

"Um, yeah. Pretty much. But it's gotten worse since..." He exhales and looks out the window, apparently not planning to finish his sentence.

"Since what?" I prompt.

But Keane doesn't reply. He's looking out the window, his face turned away from me.

"Since the voices started telling you to chop people up?" I venture. But Keane doesn't react. "Since your cat told you to buy a Powerball lottery ticket?" I ask, peeking at him. Still nothing. "Since you started collecting other people's toenail clippings?"

That last one elicits a chuckle from Keane. He turns to look at me, a crooked smile on his face. "You just pull those out of thin air, or is there something you'd like to tell me?"

I beam a smile at him.

"Nah, it's nothing quite as exotic as collecting other people's toenail clippings," Keane says. "I've just had a bit of a hard time since I stopped playing baseball, that's all."

"Why'd you stop playing? If you like it, then you should keep playing."

Keane looks out the window again.

And just like that, I realize we're not having a lighthearted, casual conversation any more. Clearly, whatever Keane's telling me is something deeply important to him.

"Keane, why'd you stop playing?" I ask softly, the hairs on the nape of my neck standing up.

Keane exhales. "Because I got hurt." He absently touches his elbow on his left arm and looks at me. "My elbow crapped out on me. My pitching motion got fucked up. And that was that."

"But you're so young and in such good shape. I mean, jeez, you just walked on your hands for me. It seems like you could swing a bat and run around some bases if that's what you still want to do."

"It doesn't work like that. I was a pitcher."

"Oh. Well, can you play some other position, maybe? You know, like shortstop or something?"

"Doesn't work like that," he says softly, but there's no irritation in his tone, only explanation. "Pitchers are highly specialized. A guy can't pitch anymore, he's done."

It suddenly dawns on me Keane must have played baseball at a really high level—not just in some recreational league with friends on weekends, as I've been thinking we're talking about.

"Did you play in college?" I ask.

Keane nods. "Arizona State. I dropped out my junior year when I got drafted by the Cubs. Played in their farm system and slayed it. I was working my way up in their organization like a beast. All my coaches said I was just about to get called up to the major leagues." He sighs. "And that's when I hurt my fucking traitor of an elbow—my ulnar collateral ligament." He pauses. "Surgery didn't go according to plan. I couldn't get my fastball going and my curveball sucked ass." He shrugs, obviously deflated. "So that was it. The headline on the newspaper of my life read 'Baseball Dreams *Finito* for Peenito.'"

"I had no idea you played at such a high level," I say softly. "Wow, Keane. You were a professional athlete."

He waves at the air dismissively. "Meh, minor leagues. Not even worth mentioning to anyone. No one ever dreams of playing in the minors, trust me. That's just a means to an end—the stepping stone to the *real* dream."

"You must have been devastated when you got hurt. I'm so sorry, Keane."

"Hey, that's life, baby. Sometimes it goes according to plan, and sometimes it punches you in the balls. When your balls get punched, you just gotta wipe 'em off and figure out a new dream, right?"

The look on Keane's face is making my heart physically hurt. If I weren't driving, I'd throw my arms around him and hug him to me.

Keane stretches and exhales loudly. "So, anyhoozles, baby doll. Enough about me and my saga of woe. Let's talk about you. Specifically, let's talk about the fact that you're totally and completely full of shit, shall we?"

I'm sure my face registers my surprise.

"You said you usually have a hard time talking to new people, but you seemed awfully smooth talking to Brian in the minimart—and you've been smooth as a morning lake talking to me all day."

Keane's body language doesn't match his lighthearted words. But, clearly, he's not in the mood to talk about the loss of his baseball dreams anymore.

"What the hell is your obsession with Brian?" I ask. "It's getting weird, Keane."

"I'm not obsessed with Brian. I'm obsessed with solving the puzzle that is Maddy Milliken. And so far, your supposed shyness can be filed along with the Loch Ness Monster."

"Keane, I'm not socially *inept*—I'm *shy*. Well, okay, yes, I'm socially inept at times." I sigh. "Any of my old tap-dancing videos would confirm that."

"You tap-danced?"

"For years."

"And there's video to prove it?"

"Tons and tons."

"Tap-dancing can be pretty dope."

"Not the way I did it."

Keane laughs. "Add those tap-dancing videos to the Maddy-Keane Film Festival, brah. I'll watch those bad boys tonight."

"Ha!" I say. "That will *never* happen."

"Oh, I've got my ways," Keane says. "So, anyway, nice attempt at deflection, baby doll, but I still wanna talk about *Brian*. I could hear you giggling in the minimart before I even got through the front door." He makes a high-pitched giggling sound, clearly intended as an impression of me.

"Again with the Brian obsession. Dude. Give it a rest. Maybe babbling with you for five straight hours before I met Brian got me in the right frame of mind to babble to a stranger, who knows?"

Keane cringes. "You're saying I lubed you up for Brian? So I'm Brian's *fluffer*?" He laughs like he's said something incredibly funny, but I don't get the joke.

"What's a *fluffer*?" I ask.

Keane shakes his head. "Oh, sweet, innocent, sheltered Maddy Milliken."

"Is it something gross?"

"It's something *awesome*."

"What is it?"

"You'll just have to look it up, buttercup."

I roll my eyes. "You're annoying."

"I've heard that a time or two."

I shrug. "The truth is I've kind of surprised myself today. I swear I'm not normally so comfortable talking to new people, especially guys, and today I've been totally comfortable talking to *two* of them. Maybe I'm turning into a man-eater after all, huh?"

"Yee-boy!" Keane shouts. He sticks his hand up and we high-five.

"Trust me, though," I say, laughing. "You wouldn't be quite so impressed if you saw me trying to talk to a guy I'm actually *attracted* to." I snort. "I stutter and sputter and end every sentence with a question mark."

An unmistakable shadow passes across Keane's face.

"What?" I ask. "What's wrong? You don't believe me? I swear to God, I'm telling the truth. I geek out and lose all composure when I'm feeling anything even remotely resembling the urge to 'bone the fuck outta' someone. I become a total and complete dork."

Keane's mouth twists into a scowl just before he turns his head toward the passenger-side window. "So you keep telling me," he says quietly, his face turned away from me. "Maybe one of these days I'll be lucky enough to witness you in action."

Chapter 22
Maddy

Keane and I burst into our motel room and put down our overnight bags and the food, water, and beer we purchased at a supermarket down the street.

"Which bed you want?" Keane asks, motioning to the two queen size beds taking up all available space in the small room.

"Don't care," I say. "They both look equally lumpy."

"Cool, 'cause I got a thing for being on the right side."

"Knock yourself out, sweet thing," I say.

"Don't mind if I do."

Keane unceremoniously flops his body onto his chosen bed, flashing his dimples at me as he does.

Wow. Life sure is full of surprises, isn't it? When I picked Keane up in front of his apartment building twelve hours ago, I never would have believed in a million years I'd be sharing a motel room with him tonight, and yet, here we are, and I'm not the least bit anxious about it. When the motel clerk asked, "One room or two?," it felt like the most natural thing in the world for me to say to Keane, "Hey, why spend double the money for two rooms?"

"I should warn you," Keane says, stretching out to his full length on his bed and putting his hands behind his head. "I'm probs gonna stink up the bathroom in the morning, so you should plan on getting your ass in there before I bomb it to high heaven."

I laugh. "Thanks for the heads up. I'll be sure to go in there before you."

Keane flashes me his dimples again and rubs his palms together. "So, hey, let's get this film festival underway. I'm dying to see this masterpiece of yours."

160

I grab my duffel bag. "I'm gonna take a quick shower and then I'll cue it up."

"Radsicles. I'll pop a brewski and watch some baseball while I wait." He flips on the TV and begins scrolling through the channels.

"Cool," I say. "And, yes, that's most definitely 'k-e-w-l.'"

"Hey, don't fling that shit around willy-nilly, sweetheart—it's gotta mean something special when you use it."

"Oh, I know, and, trust me—it does."

We share a huge smile.

While Keane makes himself comfortable in front of the TV, beer in hand, I float into the bathroom, my duffel bag in hand, a huge smile on my face.

Twenty minutes later, I emerge from the bathroom, my hair wet, my body relaxed, to find Keane on the floor in front of the TV, doing crunches.

The minute Keane sees me, he stops what he's doing and flashes me a look of unmistakable annoyance. "Oh, for the love of fuck," Keane says, motioning to me with clear disdain. "You gotta be kidding me."

I look down. "What?"

"You sleep in a baggy sweatshirt? Jesus Christ, Maddy, first that god-awful shirt and now this? Are you even *capable* of waggling your boobs at a guy?"

"I'm chilly."

"Bullshit. It's a hundred degrees in this room."

"It is? Oh. Well, I'm chilly."

"Liar."

"Not lying."

"*Liar.*"

"I'm *not* lying, Keane."

But, oh my God, I'm totally lying.

I'm hot as hell in this goddamned sweatshirt.

But after the big deal Keane made about surveying my "merchandise," I'm too self-conscious to reveal the tight-fitting "Adventure Time" tank top I'm wearing underneath my sweatshirt.

Keane rolls his eyes as he pops up from the floor, grabbing his duffel bag as he goes. "I'm gonna take a quick shower and when I come out, I want *Shoot Like a Girl* cued up on your laptop and those boobs of yours in full waggle-mode. I gotta see what we're working with here, man-eater."

I scowl at him.

"Hey, easy with daggers, babe. How the fuck else am I gonna help you attract hotties who'll make your motor run if I haven't seen what you've got to hook them with?"

"I never asked you to help me 'hook' the hotties."

"Yeah, but I'm a giver, baby. It's a blessing and a curse."

"What if I don't want or need your help? Maybe I'm gonna 'hook hotties' with my sparkling personality alone."

Keane pauses for a beat just outside the bathroom door, apparently letting what I've said sink in, and then he throws his head back. "Bwahahahaahaaaaaa!" he bellows, just before closing the bathroom door behind him.

I roll my eyes, even though Keane's no longer in the room to witness the gesture, and pull out my phone. Not surprisingly, I've got a text from my sister.

"Howz it going, sissy?" Hannah writes. "Check in, please."

I punch the button to give my sister a call.

"Hellooooooooo," Hannah says when she picks up my call.

"Hi, Banana," I say. "I'm safe and sound. Made it to a motel near Medford without anyone attacking me."

I hear the shower in the bathroom turn on.

"Excellent," Hannah says. "This pleases me. And how's it going with your bodyguard? Are you still mad at me for forcing you to bring him along?"

"Not mad at all. Keane's awesome. We're having fun together."

"Oh, *really*?"

"Yep. We clicked right away. Well, almost right away. Tiny stumble at first."

"So he's nice?"

"Um, 'nice' isn't a word I'd use to describe Keane Morgan. That's not nearly descriptive enough."

"Oh, *reeeeeeally*?" Hannah says, her tone laced with innuendo.

"No, no. It's not like *that*. Keane's a sweetheart, but he's definitely just a friend. It's so weird—I already feel like I've known him forever. You wouldn't believe how easily I just babble and babble with him for hours on end about everything and nothing."

"You're using your happy voice, Madelyn."

"Probably because I'm extremely *happy*. We just had pizza at this adorable little place with *Lady and the Tramp* tablecloths and now we're settling in for the night at our motel. We're gonna watch *Shoot Like a Girl* on my laptop."

"Oh, *reeeeeeeeeaaaally?*" Hannah says. "You two went out for dinner like *Lady and the Tramp* and now he's gonna watch your movie?"

"Yeah, he seems genuinely excited. I didn't even have to twist his arm to watch it."

"Oh, *reeeeeeeeaaaaaally?*" Hannah says.

"Listen to me, Linda," I say. "I told you: it's not like that with Keane. We're *friends*. For some inexplicable reason, Keane and I just hit it off. You'll see when you meet him. He's so easy to like. Super funny. Silly. Sweet. Definitely one of a kind." I snort. "He's Batman with Robin's personality."

Hannah doesn't reply.

"Hannah, stop it. We're *friends*, I swear. If you saw him, you'd understand. We'd never go for each other in a million years."

"Mmm hmm. Your tone of voice suggests otherwise."

I scoff. "Hannah, you don't understand. Keane lights up any room he's in. People fall all over themselves in his presence. We went to a diner for lunch and the waitress practically fell onto the floor giggling at every stupid thing he said. Everyone's drawn to him. It can't be helped."

"He sounds wonderful."

I hear the shower turn off in the bathroom. Damn, that was fast.

"He is. But don't tell him I said that because he's also a cocky bastard with the biggest ego of anyone I've ever met—a total narcissist. Oh, and he's super flakey. And annoying. And immature. He might also be a megalomaniac, though I'm not certain about that yet. He's definitely verging on psychotic, though. Oh, and he's also most definitely a pig—though that seems to be a hot-button word with him so don't tell him I called him that."

"He sounds like a gem."

I sigh. "He is. He's not like anyone I've ever met." I glance toward the bathroom door, making sure Keane's not about to enter the room and overhear this next part. "I think he's a bit lost right

163

now," I whisper. "You know, trying to figure out what he wants to be when he grows up."

"Aren't we all," Hannah says.

"Yeah, but, I mean, I think he's at a real fork in the road. He's kinda breaking my heart just a little bit."

"Oh, honey. You've always loved lost puppies, haven't you?"

"They're just so fun to rescue."

"Oh, Maddy."

Without warning, the bathroom door swings opens wildly and Keane bursts into the room like a superhero, literally beating his chest—*his shirtless chest*—and my jaw drops to the freaking floor at the sight of him.

"Sweet Sassy Molassey," I breathe into the phone. "Gotta go."

"Hang on. Have you talked to Mom—"

"I'll call you tomorrow."

"*Wait.*"

Keane plops himself down onto the bed next to mine, stretches his glorious body to its full length, rests his cheek on the palm of his hand, and flashes me his un-freaking-believable dimples. "Hi, hot stuff," he whispers. He winks.

"Did you talk to Mom?" Hannah says into my ear. She giggles. "She called me and was, like, 'Ohmigawd, Smith is so amaaaazing! He's—'"

"I'll call you tomorrow," I bark at Hannah like a total bitch, cutting her off. "I'm fine, Hannah. I'm safe. Kissy-kissy. Love you lots. Best sister ever. Bye." I hang up my phone. "For the love of fuck," I say to Keane. "Abso-frickin-lutely *not.*" I motion to his bare torso like his sheer perfection pisses me off.

"What?" he asks innocently. He touches his rock-hard abs. "You're not a fan of the Seahawks?" My gaze drifts from his un-*freaking*-believable abs to his black sweatpants, emblazoned near the waistband with the Seattle Seahawks' logo.

"I have no problem with the *Seahawks*," I say. I point to his bare torso—to his stunning pecs and abs and ridiculously gorgeous arms and shoulders and perfect nipples and insanely attractive forearms (what the hell is up with those *forearms*?). "I have a problem with"— I make a presto-change-o motion in front of his eight-pack—"*all that.*"

"All what?" He stretches out his right arm, displaying his triceps muscle. "Oh, you mean *this*?" He rotates his arm and his bicep bulges right in front of my face. "Or do you mean *this*?" He flexes his washboard abs.

"Dude, I'm not gonna sit here for an hour and a half, watching my movie next to a half-naked Adonis on a bed. Cover that shit up *right now*."

A huge smile spreads across Keane's handsome face. "You think I'm an Adonis?"

"Figure of speech."

"Maddy, this is how I *sleep*," he says, rubbing his palm across his naked chest. "You're wearing your preferred jammies; I'm wearing mine."

"When it's time to sleep in your own bed, wear whatever the heck you want. But for now, if you're planning to come over to *my* bed to watch *my* movie, and sit two inches away from *my* body in a motel room, then cover that shit the fuck up. This isn't one of your gigs, Ball Peen Hammer."

Keane laughs, leaps up from his bed, and stands at the edge of mine. "Scoot over, sweet meat," he says, swatting my thigh. "I'm dying to see this masterpiece of yours."

I don't budge. "Keane, I'm not joking. I can't sit here next to the most perfect male specimen ever created while he's barely clothed and calmly watch my movie like lah-de-dah-this-is-so-normal. Now cover that shit up right the fuck now, Ball Peen Hammer. I'm not gonna ask you again."

"This is ridiculous," Keane says, still smiling. "What if we were at the beach? Or a pool? What if I were *European*? I'd be wearing way less than I am right now. At least I'm wearing full sweat pants. I normally sleep in my briefs or nothing at all." He winks.

"We're not at the beach or a pool—and you're not European. You're from freakin' Seattle. And we're in a motel room. *On a bed.* Just the two of us, after knowing each other for one freaking day. Now cover that shit up or I'm gonna slap the motherfucking shit out of you."

Keane crosses his gorgeous arms over his spectacular chest. "I've never heard you curse like this, Madelyn Milliken." He flashes a huge smile. "I *like* it."

"Oh, yeah? You like it, huh? Well, then, how 'bout this—put your *fucking* shirt on, motherfucking Keane Morgan. What's your middle name?"

His smile is at full-wattage. "Elijah," he says.

"Okay. Put your *fucking* shirt on, Keane Elijah *Fucking* Morgan."

Keane laughs. "What's your middle name?"

"My middle name is 'Put Your *Fucking* Shirt On, Keane Elijah *Fucking* Morgan,'" I say.

Keane laughs uproariously. "God, you're adorbsicles, Maddy, just like Zander said you'd be."

"And you're annoy-sicles."

Keane laughs again. "Tell me your middle name, sweet meat."

I twist my mouth, trying not to smile, but it's hard not to react to the glorious smile on Keane's face. "Elizabeth," I say.

"Elijah and Elizabeth," Keane says. "We sound like some old timey Amish couple. Eliza!" he bellows in some old timey Amish voice. "I'm going out to hitch the oxen to the plow 'fore the rains come—looks like a mackerel sky!"

"*What*?" I say, laughing.

Keane flashes me his dimples. "Madelyn Elizabeth Milliken," he says reverently. "That's pretty. Just like you."

I feel myself blush. Goddammit, my cheeks are freakin' traitors. "Thank you, Keane Elijah Morgan," I say evenly. "Now put your *fucking* shirt on. *Please*."

Keane assesses me for a beat. "You're serious?"

I flash him an expression that confirms my seriousness.

Keane exhales. "Well, *shit*. I'm not gonna be able to sit and watch a movie next to a fucking *Yeti*." He motions to my sweatshirt, a scowl on his face. "You're making me hot just looking at you in that goddamned thing—and I don't mean 'hot' in a good way. I mean 'hot' like you're causing searing pain behind my eyes."

I squint at him and he squints right back.

"You give me the evil eye, I give it back bigger, better, and evil-er," he says. "You forget I've got four brothers and a demonic sister. You're gonna have to be a shit-ton scarier than *that* to make me jump."

"Why the heck do you care if I'm wearing a sweatshirt?" I ask.

"It annoys me."

"You just wanna see me waggle my boobs," I say.

"This is not a secret."

There's a beat.

"Pig," I say.

"Yeti," he says—and then he grins from ear to ear.

"I'm not gonna take my sweatshirt off just so you can 'survey the merchandise,'" I sniff. "I'm a bit chilly. If that changes, I'll remove my sweatshirt. My comfort is more important than your piggish desire to see me waggle my boobs."

Keane rolls his eyes. "You can't possibly be chilly."

"I am."

Keane exhales. "Fine, you freak." He reaches into his duffel bag and pulls out a T-shirt, clearly annoyed by the effort.

"Thank you," I say primly. I turn away from him to attach my hard drive to my laptop, a smug smile of victory on my face.

A moment later, Keane's sitting next to me on my lumpy bed, his tight gray T-shirt leaving nothing to the imagination, his skin smelling deliciously of soap.

"Are you ready to commence the inaugural Maddy-Keane Film Festival?" I ask, clicking into my hard drive.

"First things first," Keane says. He holds up the Abba Zaba bar we got at the supermarket down the street before coming to the motel. "I'm gonna pop your Abba Zaba cherry first, sweet meat." Keane begins unwrapping the candy bar. "If you're feeling any pain or discomfort whatsoever, please let me know, sweetheart," he coos. "This is supposed to feel good and nothing else. Really, really *gooood*."

Heat spreads between my legs. "Okeedokey."

I'm thinking Keane's going to hand me the unwrapped Abba Zaba bar, but, instead, he surprises me by bringing the candy bar to my mouth like I'm a helpless baby chick.

My chest tightens at the closeness of his body to mine, at the expression of desire flickering in his eyes.

I open my mouth, my pulse suddenly pounding in my ears, and Keane gently places the taffy between my lips.

"Am I hurting you?" he whispers as I bite down, his eyes darkening.

I shake my head.

"Good?" he whispers.

"Good," I mumble, surprised by the combination of chewy vanilla and creamy peanut butter on my taste buds.

"Are you feeling *pleasure*?"

I nod profusely.

"Excellent."

Keeping his face mere inches from mine, Keane slowly takes a bite of the candy bar, right from the spot where I just chomped down, and we chew in silence for a beat, staring at each other.

"You're no longer an Abba Zaba virgin, Maddy Milliken," he whispers solemnly. "You're an Abba Zaba *woman* now, baby, exactly the way God intended." He reaches out and strokes my hair, causing goose bumps to erupt all over my body.

Out of nowhere, my clit flutters, making my breath hitch. What the hell?

Keane moves his hand from my hair to my cheek, brushing his knuckles against my skin, and my nipples rise and harden in response to his unexpected touch.

What the fuckity?

Keane leans toward me slowly as if to kiss me—or am I just imagining that?—and I reflexively close my eyes. Oh God. I'm suddenly hyper-aware of my lips, as if they've been stung by a thousand bees and swollen to twice their normal size. I part my lips, my body vibrating with anticipation.

I feel Keane's body heat hovering inches from my face, as if his lips are hovering over mine.

I wait, my eyes closed, my breathing shallow. But I feel nothing.

After a beat, Keane lets out an audible exhale, his warm breath tickling over my lips, and drops his hand from my hair. I open my eyes to find Keane staring at me intently, his cheeks flushed.

I let out an audible exhale to match Keane's. What the frickity-frack just happened? We're *friends*. In fact, I've never felt so securely in the friend zone with any guy in all my life. The only explanation for what just happened is I fell momentarily into some sort of hormonal trance after seeing his near-naked body on a bed. That's got to be it.

Keane clears his throat. "And that, my *honorary little sister*," he says slowly, "is the simple *pleasure* of an Abba Zaba bar."

I clear my throat the way Keane just did and swallow hard. "Thank you," I say. "Not quite as *pleasurable* as my actual de-virginization, but still highly *pleasurable*." I try to smile breezily, but I can't—my heart is still pounding like a jackhammer along with my crotch.

"Now you're speaking my language," Keane says. "Tell me all about it."

"About what?"

"Your actual de-virginization."

Aaaaaaaaaand the hormonal trance, whatever it was, is now broken.

"Was it with that first boyfriend you told me about?" Keane asks. "The guy you said was the only guy who's ever really gotten your motor running?"

Crap, crap, crap. Why on earth did I bring this up?

"What was his name again?" Keane asks.

I pause for a long moment. I don't want to talk about Justin—not now or ever.

Keane's staring at me, waiting for me to reply.

"Justin," I finally say.

"Oh, yeah. Was Justin the lucky lad who got to pop your actual cherry?"

I nod.

"Good times?" Keane asks.

I nod again.

"*Excellent*. Always good to have a *pleasurable* first time. I sure did." He snickers. "Kelsey Kerrington. Wooh! Hot little momma. She lived across the street. Damn near broke my heart when her family moved away. Thought I was gonna die of grief." He chuckles at the memory.

I feel my cheeks blaze. I have no desire to talk about Justin with Keane, or anyone. Not now, not ever. Not about how I lost my virginity to him one magical night at his parents' lake cabin. Not about how I loved him with every cell of my body. Not about how, in the blink of an eye, he was gone forever.

"So what happened with Justin?" Keane asks. He takes another bite of the Abba Zaba bar and continues talking while chewing. "Did he bone the fuck outta ya all the livelong day and then you two just flamed out or what?"

Goddammit. I don't want to talk about this. Since Justin died three years ago, I've talked about him plenty, thank you very much, including talking with a therapist once a week for three months, per the insistence of my mother, and now I'm emphatically done talking. "It just didn't work out," I say curtly.

"Young love never does," Keane says breezily. He holds the Abba Zaba bar up, offering it to me, and when I shake my head, he takes another huge bite. "How long were you and Justin together?" he asks.

My chest tightens. "Eight months."

"Hey, you beat Kelsey and me by two months. Who broke it off? Him or you?"

I exhale. "I'd rather not talk about it," I say.

"Justin did, huh? *Bastard.* You want me to track that fucker down and beat the crap out of him for you? Sic the Morgan Mafia on him? Break his legs?"

I shake my head, trying to hold back my threatening emotion.

"How old were you?" He pops the last bite of the candy bar into his mouth.

"I'd rather not talk about it."

Keane's face melts. "Aw, Maddy. Don't get all wilty-flower on me again." He strokes my cheek. "Whoa, come on, baby doll. Don't let that guy get to you—that was then and this is now. If that asswipe couldn't see what a catch you are, you're better off without him. It's his loss." He scoots closer to me on the bed, puts his strong arms around me, and hugs me to him. And, just like that, I melt into him like an ice cream cone dropped onto a blazing hot sidewalk.

"Aw, it's okay, baby doll," Keane purrs. He strokes the back of my head and kisses my temple. "That idiot was just too dumb to know what he had, that's all."

I nuzzle my face into the crook of Keane's neck, breathe in the soapy masculinity of his scent, and let my silent tears flow.

"That dude was just too young to understand what he had. Ssh. He was an idiot." He leans back from me and looks into my eyes. "Don't cry, sweetheart." He wipes the tears from my cheeks. "You're a man-eater now, remember? You eat guys like Justin for breakfast."

I wipe my tears and nod.

"Okay," Keane says. He lies back onto the bed next to me and tugs on the arm of my sweatshirt, pulling me to him. "Come on, sweet thing." He pats his impressive chest. "I got your pillow and blanket right here. Cue up that masterpiece of yours and snuggle up close. It's time for the inaugural Maddy-Keane Film Festival to begin—and I, for one, can't fucking wait."

Chapter 23
Maddy

Oh, God, it's been so long since I've felt the sensation of warm skin pressed against mine, the deliciousness of a man's taut flesh underneath my fingertips.

I run my fingers up and down, reveling in the intoxicating cocktail of skin, muscles, and warmth, my clit throbbing as I do. A strong hand skims down my back, lands firmly on my ass cheek, and squeezes, prompting me to press my pelvis forward and moan with delight.

An orgasm is building inside my mermaid-tail as the strong hand on my ass squeezes and the shaft thrusting in and out of my mermaid-crotch sends spasms of pleasure through each and every one of my scales. I moan again, my insides burning and tightening, my entire body on the verge of back-clawing pleasure.

As that hard shaft continues plunging deliciously in and out of me, I finger the flesh under my fingertips, reveling in the sensation of taut abs, a belly button, smooth, hairless skin trailing down, down, down... until I feel a waistband and then soft fabric that's—*oh, hello*—covering a rock-hard and *very* impressive bulge. Oh, God, yes. Now *that's* a bulge a girl can really grab onto.

Which I do.

I grip the fabric-covered hardness, my breathing ragged, my clit fluttering wildly, aching for my exquisite release. I can make out the shape of the tip with my greedy fingers, and then the hard shaft, and when my body clenches, on the very cusp of exploding with pleasure, I pull the straining fabric-covered bulge toward the waistband of my tail, desperate for it to penetrate my scales and burrow deep inside me.

Wait. Hang on. None of this is making any sense. How am I holding an erection in my hand while it's simultaneously thrusting in

172

and out of my mermaid crotch? I swish my tail through the warm water surrounding me for a moment, confusion gripping me.

Suddenly, the strong hand that's been cupping my ass slides with ferocious heat toward the waistband of my tail, clearly intending to slip its fingers underneath my scales and plunge them deep inside me.

Wait. Where am I? This isn't the ocean. I swish my tail again.

Am I in a *bed*?

My tail suddenly vanishes.

Is this my bed at home?

The hard cock in my hand twitches under my grasp.

A low, masculine moan of arousal sounds in my ear, jolting me awake.

Oh, shit on a Ritz cracker.

I release the hard bulge I've been stroking and lurch away from Keane's sleeping body in the bed.

Oh God, I'm so aroused, my panties are literally wet.

I come to a shaking stand next to the bed, pulling the bedspread off as I go, and dumping my laptop with a soft thunk onto the carpet. I look down at myself, my chest heaving, my clit still fluttering like crazy. Oh, thank God, I'm still wearing my pink "Adventure Time" tank top and pajama bottoms. No scales. No tail. No hard-on thrusting in and out of me or twitching in my hand. All of it was a dream. A very erotic and delicious dream. Phew. Okay, yes, now I remember exactly what happened between Keane and me last night: absolutely nothing. We watched my movie, snuggled up together in my bed, and (apparently) fell asleep.

Well, that's a relief.

Keane loved my movie, by the way. "You're a genius!" he bellowed as the ending credits rolled. "You're gonna win an Oscar one day, Madagascar, I guarantee it!" His reaction was so effusive, in fact, it must have put me under some sort of spell. Because, right after the ending credits rolled, I did the unthinkable: I said yes when Keane demanded to see *all* my tap-dancing videos. Oh my God, I even let him see the dreaded "Born in the USA" performance, the one where I looked like The Cat in the Hat on meth.

And then, apparently not even close to being finished embarrassing myself, I re-enacted the *entire* dance routine for Keane on top of my lumpy bed while Keane threw Junior Mints at me, barking at me to catch the tiny projectiles in my mouth (which, I'm proud to say, I accomplished six out of eighteen times).

"Let's watch *Hoop Dreams* now," Keane said after we'd finally stopped giggling about my *smoove* tap-dancing *mooves*—a request which, of course, made me squeal, "Yaaaaaasssssssss."

Well, now that I'm standing here, gazing down at Keane's sleeping body in the soft morning light, it's apparent I fell asleep before *Hoop Dreams* ended. And I guess Keane did, too, or else, surely, he would have moved to his own bed for the night.

I clutch the bed covers to my chest and take a long look at Keane. He's sleeping on his side, his back to me, wearing nothing but boxer briefs. Hey, when the heck did Keane take off his T-shirt and sweatpants? (Side note: Whoa, Keane's got a spectacular ass.)

I begin to move around the bed, absentmindedly dragging the bed covers with me, and a half-second later, perhaps in reaction to my movement, Keane rolls onto his back, revealing a humongous hard-on straining behind his briefs.

He opens his eyes and smiles lazily. "Well, I'll be damned," Keane says, his sleepy eyes trained on my chest, his hard-on drawing my attention like a magnet. "Maddy Milliken's got tits."

My attention snaps up from the tent in Keane's briefs to his face, where I'm met with a smile that's almost as big as his erection.

I cross my arms over my chest. "And Keane Morgan's got a penis," I say, my cheeks turning red.

Keane looks down at his erection and grins. "Good morning, The Talented Mr. Ripley." He looks back up at me. "Don't take it personally, babe, it's just morning wood." He stretches and yawns and every muscle on his body flexes for a delicious instant. "Trust me, I could have been in bed all night with Z and I'd still have a boner. It's just the way we horny boys wake up—with a salute to the sun." He scratches his ridiculously flat belly, his knuckles brushing precariously close to the tip of his hard-on. "You sleep well, honey nuggets? I sure did. Yee-boy! I was having an extra nice dream just now. Hot damn, that was a good one. Felt like it was really happening." He winks at me. "You wanna use the bathroom before I go in there and nuke it?"

I can't peel my eyes off Keane's incredible body, not to mention the awe-inspiring tent pole behind his Calvin Klein briefs.

"Um, yeah," I mumble, peeling my eyes off him and moving toward the bathroom. "Thanks."

"You gonna take the bedspread into the bathroom with you?" Keane asks.

"Oh." I come back to Keane, put the bedspread down on the bed, cross my arms over my chest again, and walk briskly toward the bathroom.

"*Hey*," Keane says sharply behind me, making me stop dead in my tracks just outside the bathroom door.

"Yeah?" I say, still turned away from him, my heart pounding. Good lord, he's got an impressive piece of equipment behind those briefs.

"Turn around, hot stuff."

"Why?" I ask, not turning around.

"Because I want to get a good, long look at you."

"I gotta pee, Keane."

"Turn the fuck around, Maddy."

I exhale and turn around, my cheeks blazing. Holy crap, that hard-on is something to behold. His entire body is absolutely spectacular. I've never seen a more stunning example of male hotness in my life, at least not in real life. "What?" I huff.

"Put down your arms."

I don't move.

"Come on, Maddy, you're a man-eater now, remember? You eat men like chips and salsa."

I don't move.

"Stop being a puss and put your arms down, dude."

I bite my lip, but, still, I don't move.

"Jesus God, lemme see the goods, you tease—throw me a fucking bone."

"Um. I think you're already well stocked in the *bone* department, dude."

Keane chuckles. "Throw me *another* one, then—a bone for my *bone*."

I can't help but smile.

"Come on, Mad Dog. I just wanna help you become the best man-eater you can be. And that means I gotta get a good look at what we're working with. Normally, I'd require a student of mine to show me her *naked* boobs, just for thoroughness, you know, but just this once, because I respect and admire you so much, I'm gonna let you keep your tank top on while I scope out the merchandise."

I don't move.

Keane exhales with frustration. "Dude. I'll never tell a single soul you wore your scandalous "Adventure Time" *tank top* in my presence, okay? It'll be our dirty, filthy, *salacious* little secret." He flashes his dimples.

Oh my God, I can't resist him. With a loud exhale, I lower my arms to my sides, and Keane's gaze immediately shoots to my bra-less chest.

"*Dude*," Keane breathes. "Oh my God. You're gorgeous."

I bite my lip and resist the urge to cross my arms, even though I'm certain my nipples are hardening under Keane's gaze.

Keane's eyes drift back up to my face. "You're hot as fucking hell, baby doll—smokin' hot. Way, way hotter than I ever suspected. You're... *Dude*." He looks at my chest again, his eyes smoldering, and lets out an excited puff of air. "Don't ever let me catch you covering those gorgeous tits up again, do you understand me? You've been doing the world a major disservice, keeping those beauties hidden all this time. Those fuckers should be in a shadow box in the Louvre.'"

"Oh my God, Keane," I say, my cheeks bursting into flames, my heart racing.

Keane puts his arms behind his head, smiling broadly, his biceps bulging. "I had a hunch you were packing heat under there, but I had no idea you were a five-alarm fire. If you ever get up the confidence to 'waggle' those motherfuckers like you keep teasing me you're gonna do, I swear on a stack of bibles you'll not only attract *pigs* like me, you'll attract any guy you even remotely wanna bang."

Blood whooshes between my legs in a sudden torrent of arousal, making me shift my weight. "Thank you," I breathe.

Keane looks pointedly at my chest again, his eyes on fire, the hard-on behind his briefs straining. "No, sweetheart," he says, his eyes blazing. "Thank *you*."

Chapter 24
Maddy

Thursday, 10:23 a.m.

After eating breakfast at a diner next door to our motel (where Keane ate an astonishing pile of bacon, eggs, sausages, and pancakes) and then shopping at the Walmart across the street (where Keane bought me three ribbed tank tops and two form-fitting T-shirts because he "categorically refused" to set foot in my car unless I was "clad in appropriate boob-waggling gear"), we're *finally* on the road again, heading southbound on I-5 out of Oregon and into California (my new home state!), the windows of my car rolled down, the indie rock playlist on Pandora blaring. And the craziest thing of all—the thing I never would have predicted in a million years? *I'm letting Keane drive my car.*

Giving someone else control of my physical safety isn't something I do lightly or often. And yet, for some reason, when Keane offered to drive as we walked back to the motel parking lot from Walmart this morning, I heard myself reply, like it was no big deal at all, "Thanks." And the most amazing part about the whole thing was that, when that seemingly normal, but oh-so-extraordinary word of surrender left my mouth, I felt like the weight of the world had been lifted off my shoulders.

I look at Keane's profile as he drives, his fingers wrapped loosely around my steering wheel. Damn, he's a handsome-as-hell human. And, damn, that was quite a hard-on behind his briefs this morning.

"I just thought of another thing *Shoot Like a Girl* made me think about," Keane says, bringing up my movie for probably the eighth time this morning. "All those years I played baseball as a kid, I just

177

assumed I'd make it to the major leagues when I grew up—which, of course, didn't pan out. But I always had the dream, you know? But now after watching your movie I'm thinking, 'Hey, what if Little G wants to play baseball?' There's no baseball for girls. Sure, she can play softball—but there's no major league for softball. Which means the dream I just *assumed* for myself as a kid doesn't even *exist* for Gracie. I mean, I'm not saying girls should be allowed to play baseball—girls and guys are just different when it comes to strength—but thanks to your movie I'm thinking deep thoughts like, 'Hey if Gracie decides she wants to play softball, then she's gonna have to dream a lot smaller than the little boys playing the same fucking sport on the field right next door.' And that kinda sucks, if you stop and think about it."

I pause for a long beat, utterly floored. "Keane," I finally breathe. "Wow."

"What?"

"Is it possible my little documentary has turned you into a... *feminist?*"

Keane scoffs. "Hell no. Your little documentary didn't turn me into shit, baby doll. I already was a feminist—I just didn't know it until I saw your movie. I guess I just needed my inner feminist to be *awakened* by the right chick." He winks.

I stare at him, my mouth hanging open, rendered speechless.

"Hey, hand me that bag of popcorn, baby doll," Keane says, pointing to the bag by my feet. "It takes a lot to keep this body lookin' like manna from heaven."

I open the bag and hold it out to him, still incapable of speech.

"Thanks." He plunges his hand into the bag. "So, hey, you wanna chillax in front of *Magic Mike* tonight?"

"Uh... yeah," I say, finally getting ahold of myself. "Now that I know you don't rub your crotch against women like a cat on a scratching pole or pop woodies like a middle-schooler with a Victoria's Secret catalog, I'm dying to know what you actually *do* for those dollah billz."

"Prepare to be rendered speechless."

"I can't imagine *Magic Mike* will render me speechless any more than what you just said about the right 'chick' awakening your inner feminist. Jeez, Keane."

"I dunno, Mad Dog. You might be surprised. Channing Tatum's got some pretty *smoove mooves*."

"Do you do any of his moves when you perform?"

"Are you kidding? All of 'em. I even use Channing's signature song. Why reinvent the wheel, right?"

"What's his signature song?"

"'Pony' by Ginuwine."

I snort with laughter.

"Hey, dude, don't be a Judge Judy. It's a beloved classic."

"If you say so."

"I do." He stuffs more popcorn into his mouth. "Frankly, I don't give a shit what you think of my song selection. You're not my target demo, remember?"

"Yeah, well, I guess the pickles and puppets and earthquake-sensing dogs in your target demo are easy to please, like you keep telling me."

"Whoa, whoa, whoa. I never said women are 'easy to please.' What I said was they're not complicated once you've got the owner's manual, which I do."

I hoot with laughter. "You think you've got the 'owners' manual' for all womankind?"

"Pretty much, yeah."

"And you're the only one who's got it, I presume?"

"Not the only one. Of course not. But from what women tell me, guys with owner's manuals are definitely few and far between."

"Well, gosh, Ball Peen Hammer, maybe it's your destiny to - supply the owner's manual to the ignorant masses, huh?"

"Maybe it is," Keane says, his tone not matching mine at all.

The hairs on the back of my neck stand up—one of the surefire signs I'm having the initial stirrings of a brilliant idea. I pull out my phone. "Let's do it," I say. "'Ball Peen Hammer's Guide to Sex.' We'll do a bunch of short videos in which you tell the men of the world everything they need to know."

"Meh. It's not like I know any government secrets. All the info's out there on the Internet—all a guy has to do to figure this stuff out is a little research followed by testing out the techniques for himself to figure out what works and what doesn't."

"But that's the thing, Keane. Most guys don't have pickles

179

falling at their feet like you do, so they can't test stuff out the way you can. And, yeah, maybe the info's already out there, but the sheer volume of information on the Internet is overwhelming. Guys need an expert to *curate* the information for them—someone to tell them what works and what doesn't." Oh, man, I'm suddenly getting very excited about this idea. "I think this could be really cool," I say, holding up my phone. "You willing to give it a whirl?"

Keane purses his lips for moment, apparently considering what I've said. "Yeah. Okay. Sure."

"Awesome. Oh my God, I'm so excited." I hold up my phone. "Okay, for the first video, let's keep it short. One concept per video. Really basic. I want you to assume you're talking to a guy who knows nothing about how to 'operate' a woman. Like, literally, *nothing*. Just give him a basic primer."

"Okay," Keane says, shrugging. "But this is gonna be me talking, just plain ol' Keane Morgan. Ball Peen Hammer doesn't actually partake in the dabble, as you know."

"Yeah, but 'Ball Peen Hammer' is marketing gold. He's way better for branding. Plus, you might want to maintain some anonymity if this thing gets huge."

"*Branding*? What the fuck am I branding?"

"You," I say matter-of-factly.

Keane chuckles. "Okay. Whatever you say, Scorsese. But it shouldn't be 'Ball Peen Hammer's Guide to *Sex*'—it's more like 'Ball Peen Hammer's Guide to a Handsome and Happy *Life*.' Because no one can be truly happy in *life* unless they're having awesome sex."

I can't keep a massive smile from spreading across my face. "Every damned thing you say is entertainment gold. Okay, fine. 'Ball Peen Hammer's Guide to a Handsome and Happy Life.' Start with the absolute basics, okay?" I train my phone on Keane and press record. "Action."

Keane takes a big breath and then launches right in. "Hey, dudes. Listen close because what I'm about to say is gonna change your life and make you a handsome and happy lad. I want you to imagine a world where you've got the hottest girlfriend in the universe. And this hot chick of yours, she wants to ride your pony every single day—three times a day—morning, noon, and night. Yee-boy! But, check it, your cowgirl's got one condition to the rodeo: you're not allowed to come when you bone with her. Oh, she'll let you hit it as much as you want, any position, any which way, as dirty as you like it, but *never* with a pay-off for you in the end. Torture, right? I'm guessing it wouldn't take long before you'd say, 'I love ya, cowgirl, but this ain't working for me.' Because no matter how hot your chick is, or how sweet, or how much you like foreplay, you'd start feeling like something major was missing for you, sooner rather than later, right? So, okay. Now imagine that same hot girlfriend of yours says, 'Okay. We can do the chitty-chitty-bang-bang as much as you want, any which way, blah, blah, blah, but you can only come *once* in ten times.' Still not gonna work for you, right? What about *five* outta ten times? You get where I'm headed with this? You wanna reach the finish line every time you run the race, right? Well, guess what, fuckwit? *So does she.* So that's lesson one: if you're not getting your woman off, every fucking time, the same way *you* expect to get off, then you're *failing* at fucking. But it's okay. Don't despair because I'm here to help you. I've figured out everything you need to know to get her there every time. And then, once you've got that mastered, you can move on to getting her off multiple times per sesh, which is the ultimate ticket to a handsome and happy life. A happy woman in the sack will make you a happy lad, trust me. Don't worry, guys. I'll be your Master Yoda and teach you all the tricks. So stay tuned." He winks.

I turn off the video recorder, my mouth hanging open.

Keane glances at my phone in my lap, his brow furrowed. "Not what you were looking for? I was just spit balling, like you said to do—you know, starting at the very beginning. I can do something different if that was too basic."

"Oh my God, Keane," I breathe. "That was *brilliant.*"

Keane flashes me a mega-watt smile. "*That*?"

"Keane, you're amazing. What you said—and the *way* you said it..." I rub my hands together. "Oh man. We're definitely on to something here."

Keane laughs. "And what would that be, exactly?"

"I don't know yet. All I know is there's no one else like you on this big, blue marble—and that what I just saw was the perfect marriage of personality and content." I shake my head. "Oh man, I'm starting to get a *feeling*, Keane."

"Oooh. Is it the kind of *feeling* that makes you wanna waggle your boobs, by any chance?"

"I'm choosing to ignore that comment." I exhale with excitement. "Oh my God. I'm having the same kind of feeling I had when I got my idea for *Shoot Like a Girl*."

Keane's face lights up. "Seriously?" A devilish smile overtakes his lips, his eyes still trained on the road. "Say it, Maddy Milliken. Tell me I'm yet *another* 'quiet moment of magic' or I'll never make another video for you as long as I live."

I laugh. "You're *another* quiet moment of magic, Keane Morgan."

"Thank you."

"So it's okay with you if I upload this video to the channel I made yesterday?"

"Knock yourself out, Spielberg."

I log into the Ball Peen Hammer YouTube account I created yesterday and my eyes practically pop out of my head. "Oh my God!" I blurt. "Keane, your video about The Ten Year Rule already has over twenty-three *thousand* views since *yesterday*!"

"*What*? You're shitting me."

"I shit you not."

"Holy guacamole."

"You see? I'm totally right. We're on to something big here. Something *huge*."

"Dude, you look like a madwoman."

"I feel like one," I say.

"Oh my God. I'm your *muse*."

I laugh and swipe into the browser on my phone. "Okay, I'm gonna do a little research on your target demographic. I gotta know who I'm targeting with this."

"Knock yourself out."

I sit back in my car seat and begin reading articles on the *Magic Mike* phenomenon and the male-stripper world in general, and then I move on to researching the top YouTubers and Instagram hotties and male sex symbols, studying what they post and how often, and, suddenly, it's like I've been hit over the head with an inspiration-sledgehammer. I look up from my phone. "Oh, God. I think I'm getting an idea for a documentary," I say.

"What?"

"Too early to say. But when I figure it out, are you willing to be a part of it? Maybe let me interview you at length?"

"Of course. What about?"

"I'm not sure exactly. Stripping. Life. Men and women. Sexuality. Not sure."

"Hell yeah. Make me a brick in your Wall of Gender Equality any time, babesicles."

I laugh. "That's the crazy-ass thing. You're obviously being snarky when you say that, but everything you just said a minute ago about women deserving the same kind of sexual satisfaction as men *is* about gender equality in its own way. Whether you know it or not, you're an advocate for female empowerment, Keane. You truly *are* a feminist."

Keane makes a funny face. "Um. *No*. I just like making women come."

I laugh.

"But, hey," he continues, "if you think there's something deep and meaningful in the bullshit I'm spewing, then I'm at your service, babe. Whatever you do, I wanna be a part of it. I believe in you, boo."

Heat spreads throughout my core. "Thank you," I say softly, my skin on fire. "I believe in you, too, Keane. I really do."

"Thanks, Maddy."

Oh my God, my entire body is electrified.

"Hey, can I make another quick video?" Keane asks, motioning to my phone. "I wanna say this next part while I'm on a roll."

"Sure." I point my camera at him. "Action."

Keane glances at my camera and then looks back at the road. "Okay, lads, just to recap: your woman deserves to come every sesh for starters—and then the next level is making her do her multiplication tables for ya in the sack. That's so basic, it makes my balls hurt to think you're not doing that for her."

I burst out laughing and Keane flashes me his dimples in reply.

"That was Maddy Behind the Camera giggling, if you're wondering. She's a cutie, guys. Cute little freckles on the bridge of her nose. Big ol' brown eyes like Tootsie Pops. Hot little bod. Haven't seen her waggle dem boobs yet, but I'm working on it."

I blush.

"But anyway," he continues, like he didn't just make my heart lurch inside my chest and my clit zing in my panties, "I bet you're wondering *how* to get your woman doing her multiplication tables and speaking in tongues. It's simple: you gotta master more than your girl's clit. You work on nothing but her 'bald man in the boat' the whole time, you're gonna get her off, for sure, but only once per sesh, no matter how hard you try, *plus* it's probs gonna take you a fuckload of time to get her there, too—time you should have been spending getting her off three or four times."

I'm suddenly flooded with an insane volume of adrenaline and arousal, all at once. "Wait," I blurt. I swallow hard and say the next part at a whisper. "I've always thought the... clitoris is everything."

"Hey, Laura Ingalls Wilder is talking about her 'clitoris'!" Keane says, but when he sees my facial expression, he stops. "Sorry. Glad you asked that, Maddy Behind the Camera." He clears his throat. "Lemme be clear about something. I got nothing against the bald man in the boat. That's the cherry on top of an awesome sundae, no doubt about it—and who doesn't love macking down on a sweet cherry? But if you wanna get your girl off *multiple* times in a sesh, which, as I've told you is the goal here, her clit gets really sensitive after the first O and closes up shop, so that's definitely not the path to prolonged glory. So that's why I'm here to teach you how to get your girl off by working her G- and A-Spots, too."

I'm absolutely mind-boggled. I've never heard any of this before. "Does 'A-Spot' refer to a woman's ass?" I ask, trying not to sound like Laura Ingalls Wilder but failing miserably.

Keane smiles wickedly. "You don't know where your A-spot is?"

I blush and shake my head, somehow still managing to train my phone on Keane's handsome face.

"It's the place where I solve the crimes and spit out the rhymes, baby."

"That's not exactly a GPS location."

Keane bursts out laughing. "Isn't she funny, guys? Damn, that girl is funny." He glances at the camera, bestowing his audience with a smirk that can only be described as panty-melting. "Okay, let me be more specific: the A-spot's as deep inside a woman as you can possibly get."

Keane goes on to describe the location of the A-spot in detail, and then he moves on to contrasting it with the G-spot. "The G-spot's awesome, but not quite as easy to trigger as the A-spot," he concludes. "So that's why I always say, if you're looking to blow shit up right from the start, especially with someone you're just getting to know, then go for the A-Spot." He goes on to describe what to do when you find the spot. "If a guy knows how to touch that spot just right—exactly the way I just told you—then, trust me, it's gonna be 'Ka-bam, son!'—*Lionel Richie style*."

I look at Keane blankly for a beat. "Lionel Richie style?"

Keane chuckles and then bursts into singing the chorus of "All Night Long."

I turn off my camera and put my phone in my lap, adrenaline coursing through me. Oh my God. This creature sitting next to me is like nothing the world has ever seen—and, holy hell, on a personal note, I sure as hell want someone to touch me "Lionel Richie style" in the magical way he's just described in astonishing detail. Holy crap, I feel like half my body's blood volume has suddenly pooled between my legs. "How do you know all this stuff?" I ask. "Do you just watch a staggering amount of porn?"

Keane scoffs like that's the stupidest thing he's ever heard. "No, Steve Sanders, I don't watch *porn*. Watching porn is like watching a cooking show where they demonstrate how to cook lasagna using plastic noodles and rubber cheese. I watch *instructional* videos, son— and then I trade 'recipes' and 'cooking tips' with my brothers and Z." He flashes a wicked smirk. "And after all that, once I got the best recipes and ingredients for my lasagna all lined up, the only thing left to do is get my ass into a kitchen and whip up a culinary masterpiece." He winks.

When I don't reply—because, really, what can a girl possibly say in reply to that?—Keane glances away from the road again and flashes me yet another huge smile. "Uh-oh, Maddy Milliken, you're blushing like crazy. Whatever mental image of me just crossed your mind must have been an *especially* good one." He chuckles. "Better sign another waiver, baby doll. I think you're about to become hopelessly obsessed with me."

Chapter 25
Maddy

"Can I drive?" Keane asks.

"*Si, señor*," I say, handing him my keys.

"*Gracias, chiquita bonita.*"

"*De nada, señor guapo.*"

"Dude, we're totally bilingual," Keane says. "They should totally put us in charge at the United Nations."

"Totally," I reply.

We're walking toward my car after having just finished eating tacos at a cute little hole-in-the-wall in Sacramento, chatting the whole time about our families, childhoods, best friends, Keane's baseball days, and, of course, my movie (the one topic Keane keeps going back to), followed by us recording several more Ball Peen Hammer videos about all sorts of topics, not just sex, including one in which Keane instructs his viewers about the "fine art" of sending "subliminal messages" to the "pleasure center" in a woman's brain (a technique I *instantly* recognized as one Keane's used on me multiple times, the sneaky bastard).

"I'll edit the videos tonight before I upload them," I say, my arm linked comfortably in Keane's as we stroll to my car. "I'm thinking we should post one video per day for the next two weeks to really jumpstart your following."

"Whatever you say, Mad Genius."

"I'm thinking of adding some graphics to the videos," I continue, laying my cheek on Keane's shoulder as we walk together. "Maybe some titling or funny little bubbles of commentary? And maybe some sort of Ball Peen Hammer logo? What do you think of a cartoon-hammer with a Prince Charming face and a shock of blue hair, maybe a cute little cleft in its chin?" I giggle.

"Hilarious," Keane says, laughing. He slides his hand into mine. "But, hey, will you promise me something, Scorsese?"

I lift my head from his shoulder and look at him, my hand resting comfortably in his.

"Promise you won't feel obligated to do any of this stuff, okay? You should be using your gigantic brain to think about your next Oscar-winning documentary, not trying to make me into some sort of YouTuber."

"Are you kidding me?" I say brightly, squeezing his hand as we continue to walk. "I'm having a blast. I'm loving all the comments to the videos we've already posted. Plus, I've got a master plan to monetize the whole thing. Trust me."

Keane squeezes my hand. "Cool. If you're digging what I'm slinging, then I'll keep slinging it. But if you get sick of doing it or bogged down, feel free to pull the plug."

"Keane, no one can pull the plug on Ball Peen Hammer but you—he's yours."

We've reached my car and Keane turns to face me, his hand still holding mine. He looks earnest. "Why are you doing this?" Keane asks. "It's awesome and all, but... Why?"

I pause, considering my answer for a beat. "Because it's insanely fun. And because I like you."

Keane grins. "Thank you. I like you, too."

I bite my lip, but I can't stop my mouth from twisting into a crooked smile. "It gives me great *pleeeeeeeasure* to help you, *Keeeeeeeane.*"

Keane's mouth contorts into a smile that matches my own. "*Hey.* Did Maddy Milliken just send a subliminal message to the pleasure-center in my brain?"

"Did it work?"

"Oh, yeah," Keane says. "Big-time."

Without warning, he leans toward my face, licking his lips, and every hair on my body stands on end with excited anticipation—*is Keane about to kiss me*? But, no, his lips skim past mine and land gently on my cheek. "Thanks for doing all this," he whispers, his warm breath tickling my jawline.

"No need to thank me," I whisper back, my skin suddenly electrified. "I'm a man-eater now, remember? I only do what I want."

Keane looks me in the eyes, biting his lower lip. "I'm having a blast with you, Maddy."

"Me, too."

"If by some crazy chance this Ball Peen Hammer thing starts making money, we're a team, okay? Fifty-fifty. I'm the bullshit-slinger and you're the brains. It's a partnership."

My heart leaps in my chest. "Awesome. I'd much rather do Ball Peen Hammer stuff with you than shoot wedding videos." Man, his eyes are so damned gorgeous. And that little cleft in his chin is so cute. I suddenly feel the bizarre urge to kiss him, which makes absolutely no sense, so I throw my arms around him and give him a hug, instead.

Keane kisses me on the cheek again, pressing his body into mine, but this time he lets his lips linger on my cheek, his arms wrapped around my back.

I take a step back from our embrace, my entire body tingling. "You ready to go?" I ask, motioning to my car, my heart clanging in my chest.

Keane looks flustered. "You bet," he says, his cheeks flushed. "Cool."

"Cool?" I say. I clear my throat. "*Cool*."

Chapter 26
Maddy

"Okay, I have another question about *Shoot Like a Girl*," Keane says after we've been driving on the freeway in silence for about twenty minutes. "Did any of the guys on the basketball team hit on you during filming?"

I open my mouth to reply but shut it again, my cheeks rising with heat.

"I knew it!" Keane says. "Which ones?"

"Not *ones*. Just *one*."

"Freddie?"

"How'd you know?"

Keane chuckles. "Because whenever Freddie talked directly to the camera, he was obviously digging whoever was behind the camera asking him questions—which I'm assuming was you."

"Oh, please," I say, rolling my eyes. "Freddie would flirt with a house plant. He's got a huge personality, no matter who he's talking to."

"Maddy, are you *choosing* to be stupid? Freddie might have a huge personality, but he was turning on the charm *especially* for the girl behind the camera. You couldn't see that?"

"Not at all. When Freddie hit on me, I was shocked."

"Oh my God, you're hopeless. Deaf, dumb, and blind to guys' signals. No wonder you're a born-again virgin." He shakes his head. "Well, don't you worry, Helen Keller. I'll help you figure your shit out so you can bag yourself a hottie any time you please."

"Gosh, thanks."

Keane motions to my chest. "Trust me, now that you're showing your girls off a bit, you're gonna need a two-by-four to fend off all the dudes coming at you twenty-four-seven."

"That's a lot of numbers in that sentence."

"Hey, that tank top inspires numerical *superlatives*."

I laugh.

"Now if I can just get you to waggle those beauties, we'll really be in bid-nass."

Rolling my eyes, I turn on the radio to full blast. "Dream on, dude."

"Maddy Milliken, Professional Eye-Roller."

The song on the radio is Hozier's "Like Real People Do."

"Is this song following us?" I say. "I feel like we keep hearing this one."

"Seems that way," Keane says.

As Keane drives, we sit and listen to the beautiful song in silence. But when Hozier's lyrics about kissing make me think about kissing Keane, I abruptly change the station. "Good song," I say. "Just need a break from it."

We drive without speaking for a long moment.

"So did you give poor Freddie a shot or what?" Keane asks, breaking the silence between us.

"No. I told him it would be best if we remained friends."

"What the...?" Keane blurts. "Jesus Christ, woman, are you actively *trying* not to get boned ever again?"

"*No*. I'd love to 'get boned,' believe me. I'm just a relationship-girl, that's all. If I don't see the potential for more than one night, I don't feel the need to pursue anything at all. It's just a waste of everyone's time."

Keane rolls his eyes. "You're too young to be thinking that way."

"I can't help it. It's just the way I am."

"Okay, even so. Don't you think you should maybe widen the net a bit? I mean, how the hell are you so sure you can tell if someone's 'relationship material' if you haven't even gone on a single date with them?"

I twist my mouth, considering that.

"You should have said yes to my man Freddie. He seems like a cool dude. Quite a basketball player, too—he's got a perfect shot. This type of thing is exactly what I was talking about yesterday. If you've got a guy like Freddie sniffing you, why not jump in the sack and see if he *might* get your motor running? What have you got to lose?"

"Um. My self-respect?"

Keane scoffs. "Lame. That's Puritanical thinking."

"Wow, big word, Peenie."

"Zander."

"Well, regardless, with Freddie, it was a nonstarter. I was focused on making my film. If things didn't work out between us, I didn't want it to get super awkward for the rest of filming."

"Okay, fair enough. But what about the other guys on the team who weren't involved in the movie as much as Freddie? You were surrounded by basketball players for *months* and you didn't let *one* of 'em nail ya just for yucks?"

"First off, I don't let people 'nail me for yucks.' And, second off, jocks just aren't my type, like I keep telling you."

Keane sighs with extreme exasperation. "Enough already with the 'not my type' shit. *I'm* not your type; *Brian's* not your type; Freddie's not your type; and now every guy with an ounce of *athleticism* isn't your type? I mean, seriously, who the fuck *is* your type?"

I look out the window of the car, not wanting to reply.

"Tall, dark, and handsome? Short, fat, and mean? One-legged ventriloquists? Yodelers in lederhosen? Guys with rock-hard abs and blue hair?" He flashes me his dimples on that last one.

"It's not specific like that. I've felt attraction to all sorts of physical types. It's just something I *feel*. Impossible to explain."

"Bullshit. My bet is you like hipsters. Am I right? Artsy dudes with man-buns who go on and on about fucking *Nietzsche* all the livelong day?"

"Whoa. Keane Morgan knows who Nietzsche is?" I say.

"Dude, I went to college for two years. I'm not a *complete* idiot."

My skin pricks. "I know you're not. I don't think you're an idiot, Keane. I was just teasing you."

"It's okay. Even my own family thinks I'm an idiot. It's fine."

"Well, I don't. Really."

I'm telling the truth. Despite my less-than-stellar first impression of Keane's intellect, I've come to realize he's incredibly intelligent—

191

clever and bright and witty and perceptive—way, way smarter than I originally gave him credit for. Brilliant, I'd even say, just not in ways tested by standardized IQ tests.

After a moment, Keane lets out an audible puff of air. "Okay, confession? I don't actually know who Nietzsche is. All I know is he's the guy I'm supposed to name-drop whenever I wanna sound super smart."

I belly laugh. God, he's adorable.

Keane flashes his killer dimples. "So, come on, Mad Dog. How 'bout this? Tell me about the perfect guy who'd turn you into a sputtering, incoherent dork if he walked up right now and said, 'Hey, baby doll, can I buy you drink?'"

"Well, first off, my perfect guy would never call me 'baby doll.'"

"Sure he would."

"Well, okay, *maybe*. But definitely not within one second of meeting me."

"Quit stalling," Keane says. "Tell me about Mr. Perfect."

I sigh. "It's totally cliché. You'll make fun of me."

"I won't make fun of you. But if I did, who cares? I don't even know who Nietzsche is."

I puff out my cheeks.

Keane sighs loudly. "Spoiler alert, babe: we're not gonna live forever. Time's a-wastin'. Come on."

I roll my eyes. "I always seem to be attracted to James Dean types—brooding, artsy types. Guys with tormented, poets' souls who care more about creating their 'art' than having a doting girlfriend— and, hey, if the guy plays guitar and drives a motorcycle, even better—I'm a babbling goner."

"Ha! That's funny. You just described my brother Dax to a tee." He snorts.

I freeze, my heart lurching into my throat. I look out the passenger window, pressing my lips together. *Shit*. I feel Keane's eyes on me, but I don't look at him.

"Oh my *shit*," Keane says slowly, realization apparently dawning on him. "You've totally got the hots for my baby brother."

I swallow hard.

"Maddy?"

I don't reply.

"Oh my God. You *do*."

"That's ridiculous," I finally manage to say. "I've never even met your brother."

"Yeah, but you talked to him, right?"

"Yeah, briefly. About me bringing your sorry ass to L.A."

"Had you seen him before you talked to him? Did you know anything about him?"

I don't reply.

"Oh my shit. You knew all about him, didn't you? And were you a babbling, pathetic pile of goo who couldn't string two coherent words together when you talked to him—the way you said you get whenever you talk to a hottie?"

Again, I don't reply.

"Have you seen him performing with his band? Is that what you saw?"

I remain quiet.

"Ho-lee shit. You cyber-stalked the fuck outta my baby brother, didn't you?"

I open my mouth to deny it, but lying has never come naturally for me, so I shut my mouth without speaking.

"Oh my fucking God, now it all makes sense," Keane breathes.

"What are you talking about?" I ask, indignation rising in my voice. "I talked to Dax twice on the phone—once about me using his parking spot and another time about me driving your sorry ass to L.A. How could I possibly have the 'hots' for someone I've talked to twice on the phone?"

"Because you watched videos of him and saw he's your ideal type of guy and then you talked to him on the phone and he was his usual, rock-star self and then your ovaries exploded and now you're obsessed with him."

I press my lips together. "*No.*"

"Which part is off the mark?"

I don't reply.

"Oh my God. I'm totally right. You're jonezing for my baby brother. You should see your face."

I feel my cheeks blast with color, so I turn my head and look out the passenger window again. *Shit.*

193

"Now everything makes perfect sense," Keane says. "*That's* why you're not hurling yourself outta your pickle jar at me—you don't wanna blow your future chances with my baby brother when you get to L.A."

"Oh my God," I blurt. "Ridiculous."

"You're not immune to my *ebullient* charm," Keane continues, "and you're not 'outside my target demo.' You're just *unavailable*."

"Oh my *freaking* God," I say. "You're the mayor of Crazy Town, USA. I've never even met your brother. I talked to him on the phone twice and, yes, I watched a couple of his videos, but only because he asked me to shoot a video for him and I was doing *research*. I was *not* cyber-stalking and I'm not 'jonezing' and I'm certainly not obsessed with him."

Keane glances away from the road to look at me. "You totally wanna bone the fuck outta my brother."

I roll my eyes.

"It's written all over your face, Maddy," Keane whispers, his voice intense, his eyes smoldering.

"Redonkulous," I manage to say.

"You're full of shit," he grits out.

"No," I say emphatically. "I'm telling the truth, Keane."

But I'm not. I'm totally lying. I wanna bone the fuck outta Keane's baby brother. Oh, God, yes. Watching those videos of Dax performing with his band, seeing the passionate way he played his guitar and sang his songs, finding out Dax is the one who writes all his band's heartfelt lyrics, seeing the way his taut muscles strained under the stage lights with each passionate note he sang—wooh! All of that made my ovaries tingle like crazy, if not downright explode. And then, on top of all that, when Dax gave up his parking spot for me and volunteered his brother to accompany me on my drive simply to appease my overprotective big sister, my heart got in on the feels along with my ovaries.

Okay, maybe what I was feeling for Dax was nothing but full-bodied lust. But, even if that's the case, it's nothing to sneeze at, seeing as how I haven't felt even a glimmer of that particular emotion since Justin. Sure, I've had sex during the past three years with my two boyfriends after Justin (both of whom were very nice guys), and I've enjoyed it, but my feelings for them were more "gee, this is very pleasant and you're very sweet" than actual *lust*.

So, fine, I admit it. I wanna see if that initial spark I felt about Dax from afar might lead to a forest fire when I meet the guy in person (despite the fact that, yes, I'm well aware Dax has already pushed me firmly into the sister-zone).

But why should I tell Keane any of this? The fact of the matter is, even if I'd never laid eyes on Dax, Keane would still be a nonstarter for me in the romance department. First off, Keane's a jock, through and through. True, one could argue Justin was nothing but a jock, too, since he played competitive hockey his whole life, but, unlike Keane, Justin had his music and songwriting to keep his athlete's ego in check.

Second off, to put it bluntly, I don't do manwhores. And Keane? Um, yeah.

I mean, philosophically speaking, I have no problem with promiscuity. If (safe) casual sex is what other people (including Keane) enjoy, then more power to them. But I personally don't have any desire to hop from person to person or to become yet another nameless, forgotten notch on some promiscuous guy's belt.

And third off, as if all that weren't enough to put Keane firmly in my friend zone, Keane's just... *Keane*. There's no other way to say it. Yes, he's gorgeous. Duh. And, yes, okay, I'd even go so far as to say he's sexy. In fact, yes, I admit, I'm even a little curious what it'd feel like to kiss him once. And, yes, I haven't met anyone since Justin who's made me laugh and let go and forget my dorkitude so completely the way Keane so easily has. But now that I've found such a unique and unexpected friendship with this crazy baby-dolling-stripper-man, and especially now that we've decided to keep making Ball Peen Hammer videos together and see where that might lead, I would never risk ruining our amazing friendship for one meaningless night that wouldn't amount to anything but a "it was nice knowing you" slap on my back from Keane.

I glance at Keane on the other side of the car. He's staring straight ahead as he drives the car, but when he senses my eyes on him, he glances away from the road to flash me a look that could cut steel.

"I just figured the whole thing out," he says, his jaw clenching.

"You figured what out?" I ask, the hairs on my neck standing up.

"I said I can get any woman I want, as long as she's *single* and

195

available. You're not drooling over me like all the other pickles because you're simply not *available*."

"What the heck are you babbling about? I'm not drooling over you like all the other pickles because I'm not *attracted* to you in that way. We're *friends*, Keane."

"Pfft. You can be my friend and still drool over me. I'm your friend and I'm drooling over you."

"*What*?"

But Keane ignores my flabbergasted reply and forges right ahead. "You're not drooling over me because you're subconsciously keeping the door open for my baby brother."

My mouth is hanging open. "You're *drooling* over me?" I whisper.

"Fuck yeah." He motions to my chest. "Look at those gorgeous tits of yours. What guy wouldn't be losing his mind over those things? I can barely keep my eyes on the road with those things taunting me over there."

I cross my arms over my chest. "You truly think some supposed crush on a guy I've never even met is the sole reason I'm not hurling myself outta my pickle jar and attacking you?" I ask.

"One hundred percent."

"Well, you're crazy, then."

"I'm crazy, but not about this."

"I'm not attracted to you that way, Keane," I say, my cheeks flushing. "It has nothing to do with anyone else, least of all a guy I've never met. I'm not attracted to you the same way you're not attracted to me—other than to my 'gorgeous tits, ' apparently."

Keane doesn't reply. He just keeps staring at the road, his features tight and intense.

"I think you're forgetting an important part of the equation," I say. "You said you can get any woman you *want*, remember? Not just any *woman*. Maybe I haven't been responding to your *ebullient* charm like other women because you're clearly not interested in *me*—besides my 'gorgeous tits,' of course. Maybe guys like you who drool over my 'gorgeous tits' are a dime a dozen. Ever think of that?" I snort. "Get in line, son. Maybe my 'gorgeous tits' have groupies— *hordes* of groupies, just like Ball Peen Hammer. The simple fact is you're not attracted to me and I'm not attracted to you, no rock-star brother required." I glare at Keane, awaiting his response, my chest heaving, but he doesn't speak.

I wait.

But Keane remains quiet.

Jeez. I thought he'd hit me with some crazy Keane-ism after a speech like that. His silence is disquieting. "Keane?" I say. "Hellooooo?"

Another long beat.

"Well," Keane finally says, his voice barely audible. "Good thing we both feel the same way, huh? Woulda sucked if you were crushing on me and I had to let you down easy."

Chapter 27
Keane

Thursday, 10:16 p.m.

Oh, motherfucker.

Everything's all fucked up.

I can't think straight.

For the past two hours, as Maddy and I snuggled up together drinking beer and watching *Magic Mike*, I couldn't concentrate worth a shit. I felt distracted the whole time—hyper-aware of every breath Maddy took, every time the top of Maddy's hair rubbed against my jawline, every time even a square inch of Maddy's bare skin brushed against mine. Oh, and the most distracting thing of all? The way Maddy's gorgeous tits jiggled in her tank top every time she giggled at the movie (because, apparently, Channing Tatum's hilarious, even when he's dry-humping a stage in a red G-string).

The sound of the shower being turned on draws my attention away from the baseball game on TV and toward the bathroom door. Just behind that closed door, Maddy's standing under a stream of hot water completely naked, her gorgeous tits slick and wet and turning pink. If I stripped off my clothes and wordlessly joined Maddy in that little shower, touching her naked body in ways it's never been touched before, would she want Dax then?

Fuck.

I take a long swig of my beer and return my attention to the game. The pitcher steps up to the mound, looks to first base to freeze the runner, nods at his catcher, winds up and releases a curveball straight over the middle of home plate. A swing and a miss by the batter. Strike two. Nice pitch.

When I first figured out Maddy's got a lady-boner for Dax, I was

198

initially shocked, to be honest, just 'cause I didn't see that one coming. And then, for a split-second, I was relieved because that meant my universal appeal to all *available* womankind was still intact. But then, out of nowhere, an unexpected third emotion gripped me and wouldn't let go, an emotion that's kept me in its iron claw ever since: *jealousy*.

I take a long swig of my beer.

Why the *fuck* does Maddy wanna bone my brother instead of me? Sure, Dax is better looking and smarter than me and, sure, he's a fucking rock star, I get that—but I'm Ball Peen Hammer! Women hit on me right and left and sideways and backwards. I don't care if I sound like a prick for saying that—it's the goddamned truth. *Females want to fuck me*. You can set your clock to it. Which is why, fifteen months ago, when I suddenly found myself with no pitching arm, no college degree, no income, no dream, and no marketable skills—I said to myself, "Fuck it, might as well try to make a living doing the one thing I know how to do besides throwing a baseball."

I take another sip of my beer and watch as the pitcher hurls his next pitch. It's a sitting-duck fastball, total junk. Not surprisingly, the batter swings and connects, sending a rocket to the left side.

Yeah, I know Maddy's not impressed by the whole male stripper thing—she's made that abundantly clear, and, yeah, I know the fact that I was a pro athlete for a nanosecond is as unimpressive to her as my eight-pack. But do I really have *nothing* to make that chick pop a lady-boner? Not even my sense of humor, which chicks tell me all the time melts their panties every bit as much as my dimples? Speaking of which: *why the fuck don't my dimples make Maddy want to bone the fuck outta me*? She's the one who called them "killer," after all, and I don't believe for a second she was being *sardonic* when she said that.

The pitcher nods at his catcher and throws heat to the outside corner, making the batter look like a fool. Ka-bam, son!

I take another gulp of my beer.

If I were still pitching, I bet Maddy wouldn't be able to resist me then, no matter what she says about jocks not being "her type." Not that I want Maddy to *not* resist me, of course; I made a promise not to fuck her and I plan on keeping it. *But, still*. It would be nice if Maddy would behave like a normal, red-blooded female for a change and throw herself at me. Then at least I'd know the world was still spinning on its fucking axis.

Goddammit!

It bruises my balls to find out Maddy would rather fuck my *brother* than me. I taught my baby brother every goddamned thing he knows about women. I'm his Master Yoda! Sure, Dax is a rock star *now*, but growing up, who was the rock star? *Me.* I was an All-American, for fuck's sake! Not to be a dick about it, but growing up, while Daxy sat in his room all by himself, teaching himself to play his goddamned guitar twenty-four seven, and writing depressing songs, and pining for a fucking "soul connection," whatever the fuck that means, I was out in the world, pitching like a beast and getting laid six ways from Sunday by la crème de la crème of the hot-chick brigade. And what'd I do the minute I figured out the very best tricks for ringing the bell? I taught every last one of 'em to my baby brother. Of course, I did—*because I'm a giver*. And this is how he repays me?

And besides all that, it just plain irks me to find out Maddy's wasting her time jonezing for a guy who's not gonna give her a second glance. Even if Maddy were fair game for my brother (which she's not, for all the same reasons Maddy's off-limits to me), Dax still wouldn't go for Maddy, not a chance, because my baby brother, unlike me, likes himself the edgy girls—the chicks with demons who feel the need to make a guy suffer to prove his worth. And straight-shooting, tap-dancing, "Adventure Time"-pajama-wearing Maddy Milliken wouldn't know how to make a guy suffer if her life depended on it.

I lower my beer bottle from my lips, my mouth hanging open.

Oh my God.

I think I'm having what Zander would call an "epiphany."

When Dax meets Maddy and she throws herself at him like a pickle hurling herself outta jar, he's gonna say "no thanks" and send her on her merry way—and that's gonna make her feel like shit.

I reflexively glance at the bathroom door, my pulse pounding in my ears.

I don't want Maddy getting rejected and feeling like shit. Hell no. I want that awesome girl feeling like she could bag any hot dude she wants.

But, motherfucker, I absolutely *don't* want Maddy *not* getting rejected by Dax. Just thinking about Dax putting the moves on Maddy makes me want to pummel the shit outta my brother's pretty fucking face like Rocky banging on a side of beef. If any dude's gonna put the moves on my honorary little sister, it's sure as hell gonna be *me*.

Oh my fuck.

What the motherfuck am I thinking?

I glance at the bathroom door again, my heart racing. I can hear Maddy in the shower, singing "Stressed Out" at the top of her lungs. Dude. She's singing my theme song. I'm so fucking stressed out, I feel like I'm gonna explode. Which means there's only one thing for me to do: pick up the phone and call the one person who always knows exactly what to say to calm me the fuck down.

Chapter 28
Keane

"Hey, baby doll," Zander says, answering my call. "You fuck Maddy Milliken yet?"

"Naw," I say, foregoing any kind of formal greeting. "She's been declared off-limits, remember?"

"I must admit I don't see that as a substantial impediment."

I exhale into the phone. "I'm in bad shape, sweet meat. I need your expert counsel."

"Tell me all about it, pretty baby. I'll be your shoulder to cry on."

"Dude, I'm fucked up in the head."

"Tell me."

"I don't want this chick, Zander, I really don't. She's not like anything I ever go for. First off, she's super smart and you know I don't dabble in smart girls. I mean, dude, get this: Maddy's so smart, she hasn't fallen for *any* of my tricks."

"*None* of them?"

"Not a one."

"You flash her the dimples?"

"A million times. With extra sauce."

"You flash her the abs?"

"Of course. I even did the thing where I walk on my hands."

"Ooph. How'd your elbow hold up?"

"It hurt, but I didn't care."

"And she didn't go nuts over your abs?"

"She clapped and cheered like I was a seal at the circus."

"But did your T-shirt ride up when you were upside down?"

"All the way up."

"Impossible."

"See? That's what I'm telling you. The girl's not human. I flashed that woman my *entire* eight-pack for, like, fifteen solid seconds—and then, check it, right after that, I flashed my dimples at *full wattage*, and *then* I sent her a subliminal message *straight* to the pleasure-center in her brain—*and she practically yawned.*"

"*What?*"

"And *then*, later that night, I came outta the bathroom in our motel room wearing nothing but motherfucking sweatpants."

"And?"

"*And she yelled at me to put my fucking shirt on!*"

"*What?*" Zander makes a "mind officially blown" sound. "This makes no sense, Peenie."

"That's what I've been trying to tell you. *It makes no sense.*"

"What *is* she?"

"A *monster*." I groan in frustration.

"Hmmm. This is a very, very interesting turn of events." Zander pauses for a very long moment. "But, just to be clear, you care about Maddy not falling for any of your tricks because... ?"

I glance at the bathroom door. Maddy's still in the shower, singing "Stressed Out."

"Because Maddy's got girl parts and I'm *me*—which means she should want to fuck me. Period. I'm just following God's master plan, trying to stave off the End of Days, brah. Simple as that."

"But you're not allowed to fuck her," Zander says slowly, like he's telling a preschooler not to eat his own poop.

"So what? Making women *want* to fuck me, even if they can't have me, is what makes mathematical sense in the universe, kinda like how your arm span equals your height or a *pound* of feathers weighs the same as a *pound* of pennies."

"Yeah, I know, sweet meat, but Maddy's off-limits, remember?" Z says. "So this *one* time it's probably for the best if this *one* girl doesn't want to fuck your brains out, you see what I mean? Maybe under the circumstances, you should be glad Maddy's not throwing herself at you the way other chicks do. See what I'm saying, Steve Sanders?"

I exhale with exasperation. "It's a matter of *principle*," I say. "Some things in the universe can't be trifled with, son."

Zander exhales but doesn't say anything.

"What?" I ask.

"Oh, Peenie Weenie."

"What?"

"You like her."

"Well, yeah, I *like* her—as a *friend*. She's super cool."

"Mmm hmm," Zander says.

"If you met Maddy you'd understand," I say. "She's nothing like the chicks I go for. She's *smart*. Funny. Doesn't play games. And, sure, she's *pretty*—really pretty, actually—but she doesn't look, you know, like a *supermodel* or anything—other than her tits; her tits are definitely supermodel-quality. But, other than that, she's just this cute, sweet, adorable girl."

"She's *adorbsicles*, isn't she?"

"Totally."

"Ha! I totally called it! Remember? The minute she called you 'jerksauce' and followed it up with 'dickweed,' I said 'Maddy Milliken's adorbsicles.'"

"Yeah, you called it, brah. She's definitely adorbsicles. A cutie patootie, I'd even say."

"A cutie *patootie*? Holy shit. That's next lev. She must be awfully cute."

"She is. Best girl ever. But just as a friend, you know. An adorbsicles, cutie-patootie *friend*." I pause. "But the thing is, Z..." I let out a long, tortured sigh. "I really, *reeeeeeeally* wanna fuck the living hell outta my adorbsicles, cutie-patootie friend."

Zander laughs. "I knew it!"

"No, no, no. Not the way you think. I don't want to fuck her because I wanna *fuck* her; I wanna fuck her because I'm not *allowed* to fuck her. 'Cause she's forbidden fruit." I grunt. "I know that's the game my head is playing with me, but I can't make it stop. I don't actually wanna fuck *Maddy*; I wanna fuck the chick I can't have. You follow me?"

"But you said she's got nice tits."

"Dude, they're not *nice*; they're *gorgeous*. Oh, shit, she's got the most perfect tits you ever saw, Z—totally real, too."

"*Nice.*"

"I know. I was beginning to think real ones had gone the way of the dodo bird. Took me a while to get to see hide nor hair of 'em, though, 'cause she was wearing this god-awful shirt all day yesterday that made her look like the fucking sun, but, yeah, I bought her a tank top to wear today so I've had a nice view of her tits all day long and, holy guacamole, baby doll, they're perfect."

"Excellent."

"*Not* excellent. She's off-limits, remember? What good are perfect tits to me if I can't touch 'em or lick 'em or fuck 'em?"

"So touch 'em and lick 'em and fuck 'em."

"I can't! She's off-limits!"

Zander exhales. "It's a predicament, for sure."

"And even if she weren't off-limits, I still couldn't touch 'em or lick 'em or fuck 'em, anyway. Not *now*."

"Why not *now*?"

"Because I've gotten to know her, and now she's not just some chick to me—she's *Maddy*."

"Oh, shit. She's got a name? That's fucked up."

"Come on, Zander, you know what I mean."

Zander laughs.

"I really *like* her, Z—maybe more than any chick I've ever met."

"Oh, shit, Peenie. Are you serious?"

"Yeah. And she told me herself she's a relationship-type girl—never even had a one-night stand, this girl. I can't fuck a girl like that and never call her again—she'd hate my guts."

"True."

"And I most certainly can't fuck her *and* call her again *and* really like her, either. That's what Dr. Phil calls a *relationship*, son. And that's not in the cards."

"And why is that again?"

"Because I float like a butterfly, sting like a bee, do whatever handsome and happy thing I please."

"Yeah, 'whatever happy and handsome thing you please' except fuck Maddy Milliken, apparently."

"*Fuck*." My shoulders droop. "I *really* wanna fuck her, Z."

"Then fuck her."

"I can't. I don't want her to hate me."

Zander sighs with resignation. "Yeah, then you definitely can't dabble with this one. Definitely off-limits."

"That's what I've been telling you. I can't do it." I grunt. "But I *wanna* do it, Z. I wanna fuck Maddy so fucking bad, my balls physically hurt."

"Then fuck her."

"Would you stop screwing with me? I need your sage counsel, Z. I'm dying here." I let out a tortured moan. "Oh, God. My balls hurt so bad."

Z exhales loudly, just as the shower water turns off in the bathroom. "Dude," Z says. "Here's the bottom line: You can't fuck Maddy Milliken. First off, she doesn't do casual sex and you know it. Second off, Daxy and Ryan said she's off-limits. And, third off, you like having her as a friend. So, there you go. You one hundred percent *cannot* fuck this girl, no matter how gorgeous her tits might be."

"There ain't no 'might' about them tits, son. They're smokin' hot *perfection*."

"You can't fuck her, Peenie Weenie," Z says firmly.

I sigh again. "Yeah, I know. I just needed to hear it out loud. I was starting to go a little bit insane."

"That's what always happens to you when your balls start hurting, baby doll. Ain't no thang."

"Yeah, I know." I sigh yet again. "Thanks for the wise words, Z. You da best."

"Glad I could be of service."

I take a long swig of my beer, considering. "It's a moot point, anyway. I just found out she's got the hots for Dax."

"Aw, *shit*. That's a monkey wrench, for sure."

"Why is that a monkey wrench? We just agreed I'm not gonna fuck her, either way."

"Yeah, but you're *you*, Peenie. You were totally gonna fuck her, no matter what we just said."

"Shit, Z. Don't say that. *Fuck*. I was just getting my mind wrapped around *not* fucking her. Why you gotta mess with my head like that? My balls are about to explode."

"Look, can I be straight with you, love muffin?" Zander asks.

"Always."

"All that's going on here is this: it's *killing* you this girl doesn't want to fuck you. I don't know why she doesn't, but she doesn't. And that's what's got your balls hurting so bad, not her gorgeous tits."

"You're right. Why the fuck doesn't she wanna fuck me, Z?"

"And add to that, she wants to fuck your brother? Your balls are probs a ten outta ten on the pain scale."

"Eleven. I'm in so much pain, I wanna punch a fucking wall, not to mention my baby brother's rock-star face."

"Shit."

"Shit," I agree.

There's a long pause, during which a hair dryer begins blaring from the bathroom, followed by Maddy singing "Blue Jeans" by Lana Del Rey at the top of her lungs.

"So how's tricks for you?" I ask Zander, sighing with my agony. "Do you miss me something awful or what?"

Zander chuckles. "Hell no, I don't miss you. Ain't no time to miss my wifey when I'm fucking my future wife Lionel Richie style, son."

"Things are going well with Daphne?"

Zander sighs wistfully. "I'm in *love*, baby doll."

"Damn, that was fast. You sure you're not just in lurve?"

"Nope, it's straight-up *love* this time. I'm sure of it. This girl's my primordial destiny."

"I've been meaning to ask you: what the fuck does that mean?"

"It means Daphne's been fated for me since a time when humans were nothing more than little blobs of goo floating around in a primordial goop."

"Wow. You know that this fast? You just met her."

"Don't need *time* to know how I feel. I just *know*."

"But you haven't told her you love her, right? I hope and pray?"

"Of course, not. I'm not a fucking idiot." He sighs. "But, damn, she's amazing. I've seriously never felt like this before. It's like I'm drugged."

"You sure she didn't slip something into your beer?" I snort.

"If she did, I don't care."

"I sure hope she doesn't turn out to be batshit crazy like the last one," I say.

"Who the hell knows?" Zander says. "She might be planning to chop me up into little tiny pieces and put me into seven garbage bags in her garage for all I know. I barely know the girl." He laughs.

I join Zander laughing.

207

"I don't need to *know* her to *love* her," Zander adds. "But, yeah, fingers crossed she doesn't murder me in my sleep and feed me to her cats." He sighs happily. "But if she does, it was well worth it."

"Wow. How do you do that?"

"Do what?"

"Go all-in like that, so fucking fast?"

Zander audibly shrugs. "I just trust my feelings. No regrets that way. If I'm wrong, fuck it. It's more fun this way. So, anyway, where are you?"

"At a motel in San Luis Obispo, about three and a half hours north of L.A. We could have pushed forward instead of stopping for the night, but we both said, 'What's the rush?'" I bite the inside of my cheek. "Honestly, man, I'm having such a good time hanging out with this girl, I didn't want the road-trip to end just yet. She did this tap-dancing routine on top of the bed last night that had me in stitches, brah; you shoulda seen her. Talk about 'adorbsicles.'"

"So, um, what do you and Maddy plan to do *tonight* on top of the bed in your motel room? More tap-dancing or...?"

"Well, when we first got here, Maddy edited some videos she shot of me today." I tell Zander about the videos Maddy and I have been doing and he says the whole things sounds awesome. "Then we watched *Magic Mike*," I continue. "And when Maddy gets out of the bathroom we're gonna watch this documentary about a spelling bee she was telling me about."

"Um... *what*?" Zander says.

"What?"

"Peenie. Sweetheart," Z says. "You just said you decided to stop at a motel with a woman with perfect tits instead of driving straight through to your destination so you could watch *Magic Mike* and a documentary about a spelling bee. Peenie, you said that shit *out loud*."

Blood whooshes noisily into my ears. Oh my God. *What the motherfuck is happening to me*? "Shit," I croak out, cringing.

"Please tell me you're stoned outta your mind?"

"No. Maddy and I drank a couple beers while watching the movie, but that's it."

Zander sighs. "Then please tell me Maddy Milliken has surgically removed your aching balls from your body and put them into a jar on the nightstand?"

I don't reply.

"Look, baby doll, it's okay," Zander says. "God only knows what survival strategies you've had to employ for the past thirty-six hours to keep yourself from boarding the bone-train with this girl, but your subconscious *obviously* wanted another night alone with this chick to take another shot at her. Either that or you sincerely wanted to take a woman with gorgeous tits to a motel room for no other reason than to watch *Magic Mike* and a movie about a fucking spelling bee."

I pause, considering. "Well, in my defense, Maddy's never seen *Magic Mike*, and the movie about the spelling bee—"

"Peenie!" Z barks at me. "Snap the fuck out of it! You wanna fuck this girl and you're using Channing Tatum as your wingman!"

I bow my head in instant shame, even though Zander's not here to witness the gesture. "You're right," I say. "This is a new low, even for me. Jesus."

"Aw, don't be too hard on yourself, baby doll. Now that you know what your subconscious is up to, you can put the kibosh on it," Z says. "Use your head, not your head, son."

"Okay. You're right."

"You can do it, Peenie."

The hair dryer in the bathroom turns off and Maddy stops singing.

"Okay, Z," I say. "I'll grab the reins from my horny subconscious and show it who's boss. Thanks for the sage counsel."

"You bet. So, hey, did you talk to that talent agent yet?"

"Uh, yeah. I'm dancing at a club in Hollywood tomorrow night. The agency guy will be there, plus a ton of peeps from the entertainment industry. Sounds like it's kind of a big deal."

"No shit? Congrats."

"Nothing to congratulate me about yet. It's just an audition."

"Why do you sound like that? You're gonna do great."

"I dunno, Z—it's L.A. I might be a little fish in a big pond down there."

"No way. You're gonna blow everyone away. You're the legendary Ball Peen Hammer, for fuck's sake—ain't no one better at shaking his ass in a G-string than my beloved wifey."

"Yeah, but L.A. is next lev. Might turn out I'm a guppy swimming in a shark tank."

"Pfft. No fucking way." Zander pauses. "Hey, I tell you what, Peenie Weenie, how 'bout I come down to the land of milk and honey tomorrow and cheer you on? I can hop a flight after my morning clients and then we can fly back to Seattle together on Sunday night."

"That'd be awesome."

"Cool. I'll book it."

"You da best, ZZ Top. That's why I love you da most."

"No problemo, Chiquito Banano."

"Maddy's gonna be stoked to meet you."

"I'm excited to meet her, too. I already adore her from afar, as you know."

I let out a huge exhale of relief. "I'm glad you're coming, man. Thanks."

"I always got you, baby doll, even if all you need is someone to cheer you on extra loud while you're shakin' your ass."

"Thanks, brah."

Without warning, the bathroom door swings open, and Maddy strides out, instantly blasting the small room with the scent of flowers.

"Hey, so did I tell you what Daphne said to me yesterday about..." Zander begins saying in my ear, but I'm too distracted by Maddy to hear another goddamned word he's saying.

Because along with Maddy's "Adventure Time" pajama bottoms, tonight Maddy's wearing one of the tank tops I purchased for her—the pale yellow one, to be exact. And thanks to the shirt's light color and the thinness of its fabric—plus the fact that the room is chilly and Maddy's clearly not wearing a bra—I can, for the first time plainly make out the unbelievably perfect shape and size of Maddy's very real boobs... as well as the jutting, boner-inducing outline of her two rock-hard nipples.

"Uh huh," I say, not listening to a word Z's saying.

Maddy approaches me on the bed, smiling.

"Gotta go, Z," I bark. "Text me your flight info. Blah, blah. Bye."

Chapter 29
Keane

Maddy hugs herself. "Is it chilly in here?"

"No," I reply, even though, yeah, it's totally chilly in here.

"Have you seen my sweatshirt?"

"No," I say, even though I saw Maddy's sweatshirt on the carpet on the far side of the bed.

"Who were you talking to?" Maddy asks.

I put my phone on the nightstand. "Zander," I say. "He's gonna fly down to L.A. tomorrow."

"Really? Awesome. I can't wait to meet him."

"He feels the same way. In fact, I'm pretty sure he's coming to L.A. to meet you, although he *claims* he's coming to watch me perform."

"You're performing? You didn't tell me that. Where?"

"Oh. Yeah, I'm performing in a showcase at a Hollywood club tomorrow night. It's an audition for that talent agency I told you about."

"Really? That's cool," Maddy says. She giggles and plops herself next to me on the bed, smelling like a flower garden. "They're gonna love your blue hair."

"You think?"

"Of course," Maddy says. "Makes you different—memorable. So, hey, can I come watch your show?"

"Of course. I'd love to have you there."

Maddy's bare arm rubs against mine. "It's an audition?" she asks.

"Yeah, for that agency I told you about, to see if they wanna rep me. Plus, there's gonna be a bunch of talent scouts there for other stuff, too. It won't be your kind of thing, obviously—it's gonna be

Magic Mike type stuff—but, yeah, you're welcome to come if you think you can stomach it."

Maddy leans back onto her forearms on the bed and my eyes immediately train on her boobs as they settle into their new position. "I won't have to 'stomach' it," Maddy says, her tits on dazzling display. "I liked *Magic Mike* a lot, believe it or not. I loved how Channing Tatum and all those guys were having so much fun. Do you have fun like that when you perform?"

My eyes dart from Maddy's chest to her face. "Uh, yeah. I have a blast."

"Male stripping isn't at all how I expected it to be, at least not if it's anything like how it was depicted in the movie. I thought it'd be like female stripping—you know, kind of sad and smarmy and exploitative—but it's just a big, fun party."

Maddy's nipples are rock hard. Jesus Christ, I wanna touch and suck those motherfuckers. "Uh, yeah," I say, my eyes darting back to her face again.

"Is it okay if I bring Hannah and Henn to watch the show?" she asks, apparently unaware of the magnetic pull her nipples are having on my fingers and tongue.

"Um," I say, clenching my fists. What the fuck did she just ask me? "Sure. Bring whoever you want. The more the merrier. Like you said, it's just a big party."

"Cool!" Maddy chirps. She does a happy little shimmy and her boobs jiggle softly with her movement.

Oh my fucking shit—did Maddy Milliken just *waggle* her boobs at me? Did she *mean* to do that? 'Cause it was *spectacular*.

"So what are you gonna do in the show tomorrow night?" Maddy asks, seemingly oblivious to the show her gorgeous tits just gave *me*.

"Uh. It's just a one-song slot, no big deal. I'll just wing it—probably do my *Magic Mike* rip-off."

I lean back next to her on the bed. Damn, she smells good. And those freckles on her nose are so goddamned cute. And, damn, I love the way her Tootsie Pop eyes sparkle when she's smiling at me like she's doing this very second. What I wouldn't give to be the guy who makes those pretty brown eyes of hers roll back into her head with pleasure.

"You're gonna do a *Magic Mike* routine—like, literally?" Maddy asks. She bites her lip, drawing my attention to her mouth.

"Uh, yeah, I have a routine where I basically steal all Channing Tatum's moves from when he danced to 'Pony.' Makes things easy for me and women go crazy for it."

Maddy's bare arm brushes against mine again.

"Oh my God. I can't wait to see you do that," Maddy says. "Word on the street is Ball Peen Hammer is amaaaaaaazing. Of course, it was Ball Peen Hammer who started that rumor, so take that with a grain of salt." She snickers.

God, Maddy's hair looks so soft and smooth. Without thinking, I reach out to touch it, but then sharply pull my hand back like I've touched a hot stove. *Fuck*! I need to stop this shit right now. This isn't gonna end well and I know it.

I clear my throat. "Yeah, well, believe the hype. Ain't no one better at dolin' out lap dances and *smoove mooves* than Ball Peen Hammer, son."

"So I hear, *son*."

There's a beat.

Shit.

My balls hurt so fucking bad.

Maddy pokes my forearm with her index finger. "So, come on, tell me the truth: doing those *smoove mooves* for horny, screaming women turns you on at least a little bit, doesn't it?"

I shake my head.

"Not at all?"

I sit on my hand to keep myself from stroking Maddy' hair. "Ain't no time to pop a woody when you're doing a flip."

"But what about the part of your routine where you pull someone out of the crowd and give them a lap dance?" she asks. "You do that like in the movie, right?"

"Yep."

"And that doesn't turn you on?"

"Not at all."

"You're seriously not into it *at all*?"

"Oh, I'm *into* it—totally into it—I'm just not turned on *sexually*."

Maddy looks thoughtful. "Hmm. Now that I've seen the movie, I must admit I'm excited to see you in action. I'd love to see you do Channing Tatum's smoove mooves."

I close my eyes. I shouldn't say what's on the tip of my tongue. But my balls have a mind of their own. "How about I give you a little preview right here and now?" I blurt.

Shit. Bad Peenie! Bad, bad, bad!

Maddy's face lights up. "Really?"

"Why not?" I say, my pulse raging in my ears. *Why not? Gosh, Keane, maybe because you're only suggesting this to make her want to fuck you—which you absolutely can't do!* "It's only fair, right?" I hear myself saying, my voice as smooth as silk. "You tap-danced for me last night—the least I can do is return the favor and dance for you." I flash her my dimples.

"Excellent point," Maddy agrees. "But keep in mind you'll be popping my lap-dance cherry, so be gentle with me."

"Sorry, baby doll, there ain't no such thing as a *mild* lap dance when it comes to Ball Peen Hammer—only *wild*."

Color floods into Maddy's cheeks. She abruptly sits upright on the bed, fidgeting. "Oh my gosh. So, how do we start? Where should I sit?" Maddy looks down at her tank top. "Is this okay for me to wear? Oh my God, this is so exciting. Gah."

I put a hand on her forearm. "Calm your gorgeous tits, baby doll," I say. "Your only job is to sit-and-submit."

"'*Sit and submit*?'" Maddy giggles. "Oh my God, Keane. You gotta say that in a video. That's hilarious."

My skin is suddenly on fire. "Dude. Are we gonna do this or *talk* about doing this?"

"Sorry, yes, we're totally gonna do this." Maddy makes a big show of shimmying her shoulders and shaking her hair, apparently readying herself for her lap dance like a method actress preparing for an emotional scene, and her boobs jiggle delectably with her effort.

Okay, holy motherfucking shit. Maddy totally meant to waggle her glorious boobs at me that time, I'm sure of it. I mean, she can't possibly be so clueless as to not realize when she's waggling her braless tits at a defenseless man, can she?

Maddy places her palms together after she's done shaking her body. "*Namaste*," she says. She shoots me a solemn expression. "Okay, Ball Peen Hammer, I'm ready to 'sit and submit' now."

Wow. It turns out Maddy Milliken is sexy as hell. Who knew? Which means I should stop this shit right now.

Yep.

That's the right thing to do.

"Okay, let's do it," I say eagerly, rubbing my palms together. "First off, let's take care of bid-nass, shall we?" I hold out my palm to her. "You wanna see Ball Peen Hammer shake his ass, you gotta pay for the privilege."

"What?" She laughs.

"Pay me," I say evenly, shoving my open palm at her. "I'm a professional." *And if you're a paying client, I can't fuck you.*

Maddy slaps my open palm with hers. "Here you go, hot stuff— an imaginary buck. Go buy yourself an imaginary cuppa coffee from 1991, on me."

"I'm not kidding. Pay me. It can be a buck, a penny, whatever— but real money must exchange hands for this lap dance to occur." *Because if you're a paying client, I can't fuck you.*

Maddy rolls her eyes. "Okay, fine, you dork." She pops off the bed and rummages around in her purse. She pulls out a crumpled dollar bill and lays it in my palm. "Here you go, hot stuff. Now go buy yourself a *real* cuppa coffee from 1991. Boom."

"Thanks." I toss the bill onto the nightstand next to our empty bottles of beer and look around the small room, trying to figure out how the hell I'm gonna do my *Magic Mike* routine in such a cramped space. "Okay. It's gonna be hard for me to do what I usually do in this tiny room," I say, my pulse pounding in my ears. I pull the only chair in the room out from under a small desk next to the dresser. "I'd normally have a speaker with a full light show, so you'll have to use your imagination a bit." I lead Maddy to the chair, place my palms on her bare shoulders and guide her to sitting.

"A *light* show?" Maddy says, settling herself into the chair. "Wow, you really *are* a pro. Gosh, should I be scared?"

"Not at all. I'm just gonna show you a good time." *And make you want to fuck me.*

Maddy giggles. "What exactly are you gonna do to me?"

Make you want to fuck me. "Well, since you're a newbie," I say, "I'll keep it simple. I'll just serve up a little fried eggs, bacon, and toast with jam."

215

Maddy giggles again. "Which would be... ?"

"What you saw in the movie. I'll dance, tease you a bit, turn you upside down, flip you over this way and that, and then strip down to my briefs and shake my ass." I pause. "Unless, of course, any of that makes you uncomfortable, in which case, I'll only serve up what you think you can handle."

Maddy's eyes are sparkling. "What I can handle? I'm a baller, baby. Bring it Salt-N-Pepa style, son." She winks.

I look at her blankly.

"'Push It,'" she says.

"Now who's the dork?"

She giggles. "Just treat me like any other paying customer, Ball Peen Hammer. No holding back."

"You sure?" I ask. *Because when I'm done with you, you're gonna wanna fuck me.*

"Hell yes!" Maddy shouts, pumping her fist into the air like a cheerleader. "Hit me with your top-of-the-line *smoove mooves*. Don't think of me as Maddy; just think of me as another nameless pickle with a dollar bill."

"All right. But fair warning: you're gonna be obsessed with the idea of sleeping with me when I'm done."

"Yeah, yeah, Ball Peen Hammer," Maddy says, smirking. "So you keep telling me." She makes a signing motion in the sky. "Another waiver signed. Now hit me with your best shot and I'll take my chances about what happens next."

Chapter 30
Maddy

Keane looks around the small motel room while I sit in a rickety chair, watching him. He seems nervous, though I can't imagine why. Isn't this what he does for a living?

"There isn't a lot of room to maneuver in here," Keane says, biting the inside of his cheek. "I'm not gonna be able to do most of my usual moves."

"No judgment here," I say. "Just jiggle a little bit and I'm sure I'll be duly impressed."

Keane rolls his eyes. "I don't *jiggle*, Maddy. I *dance*."

"Okay, *gyrate*. Writhe. Shake your booty. Whatever. I'm just saying I'm easy to please."

Keane twists his mouth, still surveying the small space. "I can't do any of my acrobatics or flips in here. This is gonna be pretty lame, actually." He sighs. "And I'll definitely have to use the bed for some stuff. Okay? Otherwise, there's no place to maneuver."

I bite my lip, trying not to smile. "Do whatever you think is best," I say. "I won't know the difference. It's my first lap dance, remember?"

Keane furrows his eyebrows adorably. "Okay. But just so you know I'm usually way more exciting than what you're about to see."

I purse my lips and flare my nostrils, trying to keep a huge smile at bay. Why the heckity-heck does Keane seem so freaking *nervous*? "Don't worry," I say. "I'll mention the cramped performing space when I write my Yelp review."

"Hang on." Without warning, he leans over me, giving me a whiff of his delicious, soapy scent, grabs ahold of either side of my chair, and rotates me a quarter turn so I'm facing the length of the narrow "alley" between the beds and the dresser. "Okay, that's

217

better," Keane says. "Gives me a little more room to work with." He grabs a shirt from his duffel bag and throws it over the lamp on the nightstand, further dimming the already low lighting in the room. "Can I use your laptop to play some music?"

"Sure." I motion to my computer on the bed and tell him the password.

After calling up something on my computer, Keane places the laptop onto the dresser to my left. "Press play on the song when I cue you," he says.

"Yes, sir."

Keane positions himself a few feet in front of me, his head bowed, his hands clasped in front of his crotch, his legs spread into an athletic stance, but before he can do anything else, I burst into a manic giggle.

Keane looks up. "You okay?"

"Yeah. Sorry. I just realized I've paid a male stripper for a private lap dance in a motel room." I snicker. "Okay. I'm good now. Proceed." I exhale and shake out my arms.

After a beat, Keane puts his head down again, but then immediately raises his face to look at me again. "Picture colorful lights swirling around the room, okay?"

"Ooooh. Aaaaaaah. Pretty."

Keane levels me with the most hilariously annoyed expression he's ever flashed at me (which is saying a lot). "Are you gonna be *sardonic* this entire time, or can you at least *try* to act like a normal pickle with a dollar bill?"

"Sorry. I will most definitely relax and act like a normal pickle with a dollar bill, starting now."

"Thank you." He takes a deep breath, shakes out his arms, clasps his hands in front of his crotch again, and lowers his head. "Cue music," he says.

I dutifully reach over to my computer and press play on the song Keane's got cued up on YouTube: "Pony" by Ginuwine, of course.

The song begins blaring in the small room. But Keane doesn't move. To the contrary, through the first familiar chords of the iconic song, Keane remains stock-still, apparently letting anticipation build the same way Channing Tatum did when he danced to this song in *Magic Mike*. And I must say his tactic is working like a charm: I'm transfixed.

But, still, Keane doesn't move, other than to subtly flex the muscles on his forearms.

Finally, after a few bars of the song, Keane begins moving his hips and slowly touching his chest over the fabric of his tight black T-shirt—an understated move that most definitely piques my interest—and when the song reaches Ginuwine's vocals, Keane's magnificent body finally springs to animated life, jerking and gyrating to the beat of the music.

Whoa. *Hotness*. I had no idea Keane could move like this. He's as fluid as mercury.

"Woohoo!" I scream. "Yeah, baby! Now *that's* what I'm talkin' 'bout!"

Keane smirks at me, as if to say, "You ain't seen nothing yet." He thrusts his pelvis in rapid succession and then glides back a step, his body shuddering.

"Channing's got nothing on you, baby!" I shout.

Keane's body is bending and twisting now, undulating like an upright worm along with the song.

"Yeah, baby!" I shout.

In one easy motion, Keane leans completely back, touches the ground with his fingertips, and then pops back up to standing.

"Wow!" I scream.

Keane's suddenly on his hands in the tight space and then back on his feet, and then he's dry humping the floor with jaw-dropping thrusts, much to my shrieking delight. Then he's back on his feet, peeling off his T-shirt while thrusting his pelvis into the air like he's in the throes of extremely rough sex. Holy hell, Keane's sweatpants are riding so low on his hips, it's a wonder they're not falling off when he's moving like that.

"Woohoo!" I shriek, laughing gleefully.

Keane throws his T-shirt onto the bed and shoots me a smolder so intense, my breathing hitches.

"Sexy," I whisper, my voice barely audible, though I'd intended to scream the word.

In a flash, Keane's standing over me as I sit in my chair, his body heat wafting over me. Right in time with the music, he picks my chair up off the ground with me in it, making me shriek, and then quickly releases my seat to the ground while holding my body up by my ass.

219

I open my mouth to say, "Hey, I remember that from the movie," but before I can get the words out, Keane's got my thighs on his shoulders and my crotch in his face.

"Oh my..." is all I can manage to eek out as Keane shakes his head into my crotch like a voracious dog with a bone. But before I can say anything more, Keane's strong arms are cradling my back and lowering me confidently onto the bed.

"Oh my God," I gasp. "Wow."

In a flash, Keane's on top of me, his forearms resting on either side of my head, his pelvis dry-humping me to the beat of the song.

"Whoa. At least buy me a drink first, big guy," I say.

Keane flips me onto my stomach and, an instant later, his pelvis is driving into my ass in cadence with the sexy music.

"Okay, now I'm gonna need dinner and dessert," I say.

Keane exhales from behind me and stops moving. After a beat, he flips me over onto my back and straddles me with his strong thighs, his knees on either side of my hips, his sweatpants riding low. "Are you not feeling this *at all*?" he asks, his breathing labored.

"Oh," I say, taken aback. I feel my cheeks blush a deep crimson. "Am I supposed to be reacting differently? I'm sorry."

"No, I just mean..." He stares down at me for a long beat, his blue eyes blazing, his muscles tensing. "This isn't turning you on *at all*?"

"*Oh*. Um. Of course, it is. I mean, you're gorgeous. Look at you. And your *smoove mooves* are amazing. I especially liked that back-door-action simulation."

There's a long beat of silence as Keane stares at me, apparently rendered speechless.

Damn. I feel like I'm saying exactly the wrong thing here. "And, hey, you did that oral-sex simulation from the movie even better than Channing Tatum," I add, filling the awkward silence.

Keane's eyes are burning. Wordlessly, he grabs my hands and places them above my head on the bed, his eyes boring holes into my face like laser beams. But he doesn't speak.

"Um," I say. I swallow hard. Whoa, this is kinda hot all of a sudden. "And, um, when you ripped off your shirt," I whisper, my heartbeat suddenly raging in my ears, "that part was really..." I trail off, too flustered to finish my sentence. Wow, this is suddenly really, really hot.

Keane lets out a shaky breath but, still, he doesn't speak. He slides his palms into mine and clasps my fingers. "That part was really *what*?" he finally asks softly, his eyes flickering with heat.

"Cool?"

Keane smirks. He releases my fingers and slides his palms out of mine, down past my wrists and forearms, over my armpits, all the way down to my ribcage, where he finally lets his hands come to a rest mere inches from my breasts.

I open my mouth to speak, thinking I should fill the silence between us, but I'm suddenly too overcome to form words. Every inch of the flesh Keane just touched is tingling like crazy. And I'm hyper-aware of the placement of his warm, strong hands on my body. If he moved them a mere inch, he'd be touching my breasts.

"Did I do anything at all to get your motor running?" Keane asks softly, his eyes locked with mine, his pelvis heavy on top of me.

I let out a long exhale to steady myself. I'm really not sure how to answer Keane's question. Honestly, this thing he's doing to me right now is getting my motor running ten times more than the actual "lap dance" he performed a few minutes ago.

When I don't reply to his question, Keane slides his hands up from my ribcage—over my armpits, past the sensitive undersides of my arms, across my forearms and wrists—and into my palms again.

But he remains quiet.

Good God, what's he doing to me? He's wreaking havoc on my body with the simplest of touches.

Keane leans over me, his eyes burning like coals, his fingers intertwined in mine. "You weren't feeling it *at all*?" he whispers.

"Oh, no, I totally was," I sputter. "It's just that... um..." I begin. I take a deep breath, gathering myself. "When you did your whole stripper-thing, it felt like you were doing a Channing Tatum impression—like you were playing a character, rather than just being *Keane*." I swallow hard. "And... um." I shut my mouth. Keane's begun gliding his hands from my palms down toward my torso again, and I'm too overcome with tingles to speak further.

"And...?" Keane coaxes as he runs his hands down and then back up my arms, his body hulking over mine.

My heart is pounding like a freakin' jackhammer. And so is my crotch. What the heck is this shirtless boy doing to me, pinning me

221

here on the bed and caressing my bare flesh like that? He's turning me into a freakin' pile of goo. "And..." I swallow hard again.

"Tell me," Keane says.

Shoot. I really don't think I should say the words on the tip of my tongue. Once I say them, I won't be able to stuff them back in again, after all—and, as sexy as Keane is—and, damn, he's most definitely sexy—I have no intention of nudging this friendship of ours outside the friend zone.

Or do I?

"And...?" Keane prompts again, his face on fire.

I bite my lip. Okay, it's clearly time for me to figure my shit out. What the hell am I doing with this boy? If I'm being honest with myself, what the heck was I hoping to achieve tonight when I came out of the bathroom in my thin yellow tank top and no bra and scooted into bed with a guy who'd been going on all day about my "gorgeous tits"? Hmm? Was I just giving the guy a naughty little peek to boost my ego? And how about when I shimmied for him and let the girls jiggle like Grandma's Jell-O mold for him? What was I doing then? Hmm? Did I maybe wanna make him drool just a little bit more to cap off a day full of drooling? *Or was I subconsciously intending to give Keane the green light to make a move on me?*

"And...?" Keane prompts again. "Come on, man-eater. Tell me."

I exhale a long, shaky breath. *Yeah, I was totally giving this sexy boy the green light to make a move on me*, I suddenly realize. *Most definitely.* "And I think," I begin, my tongue thick and clumsy in my mouth. "Um. It turns out... I think Keane Morgan is... much... sexier... than Ball Peen Hammer." I take a deep breath. "Much, *much* sexier."

Keane's eyes darken.

My heart is absolutely racing, but I forge ahead. "Like when you sang along to 'Trip Switch' in my car? For me, that was..." I trail off. Okay, yeah, I can't do this anymore. I've said all I can manage. I'm done being a man-eater now. I tried.

Keane smirks. "When I sang 'Trip Switch' that was... *what*, Maddy?" Keane asks. He bites his lip. "Hey, don't turn into Shy Maddy on me now, baby doll. It's just me, remember? Tell me what you were gonna say."

I swallow hard. Oh, God, I can barely breathe. "That was... sexy as hell," I whisper.

Keane unclasps his fingers from mine and runs his warm hands down the length of my arms again, all the way to my torso, bringing his thumbs to rest precariously close to the sides of my breasts. "You thought *that* was sexy as hell?"

I nod, barely able to breathe. Oh, crap. I can feel my nipples hardening into little pebbles.

Keane licks his lips. "You thought me singing along to 'Trip Switch' in your car was sexier than all that stuff I just did for you?"

I nod again.

Keane chuckles softly to himself. "Ho-lee shit." He takes a deep breath. "Okay, don't move, baby doll. I got another lap dance for you." He leaps off me, strides to the desk across the small room, and fiddles with something on my laptop. "Let's see if I can't get your motor running to full-throttle this time, sweetheart."

Chapter 31
Maddy

I remain frozen on the bed, my arms above my head, my eyes wide, my nipples hard, watching Keane's muscular backside in the dim light as he bends over my computer, the waistband of his sweatpants riding impossibly low on his trim hips.

When "Trip Switch" begins blaring, Keane turns around and stands at the edge of the bed, his chest heaving, his muscles taut.

I hold my breath, waiting for him to start dancing. But he doesn't move. He just keeps standing at the edge of the bed, commanding my attention with nothing more than his smoldering gaze.

I rise up onto my forearms, my chest heaving in synchronicity with Keane's, anticipation killing me—but still, Keane does nothing but glower at me like a vampire assessing his next meal.

Finally, mercifully, when the song reaches its first chorus, Keane begins moving his body, his eyes still trained on mine. But this time, unlike the way Keane danced to "Pony" a few moments ago, his movement isn't flashy. It's raw. Sensual. *Honest*. It seems Keane's not *performing* to this song—he's *revealing* something to me. Something intimate—a secret just for me.

I part my lips, suddenly overcome with desire.

After several understated moves, Keane bends down and peels off his sweatpants, his eyes still locked with mine, and when he straightens back up in nothing but grey boxer-briefs, my breath catches.

"Wow," I whisper.

But Keane's got his game face on. He crawls onto the bed like a panther and, starting at my bare feet, his body gyrating subtly to the beat of the music, he slithers up the length of my pajama bottoms, skimming his nose and mouth up my shins and knees and inner thighs. When his face arrives at my crotch, he pauses ever so briefly right above my aching clit.

I widen my legs at the sensation of his warm breath on my bull's-eye, but even as I do it, he's on the move again, his nose and lips skimming up the length of my torso toward my breasts.

Good God, we're not even a full minute into the "Trip Switch" portion of this lap dance and Keane's already got me spreading my legs for him? What am I doing? I feel like I'm under a spell.

Keane's face nuzzles briefly into my cleavage and then skims over to my hard left nipple jutting up from underneath my tank top. He hovers over the erect bud for a long beat, his labored breathing warming the fabric over my breast, until, without warning, he nips at the outline of my nipple, making me moan softly in shock and arousal.

Keane looks up from my chest, his eyes blazing, perhaps looking to gauge if I'm comfortable with the new direction of this lap dance, and I nod, encouraging him. He smiles wickedly and, without hesitation, lowers his head and buries his face in the fabric-covered valley between my breasts again, this time with ferocious enthusiasm. I run my fingers through Keane's hair as he makes my breasts jiggle and my nipples harden to steel.

But, quickly, Keane's face is on the move again. He lays soft kisses on my collarbone and up my neck as his hand fondles my breast from the outside of my shirt.

I arch my back, moaning with pleasure, my body on fire. Every fiber of my body wants to reach out and grope Keane the way he's doing to me, but I'm not certain about the rules of this "lap dance." Keane's clearly told me the pickles are never allowed to touch him when he performs... and I'm honestly not sure if I'm a pickle right now or if I'm just... me.

I've no sooner wondered about the nature of this "lap dance" than Keane covers my body with his, presses himself into me, and grinds a massive hard-on straight into my crotch.

I let out a soft moan, relieved and excited to discover Keane's as turned on as I am. I throw my arms around his back and hike my legs around his gyrating hips and grind myself into him feverishly. "Keane," I whisper, excitement surging inside me.

"Touch me, Maddy," Keane whispers into my ear, his hips coaxing mine into sensual movement to match his, his hands exploring my breasts. I slide my fingertips down Keane's muscled lower back, over the waistband of his briefs, and caress and squeeze his hard ass from outside his underwear as he gyrates deliciously on top of me. Oh my God, this feels incredible.

In response to my grip on his gyrating ass, Keane slides his hand under my tank top and caresses my naked breast, sending electricity shooting through my entire body. "You're sexy as hell," Keane whispers, his fingers pinching my nipple. "I gotta see 'em," he says. "I'm dying to see 'em."

"They're all yours," I whisper.

Keane deftly repositions himself until he's straddling me, his knees resting on either side of my hips, his erection poking monstrously from behind his gray briefs. He takes a deep, shaky breath and slowly lifts my tank top to my neck, his palms brushing against my naked skin as he lifts the fabric. "Gorgeous," he breathes. "Holy fuck. They're perfect." Without hesitation, he leans over me and swirls his tongue around my rock-hard nipple.

When Keane's mouth moves to my other breast, I slide my fingers straight down his back, burrow them underneath the waistband of his briefs, and grope every square inch of his bare ass.

At the touch of my greedy fingers on his flesh, Keane shudders on top of me with obvious arousal. "I shouldn't be doing this," he breathes. "Oh, shit." He slides off me, taking his ass away from my reach, and stretches his body next to mine on the mattress, and, before I can pout about him pulling his bare ass out of my reach, he reaches between my legs and begins massaging my clit from the outside of my pajama pants.

At his confident touch on the most sensitive spot of my body, I arch my back and widen my legs and literally growl with pleasure.

"Does that feel good?" Keane whispers, his fingertips stroking me fervently, his steely hard-on grinding into my thigh.

"So good," I gasp, jerking underneath his hand.

I reach over and stroke the bulge straining behind his briefs, and he lets out a loud groan at my touch. Oh, God, I'm dying to slide my fingers inside his briefs, or, hell, to slide those damned underwear right off and see Keane's naked body in its full, erect, breathtaking glory, but I refrain. Keane's not slipping his fingertips inside my underwear, after all, so I suppose I'll follow his lead.

"Trip Switch" ends and the next song cued up on YouTube automatically begins playing. It's a song I don't recognize, though I can tell it's also by Nothing But Thieves, and, holy hell, it's a sexy freakin' song. I begin stroking Keane's fabric-covered hard-on more fervently, aching to give him pleasure the way he's doing for me.

After a moment, Keane lets out a guttural groan and his entire body shudders. "Stop," Keane blurts. "You gotta stop that. I'm too turned on. I can't... You gotta stop."

I stop touching him, though it pains me to do it, and place my hands by my sides.

"What the fuck are you doing to me?" Keane whispers, his fingers working me into a state of delirium. "Oh, fuck, I *really* shouldn't be doing this." He presses his hard-on urgently into me, his extreme arousal evident. "Fuck, Maddy. What am I doing?"

"Keane," I murmur. "I'm so close. Oh my God."

"You're so fucking sexy. Look at you. *Fuck*. I'm such a fucking idiot."

"Oh my God," I gasp. I beat my fists against the mattress like a wild woman and let out a strange noise. My body is tightening and coiling sharply from deep inside, on the very cusp of releasing ferociously.

"Oh, I'm fucking up so bad," Keane whispers, even as he increases the speed of his hand on my clit and kisses my breast. "What the fuck am I doing?"

I moan and buck, my skin prickling. I'm on the ragged edge. "Don't stop. Oh my God. Here it comes." I feel like I'm losing control of my limbs. I grip the bed cover underneath me and arch my back, writhing at the outrageous pleasure he's giving me. Oh my God, Keane's fingers are fucking magical. And now he's sucking on my nipple so fucking hard, it hurts. Oh shit, I'm so effing close. This is the most turned on I've ever been in my life.

Keane increases the speed of his magical touch. "You're so fucking hot," he breathes, his excitement turning me on. "Come on, baby. Let go. Come for me. Concentrate on how good it feels." His lips travel from my breast to my neck as his fingers continue working me.

227

"Oh, God," I say, my voice breaking. I'm right on the edge. Keane's fingers are owning me. His lips and tongue are giving me goose bumps. His hard-on pressing against my hip is divine. His scent. The song. Holy shit, this *song*.

"Listen to the song," Keane whispers, reading my mind. "It's called 'Itch.' Scratch your fucking itch, baby. Listen to the lyrics and scratch your fucking itch."

I do as I'm told, and after a brief moment of listening to the words of the song, my body releases with the strongest orgasm of my life. "Oh my God," I groan loudly. "I'm coming so hard. Oh, God."

"Oh, Jesus," Keane says, clearly outrageously excited by my climax. And those are the last words he says before all hell breaks loose.

He climbs on top of me and kisses me voraciously. He's groping every inch of me. Pressing his hard-on feverishly into my crotch. We're panting. Clutching at each other. Dry-humping each other like lunatics. Kissing voraciously. Oh good lord, this is the most intense moment of my life. I'm literally dizzy—euphoric. I've never been kissed like this—with such urgent, desperate *need* before. It's pushing me into a state of delirium like nothing I've experienced before.

"Make me come again," I gasp against Keane's lips, my pelvis tilting and grinding. I'm desperate for him, aching for him to plunge himself inside me and burrow himself all the way. "Do that thing to me, Keane. I'm all yours. Do it now."

But, at my invitation, Keane does the exact opposite of what I'm expecting him to do: he freezes on top of me like I've stunned him with a Taser.

"Keane?" I ask after a beat, confused by his strange body language. "Make me come again," I breathe, thinking he didn't understand me the first time. "Do that thing to me, Keane. I've never come over and over before. I wanna do it."

Keane lets out a long, tortured exhale. "Shit," he says, almost inaudibly.

I'm stunned into paralysis. That's not what I expected Keane to say in response to my invitation. What the hell is happening? "It's okay," I say, my mind reeling even as my body continues writhing underneath him. "I paid you as a joke, remember? I'm not really a client. It's okay."

Keane sighs deeply, rolls off me, and lies on his back next to me on the bed. He puts his forearm over his eyes and lets out another long exhale. "I can't do this," he says softly. "Oh, shit. I've *really* fucked up."

My stomach drops into my toes. My cheeks flush. "But..." I sputter, my head spinning. "I'm not really a pickle with a dollar bill, Keane." Oh, God, I can hear how pathetic I sound, but I can't stop myself from forging ahead. "It's just me. I give you permission. *Please*."

"No, it's not the client thing, Maddy," Keane whispers, his voice almost inaudible. "It's..." He sighs, but he doesn't finish his sentence. He sits up on the bed next to me, his hair tousled, his cheeks flushed, his hard-on still raging behind his briefs. "I just can't."

"But..." I begin. But I don't know what to say. I truly don't understand what's happening. "But... that *kiss*, Keane," I finally manage to blurt.

Keane rubs his eyes. "It was amazing," he says softly. He hunches over and lowers his head, his mind obviously made up. "You're sexy as hell, Maddy. This has nothing to do with you. I've just fucked up, that's all. I took things too far. I'm sorry."

Okay, this moment is definitely brought to me by the letters W, T, and F. If I understand this situation correctly, and I'm quite certain I do, I've just blatantly thrown myself at a self-proclaimed *manwhore*—in fact, I've literally and explicitly *begged* said manwhore to pretty please do me—*and he's turned me the fuck down.*

What the frickity-frackity fuck? I know Keane says I'm deaf, dumb, and blind to guys' signals, but I'd have to be a houseplant to misunderstand the signals Keane was just now throwing at me. Right? For fuck's sake, the guy groped and licked and *bit* my breasts and nipples and massaged my clit until he brought me to the most epic orgasm of my life. And, hell, I need only look over at him to see he's *still* hard as a rock, for what it's worth. And the biggest "signal" of all, or so I thought: he gave me the kiss of a lifetime. Oh my God, that kiss! It was the most passionate, intense, heart-palpitating, soul-stirring, electric kiss of my entire life, by far. Sure I might typically be deaf, dumb, and blind to guys' signals, but what part of all those motherfucking *signals* did I fucking misunderstand this time? "Keane?" I say, my pathetic, hormone-infused brain unwilling to accept the rejection he's so clearly doling out to me.

Keane doesn't reply.

"Keane?"

And, just like that, I totally understand what just happened to me.

In fact, the situation is as clear as can be. What Keane did to me wasn't standard "lap dance" procedure for Ball Peen Hammer—that part is true, but it wasn't an actual make-out session between Keane and Maddy, either, not like I thought. At least, not for Keane, it wasn't. Nope, what just happened was a *third* option, something I didn't even realize was a possibility until just this very second: Keane was merely playing his own idea of a video game. *And the motherfucker was simply racking up points.*

I sit up in the bed, yanking down my tank top and shaking with my humiliation and rage. "You *prick*," I spit out between clenched teeth. I wipe my mouth, desperate to erase all evidence of what I'd *thought* was the best kiss of my life. "You arrogant, egotistical, insecure *asshole* of a little *prick*!"

Chapter 32
Keane

Maddy leaps off the bed, her eyes wild, her face red, and begins rummaging into her duffel bag. "Congratulations, Ball Peen Hammer," she seethes. "I hope you got what your pathetic ego needed, you motherfucking dickweed."

"Maddy, let me explain. You're taking this all wrong."

Maddy gruffly pulls some clothes out of her bag and marches into the bathroom, slamming the door in my face as I try to follow her.

"Would you calm down and listen to me?" I yell through the door. "I fucked up, okay? But not in the way you're thinking."

"You just couldn't stand it, could you?" she shrieks from the other side of the bathroom door.

"Couldn't stand *what*?"

"That there was one pickle in the entire *universe* who wasn't hurling herself out of her jar and throwing herself at you!" She makes a loud scoffing sound. "Well, congratulations, Ball Peen Hammer. Job well done." I hear clapping from inside the bathroom. "You got that last pickle hold-out to *beg* you to fuck her. Phew. Your ego's safe and sound."

Oh, Jesus Christ. I've fucked up so bad here. "Maddy, listen—"

Maddy bursts out of the bathroom wearing her jeans and one of the tight-fitting T-shirts I bought her this morning—almost breaking my nose when she swings open the door, by the way—and then she beelines to the front door of our motel room, grabbing her purse off the dresser as she goes.

"Where are you going?" I ask, panic flooding me.

"Well, unfortunately, since I've had two beers, I can't hop into my car and drive straight to my sister's like I want to do." She opens

231

the front door of the motel room and marches through it toward the street without even a backward glance at me. "So I guess the only rational thing for a girl to do under the circumstances is get shitty-ass drunk."

I follow her into the night, panting, my almost-naked body prickling with goose bumps in the cool air. "You're going to the bar?" I shout at her back, referring to the small bar directly across the street from the motel.

She doesn't reply, but the trajectory of her marching leaves little doubt about where she's headed.

"We've still got a couple beers left!" I yell lamely, but Maddy keeps marching, not even acknowledging me. "You can't go to a bar alone!" No response. "Please. Just. Fuck, Maddy, stop and listen to me. *Maddy!*" I spin toward the room like I'm gonna dart inside but immediately turn back around, not wanting to lose sight of Maddy. "Well, shit, just wait for me to get dressed!" I shout to her. But she's not waiting. She's not stopping. As far as she's concerned, apparently, I don't exist. "I'm coming with you!" I shout.

But Maddy's already halfway across the road, not even glancing behind her.

Damn, I didn't think Maddy had it in her to be this decisive and hostile. I would have figured her to sit on the bed in the motel room, crying and going all wilty-flower insecure on me about what just happened. But she's a bat outta hell.

"Wait for me!" I scream again. But it's futile. She's already made it to the other side of the road and she's striding purposefully up the walkway leading to the bar.

"Maddy!" I scream at the top of my lungs.

Without the slightest indication she's heard a word I've screamed at her, Maddy shows her ID to the dude at the door of the bar and slips inside the building, but not before three asshats standing just outside the door say hi to her and blatantly look her up and down.

Oh, shit. That's right. Cal Poly's just up the road, which means that entire bar's gonna be filled to the rafters with college guys just like those three asshats, all of them looking to get laid on a Thursday night. Jesus Christ. What the hell have I done? Maddy's gonna be irresistible to every single guy in that bar, because, not only is she adorable and pretty and rocking some gorgeous tits, she's also gonna be giving out big-time "green light" signals to every guy she meets tonight, thanks to the blue balls I just gave her.

I scramble frantically back into the motel room and throw on my clothes. Shit. Where the hell are my shoes?

My phone rings and I lurch toward it. "Maddy?" I blurt into the phone, not even looking at the incoming number.

"Do you have my fishing rod?" the voice on the other end of the line calmly asks. It's my oldest brother, Colby. "I've called you three times and you haven't returned my calls, Keane."

Oh, Jesus. The hits just keep on coming. I scour the small room, frantically looking for my shoes, my phone pressed against my ear. "Why the fuck are you calling me about a fishing rod?" I bark. "Text me that shit. You know I hate talking on the phone."

"Wow, someone's in a prick-ass mood. Do you have my rod or not?"

"Yeah. Z and I went fishing a couple weeks ago. It's in my closet, way in the back."

"Goddammit, Keane."

"No big whoop. Just go get it. It's sitting right there."

"I tried. I couldn't reach Z and Mom couldn't find your extra key."

"Oh, yeah, Rum Cake stole my extra key."

"Shit. Would have been nice to know that before I went down there and wasted my time."

"Yeah, total dick-move by Ryan, huh? He totally should have told you he took my key. Anyway, nice talking to ya, Eldest Morgan Brother, but I gotta go. I'm having a situation that can only be described as an emergency."

"What's up?"

I spot my missing shoe peeking out from under the far bed and quickly grab it. "Can't talk. Found my shoe. Gotta go."

"Come on. Three-second version."

I exhale an exasperated breath as I put my shoes on. "I fucked up with a smart girl. And now she's in a bar across the street from our motel room with a bunch of Cal Poly nerds and I gotta go over there and stop her from bonin' the fuck outta some engineering major just to show me what I'm missing out on."

"How'd you fuck it up with her? Did you cheat on her?"

233

"Fuck no. I'm a *Morgan*. Plus, you gotta be exclusive with a chick to be able to cheat on her in the first place, and that particular sitch ain't happenin' with me any time soon. Still haven't figured out how I can be Ball Peen Hammer and someone's devoted boyfriend at the same time." My shoes on, I lurch out of the motel room and stand just outside the door, my phone pressed against my ear, my eagle-eyes trained on the door of the bar in case Maddy comes out on the arm of some hipster with a man-bun and a guitar. "So, hey, Cheese, I gotta go. Nice chatting with ya."

"Just gimme a sec. I could have texted about the fishing rod."

"I don't have time, Bee. I told you—I gotta prevent a spite-fuck in progress."

"Just gimme two minutes, Keane. This is exactly the sort of thing that made me wanna call you."

"What 'sort of thing'? Me screwing up with a smart girl?"

"No. I mean how you never talk to anybody anymore. You've been doing your turtle-crawling-into-his-shell thing a lot more than usual lately. You doing okay?"

I laugh. "You're calling because you're *worried* about me? Ha! Dude, I'm fan-fucking-tastic. I'm the mighty Ball Peen Hammer. Couldn't be better."

"You sure? Because it kinda seems like maybe you're having a tough time getting past the let down on the whole baseball thing."

"Pfft. Yesterday's news, son. I'm slaying it. So, okay, is that it? Because as much as I'd love to stand here and talk about how shitty-ass my life is, I gotta go across the street and stop my off-limits, platonic *friend* with gorgeous tits and Tootsie Pop eyes from leaving a bar with some guy who's probably talking to her about Nietzsche right this very minute just to get into her pants."

"You know who Nietzsche is?"

"I don't have time for this, Cheese. My girl's probably doing a *Coyote Ugly* dance on top of the bar right this very minute."

"Who is this girl? She's got you pretty worked up, huh?"

"Her name is Maddy Milliken and I *really* gotta go."

"Oh, any relation to Kat's friend, Hannah Banana Montana Milliken from the wedding?"

"How the fuck does everyone but me put that together so fast?" I sigh. "Yeah, she's Hannah's little sister. She's starting at UCLA in a week and Dax made me drive with her to L.A. as a favor to Hannah. Long story short, Daxy declared her off-limits—not because he wants her for himself, but because he thinks there's some kind of Kevin-Bacon-six-degrees-of-separation between Maddy and the dude who owns his record label." I quickly describe the chain of people linking Maddy to Reed Rivers and explain the full breadth of my brother's ridiculous logic in designating Maddy off-limits.

"Well, that's an insane leap of logic," Colby says. "Except for the part about her living across the hall from him. That part's not crazy. He's right about that."

"Yeah, I guess he doesn't want me trifling with her and leaving a mess for him to clean up after I leave."

"But you trifled with her, anyway, I take it?"

"Well, *yeah*."

Colby chuckles.

"Don't laugh. I did my best, brah. I've been on the road all alone with the girl for a whole day and a half. And, tonight, out of nowhere, she went from cute and pretty to sexy as hell. I'm only human, Bee."

Colby chuckles again. "That remains to be confirmed after the autopsy."

"*Whatever*. I gotta go."

"No, no. Tell me the story. I'm listening."

I exhale. "So, okay, we were fooling around a few minutes ago in our motel room and then I grew a fucking conscience out of nowhere along with my boner—God knows how the fuck that tragedy happened—the *conscience*, I mean, not the boner—that's certainly never happened to me before, that's for sure—so I stopped before I'd even gotten a finger inside her 'Adventure Time' pajama bottoms and the—"

"*'Adventure Time'* pajamas?" Colby says, laughing.

"I know, right? She's such a fuckin' cutie. She also tap-dances and makes documentaries. And then, on top of all that, come to find out she's unexpectedly sexy as hell, too? A little animal, that one. Oh my God. Forget about 'off-limits,' son. That's a concoction no man could resist."

"She sounds awesome."

"She is." I exhale a ragged breath. "God, my balls hurt so fucking bad."

"So the sparks were there when you trifled with her?"

"Oh, Jesus. A five-alarm fire."

"Then why'd you throw on the brakes? Sparks like that, who gives a shit what Dax wants? You never follow the Morgan Bro Code, anyway. Why start now?"

"Are you insane? I *always* follow the Bro Code."

"Ha!"

"I do."

"Okay, Peen. Sure, you do. But humor me: was there anything *besides* Daxy's off-limits designation that made you grow a conscience along with your boner?"

Goddamn, I hate Colby. Nothing ever gets past him. "Yeah," I grumble. "She's a relationship-girl. Never had a one-night stand."

"And?"

"What do you mean 'and'? There's no 'and' to be had. This isn't a girl who does casual sex—she's said so herself—and that's all that's on the menu with me, so I grew a fucking conscience and put the brakes on."

Colby sighs. "Well, great job, dumbshit. You put the brakes on so she wouldn't hate you and now she hates you for putting the brakes on."

"Yeah, I know. That irony hasn't escaped me. Obviously, I shoulda just fucked her if she was gonna hate my guts anyway, right?"

"That's one way to look at it, I suppose—if you're an idiot."

"Fuck, Bee. She thinks I was using her just to feed my ego—you know, like I was just stringing her along and not actually feeling it. And that couldn't be further from the truth."

"You sure about that? Because it sure sounds like something you'd do, Keane."

I stop and think for a beat, still staring like a sniper at the bar across the street. There's still no sign of Maddy coming out, thank God, though who knows what she's doing inside that building. "Okay, I admit I *started* trifling with Maddy because of my ego," I begin. "But then I was totally into it, lock, stock, barrel, and boner, I swear to God. And then I threw the brakes on because I realized I like her too much to hurt her feelings."

"Who are you and what have you done to Keane Morgan?"

"I know. Trust me, that shit's never happened to me before. But for some reason I'll never fully understand, my desire not to hurt Maddy was stronger than my desire to fuck her—although, just to be clear, my desire to fuck her was, like, DEFCON-one."

"Holy shit, Keane."

"What?"

"Do you hear yourself, dumbshit?"

"What?"

"It sure sounds like you're talking about much more than a trifle to me."

My cheeks flush.

"Explain to me why you don't want a relationship with this girl?" Colby asks. "She sure sounds like girlfriend material."

I scoff. "Now who's the dumbshit? Ha! Let me count the ways why that's the stupidest thing you've ever said. First off, I just met this girl, Colby—laid eyes on her for the first time yesterday *morning*. I'm not Zander, okay? I don't leap into relationships on a wing and a prayer and simply *hope* the girl's not gonna turn batshit crazy on me a week from now. Second off, regardless, there's no such thing as 'girlfriend material' for me right now, no matter how awesome the girl happens to be."

"Why?"

"*Why*? Because Ball Peen Hammer can't do his job when he's got a girlfriend sitting at home, pissed off every time he doesn't return a fucking text. Plus, fuck everything else I just said, it doesn't matter anyway because this girl lives in L.A. Ain't gonna happen, regardless. You know me. I can't even pull my shit together enough to call Mom once a week—you really think I could keep a long-distance girlfriend happy?"

"Not a fucking chance," Colby says without hesitation.

"Well, shit. You didn't have to jump on board quite that fast," I say. "You could have at least argued it's *possible* I could do it."

"It's not possible, Keane."

I sigh. "Yeah, I know."

Colby's sigh matches my own. "Okay, the most important thing here is that you threw on the brakes with her because you didn't wanna hurt her, right?"

"Correct."

"Because you like her too much to make her hate your guts?"

"Correct again."

"Okay, then why the fuck are you sitting here talking to me? Get your ass over to that bar and explain everything to her, top to bottom, or else she's never gonna believe you weren't just mind-fucking her to boost your ego or your stats."

"But what should I say? How should I spin it?"

"Spin it? No, dumbshit. I just told you: tell her the whole truth. Everything. Even the off-limits thing. Make her understand you threw on the brakes 'cause you grew a conscience, not 'cause you were fucking with her."

"You think? Because I was thinking maybe I'd do the deny, deny, deny thing at first, just to get her to—"

"Oh my God, you're such a fucking idiot," Colby blurts, cutting me off. "Keane, listen to me carefully. Do *exactly* what I just told you to do, okay? Don't play games. Don't leave any part of it out. Tell her the truth. Be sincere and sensitive and *kind*. Trust me."

There's a beat as I consider my big brother's advice.

"Keaney, have I ever led you astray with women before?"

"Never." I sigh. "Okay, Bee. I'll head over there now and tell her the whole, ridiculous truth and put my tail between my legs. Thanks, brah. You know I love you the most, right?"

"Yeah, yeah. Good luck. Oh, hey, wait. One more thing: if you ever use my fishing rod again without asking me, I'll pummel your face."

"Gotcha," I say—but we both know I'm totally gonna use Colby's fishing rod again without asking him.

"Bye, Keaney. Keep me posted."

"Will do, big bro."

"Oh, hey, and call Mom, would you? You know she loves you the most, God knows why. Throw that poor woman a bone, Keane."

"Okay, okay. I'll call Mom as soon as my busy schedule allows, I promise. But right now, I gotta go stop a spite-fuck in progress."

"Love you, fucktard. Good luck."

Chapter 33
Keane

I enter the small bar and scan the place, looking for Maddy. It's packed to the gills with college kids. Yep, just as I suspected, this dive bar ain't just a dive bar, son. Despite ramshackle appearances, it's an unlikely hot spot for Cal Poly nerds and hipsters. Which means pretty, witty, adorbsicles Maddy Milliken with those cute little freckles on her nose and sparkling Tootsie Pop eyes and goddamned gorgeous tits is gonna have her pick of pickles tonight, especially with the "please fuck me" sign she's surely got stamped on her forehead.

Okay, there she is. She's on the far side of the room, sitting on a stool at the end of the bar, flanked by two dudes—and all of three of them are in the midst of guzzling beers like they've been best friends forever.

Well, that was fucking fast.

Jesus.

What the hell happened to Shy, Introverted Maddy, the girl who supposedly can't talk to a guy to save her life? So far, I haven't seen hide nor hair of that fabled creature. She might as well be Big Foot.

Maddy spots me across the crowded room and furrows her brow with disdain. She turns her gaze away from me to say something to the guy on her left, a hipster with, oh my shit, *a man-bun* (which, I must admit, the dude wears quite well). Maddy giggles and throws back her head like Man-Bun's said something *wildly* hilarious, but we both know she's laughing like that for my benefit, not his.

I bite my lip, watching Maddy for a long moment. Man, she's on fire, clearly hell-bent on showing me what I'm missing out on (as if I don't already know). She pivots her head and nods at something the dude on her right is saying—a dude with short black hair and no discernible muscle mass—and he laughs.

Okay, enough of this shit.

I stride purposefully toward Maddy, just as a round of shots for the threesome arrives.

"Hey, Maddy," I say.

"Oh, hello, Keane," Maddy says primly.

"Is this him?" Man-Bun asks, a smug expression on his hipster face.

"The one and only." She raises her shot glass toward me. "To you, Ball Peen Hammer. Congrats on successfully making the entire population of pickles throw themselves at you—leave no pickle behind, right?" She downs her shot and slams her empty glass on the bar in front of her, her cheeks blazing.

Wow, Maddy's never looked sexier than she does right this very minute. Holy fuck. Where the hell did this little *femme fatale* come from? "I need to talk to you, Maddy," I say calmly, though my entire body feels like it's about to explode.

"Hey, everyone, we're back," a dude says into a microphone at the other end of the small bar, and we all reflexively direct our attention toward the voice. A band of three guys—guitar, bass, and drums—is standing on a tiny stage in the far back corner, poised to rock out—which they begin doing immediately, launching into "Are You Gonna Be My Girl" by Jet, a rocking song that instantly draws a handful of people to dance on a small clearing in front of the band.

"I'm not in the mood to talk to you, Ball Peen Hammer," Maddy grits out, drawing my attention away from the band. She turns and flashes Man-Bun an alluring smile, and right on cue, he leans in and whispers something to her. She nods, and, without even a glance at me, Man-Bun grabs her hand and pulls her past me to the small dance floor.

Wow. Man-Bun's got balls, I must say.

Without hesitation, I stride to the dance floor and tap Man-Bun on the shoulder before the pair's even gotten started dancing. "Hey, man," I say. "I like your hair and that's not sarcasm—but that's the last nice thing I'm gonna say to you tonight. It's time for you to walk away or this is gonna get ugly."

Man-Bun makes a face like I just took a shit on his shoes. "Hey, she told me what happened, man. You had your chance."

Aw, hell no. I take a step forward, a maniacal grin on my face, my muscles tensing.

"Keane. Please," Maddy says, a look of horror overtaking her face. "Stop it. I'm dancing with..." She pauses. "Him."

My grin twists into a satisfied smirk: Maddy doesn't even know this asshat's name. "She's just dancing with you to piss me off," I say to Man-Bun, and take a menacing step forward. "And guess what? *It's working.*"

"Hey, I don't want any trouble," Man-Bun says, holding up his hands and taking a step back.

"No, wait," Maddy says, touching Man-Bun's arm.

Man-Bun's face is twisted with anxiety.

I lean into the guy. "Hey, just so you know, I've got balls the color of my hair right now." I flex every muscle on my body all at once. "And that's making me really cranky."

"Uh, yeah, I think I'm gonna catch you later," Man-Bun says to Maddy. "Nice to meet you."

And just that fast, he's gone.

"Real mature, Keane," Maddy says through clenched teeth. She turns away from me, apparently intending to stomp off the dance floor—damn, I had no idea Maddy could be so feisty!—but I grab her arm and force her to stay put.

"Just hear me out," I say.

"What's there to talk about?" she says, her cheeks flushing. "I threw myself at you and you turned me down. Actions speak louder than words."

The song ends and the band begins rocking out to a rocking, fast-paced version of "Ain't No Sunshine."

"Hey, they're playing your song, *Sunshine.*"

Maddy rolls her eyes.

"Come on. It's gotta be a sign. Just gimme this song to apologize to you and then, if you still hate me, I'll take you back to the room, tuck you safely into bed, and get my own room."

Maddy pauses for a beat, apparently considering her response, and then she nods curtly.

Despite the upbeat tempo of the song, I wrap my arms around her and pull her close for a slow dance, but she stiffens and pushes on my chest, forcing space between us like we're at a middle-school dance.

The band is so loud, I can barely hear myself think, so I lean into Maddy and place my lips on her ear. "Can you hear me?"

She nods.

"Okay, here's the deal, Sunshine. I fucked up, big-time, but not in the way you think. Yeah, it bruised my ego you didn't want me, I admit that, and then it bruised it even more you wanted my brother instead of me. So, if I'm being honest, I think I started giving you a lap dance because I wanted to make you want me. But then things went way beyond that for me. Maddy, I swear to God I don't get hard when my ego gets bruised or when I'm trying to make someone want me. I only get hard when I want to fuck someone. And, believe me, I wanted to fuck you—still do. So fucking bad. If you could feel how much my balls hurt, you'd send me a get-well bouquet." Her body softens in my arms, so I pull her a bit closer. I press my lips into her ear again. "I *kissed* you because I wanted to kiss you," I say. "Every single thing that happened between us was real. I was Keane Morgan the whole time, okay? Ball Peen Hammer was long gone by the time I popped wood for you, I swear to fucking God. Maddy, I was *totally* feeling it."

At that, any remaining resistance in Maddy's body melts away. She presses the full length of her body into mine and I wrap my arms around her back.

She slides her mouth against my ear. "Then why'd you turn me down?"

I pull back from her and put my fingertip under her chin. "Because you're off-limits."

Maddy scrunches up her face, clearly not sure if she's heard me correctly. "What?"

I press my lips against her ear again. "I said you're off-limits."

She leans back and flashes me a look of pure confusion, so I lean into her ear and explain every one of Dax's stupid reasons for declaring Maddy off-limits.

When I'm done talking, Maddy pulls back from me, looking utterly flabbergasted. "That's ridiculous," she shouts. "Dax has no right to declare who I can or can't have sex with. I've never even met the guy. Screw Dax."

I lean into her ear again. "Yeah, I know. At this point, I don't care about Dax's bullshit. If that were the only thing standing in the way, I'd be bonin' the fuck outta ya in the motel room this very second. But there's an even bigger reason why I threw on the brakes tonight." I pause and exhale. "Maddy, I don't want to fuck things up between you and me."

"What do you mean?" she shouts.

"I don't wanna fuck up our friendship."

At that, Maddy throws her head back. "Oh, dear God. Yet another ticket to the freakin' friend zone. It's my permanent goddamned address." She tries to break free of my embrace, but I hold her firm and force her to listen to me.

"No, no, Maddy. You're misunderstanding. I'm not friend-zoning you like *that*. I'm not saying, 'I'm just not into you.' Okay? I just told you, I wanna bone the livin' fuck outta ya, woman. I threw on the brakes because I realized something kind of crazy—or at least it was a batshit crazy thought for me: I don't want to hurt you even more than I wanna fuck you. And, trust me, I *really* wanna fuck you."

Maddy scoffs. "Oh my God. Nice try. That's the biggest bunch of bullshit I've ever heard in my life."

"No, Maddy, listen to me. I'm telling the truth."

The loud song ends and the band starts a new song, this one much more chill—"Come as You Are" by Nirvana—and, suddenly, talking is much easier without shouting.

"Maddy, listen to me," I say. "You've never had a one-night stand. You told me yourself you're a relationship-type girl. If we'd gotten to bonin', it would have been nothing but a one-night thing. A fling. And I realized when the heat of the moment was over and I went back home to do my Ball Peen Hammer thing and started hunting MILFs in the produce section and flakin' out on hitting you back, you'd feel like total shit and maybe even hate me. And I don't want that."

Maddy looks dumbfounded. "You're telling me you refused to have sex with me tonight because you *like* me too much?"

I consider that wording for a beat. Is that what I'm saying? Hmm. I guess so. Sounds kinda stupid when she puts it like that, but oh well. It's the truth. "Yeah," I reply sheepishly.

Maddy looks into my face for a long beat but doesn't speak. "This is insane."

I grab her and hug her to me, swaying with her to the new song. "Can we please just reset the clock and go back to the moment right *before* I offered to dance for you tonight?" I ask. "I'm an idiot sometimes, Maddy. Ask my brothers and sister—there's a reason everyone calls me Peen."

She doesn't speak.

I exhale a long breath. "I didn't mean to hurt you. I stopped precisely because I *don't* wanna hurt you. Obviously, I fucked it up, okay? But that's honestly what I was thinking in my pea-brain."

Maddy sighs. "I don't know why, but I totally believe you." She lays her cheek on my shoulder and her shoulders slump. "Thank you for being honest with me. I get it."

I can't understand the strange mix of emotions I'm feeling. Certainly, I'm relieved—but even more so I'm disappointed. I thought maybe she'd try to convince me I'm being stupid— that it wasn't up to me to throw on the brakes. I thought maybe she'd say, "I'm a big girl, Keane! If I wanna have sex with a guy, that's what I'm gonna do—even if the guy is you!"

I clear my throat. "So we're good, then?" I ask.

"We're good," she says. "The clock has been officially reset. The lap dance never happened. Friendship without benefits resumed."

I wrap my arms around her even more tightly and she presses her body into mine—and the minute I feel her gorgeous tits molding themselves against my chest, my cock begins to tingle with the initial stirrings of a boner. *Fuck.* I pull back slightly from her, not wanting to send the poor girl mixed signals.

"You know what? You totally made the right call," she says. "We're gonna be doing those videos together and building your brand. Plus, I'm already getting tons of ideas for my next film, and all of them seem to involve you as my star." She sighs deeply. "I don't wanna screw this up, either—whatever it is. You're totally right: I'm not a 'friends with benefits' kind of girl. When I give my body to someone, I can't help giving my heart, too. It's just the way I'm wired and I know it. If we 'boned the fuck outta each other' that totally would have screwed things up between us."

"Exactly," I agree, even as a tsunami of disappointment is crashing down on me. "Would have been a huge mistake."

"Definitely the right call," she agrees. She steps out of our embrace and flashes me a wistful smile. "Thank you for unexpectedly being the sane one of the two of us."

I try to smile back at her, but my lips feel tight. Damn. I'm surprised at how disappointed I feel. God, I wish Maddy would have insisted she could handle a one-nighter with me, no strings attached. If she'd done that, or at least *attempted* to do it, there's no doubt in my mind I'd have yanked her arm out of its socket getting her back to the motel for a marathon bonin' sesh. "Come on, man-eater," I say, sliding my hand in hers. "Let's go back to the room and sleep in our separate beds."

"Let's do a shot first," she says. "Just a little more booze in my bloodstream, and I'll surely wake up tomorrow morning not even remembering this whole thing happened."

"Sounds like a plan." We sidle up to the bar and I order a shot for her and a double for me. "So how the fuck did you hook up with those two dudes so fast?" I ask. "I couldn't believe it when I walked in here and saw you flirting with them. Where the fuck is this shy, tongue-tied girl I keep hearing about?"

Maddy shrugs. "I was so pissed at you when I stormed in here, I totally forgot to be shy."

"But what the fuck did you say to them?"

"I just bellied up to the bar to order a drink, and one of the guys said hello and asked me if I was alone. So I waggled my boobs at him and said, 'Yeah. I just threw myself at a guy in my motel room across the street and he turned me down. So now I'm gonna get shit-faced drunk and drown my sorrows.' And, just that fast, they cleared a stool for me and bought me a beer and a shot."

"Wow. How *magnanimous* of them."

"I thought so."

"Here you go," the bartender says, handing us our shots.

Maddy reaches for her purse.

"No, I got this, baby doll. I fucked up tonight. The least I can do is buy you a shot as part of my apology."

"No argument here. I hereby accept this shot as your penance."

We clink glasses and down our shots.

"Can we please solemnly agree never to speak of this horrific incident again?" Maddy says, putting her empty glass down. "This was pretty much the most humiliating thing that's ever happened to me. Literally."

My stomach clenches. "Of course," I say. "I'm sorry."

"Hey, I know what we should do," she says brightly, clearly changing the subject. "Whaddaya say we go back to the room and watch that documentary about the spelling bee I was telling you about? That's a surefire way to press the reset button on our friendship."

I look at my watch. "It's almost one. You're not even gonna make it past the opening credits."

"Sure I will."

"Dude. You won't. You look like a hobo in front of Seven-Eleven right now."

"Bull-honkey," Maddy says. "I'm totally sober." But her words are beginning to link together unnaturally. She slides her hand into mine. "Come on, baby doll. Let's go watch a documentary about speelllling and pretend tooonight never happened."

"Okay, man-eater." I kiss her on the cheek and my cock starts to tingle. "Good plan."

We walk toward the front door of the bar.

"Hey, when we watch the movie," Maddy says, resting her cheek on my shoulder. "How about we see who can spell more words: Drunk Maddy or Sober Keane?" She snorts.

"My money's on Drunk Maddy," I reply, squeezing her hand.

"Mine, too. I was being *sardonic*, Steve Sanders."

I take a long, deep, steadying breath. "Cool."

"K-e-w-l?"

"Of course."

We walk hand-in-hand out of the bar into the chilly night.

This is good, right? Mission accomplished. Friendship intact.

This is an A-plus result. Right?

Because there's nothing I'd rather do right now with sexy little Maddy Milliken than watch a documentary about a spelling bee. Nothing at all.

Unless, of course, you count the fact that all I wanna do is bone the fuck outta this girl, Lionel Richie style, to within an inch of her life. More than I wanna breathe.

Oh my fuck, my poor, poor balls.

Chapter 34
Maddy

Friday, 2:28 p.m.

Keane and I are back on the road again, traveling at full speed down the I-5, only about three hours away from my brand new home. And, as excited as I am about starting my new life in Los Angeles, with each mile we travel, a certain kind of melancholy is beginning to descend upon me.

Even if Keane and I remain friends after today, which I truly believe will be the case—and even if going forward Keane and I will still be in constant contact as we play our Ball Peen Hammer "video game" together and try to rack up points—I know in my heart things between us will never be the way they've been while we've been all alone in this bizarre little bubble. How could the quiet magic of my hatchback continue unscathed in the real world amidst friends and family and school and stripping? (Oh yeah, and *manwhoring*. Can't forget about that.)

But, considering the situation, I just keep pushing those kinds of thoughts out of my mind. What's the point in thinking about stuff like that? Like Keane said, even if he were up for a relationship, which he's not, it'd be awfully hard to start one with a guy who lives more than a thousand miles away. Plus, I'm not sure I'd even want a relationship with Keane, anyway. I only just met the guy, after all—and, thank God, I'm nothing like my mother. When it comes to matters of the heart, I'm *sensible*. I don't just leap into things and hope the feelings turn out to be real. So, anyway, I've just tried to enjoy these last hours of our unlikely bubble and not think about what's going to happen after it's popped.

I suppose my desire to savor every last drop of my time alone with Keane is the reason we unexpectedly wound up sleeping in the same bed again last night. There was no hanky panky, of course—we'd solemnly agreed at the bar last night that bonin' the fuck outta each other ain't on the menu, son, and we both stuck to our agreement. But, still, after the opening credits of the spelling bee documentary had rolled last night and I'd started drifting off to sleep, when I felt Keane slowly extricating himself from my limbs and quietly attempting to move to the other bed, I clutched his arm fiercely, suddenly yearning to sleep with my body draped over his one last time. "Don't go," I whispered.

Keane hesitated, ever so slightly.

"Please," I added.

At that, Keane wordlessly wrapped his strong arms around me and held me close. And the next thing I knew, I was fast asleep in his arms.

When I awoke this morning, Keane was already in the shower, so I have no idea if he woke up saluting the sun like the morning before—and, frankly, I don't want to know. If Keane *did* wake up with a raging hard-on, I don't want my pathetic brain interpreting that as some sort of sign Keane's looking for a loophole to last night's agreement; and if, on the other hand, Keane *didn't* wake up with a raging woody after lying next to me in a bed, just the two of us, Lionel Richie style, well, I honestly don't want to know that, either. Because, truth be told, despite what we said to each other in the bar, if Keane had made a move on me in the middle of the night, I would have stripped off my pajamas in a heartbeat and given myself to him.

I look over at Keane on the other side of the car. He's quietly driving, looking deep in thought (or, well, as deep in thought as Keane Morgan ever gets).

"Hey, you wanna shoot another video?" I ask, figuring a Ball Peen Hammer video is the surest way to jumpstart normalcy between us.

"Sure," Keane says. "I got endless bullshit for you, brah—you know that."

I grab my phone out of my purse. "Endless bullshit is good," I say, "because people are scarfing down your bullshit like Zander Shaw on a bag of white-cheddar popcorn, son."

Keane laughs.

But, man, it's no joke. When I checked the numbers on Ball Peen Hammer's social media accounts this morning, I was absolutely blown away. There's no doubt about it: the handsome and happy lad is going viral.

Keane glances at the camera. "Ready, Scorsese?"

"Hang on a sec, sweet meat." I briefly fiddle with a setting on my phone. "Okay, action."

Keane's face lights up, as it always does when there's a camera trained on him. "Hello, my handsome and happy lads in training." He winks at me and I grin back. "And, hello, Maddy Behind the Camera. You're looking awfully pretty today, I must say."

"Hello, Ball Peen Hammer," I say, looking at the mesmerizing image of Keane on my display screen: blue hair, blue eyes, and tight blue T-shirt showcasing the most beautiful arms I've ever felt wrapped around me. Oh, crap. I'm doing it again: thinking about that toe-curling orgasm Keane gave me last night. Oh, crap, now I'm thinking about that amazing kiss. I take a deep breath, forcing myself to concentrate on the present moment. "You look awfully *blue* today," I say. "So what are you gonna teach us this fine afternoon, you handsome and happy lad, you?"

"Today, I've got a real treat for you," Keane replies. "Believe it or not, I don't feel like talking about sex today, so I'm gonna teach you lads a basic survival skill: how to survive and thrive during an argument with a chick."

I snort. "Oh, this ought to be good."

"Okay, listen up, lads. When you find yourself in an argument with a chick, follow this surefire strategy and you'll come out smelling like a rose every time." He pauses briefly for dramatic effect and then speaks slowly. "Remain calm in the face of her anger or outrage—absolutely do *not* lose your cool or start screaming at her because, first off, that's just a dick-move and, second off, it shows weakness and chicks can sniff weakness like a shark smelling blood—and then *calmly* deny, deny, deny any and all wrongdoing until she either starts second-guessing herself or forgets what she's mad about all together."

I'm dumbfounded, as I so frequently am while making one of these videos with Keane. "Seriously?" I ask, incredulous. *"That's* your technique for winning an argument with a woman? 'Deny any and all wrongdoing'?"

"Correct."

"You *seriously* think if you continually deny wrongdoing in an argument, a woman will start doubting her reason for being angry or maybe even forget why she's upset in the first place?"

"Well, the most likely outcome is the self-doubting thing—women unfortunately do that shit a lot. Making her forget the reason she's upset in the first place is a bit tougher to pull off, I admit—*but* if you flash your dimples while doing the denying, it should work like a charm over half the time."

"Oh, so dimple-flashing is part of this brilliant strategy?"

Keane flashes his dimples at me. "Correct."

"Well, gosh, then is a guy shit out of luck if he attempts this tactic over the phone?"

"Hmm. Good point. I never thought about that. Lads, Maddy Behind the Camera makes a good point. You best be usin' FaceTime if you find yourself in a *telephonic* argument with a chick. Thanks for thinking of that, Maddy. See, guys? She's definitely the one with the brains in this duo."

"And, um, another kind of obvious thing, Ball Peen Hammer—I'm not sure if you've thought this part through, either—but you're assuming the guy doing the denying has killer dimples in the first place, just like you."

Keane shoots me his most beaming smile. "Aw, you think my dimples are '*killer*,' Maddy Behind the Camera?"

For a half-second, I consider replying the way I've done in the past—by claiming I've used the word "killer" sardonically. But this time, that claim simply isn't true.

"Yeah, I do," I whisper earnestly, my chest tightening.

Keane smiles wistfully as he stares at the road ahead of us. To my surprise, he doesn't hit me with a gloating Keane-ism like I'm expecting him to do.

I clear my throat. "What about just saying 'I'm sorry' to a chick after you've been a flaming asshole to her?" I say. "That seems like it would be a simpler tactic than all that denying, doesn't it? At least if you're dealing with a particularly hard-to-please chick? A *nitpicky* chick?"

Keane snorts. "Nitpicky chick."

"A nitpicky chick-chick," I say.

"E-i-e-i-o," Keane says softly.

He glances away from the road to gaze at me with somber blue eyes.

"But, seriously, Ball Peen Hammer," I say, my heart squeezing in my chest, "is there *any* situation when you'd advise a handsome and happy lad to give a woman a simple and sincere *apology* after he's been a total dick to her?"

Keane shakes his head solemnly. "Don't do it, brah. It's a slippery slope. Then she'll expect you to apologize every fucking time you've been a total dick, and that's the kind of thing that'll get a handsome and happy lad lash marks across his back in the distinct shape of a pussy-whip."

I can't believe my ears. I lower my camera, flabbergasted. "But... Keane. 'Deny, deny, deny' isn't at all what you did with me last night. In fact, you did the exact opposite—you told me the truth and apologized with complete sincerity. You were absolutely wonderful last night."

"I was?"

"Yeah."

"Huh. Wait. *Me?*"

"Yes, *you.* You were amazing."

"Wow." Keane purses his lips and considers for a long moment. "Well, I think there's a very good explanation for my erratic behavior last night: you're not a *chick*—you're *Maddy*. Normal rules don't apply when it comes to you."

My heart lurches. "I think what you did last night was extremely effective," I say softly. "Maybe you should teach *that* to the handsome and happy lads."

"Yeah?"

"Yeah. It'd be a helluva lot more respectful of the girl's feelings than 'deny, deny, deny.' It'd be *real*."

"Hmm."

"Do me a favor, Keane, just for yucks: do the video again, but this time, pretend you're giving instruction about what a guy should do if he's been a flaming asshole to *Maddy Milliken*. Don't say 'Maddy Milliken' in the actual video—replace my name with 'your girl' or 'a chick' or whatever when you speak—but *think* it in your head while you talk. Will you do that for me?"

Keane shrugs. "I can certainly try."

I train the camera on Keane's heart-stopping blueness again. "Okay, Ball Peen Hammer. *Action.*"

251

Chapter 35
Maddy

Friday, 5:19 p.m.

"Maddy!" my sister shrieks, throwing her arms around me.

I clutch my sister to me. "Banana," I whisper into her ear, my eyes welling up with tears.

Oh, good lord. Why the heck am I tearing up? Yes, I'm elated to finally be here to start my new life, and, yes, living with my sister is gonna be the bomb dot com. But I think my tears are flowing for another reason. When Keane and I stepped out of my car three minutes ago and began walking up the pathway toward my sister's apartment—when I knew Keane and I would never again settle into my hatchback for another leg of our drive, just the two of us—I felt such an overwhelming sense of loss, I thought I was gonna cry. And now, it seems, at the sight of my sister's sweet face, her big brown eyes peeking at me from behind her glasses, I'm doing just that.

Hannah pulls back from our embrace. "Aw, Madelyn." She wipes my tears. "Tears of joy, I hope?"

I nod.

Hannah turns her attention to the force of nature to my right. "And you're Keane, right? We met at the wedding."

"Oh, yeah. Great to see you again." Keane puts out his hand, but Hannah goes in for the hug.

"Thank you for taking such good care of my little sister," Hannah says as she pulls out of her embrace with Keane.

"Oh, believe me, Hannah, it's been my..." Keane begins, but he stops talking midsentence and starts anew. "I've loved every minute of hanging out with Mad Dog here," he says.

I smile at Keane through my watering eyes.

Of course, I know what word Keane was about to say to my sister: *pleasure*. And I also know, seeing as how I'm now an (honorary) handsome and happy lad, that Keane Morgan believes uttering that word to a woman, coupled with calling her by name and flashing his killer dimples (which he's doing right now), would send a subliminal message about his unparalleled sexual prowess to the pleasure-center in that woman's brain. Well, obviously, Keane's not willing to send that particular message to my sister.

"Which one is my brother's apartment?" Keane asks, and Hannah points to a door directly behind us.

"Wow," I say. "You weren't kidding when you said Dax lives *right* across the hall."

Keane leaps to his brother's door like a kangaroo on cocaine and pounds on it loudly. "Hey, Rock Star! Open up! It's your favorite brother!"

After a short beat, the door swings opens and there he is—Dax Morgan himself, the golden god who took my breath away while watching an hour's worth of his videos. And, wow, I must say—the guy is every bit as gorgeous as his videos promised he'd be.

The two brothers hug enthusiastically and exchange a rapid-fire flurry of greetings and compliments and jabs, including Dax laughing his ass off about Keane's hair, and, finally, Keane turns away from Dax and introduces him to me.

"Great to meet you, Maddy," Dax says, putting out his hand.

I shake it. "You, too."

"I'm excited about the video we're gonna do."

"Me, too."

Wow. If I were thirteen years old, a poster of Dax Morgan would be hanging on my bedroom wall. He's physical perfection, even more so than his big brother, if that's even possible. And yet, I'm surprised to realize there are no butterflies flapping around in my stomach at the moment. No crazy heart palpitations squeezing my chest.

Well, actually. Wait. That's not true. I *do* feel butterflies and heart palpitations. Most definitely. But it's not Dax Morgan who's causing them.

No, seeing Dax and Keane standing together like two blue-eyed salt and salt shakers, it's suddenly crystal clear to me it's not my fantasy guy who's causing my body to zip and zap like a live wire;

it's the real-life guy—the quirky dude with blue hair and killer dimples and the softest, most delectable lips I've ever tasted in my entire life—not to mention the strongest arms that have ever held me through the night—who's most definitely doing the honors.

Chapter 36
Maddy

Friday, 10:12 p.m.

So, apparently, this is what I do on a Friday night in my new life instead of editing wedding videos in my bedroom all by myself: I sit in a Hollywood nightclub drinking a blue-colored alcoholic beverage (in honor of Keane, of course) with Hannah, Henn, Zander, and Dax, and I watch male strippers make a whole bunch of *extremely* enthusiastic women lose their freaking minds.

Oh, and I also laugh my ass off, pretty much nonstop.

Aaand people-watch like cuh-raaaaaazy.

Aaaaaaaaaaand I also get buzzed, too—which is a mighty good thing because it means I'm only obsessing about last night's make-out session with Keane every thirty seconds instead of every three. Yay! Thank you for slowing my brain function, Mr. Blue Sky Martini!

I check out the stripper onstage, a muscular dude dancing to "Let's Go Crazy" by Prince. The guy's got a nice body with all federally recommended ripples and ridges as well as pretty good dance moves, but as with the four performers before him, he's got absolutely no stage presence to speak of—nothing to make him stand out in a ripples-and-ridges crowd. To put it bluntly, he's no Keane Morgan.

"So, hey, Dax," Zander says, sipping his blue martini. "Is 22 Goats playing anywhere while I'm in town? I'd love to check you guys out."

"Yeah, actually, we're playing tomorrow night at The Viper Room."

"Cool. I'll take the wife for a romantic night out. You wanna come, too, Maddy? You can be my mistress."

I giggle. "Of course."

"Hey, Maddy, maybe you could shoot some footage for our video at the show tomorrow?" Dax says.

"Great idea," I reply. "I'll get performance footage tomorrow and then capture interviews and B-roll this coming week."

"Sick. Hey, why don't you hang backstage with the band before the show so you can shoot some 'behind the scenes' stuff there? That'd be cool, right? Green rooms always look super backstage-legit."

I nod vigorously, simply because I'm too excited to speak.

"Hey, I wanna see you guys play, too," Hannah says. "Whaddaya say, Henny?"

"Hell yeah," Henn says.

"Cool. I'll put all your names on the list at will call," Dax says.

"Awesome," Hannah says. "Thank you."

Everyone thanks Dax and he replies graciously that he's happy to do it.

I take a sip of my drink, my heart pounding. I can't stop staring at Dax's shockingly gorgeous face, especially his lips. They look so much like Keane's beautiful lips, it's insane. Aaaaaaaand now I'm thinking, yet again, about my passionate kiss with Keane last night. Oh, God, it was the most electrifying kiss of my life.

"So, Dax," Hannah says. "Sorry if you get asked this every day of your life, but why the hell are you guys called 22 Goats?"

Dax chuckles. "It's a stupid story, actually."

"Oh, I love stupid stories," Hannah says.

"It's true. She loves all my stories and they're all stupid," Henn says, making Hannah giggle.

I take another long sip of my martini, my cheeks hot, remembering the sensation of Keane's body on top of mine, his hard chest pressed against my soft breasts, his fingers working between my legs with incredible skill.

"So, Fish, Colin, and I were partying with these girls one night after a show," Dax begins, "and one of them had grown up on a farm in Nebraska or wherever and she was telling us all these weird factoids about farm animals." He chuckles. "So she was like, 'Did you know goats *smile*?' And, of course, we were all like, 'Are you shitting me? Is this a Chinese proverb?' So she goes, 'No, no, goats

actually *smile*. Google it.' So we search 'goats smiling' and this
Buzzfeed article pops right up called '22 Goats Smiling at You.' And,
holy shit, guess what? Goats totally smile at you." He laughs. "And
for some reason we all thought those twenty-two goats smiling at us
were the funniest things we'd ever seen." He leans forward like he's
telling a secret. "I should at this point in the story mention we were
smoking the finest weed."

Everyone laughs.

"Found it," Henn says next to me, looking down at his phone.
He bursts out laughing. "Oh my God—it's true. Goats really do *smile*
at you." Henn passes his phone around the table, and everyone
marvels and laughs at the silly photos.

"So, anyway, Fish was like, 'That should be our band name,
dudes—*22 Goats Smiling at You*.' Right before then we'd decided
our band name sucked and we wanted to change it to something super
awesome, but up to that point we'd only come up with lame and self-
important shit like, 'Masters of Profundity' and 'Darkness
Descendant." He belly laughs at that and we all laugh with him. "So,
anyway, that's what we became—'22 Goats Smiling at You.' But
then my brother Colby said the name sounded like a Dr. Seuss book
on acid and then my other brother Ryan said we sounded like a band
of pedophiles who play little kids' birthday parties only to scout out
our next victims."

Everyone laughs uproariously for a solid minute at that.

"So we shortened it to 22 Goats," Dax finally says. "And there
you go."

"What was your band name before that?" Henn asks. "You said
it sucked."

"Okay, don't judge. Fish, Colin, and I came up with our first
band name back in tenth grade."

We all hold our breath, waiting for whatever bomb Dax is about
to drop.

"Dax Attack," Dax finally mumbles, clearly embarrassed, and
we all burst out laughing again.

"Ladies and gentlemen!" the emcee suddenly bellows onstage,
interrupting our collective laughter.

Zander looks at his watch, his eyes lighting up. "Oh, I bet this is
gonna be Peenie."

The emcee continues: "Put your hands together for a spicy hot dancer who's gonna bring the *caliente* to you tonight: the one and only—Latin Lover!"

The crowd applauds enthusiastically and an attractive Latino dude comes onstage and begins shaking his ass to Pitbull's "I Know You Want Me."

I sip my drink and watch the guy politely for a grand total of twenty seconds. And then I'm bored out of my mind. *Meh.* So I shift my attention from the guy onstage and do what I've been doing all night: I watch the frenzied women in the audience as they watch the performer onstage.

Oh, how the women in this club love themselves some nearly naked, gyrating man-meat. I had no idea women went this nuts over male strippers, and I must say I'm fascinated. I can't help thinking the uninhibited female revelry I'm witnessing wouldn't fly *at all* if the genders in this room were reversed. I mean, seriously, if the stripper onstage were a woman and the audience full of men—and if even *one* guy in that hypothetical male audience behaved the way this *entire* female audience is behaving—that skeevy guy would no doubt find himself bounced out of the club faster than he could say, "Show me your tits!" Frankly, he might even be arrested for sexual assault.

Oh my gosh.

My eyes widen to the size of saucers.

My chest tightens.

I put my drink down.

Eureka.

The vague swirl of ideas percolating inside my brain since yesterday has just crystallized into an actual *idea*—and a *brilliant* one, at that, I do believe.

"By George, I think I've got it!" I blurt, slapping my palm onto the table.

All conversation at my table ceases and everyone looks at me expectantly.

"Oh, she's got an idea," Hannah says to everyone, her eyes lighting up. "What is it, honey?'

I can't speak. My brain is whirring and clacking like factory equipment roaring to life after a power outage.

"What kind of idea?" Dax asks, looking genuinely interested.

"For your documentary, honey?" Hannah asks.

I nod.

"Awesome!" Hannah squeals. She looks at the group. "Maddy's got to turn in a huge film project by the end of the year for her documentary filmmaking class and she's been trying to come up with her 'big idea' all summer." Hannah looks at me, her face aglow. "So what's your big idea, lil sissy?"

My heart is absolutely racing with excitement. I can barely speak. I take a deep breath to collect myself. "What if I do a sequel to *Shoot Like a Girl*, only this time set in the world of *stripping* instead of basketball?" I blurt. "The exact same concept—looking at a popular activity slash cultural phenomenon and examining it through the prism of gender? Only this time with *strippers!*"

"Omigosh! I love it!" Hannah gasps, and everyone at the table echoes her enthusiasm.

My pulse is absolutely pounding. "I can feature interviews with strippers of each gender, the same way I did interviews of male and female basketball players, and then I'll juxtapose the fun and lighthearted world of male stripping with the darker, more exploitative world of female stripping—and then dig into the million-dollar question of *why* the difference, you know?" I'm practically panting. Oh my God, I love it when my brain explodes with inspiration like this.

"I'd totally watch that movie," Dax says.

"Me, too," Zander says. "But, um, just double-checking before I pay the price of admission—there'll be at least a *glimpse* of a woman on a pole in this documentary, right?"

Everyone laughs and Zander flashes me a huge smile, telling me he's just messing with me, and I melt under his adorable gaze.

God, I love Zander Shaw. The moment I met him in Dax's apartment a few hours ago, I instantly understood why Keane adores the hell out of him. Which he *so* obviously does, oh my freaking God. Have you ever seen one of those videos where a solider comes home from deployment and is reunited with his beloved Labrador—and the dog is so overcome with joy, his entire body wags? Well, that's exactly what it was like when Keane was reunited with Zander this afternoon (and, yes, just in case you're wondering, Zander was most definitely the returning soldier and Keane the Labrador).

I flash Zander a huge smile across the table. "Well, I make no promises, Z," I say, "but I'd think at least *glimpsing* a woman on a pole in a movie about strippers is a pretty good bet."

"Then count me in."

I laugh with glee, suddenly overcome with excitement. "I really think I'm onto something here. I read up on stripping a little bit while Keane was driving yesterday and what I've learned about the male-female dichotomy is intriguing. It seems male strippers do the job mainly for fun and to boost their egos, way more so than for money, while female strippers, on the other hand, overwhelmingly say they're in it for the money and nothing else. In fact, women overwhelmingly say the job actually *degrades* their self-esteem."

"Wow, you've already researched all that?" Zander says.

"Sounds like you already had a pretty firm grasp on your idea before coming here tonight," Hannah says.

"Not really. It took coming here and seeing this crowd for the idea to click into place."

"Ah, inspiration," Dax says wistfully. "So hard to pin down. I can certainly relate." He grins at me.

"It's gonna be *so* good, Maddy," Hannah says.

"Indubitably," Henn agrees.

"Hey, you could call it *Strip Like a Guy*—that sounds kind of sequel-ish, doesn't it?" Hannah says.

"Omigosh, I love it!" I shout.

Everyone at the table agrees that title rocks.

"Leave it to the PR woman to come up with the badass title," Henn says, looking lovingly at Hannah. He kisses her on the cheek. "You're a fucking genius, babe."

"Aw, Henny," Hannah says, her cheeks glowing.

Henn raises his blue martini to me. "Here's to you, Maddy. It sounds like we're gonna be cheering you on at the Oscars in a couple years, huh? I'll get my tux pressed now, just in case."

Everyone clinks my glass and offers me best wishes, making me blush.

"Thanks so much, guys," I say. I shoot a special smile to Henn. "Thanks, Henn."

He grins at me. "You betcha, pretty lady. Go forth and conquer. We're all cheering you on. If you ever need my help with anything, just lemme know."

"Aw, Henny," my sister says again, sighing. She lays a big kiss on her adorable boyfriend's cheek. "I love you."

Henn lights up at my sister's words of affection. "I love you, too, Banana," he whispers. He turns his face to Hannah's, nuzzles her nose gently, and then plants a soft and sexy kiss on her lips that sends blood whooshing into my crotch. Damn, that nerd can *kiss*.

Aaaaaaaaaaaaaaaaaaand now I'm thinking about last night's incredible kiss with Keane. *Again*. Why does *everything* I see make me think about that damned kiss?

I put my hands over my face, trying to get a grip, but my body is reacting to the memory of last night's passionate kiss with Keane like it's happening right now. For the love of God, I can feel my nipples hardening in my bra. Aaaaaand now I'm thinking about how Keane took my nipple into his mouth, just before I came. Oh, Jesus. Now I'm thinking about the delicious *orgasm* he gave me that rocked my world. And the way he held me on the dance floor in the bar when he told me he liked me too much to treat me like just another notch on his manwhoring belt. And then held me in his arms Lionel Richie style last night.

I sigh wistfully, lost in my thoughts, until an explosion of screams and applause draws my attention to the stage. Oh. It seems the Latin Lover has just finished his *caliente* performance. After blowing kisses to the audience, the guy gathers his clothes off the floor of the stage and makes his way to a cordoned-off table—a table Keane told us earlier is filled with talent scouts and agents, including an agent from the huge talent agency Keane's hoping will sign him tonight.

As the Latin Lover approaches the VIP table, I observe the tepid body language of the people seated there. I could be wrong, of course, but it seems to me they weren't any more enthralled by the Latin Lover than I was.

A wave of nerves crashes into me for Keane. God, I hope he knocks it out of the park tonight. If the industry people at that table see even one-tenth the star potential I see in Keane, who knows what opportunities might come his way?

Zander looks at his watch. "Peenie should be on next."

"He's gonna make everyone else look like chumps," Dax says, sipping his drink.

"He said he's gonna do his *Magic Mike* routine," I offer. "The one where he dances to 'Pony'?"

"Good," Zander says. "That one always slays. Wait 'til you see our boy in action, Maddy—he's gonna blow your mind."

Well, yeah, I know, I think. *I already saw our boy in action last night in the privacy of my motel room and he most definitely blew my mind.*

Aaaaaaaaand now I'm thinking about last night again. The orgasm. His body smashed against mine. His arms. His wet tongue on my breasts. The way he pulled up my tank top and lay on top of me and how my soft, naked breasts molded into his muscular chest. *And that kiss.*

Gah!

I've got to stop this. Keane and I have mutually decided to be *strictly* friends and I've simply got to move on and accept that fact, no matter how much my crotch throbs every time I think about last night's deliciousness.

I take two huge gulps from my glass and drain it.

"Whoa, you want another one, Maddy?" Henn asks, and I nod vigorously.

Henn signals the cocktail waitress. "You okay?" he asks, leaning into me with concern.

I nod again, but I'm a freakin' liar. *I'm not okay.* I'm a woman on the verge of a lust-induced, clit-throbbing nervous breakdown.

"Ladies and gentlemen," the emcee onstage bellows into a microphone, making me shoot upright in my seat. "Put your hands together for a talented gentleman who's come here all the way from the Emerald City to entertain you!"

"Oh, shit, here we go!" Zander yells, rubbing his hands together.

I grab my phone off the table and scramble to set it to record, my hands shaking with nervous excitement.

The emcee continues: "Let's give a warm and rowdy welcome to the man from Seattle with a hammer-in-his-pants... the one and only *Ball Peen Hammer*!"

Chapter 37
Maddy

When Keane swaggers onto center stage like he's the undisputed heavyweight champion of the world—his astonishing blue eyes blazing, his hair spiked to perfection, his chiseled features and bulging muscles accentuated gloriously under the colored stage lights—the audience erupts, already sensing this blue-haired creature standing before them is going to deliver something unlike anything else they've seen tonight.

I hold my phone at the ready as I await the first familiar chords of "Pony," my heartbeat pounding in my ears. But when the music starts, to my surprise the song isn't "Pony." It's the sexy song that auto-played last night after "Trip Switch" had ended—"Itch" by Nothing But Thieves—the song that played when Keane kissed me and made me climax.

Keane lifts his head and scans the room, apparently searching for something specific, and when his eyes land on me, they stop searching.

Without thinking, I put my phone down on the table with a thud and give Keane my undivided attention. *He's looking right at me.* Oh my God.

The sultry vocals of the song begin and, much to the screaming pleasure of the audience, Keane begins moving his hips and touching his torso, his eyes still trained on me.

I put my hand on my chest. Holy hell.

Keane rips off his shirt and throws it down like it's searing his flesh, and the audience explodes into shrieking excitement. A moment later, the chorus of the song kicks into gear and Keane's off to the races. He dips down to the floor, and then onto his hands. He dry-humps the floor with a fierceness that blows last night's display

263

out of the water. And then he hops back up and gyrates his body like a man freakin' possessed.

Wow, the crowd is going absolutely crazy for him. And so am I, though I can't seem to move a muscle.

Keane does an effortless backflip off the edge of the stage and strides with cat-like grace to the front row of the audience. In jaw-dropping, rapid-fire succession, he gives brief lap dances to several women in the front row, acquiring a flurry of crumpled dollar bills in his waistband as he goes, until, finally, he pulls a pretty brunette out of her chair and escorts her to the stage, shaking his ass in his low-riding sweatpants as he goes.

Once Keane's onstage with his pretty brunette, he lays her onto the floor with gentleman-like care, brushes his knuckles against her cheek like she's the great love of his life, and then rises to standing over her, gyrating deliciously the whole time.

First things first, Keane bends down to remove his sweatpants, a move that sends the dollar bills peeking out of his waistband fluttering to the ground—and when he straightens back up in nothing but the teeniest black G-string, every woman in the room, including me, gasps at the jaw-dropping sight of him. Holy hell.

For a long beat, Keane goes stock-still, his almost-naked body hulking over the giggling, prostrate woman onstage beneath him, his chest heaving, his muscles taut under the colored stage lights. He looks pointedly toward the back of the club again—and, this time, when he locates me, his eyes burst into freakin' flames.

And so do my panties.

Oh my God.

Keane moves to the floor alongside his human prop and then proceeds to... well, there's no other way to put it: simulate bonin' the fuck outta her. *Ho-lee shit.*

First, Keane simulates eating her out with shocking zeal, and then he motorboats her breasts. Finally, he places her thighs against his chest, turns his head to stare right at me, and thrusts in and out of her crotch with grinding movements that make me shudder with yearning.

After the thrusting portion of his program is over, Keane leaps up, pulls the blushing, trembling brunette to standing, and positions her facing the crowd. With his eyes trained squarely on mine *again,* he saunters behind the woman (giving the audience an incredible view of his bare ass cheeks as he goes), wraps his muscled arms around the woman's torso from behind, and begins simulating touching her, his hands simultaneously hovering an inch above her breasts and crotch like he's massaging her to orgasm.

Holy crap.

Gimme that.

I feel like I'm on the cusp of a tiny orgasm, just from *watching* him.

When Keane's done "pleasuring" his plaything, he grips her shoulders and shakes her, apparently portraying her body-quaking orgasm, and the entire place leaps to its feet with shrieking appreciation.

But Keane's not done yet. With his scorching eyes still trained on me, he bends his new doll over at the waist, his large hands gripping her hips with dominating authority, and he proceeds to bone the living hell outta her from behind.

Oh my God. I'm transfixed. And soaking wet.

I'm not imagining the meaning of all this, right? He's staring right at me. Playing the song from last night. Fake-fucking a brunette. There's no other interpretation, right? *He's showing me what he wants to do to me.*

And, hell to the yes, I want him to do it. Right effing now.

Keane bends over the woman's back, grabs a fistful of her dark hair, and thrusts into her one last, beastly time, his eyes searing holes into my flesh as he does.

And that's it. I'm gone. Put a fork in me. I'm done. I've got to have him. I don't care what I said last night. And I certainly don't care about his goddamned stupid brother. In fact, I don't care about anything or anyone except *me* and what I want.

And what I want is him.

I want to kiss him. And have sex with him. And then do it again. I want to touch and kiss and lick and suck every inch of that insane body of his, and then do it again. And I want him to touch me, every inch of me, inside and out, all the way inside the deepest, most secret places of my body, and make me come again and again. And then fuck me. And lick me. *And then do it all again.*

No matter what we said to each other last night, or how my

heart's inevitably going to shatter when the pleasure's all gone and there's nothing left but pain, in this moment, I want him like I've never wanted another man.

And, by God, I'm going to get him.

Right freakin' now.

Chapter 38
Maddy

Everyone's laughing and talking excitedly around me at the table about the sheer savagery of Keane's performance, but I can't join them. I'm speechless, my entire body wracked with outrageous desire.

Onstage, Keane gathers up his clothes, slips on his sweatpants, and gallantly escorts his brunette plaything back to her seat. He gives the gushing woman a post-coitus peck on her cheek, flashes his killer dimples, and strides toward the VIP table at the foot of the stage, slipping his T-shirt on as he goes.

When Keane reaches the table, I'm not surprised to observe every single talent scout leaping up to greet him, their enthusiastic body language in stark contrast to the lukewarm reception they've given all prior performers tonight.

After a moment, Keane turns away from the VIPs, looks toward my table way in the back, beckons vigorously, and mouths what looks like, "Maddy."

I'm frozen in my chair. Keane couldn't possibly have just called *me* down there, could he?

"Hey, Maddy," Zander says. "I think Peenie wants you to go down there."

Keane beckons again, this time with unmistakable urgency.

"Yeah, Maddy," Dax says. "Keane definitely wants you."

And I want him, I think. *So take your 'off-limits' proclamation and shove it up your gorgeous rock-star ass, Dax Morgan.* Without saying what I'm thinking (though it would have been so freakin' badass), I rise from my seat and glide across the club toward Keane like he's pulling me on a string.

When I reach Keane, he grabs my hand and pulls me into him.

"This is Maddy Behind the Camera," he says proudly to the VIPs. "Madelyn Milliken."

Everyone says hello to me, and I return their greetings, though I'm utterly confused as to why Keane's introducing me at all.

"Maddy goes to UCLA film school and she won a huge award at a film festival last year for this mind-blowing documentary she made," Keane says. "What was the name of that festival, Maddy?"

I say the name of it and it's clear the VIPs recognize it as something prestigious.

"Maddy's the one who shot all those videos of me," Keane says, flashing a charming smile at the group. "I sling the bullshit and take my clothes off, but Maddy here is the brains behind the operation."

Okay, I think I get what's going on here. Clearly, these talent scouts have seen Keane's videos, and, understandably, their interest in him (and the fan base he's so quickly attracting) is piqued. Well, let's see if I can pique their interest in this blue-haired stripper-man even more.

"I have very little to do with what you see on those videos," I say breezily. "Keane's the one who comes up with everything you see—and all of it on the fly, I might add. After having spent two days on a road trip with this guy to get here from Seattle, I can assure you that what you see on those videos is just the tip of an incredibly talented iceberg. There's no one like Keane. He's a complete original. Endlessly entertaining. Funny. Insightful. At times, totally idiotic. But, always, as you just saw, completely mesmerizing."

Keane blushes a deep crimson and squeezes my hand.

"I'm actually planning to make him the star of my next documentary," I add. "He's just that compelling."

Several VIPs at the table pull out business cards and say they want to arrange auditions with Keane early this coming week, which prompts a dark-haired guy to leap up and proclaim his agency now represents Keane and any and all auditions must be scheduled through his office.

Keane suddenly looks like he could tip over.

"You okay?" I whisper, gripping his hand.

Keane nods.

After the VIPs have shaken Keane's hand and repeated their various intentions to audition him for a bunch of projects early this week, it's obviously time for Keane and me to blow this popsicle stand and let the VIPs watch the next guy onstage, a guy in a firefighter outfit dancing to "Disco Inferno." Keane grabs my hand, pulls me into his body, and begins leading me toward the back of the club.

"Well, that went well," he whispers under his breath. "Ho-lee shit."

"They absolutely loved you," I say.

"We'll see. Nothing in ink yet. Hey, thanks for saying all that cool stuff about me. They ate it up—especially since it was coming from a brilliant, award-winning filmmaker." He squeezes my hand.

"Keane," I blurt, unable to contain myself a moment longer. We're about ten steps from the VIP table, headed to the back of the club where our group is waiting. "I need to talk to you for a second." I swallow hard. "*Alone.*"

Keane abruptly stops walking and looks at me expectantly. "Everything okay?"

I glance around at the screaming audience members surrounding us on all sides, and then at the table filled with our peeps on the far side of the club. "I can't talk about it here," I whisper, my cheeks blazing. "Somewhere where our peeps can't see us."

Keane glances in the direction of our table in the back and then, without a word, pulls me toward the side of the club and around a corner at the end of the bar. Once he's got me nestled into a little alcove that's out of sight from our table, Keane guides my back firmly against a wall and leans his body into mine, his palms on either side of my head. "What's up?" he whispers, his blue eyes smoldering.

My heart is racing. My crotch is throbbing. I can barely breathe. "I can do it," I blurt.

Keane bites his lip, clearly trying to keep a smirk from spreading across his lips. "Do what?"

"Friends with benefits." I let out a shaky breath. "I can totally do it. Oh, God, Keane, I want you."

Keane's eyes darken but he doesn't speak.

"Don't worry—we won't tell a soul," I continue, my breathing ragged. "I promise I won't feel upset or rejected when you go back to Seattle and go back to your manwhoring life. We'll have a no-strings *fling*, just while you're here in L.A., and when you leave, we'll go back to being nothing but friends again." Oh, God, I know I'm rambling, but I can't control myself.

Keane leans forward into me, closing the tiny gap between our bodies. "I'm not up for a relationship," he says, his face an inch from mine. "You know that, right?"

"I don't care about a relationship. I don't want one, either. I'm a man-eater now. New city, new school, new Madelyn." Oh God, I'm trembling. "We'll bone the fuck outta each other while you're in L.A. and when you go back to Seattle, you'll go back to manwhoring and I'll start my downward spiral into utter debauchery, jumping into the sack with any stupid hottie who comes my way and—"

Keane cuts me off by pressing his lips into mine. I throw my arms around his neck and press myself into him, devouring him. When I feel the sensation of his hard-on grinding into me, I press myself into him even harder and moan softly into his mouth, my tongue swirling greedily with his.

After a moment, Keane pulls out of our kiss with a sexy suck on my lower lip, his erection firmly lodged against my crotch. "You're sure you can handle this?" His body is trembling against mine.

I nod, grinding myself into him. "I want you."

"But, listen to me, Maddy. I party for a *living*. I'm not looking for a girlfriend with my life the way it is, especially not a long-distance one. That's not gonna change, no matter how awesome the sex is, which, holy fuck, it's *so* gonna be."

"I understand. I don't want a relationship, either—with you or anyone. I'm turning over a new leaf. I'm a man-eater now." I bite my lip. "And my first meal is *you*."

Keane's eyes flash with heat. "When the fuck did you become *sexy*, Maddy Milliken? Good lord, woman, you turn me on." He takes a deep breath. "Okay, fuck yeah, let's bone, baby doll. Oh my God, I wanna fuck you so bad, my balls are the color of my hair. Come on." He grips my hand and, much to my surprise, pulls me straight toward our table in the back. "First things first, though, we gotta show our faces to Dax or he's gonna think I'm off fucking you in some dressing room." He snickers. "Which is exactly what I'm gonna do as soon as I throw Daxy off the scent."

"We could say we're going backstage to interview some strippers for my next documentary. Right before you went on, I told everyone what I'm gonna do for my next project. Keane, I'm gonna do a sequel to *Shoot Like a Girl*—only this time with strippers."

"Oh my God, babe, that's genius." He squeezes my hand enthusiastically. "Brilliant."

"You'll be in it, right?" I ask, my heart racing. "I want you to be the star of the film the same way Freddie starred in the basketball version. I'll build the story around you as my narrator."

Keane abruptly stops walking. "Are you serious?"

I nod. "We'll see the world of male stripping through your eyes. You'll be on-camera and in voice-overs throughout."

"Wow, I'm honored, Maddy. Yeah, *of course*. Thank you so much."

"Don't thank me, Keane. Thank *you*. You're gonna be a star, I know it. Having you in this film is gonna be a huge coup for me by the time it comes out, I guarantee it."

"No, Maddy. You're the star. Those talent scouts kept asking me about the videos," he says. "They said they loved my performance onstage, but it was the videos that grabbed their attention the most. None of this would be happening without you."

I bite my lip and touch his cheek. "I believe in you."

His cheeks flush. "Thank you. I know you do. I can feel it." Keane lets out an audible sigh. "Oh my fuck. My balls hurt so fucking bad."

I laugh. "Well, then, come on. Let's stop talking and bone, for fuck's sake."

"Yee-boy. First things first, though, let's keep the Morgan Mafia off my ass."

Chapter 39
Maddy

When Keane and I arrive at the table filled with our peeps, everyone leaps up to hug Keane and congratulate him on his take-no-prisoners performance.

Quickly Keane gives everyone the scoop about what just went down at the VIP table and follows that up by telling them our cover story. "So we'll plan on meeting up with all of you when I'm done introducing Maddy to some of the guys backstage," Keane concludes. "Just text us where you're at and we'll find you."

Dax squints at his older brother, clearly suspicious. "So you're gonna go backstage with Maddy to introduce her to strippers?" he asks.

"Yup," Keane answers smoothly. "So she can gather some background info and arrange some future in-depth interviews. Hey, Zander, you wanna hang out with Maddy and me backstage while we schmooze the stripper-brigade?"

I'm shocked. Why the heck did Keane just invite Zander to our private party?

"Awesome," Zander says.

Dax visibly relaxes. He turns his attention to Henn and Hannah, his suspicion apparently quelled. "So you guys wanna maybe go see a band? I think Maps and Atlases is playing with Finch at The Roxy at midnight."

"Why don't we party at my place?" Henn suggests. "I just bought a house around the corner—we'll make it an impromptu housewarming party. Why don't you call Fish and Colin and tell them to bring whoever? I'll call Reed. He just texted me he's back in town and wants to hook up. I'm sure if I promise him I'll breakdance for him at the party, he'll come running with a whole crew of people."

Hannah giggles, apparently in on the joke.

"*Awesome*," Dax says. He looks at Keane. "Hey, Peen Star, you cool with heading over to Henn's place after you three are done here?"

"You bet, Rock Star," Keane answers smoothly. "We'll just Uber it. Go ahead."

"Cool. I'll text you the address," Henn says.

"Thanks."

"Bye, sissy," Hannah says, getting up from her stool. She wraps me into a warm hug and nuzzles her mouth against my ear. "I'll stay at Henn's tonight so you and Magic Mike can have the apartment to yourselves," she whispers.

I stiffen in Hannah's arms. "How'd you know?" I whisper back.

"Oh, Maddy, it's written all over your face."

My stomach clenches. "Don't tell anyone, not even Henn," I whisper softly, my lips pressed into Hannah's hair. "Long story but no one can know. I'll tell you later."

"Roger," she whispers.

"Rabbit," I reply.

Hannah giggles. "You've got your brand new key, roomie?"

I nod. "Thanks, Banana."

Hannah pulls out of our hug. "Have fun hanging out with the strippers, guys," she says at full voice.

"Thanks," Keane, Zander, and I say in unison.

The minute everyone's gone, Keane turns to Zander. "Thanks, wingman. Now go away."

"What?" Zander asks, clearly surprised.

"You're on your own tonight, Z. I just needed to throw Daxy off my scent—he was looking hella suspicious."

Zander laughs. "Oh, Peenie. You're so predictable."

"I like to think of myself as *consistent*."

"What the heck?" I say, heat rising in my cheeks. "I thought this friends-with-benefits thing was supposed to be a gigantic secret?"

"Well, *yeah*, it is—but I tell Z everything. He doesn't count."

"Oh, well, then, I guess I should mention my sister just figured us out. Apparently, she took one look at the expression of unbridled lust on my face and said she'll sleep at Henn's tonight to give us complete privacy." I snicker. "She asked if I have *this*." I hold up my apartment key, my eyebrow raised suggestively.

"*Excellent*," Keane says, his naughty facial expression surely mirroring mine.

I look at Zander. "Which means there's an open bed for you in Hannah's room, Z. No couch-sleeping required tonight."

"Thanks, Maddy. Much appreciated."

"But don't be running back to Maddy's apartment to crash any time soon," Keane warns sharply. "Maddy and I are popping the cork on this bottle for the first time tonight and I'm betting this girl's a screamer."

I gasp. "*Keane*."

"Get used to it, Maddy," Zander says, laughing. "The boy's got zero filter." He scowls at Keane. "But, shit, Peenie. What the fuck am I gonna do for hours by myself? I come all the way down to L.A. to support you and now that you've made me your alibi, I can't go to Henn's party."

"Oh, waah waah," Keane says. "You're in fucking *Hollywood*, Z. Go wander down Hollywood Boulevard and chat with the hookers. Go see a band on The Strip. Or, fuck it, sit in a dark corner of a club and have phone sex with Daphne while watching hot women dance. I don't give a shit what you do, just don't come back to the apartment before the break of dawn."

Zander exhales with frustration. "Shit, I knew I shoulda brought Daphne to L.A. with me," he grumbles.

"For fuck's sake, Z, quit your bitchin'," Keane barks. "Have I *ever* asked you to be my wingman before?"

"No," Zander concedes.

"Not *once*. And I've been yours a thousand times. Well guess what, brah?" Keane points emphatically to his blue hair, his eyes blazing. "*Paybacks are a fucking bitch*."

Chapter 40
Maddy

After a quick detour to the all-night drugstore down the street to stock up on necessary supplies—condoms (self-explanatory), lube (because, according to Keane, "*everything* feels better with lube, baby doll,"), plus a crap-ton of snacks and beer (because, per Keane, "we're gonna need to fuel up at least twice during our marathon sesh")—Keane and I are finally—*finally*—barreling through the front door of my sister's apartment, both of us grunting like gorillas as we kiss and grope each other and tumble through the living room. Once we've crossed the threshold into my bedroom and I've closed the door behind us, I turn around to discover Keane's already naked as the day he was born, just that fast, his hard-on straining like a rocket awaiting final countdown.

"Wow," I breathe, looking at Keane's insane body in the moonlight.

"I wanna fuck you so fucking bad," Keane says, his voice dripping with arousal, his erection massive.

I motion to his dick, my entire body tingling with excitement. "I can see that."

Keane grabs his balls, his eyes smoldering. "You make my balls hurt so fucking bad, baby doll. Do you have any idea what you do to me? Oh my God. You're a monster."

I bite my lip. "Gosh, I'm sorry."

"No, you're not," Keane says, embracing me and kissing my neck. "Hey, how 'bout some tune-age for the festivities? The Talented Mr. Ripley loves music."

"I actually made a playlist this morning in the car," I breathe, my

275

knees buckling with anticipation. "All the songs that remind me of our road trip."

"Well, cue that fucker up. It's bonin' time, baby." He reaches around me and squeezes my ass. "Oh, God, this is gonna be good."

I scramble to my laptop on the dresser, wobbling on my rubbery knees as I move, and quickly cue the music.

At the first notes of my selected kick-off song—"Trip Switch," of course—Keane's face bursts into flames, and before I've even taken two steps away from my computer, he raises my arms above my head, rips my shirt off, and makes quick work of unclasping my bra.

"Perfect," he breathes when my naked breasts bounce free of their bondage. He bends down and takes my left nipple into his wet mouth, growling with desire, and my knees buckle underneath me. I touch his head, steadying myself, and then rake my fingertips through his tousled hair.

Keane unzips my jeans and lowers them to the floor. "I'm gonna make you feel so good," he whispers. He falls to his knees before me and begins licking and nipping at the crotch of my hot pink underwear for a moment, teasing me, torturing me, making me whimper with anticipation, until, finally, *blessedly,* he lowers my underpants to the floor with his teeth.

"Son of a beach ball," I murmur when my knees buckle with desire, making him laugh.

When he straightens up and assesses my naked body, his face is on fire. "You're perfect," he whispers, looking up at me from his knees. "Do you know that?"

I don't know if I should nod or shake my head in reply to that question, so I do neither. "I want you so much," I whisper.

Keane smiles. "Back at ya, baby." With that, he licks his lips, leans into my naked crotch, and devours the living fuck outta me.

"Oh my God," I breathe, my body on fire. I reach behind me and grasp the dresser at my back to steady myself. Oh, sweet Jesus, my entire body is already warping with pleasure.

Keane lets out a sound that makes it clear he's enjoying the meal he's enthusiastically eating between my legs, and I spread my legs wider, making it as easy for him as possible to devour every inch of me. When a body-clenching pressure begins building inside my abdomen, I grab a fistful of Keane's hair and yank roughly, desperate for my release.

Keane moans between my legs, and the sound of his arousal sends goose bumps up my spine.

"You taste so good," Keane growls from between my legs, his fingers sliding in and out of my wetness as he eats me. "You're delicious."

Oh my God, no one's ever touched and licked and sucked me the way Keane's doing, not to mention doing all of it while whispering to me that I'm "delicious." I've never been so turned on, so deliriously high on arousal in all my life.

Keane nips at my clit, skimming it with his teeth, and it spasms violently in response.

"That's it," Keane growls. "Come on, sweetheart." He ramps up the motion of his fingers inside me. "Come to papa." He slides his wet fingertip from my crotch straight into my ass crack and presses it firmly against my anus—a move that tells me he thinks the finish line is coming any minute now.

Knowing Keane's poised and ready to feel an orgasm ripple through me instantly becomes a self-fulfilling prophecy. In a torrent of outrageous pleasure, my clit and everything connected to it clenches and releases forcefully, prompting me to grip Keane's head with white knuckles and shove myself fervently into his hungry mouth.

"That's right, baby," Keane coos. "Oh, God. Nice one."

When my climax ends, I open my mouth to beg Keane to "make love to me," the only words I've ever used in moments such as this in the past, but, immediately, I stop myself. Obviously, those words are completely wrong for a no-strings fling with a baby-dolling stripper-man.

"Fuck me, Keane," I grit out, yanking on his hair, my pelvis thrusting and writhing with my desire. "Bone the fuck outta me."

Keane growls his approval as he comes to a stand. "Patience, sweetheart. First things first." He kisses me deeply and leads me to the bed, just as the next song on my playlist—"Like Real People Do" by Hozier—randomly starts playing.

Keane lays me down on my back and climbs on top of me, his erection spearing me just to the side of my wet entrance. Perhaps inspired by the lyrics of the beautiful song, Keane begins kissing me passionately, stroking gently between my legs, and quickly sending me into a desire-induced stupor. *Oh my God.* If there's a greater pleasure in the world than this sensuous touching and kissing I'm experiencing right this very moment, then—

Oh.

Shit.

Scratch that.

There's *definitely* a greater pleasure than the kissing and gentle touching from two seconds ago—it's the way Keane's touching me *right this freaking second.*

Keane's fingers are deep, deeeeeeep inside me and he's touching me in a way I've most definitely never experienced before. Holy hell, whatever he's doing is freakin' amazing. He's swiping at some specific spot deep inside me like a tiny windshield wiper, over and over, kissing me as he does. His strokes are firm and confident. His tongue in my mouth is confident but not overbearing. Ooph, this feels good.

"You're so fucking hot, Maddy," Keane says into my ear, his fingers working me. He nuzzles his nose into my hair and inhales deeply. "You're sexy as hell, baby. Your pussy is getting so wet for me."

Jesus Christ. This feels good. What the hell is he doing to me?

I reach down and stroke Keane's hard-on with fervor, sucking on his lower lip as I do, bucking underneath him with my rampant desire, and he shudders with excitement.

The song switches to the rocking "Are You Gonna Be My Girl" by Jet just as my body hits some sort of overload. Oh, Jesus. I'm gonna come.

I increase the speed on the hand job I'm giving him, writhing like a madwoman, spreading my legs desperately, aching to relieve the insane pressure building so pleasurably inside me. When a bead of sticky wetness oozes from the tip of Keane's penis onto my hand, I moan with excitement.

"Oh shit," Keane chokes out. "You gotta stop that. Fuck, I'm gonna lose it. Stop."

I stop, though every fiber of my body craves sending him over the edge.

Keane's fingers are still going. He leans over and kisses my breast, swirling his wet tongue over my nipple.

Oh my... hell. I'm so aroused I can't breathe.

All of a sudden, there's a slushing sound coming from deep inside me... wait, what the hell is that sound? It's the exact noise someone would make if they were sloshing across the floor in rain-filled rubber boots.

"There you go, baby," Keane says, his eyes blazing. "Can you feel how wet you are now?"

Oh my God. What's he doing to me?

"Ever been this wet before?" Keane asks.

"No," I choke out. "What's happening to me?"

"You're gonna come in a whole new way," Keane growls, his fingers still strumming that same precise spot inside me. "Hardest you've ever come. You feel it coming?"

I whimper and nod, on the verge of shrieking like a madwoman.

"You feel tight inside? Like you're gonna rip apart?"

I can't reply. I shriek and moan again.

"Let it go, baby," he coos. "Think about nothing but how good this feels," Keane commands, sucking on my nipple. "Let your body go for me. Sit and submit, baby doll. Do as I say."

I growl, trying to hold back what feels like impending insanity. "Yes," I breathe. "Oh, God. *Yes.*"

"Grab my cock again. Feel how hard and wet I am for you. How much I wanna fuck you."

I grab his erection and stroke him furiously, my arousal turning into an acute ache.

"You feel how hard I am for you?"

"Yes," I grunt out, my back arching.

"That's for you. 'Cause you turn me on so fucking much."

I can't take it anymore. Without meaning to do it, I let out a guttural wail.

"That's it. You're gonna come harder than you ever have," he whispers. "A whole new way. Gonna change your life. Feel my hard cock. Feel how much I want you. Imagine me fucking you with it, in and out, making you feel so fucking good."

"Keane," I gasp.

That slushing sound is getting embarrassing, but I can't control it. I'm beginning to convulse. Oh, God, my core is doubling over upon itself, coiling, ratcheting, folding like a defective deck chair possessed by demons. I hold my breath, instinctively bracing for the tidal wave that's surely about to slam into me and rock my world.

Without warning, a fingertip glides with ease up my anus, as that same magical hand continues its steady swiping movement deep inside me, and it's like he's tripped a switch I didn't even know I had.

I scream and let go of Keane's erection, suddenly unable to control my limbs. Out of nowhere, I'm wracked with the most violently pleasurable orgasm of my life—a full-bodied seizure emanating from a place so deep inside me, it feels like it's ripping me in two.

Without meaning to do it, I begin thrashing wildly next to Keane, overcome by the agony of the pleasure I'm experiencing. I slam my palms down on the mattress, arch my back, and grip the bedspread with white knuckles. I feel my eyes rolling back into my head, but I can't stop them. "*Keeeeeeeeeane!*" I scream, my entire body quaking.

"That's it," Keane purrs into my ear, his voice low and intense, his wet hard-on sliding against my skin. "Your nipples look amazing, baby. Ooph, you're hot as fuck. I can't wait to fuck this wet pussy and feel you from the inside-out."

"Oh, shit," I cry out at top volume. "Yes!" I shriek. "Keane!"

Oh, Jesus God. I'm flopping like a dying fish, bucking and convulsing without control. Gibberish is spewing out of my mouth.

"That's it, baby," Keane says calmly. "You're speaking in tongues, baby."

When my body finally stops shuddering and my limbs are my own again, I wipe at my eyes, gasping for air, and I'm shocked to feel wetness streaming down my cheeks. Oh Mylanta. Keane made me come so freaking hard I *cried*?

"Keane," I whisper, my body splayed on the bed in a mangled heap. "*Thank you.*"

Keane kisses me tenderly, pressing the full length of his glorious body against mine, molding my soft curves into his body's hardness. "Did that feel good?"

I nod, unable to speak.

Keane bites my earlobe. "Welcome to the big leagues, sweetheart," he whispers, his erection grinding against me insistently. "You're A-spot cherry's officially been popped."

"Fuck me," I gasp, clutching at him desperately.

"Oh, God, that's all I wanna do," he groans. "But not yet." He exhales a shaky breath. "I'm gonna give you a night to remember, sweetheart."

"Keane, no. There's no way I can—"

He slides his fingers inside me again and I immediately stop talking. *Oh.*

That feels amazing.

I don't know how it's possible, but Keane's working his unbelievable magic on me *again*—and this time my body's ramping up twice as fast as before.

Wow.

Somehow, I'm not ultra sensitive like I usually am after an orgasm. I'm only ready and aching for more.

Approximately four minutes later, I'd guess, I'm shrieking at the top of my lungs again as my body convulses with an even more forceful orgasm than the one before.

"How the hell are you doing this to me?" I choke out when the waves of pleasure have subsided and I'm left twitching on the mattress like a fish on a riverbank.

Keane brushes a lock of sweaty hair off my cheek. "It's The Sure Thing, baby doll. I told you. Works like a charm."

"But what the hell are you doing up in there? Show me."

Keane puts his hand in front of my face and moves his middle finger in a steady and simple "come hither" motion.

"That's it?"

"Yeah—but, you know, I'm doing it *right*. I'm touching the exact spot and I'm using the right amount of pressure and speed. Oh, and I'm dirty-talking into your ear like a motherfucker the whole time, as I'm sure you've noticed—that's big. Otherwise, you run the risk of losing concentration and letting your mind drift to whether you paid the electric bill or set the DVR or some other life-shit like that." He smirks. "Plus, dirty-talk is just plain hot. I *love* it. So, yeah, I touch you like I showed you, use the right pressure and speed, dirty-talk the fuck outta ya, and that's it. Those are all the ingredients to the soup. Bam-bam-bam! Honey Bunches of O's." He winks.

I clutch my chest, sitting up. "This is life-changing for me. Do you know that? I'll never be the same again."

281

Keane's eyes sparkle. "That's the idea, babe. Now you know you can do this, you'll never settle for less."

"Let's do it again," I say excitedly. "One more, okay?"

"As many more as you want, baby doll. I got all night."

I lie back down giddily, my nipples rock-hard. "Oh my God. I'm in heaven."

"That makes two of us," Keane says. He kisses me passionately, his fingers caressing my breasts at first and then trailing down my torso and slipping inside me. And, by God, after only a few minutes of touching deep inside me and whispering all kinds of sexy things into my ear, I come *again*. Just as hard, if not harder, than before. And, after that, against all odds, he does it *again*, and then again, each time easier to achieve and more pleasurable than the last.

By the time Keane's finished with me, I'm a writhing, incoherent, sweaty beast. A cat in heat. A raw piece of meat. *And I've never felt more alive in my life.*

"I can't take it any more," I breathe, undulating on the bed. "Fuck me, Keane."

Keane rolls off me abruptly and grabs a nearby condom packet off the nightstand. "Oh my God, you're a sexy beast." He quickly rolls the condom onto his erection and moves to my laptop. "How about a little 'Itch' by Nothing But Thieves for the festivities?"

"Perfect."

Keane cues the song and turns around to face me, his eyes smoldering. "Oh my God, what have you done to my poor, poor balls, you inhuman monster?" He crawls onto the bed. "You like torturing me, is that it?" With a guttural growl of excitement, Keane opens my legs, rests my thighs on his muscled chest, and slides into my wetness like a hot knife in warm butter, groaning as he does. "Oh, thank you, God," Keane exhales, his body thrusting in and out of me. "Oh my fuck, you feel amazing. Thank you, lord above."

I'm enraptured. Oh, good lord. A man inside me has never felt this good. My body is receiving him like nothing I've felt before. I'm absolutely ravenous for him. And *so* freakin' wet. I had no idea my body could get this wet from so deep inside. Oh my God, this feels nothing like any of the sex I've had before. This is beyond pleasure. This is ecstasy.

As the song barrels into its first chorus, I grip Keane's face and pull him to me for a kiss, my body moving with his, and he responds by devouring my mouth as his erection pumps in and out of me.

"Oh, God, I love fucking you," Keane whispers into my lips.

I fucking love you, too, I think, but instantly realize my stupid brain's mistake. Oh my hell, my brain just scrambled Keane's words. I must be in an orgasm-induced stupor.

"I love *fucking* you," I reply slowly, taking great care to say the words in the correct order.

"You feel so fucking good," Keane growls on top of me. "Oh, fuck, I'm trying to hang on," he grits out. "But you feel too good."

I clutch Keane to me, concentrating on nothing but what my body's feeling.

"God, I love fucking you," he groans.

"And I love fucking you," I say again, just as carefully as the last time, making damn sure my stupefied brain's not screwing it up.

"Oh fuck," Keane says. "Fuck, fuck, fuck, so good."

"Itch" comes to an end, filling the room with brief silence, and I sigh with relief. Now maybe my crazy-ass brain will stop turning everything into a freakin' fairytale.

Keane kisses me deeply, his body clearly on the cusp of release, just as the next song starts. And fuck my life, it's Lana Del Rey's "Blue Jeans." Why the hell did I put this song on the playlist? Just because it happened to play during our road trip is no good reason to put it on a freakin' playlist!

Keane thrusts into me deeply, his kisses passionate, his body clearly reaching a boiling point, and I reply with heated gyrations and groans of my own, my body on the verge of total and complete ecstasy. But, oh my God, how am I supposed to have no-strings sex while listening to *this* song? Is Lana Del Rey trying to send a subliminal message straight to my heart? Because as Lana sings her song about eternal love and brutal heartbreak, my stupid heart is beginning to adopt her words as my own.

Yes, as Keane's body moves so deliciously inside mine and he kisses me with heart-stopping passion, I'm suddenly having a premonition about what lies ahead for me when this "no-strings fling" with Keane is done: I'm going to wind up just like Lana Del Rey in "Blue Jeans"—heartbroken.

And there's not a damned thing I can do about it.

Chapter 41
Keane

Saturday, 2:46 a.m.

I'm deep-fucking Maddy Milliken to within an inch of her life to Akon's "Smack That," and holy motherfuck, it feels good. She's bent over the bed taking every inch of me, my hands variously working her clit, fondling her gorgeous tits, smacking that round ass of hers, and grabbing fistfuls of her hair.

Who knew a pretty, smart girl I actually *like* would turn out to be the hottest sex of my life? Everything Maddy does turns me on. Every sound she makes. The way she responds so enthusiastically to every little thing I do to her. She's my new favorite toy.

"You turn me on so much," I growl at Maddy, and she moans her reply. "You're so sexy, baby. Oh, fuck, this feels good. You make me wanna come so hard," I whisper into her ear, my body on the verge of release. "God, I love fucking you."

Maddy yelps, clearly on the cusp of losing it along with me.

Damn, this is good. And totally unexpected. I knew sex with Maddy would be *good*—stealing cookies outta the cookie jar is always a fun pastime—but I didn't know 'good' and 'fun' could also be this *addicting*. If I'd known sleeping with a pretty, smart girl was gonna feel *this* amazing, I'd have done it a long time ago.

Maddy lets out a tortured wail and I can feel her muscles clenching and releasing around my cock. Oooooh, fuck, that's the best feeling in the world. Oh, shit. I can't hang on. This is too hot.

In a sudden flood of pleasure, my body releases with Maddy's until we both collapse onto the bed in a sweaty heap.

Oh my God, this cookie right here is a drug and I'm a motherfucking drugstore cowboy, baby. Wooh! Maddy Milliken is

284

officially the tastiest cookie I've ever stolen in my entire fucking life. *Yee-boy*!

I roll off Maddy and slap her ass once more for good measure, making her flinch. "Dude," I say. "This friends-with-benefits thing was a stupendously fantastic idea."

Chapter 42
Keane

"She's so hot," I say, looking across the room at Maddy. I sip my beer. "She's a stealth-hottie—just kinda creeps up on ya from outta the bushes. What's that thing that hides in bushes and then sneaks out and kills you?"

I'm talking to Zander, of course. We're sitting on a shabby couch in the green room of The Viper Room, waiting for my brother and his band to take the stage in about an hour. Maddy's across the room with the band, shooting "behind the scenes" footage for some video she promised to make for them, and I can't take my eyes off her.

"Something that hides in bushes, sneaks out, and kills you?" Zander asks. "A snake?"

"No, no, Maddy's not a *snake*. I'm talking about that little mammal thing that does that."

"A little *mammal* that hides in bushes, sneaks out, and *kills* you? You mean like a lion?"

"No, not a *lion*. Something *little*, like a... I don't know what it's called. That's the whole reason I'm asking you."

"There's no such animal, Peenie."

"No?"

"No."

"Oh, well, there is now. It's called a Maddy Milliken, son." I watch Maddy across the room for a long beat, marveling at how sexy she is. "I love watching Maddy when she's being Little Miss Documentary Filmmaker," I say, my eyes still trained across the room. "Look how her face is all *passionate* and shit. Mmm mmm! Good stuff, son." I swig my beer again. "Sexy little thing."

Zander doesn't reply.

286

Across the room, Maddy shares a laugh with Fish, the bassist in 22 Goats. She's asking him questions on camera and totally connecting with him (a fact that doesn't surprise me at all, since it seems Maddy quietly connects with everyone she meets, despite that bullshit she keeps telling me about her supposed shyness).

"Oh, hey, bee tee dubs, I meant to tell you. Just in case Dax mentions it, I told him me, you and Maddy got shanghaied last night by a horde of male strippers and got too shitfaced to stumble over to Henn's party."

"Okay. Got it."

I take another sip of beer and watch Maddy for a long beat. "It's always the quiet ones that surprise you," I say. "Oh, look at her now. She's got her game face on, brah. She's so adorable. God-*damn*, she's something else."

"Peen," Zander says softly.

I peel my eyes off Maddy to glance at Zander and I'm surprised to find him staring at me with what I'd call "what the fuck are you doing?" eyes.

"What?" I ask.

"What the fuck are you doing?" Zander asks (confirming that, yes, I can read my wife like a book).

"What do you mean?" I ask.

"I mean, 'What the fuck are you doing?'"

"Well, let's see. Hmm. Right now, I'm drinking beer with my beloved wife, waiting for my rock-star brother to take the stage in Hollywood, California, baby—*yee-boy!*—and watching a sexy little stealth-hottie sneak outta the bushes and slay me with her supreme hotness." I wink at Zander and sip my beer. "Good times."

Zander doesn't look amused. "No. I mean, what the fuck are you doing with *Maddy*?"

I smile, thinking about my marathon sesh with Maddy last night for the millionth time today. "A whole lot more than *sussing* her, I can tell you that." I snort and sip my beer.

But Zander doesn't laugh. In fact, he's strangely quiet.

"What?" I ask.

"What's going on, Peenie?"

"I'm... What do you mean? Maddy and I are doing a friends-with-benefits thing, that's all."

"Doesn't seem like it."

"Well, we are."

"Sure seems like a helluva lot more than that."

I let out a puff of air, surprised. "Nope. Just having good times with a particularly delicious cookie I stole from a jar."

Zander looks perturbed. "I think maybe you're giving out some mixed signals to this girl, Peenie."

"Pfft. Absolutely nothing *mixed* here, baby doll, except maybe a little cookie dough, if you know what I mean." I wink and flash Zander my dimples, but he's not having it. I exhale. "Dude, no worries, okay? Maddy and I had 'the talk' right from the start and we both agreed to fling from the rafters all the livelong day. No mixed signals—no one gets hurt—everything's clear."

Zander glances across the room covertly and then back at me. "At lunch with everyone today, I saw you secretly grab Maddy's hand under the table."

I feel my cheeks flush. "So?"

"So she looked *really* happy when you did that."

"Yeah? So what? A guy can't secretly hold hands with the chick he's flinging with?"

Zander shrugs. "Not usually. In fact, that little hand-holding maneuver looked a whole lot like good ol' fashioned *affection*, baby doll—like grade-school butterflies. Nothing fling-y about it. Peenie, you only let go of her hand when the food came."

"Well, yeah. I like holding Maddy's hand—so sue me. I told you the other day: she's my *friend*. Friends hold hands."

"No, they don't."

"Sure, they do. Well, sometimes they do."

"I'm your friend and you never hold my hand."

I reach for Zander's hand and hold it tenderly for a long beat. "Feel better now?"

Zander shakes my hand off. "Be serious, Peen. I'm trying to tell you something important here."

I wave him off. "You just don't understand my friendship with Maddy. It's unique. We held hands and cuddled before we ever even thought of having sex. It's just what we do. I told you—she's my adorbsicles, cutie patootie *friend*."

"Well, don't you think when you hold the hand of your

adorbsicles, cutie patootie friend *after* having sex with her Lionel Richie style, a display of affection like secret hand-holding might send a subliminal message to the *relationship*-center in the girl's brain?" Zander asks.

I clench my jaw. Zander just doesn't understand Maddy and me. When it comes to Maddy, normal rules don't apply. "Flinging with Maddy is different than flinging with some stupid chick I don't even like," I explain.

"Dude, you touch her *all the time*," Zander says. "You move her hair outta her eyes. You touch her arm to get her attention, rather than just saying her name. Shit, Peenie, on the drive over here, in the space of three minutes, I saw you rub her neck, rest your hand on the *inside* of her thigh, and then kiss her motherfucking hand like you're some sort of white knight in Camelot."

"Wow, you've been keeping track of every time I touch her? That's not creepy or anything, Z. You feeling left out, baby doll?"

"Dude, I'm not keeping track of shit—that's my entire point. I'm just living my life in the same general vicinity as you, letting my eyes wander in all natural directions the way any normal person would do—and that's all the shit I just so *happened* to witness between the two of you in a matter of *minutes*. Shit, Peenie, if I saw all *that* when I wasn't even *watching* you, then what the fuck else are you doing to this poor girl when I don't happen to glance in your direction?"

Okay, now I'm getting pissed—an emotion I don't often feel toward Zander. This is the kind of third-degree I'd expect from Colby. "*'Poor girl'*?" I seethe in an angry whisper. "Hardly. I'm giving that girl the ride of her life, believe me. So what if I've gotten into the habit of touching Maddy outside the bedroom? During our road trip, we touched and cuddled and held hands all the time. That's just how our friendship is. *We touch*. It just means we like each other. I like touching her. She's a particularly affectionate person and I like that. There's nothing wrong with that."

"No, there's nothing wrong with it, unless you're giving her the wrong idea."

"I'm not. We talked about it. She understands."

"What does she understand?"

"When I leave town and go back home, it's over."

"But can't you see the way she looks at you?"

"Yeah—like I'm an idiot." I snort.

Zander's facial expression tells me he's not amused. "No, Peenie. In fact, I think Maddy might be the only person in the entire world besides me who *doesn't* look at you like you're an idiot."

I exhale and look up at the ceiling. "So what's your point? Are you saying I've fucked up here by partaking in the dabble? Because I haven't. Maddy's the one who said we oughta do this fling-thing, *not me*. She said I could steal from the cookie jar while I'm here and she wouldn't get hurt, so that's exactly what I'm doing—I'm bingeing on cookies, but only while I'm in town. When I get back home, we've *both* agreed, like adults, that everything's gonna go back to normal and we're gonna be friends again and nobody will get hurt."

Zander sighs.

"What the fuck, Zander? I just met this girl. I don't even know her. There's no alternative."

Zander scoffs at that.

"I'm not like you, Z. I don't fall head over heels when I see someone across a crowded room."

"Too bad for you. It's fun."

"It's not normal how you do that, bee tee dubs. I've been meaning to tell you—it's totally *weird*."

Z scoffs again. "Please don't try to tell me what's normal and what's not, Peenie. I love you, man, so fucking much—but you're seriously not the right person to teach me any life lessons about what's *normal*."

I grit my teeth.

"Baby doll, I'm just telling you to watch your step. Her heart's on the line. It's written all over her adorbsicles face. Be careful."

"Goddammit, Z. Why are you telling me this? You know when I was on the road playing ball I couldn't keep a girlfriend happy if my life depended on it—and I was fucking miserable whenever I tried. If that lifestyle taught me anything it's that, if I'm gonna have a relationship with anyone, no matter who it is, it's gotta be with a girl I can actually touch every fucking night of my life. I need that Z; it's who I am. I'm not a guy who can have a girlfriend on FaceTime."

"But isn't the whole point of you auditioning with that agency 'cause you're thinking about moving to L.A.?"

"Well, yeah, *if* the right opportunity presents itself," I say. "But

I'm not counting on anything. I've been disappointed before, I could be disappointed again. No expectations, man—that's the key to happiness. Now stop stressing me out. You're bad for my chi. For fuck's sake, Zander, I'm telling you it was Maddy who suggested we—"

In the middle of my sentence, the door to the green room opens and Mr. Music Mogul himself, Reed Rivers, the man with my brother's dreams in the palm of his hand, strides into the room—and, just like that, I completely forget whatever I was about to say.

Chapter 43
Keane

After entering the green room, The World's Most Interesting Man heads over to Maddy, Dax, and his bandmates Fish and Colin on the other side of the room, not even glancing at Zander and me on the couch as he goes.

I stand, intending to cross the room and grab Maddy's hand, but Reed's comment stops me.

"No, don't let me interrupt you," Reed is saying to Dax. He motions toward the couch where Zander and I are sitting. "I'll just hang out over there with Frick and Frack 'til you're done."

"No, really," Dax says. "We can shoot another time."

"No, no, finish what you're doing. I've got an 'emergency' email to respond to real quick, anyway. Carry on. Henn and Hannah should be here soon. Get as much done as you can before they get here."

Without waiting for Dax's reply, Reed saunters over to the small refrigerator in the corner, grabs a beer, and then plops down next to me on the couch.

"Hey, Reed," I say, putting out my hand. "Keane Morgan, Dax's brother. Also known as 'Frick.'"

"Yeah, I remember you from our week in paradise. You're pretty hard to forget." He chuckles. "*Peen*, right?" He shakes my hand. "Nice hair."

"Thanks. Good to see you again."

Reed looks at Zander. "Hey, 'Frack.' You were at Josh and Kat's wedding, too, right?"

Zander nods and puts his hand out. "Zander Shaw."

"That's right. Great to see you again, Zander. As I recall, you stole all my money in a poker game the night before the wedding."

Zander laughs. "Yeah. Sorry about that."

292

"Apologies are cheap. I'll just exact my revenge on you when you least expect it."

Zander chuckles.

Wow. I'm surprised Reed remembers Zander and me from my sister's weeklong wedding-shindig in Hawaii last year. Sure, Zander and I partied with the dude plenty of times during that incredible week—my brother-in-law, Josh, rented out an entire swanky resort for all their wedding guests and we partied nonstop like it was 1999—but that was almost a year ago, after all. Plus, Reed was obviously having so much fun partying with his inner circle of best friends, Josh and Henn included, I didn't expect him to remember anyone else from that week, least of all peons like Zander and me.

"Excuse me for a sec, guys," Reed says, holding up his phone. "I've got to respond to an 'emergency.'" He rolls his eyes and looks down at his phone.

When Reed begins tapping out an email with obvious annoyance, Zander and I exchange a "wow, this dude's got so much fucking swagger" look. Even if I'd never heard of Reed Rivers and didn't know he's got the hottest indie record label in the world right now (which would mean I'm living under a rock, because the dude's all over magazines and celebrity websites on the daily), I'd nonetheless be leaning over to Zander to whisper, "Who's the guy with the big dick?"

Speaking of big dicks, The Talented Mr. Ripley's feeling mighty lonely. I glance at Maddy longingly across the room. Damn, I wanna fuck that little vixen again. I pull out my phone and tap out a quick text: "I wanna bone the fuck outta u so fucking bad, Maddy Milliken. Do u LIKE making my balls hurt, u evil woman?"

When her phone buzzes with my incoming text, Maddy grabs it from her pocket, looks at it stone-faced, types something in reply without displaying a hint of emotion, and stows her phone in her back pocket again.

My phone buzzes with an incoming text and I look down.

"Yes," Maddy's text says, and nothing more.

Ooph, talk about swagger. Damn. That's a sexy girl.

"So, hey, Keane," Reed says, drawing my attention away from my phone. "You still Seattle's answer to Magic Mike?"

"Yeah," I say, shocked Reed remembers what I do for a living.

"Still livin' the dream, dolin' out fantasies to the horny ladies one lap dance at a time."

Reed chuckles and looks at Zander. "And do you shake your ass for a living, too?" Reed asks politely. "Sorry, I don't remember what you do."

"Naw," Zander says. "I'm a personal trainer. When I shake my ass, I do it behind closed doors for one special lady at a time, no cash exchanged."

"Nice." Reed smiles. "You live in L.A.?"

Zander shakes his head. "Seattle, with Keane. We're actually thinking about moving to L.A., though. Peen's got some big auditions this week and I can do personal training anywhere."

Reed looks at me. "Auditions?"

"A bunch of different stuff. We'll see. It's all up in the air right now."

"He's being modest," Zander says. "He just got signed to one of the top talent agencies in L.A. Modeling, acting, the whole nine yards. They're big."

"Which agency?" Reed asks.

I tell him.

"Oh, a good one. Congrats. The real deal. Keep me posted—" Reed's phone buzzes and he looks down at it, obviously reading something. "Fuck. I gotta answer this. Excuse me."

While Reed busies himself on his phone again, I gaze across the room at Maddy. Sexy little thing. Ooph. I tap out another text to her. "Ur ass is sexy in those jeans," I write. "Can't stop thinking about how I slapped it last night."

Maddy pulls her phone out of her pocket and looks at it. This time she can't help but smile at the message before she stows her phone in her pocket, without replying.

Damn, that's some serious swagger. She didn't even reply? *Nice.* She's keeping me guessing. I love it. I type out another text: "After 22 Goats, right after the headliner has started their set, meet me just outside the side exit."

Maddy glances at her screen again, taps out a reply, and shoves her phone back into her pocket without even a glance in my direction.

My phone buzzes with an incoming text. "YASSSSSSSSSSS," Maddy writes.

"Oh my fucking God," Reed mumbles, stuffing his phone into his pocket. "This little diva on my roster doesn't like the bodyguard we hired for her. What a pain in the ass. I guess he wasn't 'attractive' enough for her." Reed rolls his eyes at us as if to say, "You know how it is," but, of course, Zander and I don't know how it is when an artist on our label demands a new bodyguard. Reed's eyes train on Zander. "Hey, do you happen to have any training whatsoever in any kind of fighting techniques?"

"Um, yeah. Some. I've done quite a bit of boxing and kick-boxing over the years."

"Perfect. You ever thought about being a bodyguard?"

Zander bristles. "Why? Because I'm black and I've got muscles?"

"Uh, *yeah*," Reed says without hesitation, and we all chuckle at his honesty. "You've got the perfect look—and that's more than half the job description for a bodyguard in the music industry. This isn't the secret service, man—the music biz is all about an artist having a 'dope entourage.' We leave the real security to the professionals."

"Gotcha," Zander says, smiling. "And, yeah, to answer your question, I've thought about throwing my hat in that particular ring lots of times. I was just keeping you on your toes."

"As you should." Reed pulls out his card and hands it to Zander. "Well, if you wind up moving down here, shoot me a text. Maybe I'll give you a test run with one of my particularly annoying divas—see if you've got the chops."

"Thanks." Zander shoves Reed's card into his pocket. "I will."

"Everyone loves Zander," I say. "Better make your divas sign a waiver 'cause they're all gonna fall in love with him."

Reed laughs. "Awesome. Well, definitely give me a call when you move down here." Reed turns to me. "So how's Little G? I haven't seen that kid in months."

"Oh my God, she's getting so big. Hang on." I pull out my phone and show Reed and Zander the latest video of Gracie in the bathtub with my sister.

"Whoa," Reed says, laughing. "She's *huge*. Shit, man, time's flying. I gotta get up there and say hi to that kid so she doesn't forget her favorite uncle."

"Hey now," I say. "Dem's fighting words, Reed Rivers. I don't give a shit who the fuck you are or how many platinum records you got hanging on your office wall, nobody tramples on my sacred territory as Little G's favorite uncle." I point at my hair. "No one can compete with this shit, dude, so don't even try. When it comes to being a cool uncle, I can't miss 'cause I'm practically a toddler myself."

Reed's laughing his ass off. "What's the deal with the hair, by the way? Bad acid trip?"

Zander laughs.

"Oh, you think it's funny, Z? Nice of you to laugh considering I dyed it to help you get laid."

"I can't even begin to fathom how those two things are connected."

I tell Reed the whole story and he seems highly amused.

"Wow," Reed says. "Now *that's* a wingman. You owe him one, Zander."

"Yeah, I know. Peenie's the best," Zander says, clinking my beer.

"You can party with me anytime, Keane. Sounds like you're a good dude to have around."

"I'm just a giver, Reed—it's a blessing and a curse."

Reed laughs. "So did Faraday give you a ration of shit for your hair?"

"Of course. You know him. No one's safe under the best of circumstances. Add blue hair to the mix? Forget about it. I believe Josh's comment was, 'Hey look, the entire cast of *My Pretty Pony* took a shit on Peen's head.'"

Reed chuckles. "That sounds like him. What'd your brothers say?"

I purse my lips, thinking. "Well, let's see. Ryan sang the 'C is for Cookie' song from *Sesame Street.*"

Reed busts up. "Nice."

"Dax said he wants to fuck me now because he's always had a thing for Marge Simpson."

Reed and Zander laugh pretty hard at that one.

"Well, that's interesting," Reed says.

"Someone said Thing One crapped on my head while Thing Two barfed on it. I think that was a one-two punch from Kat and someone else."

"Ah, Stubborn Kat," Reed says. "She never disappoints. Love that girl."

"You can have her."

Reed laughs. "Did anyone say, 'Hey, Little Boy Blue, where's your motherfucking horn?'"

"Shockingly, no."

"Okay, well, that's my contribution."

"Cool. Thanks for playing. You're now an honorary Morgan. In fact, I tell you what: I'll bump Kat outta the family and you can take her spot."

"Thanks."

There's laughter from the other side of the room. Maddy's got all three guys from 22 Goats cracking each other up in some sort of group interview.

"What's the video they're shooting?" Reed asks.

"Some sort of promo for the album release. I'm not sure," I say.

"Really? Well, that's not necessary. I've got an entire marketing department working on all kinds of stuff for the album release, including *professional* videos. They certainly don't need to do an amateur one—we've got it covered. In fact, that's why I'm here tonight—to tell the guys about something cool I just got lined up for them for the album launch."

I bristle. I don't particularly like the way Reed just said "professional" and "amateur," implying Maddy's some kind of hack. "Well, either way, you're probs gonna want to have this video Maddy's making in your vault, brah," I say. "Maddy's no hack. She's studying film at UCLA and she won a top award at this prestigious documentary film festival last year. I saw her film and I'm not exaggerating when I say it's fucking brilliant."

Reed looks over at Maddy, clearly surprised.

"I bet when you see the video she's doing for Dax, you're gonna want her to do more of the same for your other bands, too. She's just that good."

"Wow, I had no idea," Reed says, still staring at Maddy across the room.

"Hell yeah. She's a star on the rise. Mark my words." I tell Reed a bit about the awesomeness of *Shoot Like a Girl* and he seems genuinely interested.

"It's really that good?" he asks.

"It's incredible. I'm a complete imbecile and even I thought it was amazing."

Reed pulls out his phone. "What's it called again? *Shoot Like a Girl?*"

"Yeah. It's sick, man. She thinks she's about to get limited distribution, actually. At least on Netflix."

"Wow. Awesome."

"And her next movie's gonna be about stripping. That shit's gonna be next lev."

"Basketball and stripping?" Reed chuckles. "Now there's a girl with her finger on the pulse of what people wanna see." Oh, yeah, Reed is definitely intrigued. "Huh. I'm always looking for talented people to shoot tours and promo. I'll take a look at that movie of hers and check out the video she does for Dax and the boys. Thanks for the heads up." He looks over at Maddy again, his eyes trained like lasers on her.

"Sure thing," I say, my pulse suddenly pounding in my ears. Whoa, it's all of a sudden clear to me this Reed guy is an epic hunter—totally next level. A Master Yoda. *And he's looking at my girl.*

There's a long pause.

"Um, hey, Reed," I say. I clear my throat. I really don't like the way he's looking at Maddy. "Reed?"

It's suddenly occurring to me I have a rather unique window of opportunity in this moment to test Dax's bullshit theory about the Armageddon that would supposedly result from me fucking Maddy Milliken. I probably shouldn't say anything to Reed, I know—Dax would kill me if he knew. I glance at Dax across the room. Bah. He'll never know. "So, hey, Reed, can I ask you something?" I say.

Reed peels his eyes off Maddy and looks at me. "Sure."

"Do you give a flaming shit who I sleep with?"

Reed looks surprised. "Um..." He makes a face like I'm a lunatic. "Well, I guess it depends. Is this your way of saying you want to sleep with me?"

I laugh. "No, I'm straight."

"Okay. Well, then. Are you intending to sleep with my mother or sister?"

"No."

"Are you planning to sleep with any girlfriend of mine, past or present, or any woman who's even remotely on my radar screen?"

"Um." I get a sudden pit in my stomach. Maybe this wasn't such a good idea, after all. "That depends. Is Maddy Milliken even remotely on your radar screen?"

Reed looks across the room at Maddy again, his eyes like lasers.

I'm expecting him to reply immediately with "Of course, not." But he doesn't. To the contrary, he's looking at Maddy like he's seriously considering whether to stake his claim or not. My stomach clenches violently. Oh, shit. What have I done? This is so not good.

Reed looks back at me, his face unreadable to me. "No," he says evenly, like he's just made an actual decision—like, if he'd truly wanted her, Maddy would have been his for the taking.

I exhale with relief. "Then, no, I'm definitely not planning to sleep with anyone, past or present, even remotely on your radar screen."

Reed shoots me an amused look. "Then I believe the answer to your initial question is 'No, Keane, I don't give the slightest fuck, flaming or otherwise, who you sleep with.'"

I exhale with relief again. "Cool."

"May I ask *why* you're asking me this utterly bizarre question?"

"I'm not at liberty to say," I reply, leaning in conspiratorially. "But lemme ask you another question that might illuminate my thinking for you: What if, *hypothetically*, I were to sleep with Maddy Milliken—who happens to be the little sister of your best friend's girlfriend—and what if I were to somehow fuck it up with her and piss her off and make her hate me, which, of course, wouldn't be the plan but you never know with me, 'cause I'm kind of an idiot—would you somehow hold my fuck-up with Maddy against *Dax*?"

Reed looks baffled. "Uh, no." There's a very long beat. "So are you telling me Dax is having some sort of paranoid meltdown about the album release? Is that it?"

Whoa, smart dude. I nod. "Meltdown might be a stretch. More like a freak-out. I think maybe the stress is getting to him a wee bit."

Reed winks. "Thanks for the heads-up. Not unusual with first-timers, especially with the guys like Dax who carry their band." He smirks. "And I suppose it's especially understandable if a guy's heard some of the *rumors* about me."

"What kinds of rumors?" Zander blurts, his eyes wide.

God, I love Z. As big an idiot as I am, I never would have asked that particular question, for fear of what the answer might be. But Zander just barreled right ahead, God bless him.

Reed waves his hand dismissively. "Oh, you know, rumors that make me out to be a vindictive motherfucker when someone crosses me." He swigs his beer and chuckles. "In particular, I'm guessing Dax heard this one *rumor* about what I *allegedly* did to a guy signed to my label after I found out he'd fucked my girlfriend." Reed's jaw muscles pulse.

There's a long beat.

"Uh... any truth to that one?" Zander finally asks.

Reed smirks. "Let's just say I made sure that fucker's album went down in flames and no other label would touch him with a ten-foot pole." He smiles and winks. "But, trust me, that fucker deserved it."

My stomach clenches. "Whoa," I manage to say.

Reed shrugs. "Some things are worth more to me than money, boys." He takes a calm sip of his beer. "A lot more."

"Oh," I say, my cheeks flushing. "Sounds... reasonable."

"But Dax doesn't have anything to worry about," Reed adds breezily, his jaw relaxing, his eyes sparkling. "I'm putting the full muscle of River Records behind 22 Goats, trust me. Six months from now, they're gonna be at the top of the charts, a household name. In fact, that's why I'm here tonight—to tell them some fantastic news about something I just lined up for them that's gonna launch them into the stratosphere."

"Awesome," I say. "Dax will be stoked to hear it. I think maybe he worries you only signed 22 Goats as a favor to Josh and Kat."

Reed scoffs. "Bullshit. I'd never sign a band as a favor to anyone, not even Josh. Business is business, man. I don't fuck with the reputation of my label and my other bands by signing anyone I don't believe in one hundred percent. If I sign a band, it's 'cause I'm gonna do everything in my power to make them huge." He raises his eyebrow. "Unless, of course, a guy in the band fucks my hot girlfriend—in which case I don't give a shit how much money I've sunk into his band or how much I like their fucking music, they're going fucking down."

I clear my throat. Holy shit. This dude's intense. "Gotcha," I say.

Reed smirks. "Well, no worries like that with Dax, right?" He takes a sip of his beer. "Trust me, when Dax and the boys hear what I came to tell them tonight, they'll have no doubt about my commitment to their success. Speaking of which..." He puts down his beer emphatically and stands up. "Hey, guys, you got what you need for the video? I've got some good news you're definitely gonna wanna hear. Gather 'round, boys."

Chapter 44
Maddy

Saturday, 11:48 p.m.

The cool night air is wafting over my hot skin as Keane's magical fingers slide in and out of me and his lips devour mine in the dark shadows of the night. He's got me backed against a wall in an alley along the side wall of The Viper Room, around the corner from the main entrance where people are milling under the streetlights on Sunset Boulevard.

I've never had sex in public like this, mere feet away from where anyone might happen upon us, and, I must admit, it's utterly thrilling. I bite down on Keane's neck as my orgasm comes, trying desperately not to scream and draw attention to us.

At the sound of a condom package being ripped open, I moan with anticipation, my body undulating, my crotch dripping wet. But when I feel the tip of Keane's erection resting on my clit and not penetrating me, it's clear Keane's not done with foreplay quite yet.

His fingers slip inside me again—deep, deep inside—as his hard-on presses firmly against my bull's-eye.

"You were a badass in there," Keane whispers into my ear, his warm breath sending electricity over my skin in the cool night. "Sexy as hell."

"Keane," I breathe, my arousal ramping up ridiculously fast. "Oh my God, I'm gonna come again."

"Yeah, you are," he says, his voice commanding, his fingers strumming deep inside me as his erection pushes against my clit.

I whimper. My entire body's quaking with arousal.

"You still want my fucking brother?" Keane growls, shocking me.

"No," I blurt, gasping for air as Keane's fingers work me.

"Who do you want?"

Oh, God. There's only one conceivable answer to this question. *"You."*

"Say it again."

I must admit Dax was a veritable god onstage tonight—the embodiment of everything I thought I wanted in a sexual fantasy. And yet, during Dax's performance, all I could think about was meeting Keane in this alley to do what we're doing right this very minute.

"I want *you*," I say, my voice quavering. "Only you."

"That's fucking right." Keane's warm tongue enters my mouth as his erection slides inside me, pinning me to the cold wall, and, instantly, at the delicious sensation of his erection penetrating me, my body releases with an orgasm that curls my toes.

I moan into Keane's mouth, enraptured by the pleasure enveloping me.

Keane thrusts powerfully into me, over and over, his hips moving passionately as his muscled body pins me into the wall. "You feel so good," he growls into my ear. "I can't get enough of you."

I hear the sound of someone laughing around the corner on the main drag and my skin pricks with momentary alarm at the thought of us being discovered, but somehow, those prickles of anxiety only heighten my pleasure.

"What are you doing to me?" Keane murmurs. "When'd you get so fucking sexy?"

He slides out of me and fingers me again, deep, deep inside me on that same magical spot, bringing me to the brink of another climax, and when it's clear I'm on the ragged edge, he slides himself inside me again, his erection hitting the very same spot he's just stimulated with his fingertip.

My body tightens violently, but I hang on, not wanting this delicious moment to end.

"Let go," Keane coos, his body moving inside mine. "Focus on how good this feels." He slides his hand across my ass cheek and right down my ass crack until the pad of his finger is pressed firmly against my anus. "Come for me now," he commands, his body thrusting in and out of me fervently. "Concentrate on how amazing this feels."

I will myself to focus on the delicious sensations my body's feeling: Keane's hard shaft moving in and out of me, the way his erection is rubbing against my clit with each thrust. His soft lips on mine, his tongue leading mine in a sensual dance. The insistent pressure of his fingertip.

"I own your pussy," Keane whispers into my mouth, his breath hot against my ear in the chilly night. "It's mine and I'm commanding it to come for me right fucking now." He licks at my earlobe and slides his fingertip up my ass, his erection impaling me, and my body clicks into place, releasing warm, undulating waves deep inside my core in a torrent of pleasure.

"Yes," I gasp, clutching at Keane's broad shoulders as my body clenches and twists.

Keane lets out a mangled groan and, a moment later, his body stiffens and jerks against mine with what seems like a highly pleasurable climax.

When both our bodies have gone quiet, but for the sounds of our mutual labored breathing, Keane kisses my cheek gently, pulls out of me, and slides his condom off. "That was some awesome alley sex, Mad Dog," he breathes.

I rest my forehead on Keane's shoulder, trying to catch my breath. "Another cherry successfully popped."

Keane wraps his arms around me and holds me close. "You're more fun than a Fruit Roll-Up, you know that, sugar tits?"

I giggle. He's so effing weird. "Gosh, thanks, sugar balls."

Keane tugs on my hair, prompting me to lift my face off his shoulder. When I look up and stare into his astonishingly blue eyes, he rests his forehead against mine and places his palm on my cheek. "Hey, seriously—are we still good?"

I'm surprised by the question, not to mention his earnest tone.

"Hell yeah," I say. "We're very, *very* good."

"No, I mean..." He exhales. "We're still just, you know, *flinging*, right?" He brushes his thumb against my cheek. "You still promise you're not gonna hate me when this is done?"

I bite my lip. *Shit.* How the hell do I know if Keane and I are still just "flinging"? It sure doesn't feel like it, to be perfectly honest, but what do I know? I've never "flinged" (or is it "flung"?) with a guy before, so I have no basis of comparison. Maybe this is simply how "flinging" goes—you have tons of amazingly hot sex with an insanely gorgeous guy, laugh with him 'til your sides hurt (both in and out of bed), hold hands with him secretly under tables at restaurants, stare longingly into each other's eyes across rooms, and, frankly, feel a helluva lot like you're falling head over heels in love, as crazy as that sounds after such a short amount of time. But then, magically, when time's up and the fling's over (as mutually and maturely agreed beforehand), when the guy heads back home and reverts back to being the manwhore he's always been without a second thought, and you start your brand new life as a newly minted man-eater, all those falling-head-over-heels-in-love-feelings just... *go away*? And they're replaced by... what? Feelings of serene, asexual, platonic friendship?

Yeah, it sounds pretty unlikely to me, I must admit. But, hey, it's still *possible*, right? I guess only time will tell. But, regardless, thanks to the way Keane's worded his question, I think I can honestly answer his query without opening Pandora's Box.

"Keane," I say, my forehead resting against his, my stomach suddenly filled with butterflies. "I don't know what the hell we're doing—I've never done this friends-with-benefits thing, remember? But, to answer your question, yes, I promise you, without a doubt, no matter what this thing is called or how it ends, I'll never hate you as long as I live."

Chapter 45
Keane

Sunday, 11:34 p.m.

"Oh, that's a sick angle," I say to Maddy, referring to the footage of Dax's performance from last night we're watching on her laptop. "Ha! Dax is such a fucking rock star. Look at him. He's like, 'This is my world and you're all just living in it, fuckers.'"

Maddy laughs.

For the past hour, Maddy and I have been sitting in our underwear on Maddy's bed, eating snacks, drinking beer, and poring over the video footage Maddy captured this weekend—the stuff from last night at The Viper Room plus everything Maddy shot this afternoon when she, Zander, and I hung out with the band at the recording studio and watched them lay down tracks for another song on the album.

I'm rubbing Maddy's back as we look at her computer together, my cock tingling. Damn, I'm having fun with this smart, sexy girl. Who knew this off-limits cookie would be so *phenomenal* in the sack? Once I got Maddy's orgasms working for her like clockwork, this smart girl went DEFCON-one ballistic on me in the best possible way, begging for me to bone the fuck outta her at every possible opportunity. And, of course, I've been happy to oblige.

Jesus, when Maddy and I got back to her apartment after Dax's show last night, we boned the fuck outta each other so hard, if I'd had a heart condition going in, I'd be dead right now. And then, this evening, after Maddy and I dropped Zander off at the airport, we came back to her apartment so rarin' to go, you'd have thought neither of us had had sex in months.

"Dax has so much swagger onstage," Maddy says, munching on

306

some white-cheddar popcorn. "He's just like you—he comes alive onstage. Must be a Morgan thing." She clicks into another clip from last night—footage Maddy shot from behind the band onstage while crouched behind the drum kit. "Oh, I like the way this turned out," she says. "This angle makes the club look five times bigger than it actually is."

"So mega to see the audience looking up at the band like that," I say. "Ha! Look at that guy in the front row. He's like, 'You are my leader, Dax Morgan.'"

"Oh my God, that's the money shot," Maddy says, giggling. "The look on that guy's face is priceless. As far as promo goes, you can't get much better than a fan looking at Dax like he's a cult leader."

"Smart of you to think of shooting from behind the band," I say. "Total pro move, babe."

"Not my first time at the rodeo, son," Maddy says smoothly.

"How'd you think of doing that? Did you come up with that idea on the fly?"

"No, I've shot some music stuff before. I already knew all the cool tricks before last night." She clicks into yet another clip. "Okay, now let's watch my favorite reaction shot of all time, shall we?"

I smile broadly, already knowing exactly what shot she's referring to: when Reed told Dax and the guys they're gonna be the opening act on the upcoming world tour of Red Card Riot, the hottest rock band in the entire world right now—a band, who, as luck would have it, just so happens to be signed by River Records, too.

Maddy presses play on the clip, and I'm instantly overcome with emotion at the sight of my brother's face hearing the good news. "Look at Daxy," I say, a huge lump rising in my throat. "Wow. That's what pure joy looks like."

"Joy mixed with *relief*," Maddy corrects me.

"Yeah, no doubt. Wow. I'm so happy for my baby brother. This has been his dream forever, you have no idea. He always says he couldn't possibly do anything else with his life—that he's got no Plan B."

Out of nowhere, I remember myself saying those very words about baseball to one of my teammates not too long ago. "I got no Plan B, son," I said to my teammate on a long bus ride home from a game, utterly clueless about the twist of fate awaiting me a mere two months later. "This is the only thing I've ever been good at," I continued to my teammate, "the only thing I ever wanna do."

"Your brother's life is about to change forever," Maddy says, drawing me out of my memories. "Releasing an album and opening for Red Card Riot, all at the same time, is gonna launch 22 Goats to the highest level. It's gonna be banana-pants."

"Yeah, it's gonna be awesome," I agree.

We finish watching the rest of the footage for another forty minutes or so, and when we're done, I stare at Maddy in awe. "You got so much incredible stuff."

"Yeah, I think the promo piece is gonna be great once I edit everything together. I'm thinking I'll offer Reed all my raw footage, too, just in case the label wants to use it for something down the line."

"You're so fucking good at this," I say.

"Thanks." Her cheeks flush. "I feel like it's my life's purpose, you know? Oh, hey, speaking of people fulfilling their life's purpose..." She pulls out her phone. "Come on, Ball Peen Hammer, let's get your reaction to your brother's tour announcement. I'll tag 22 Goats and Red Card Riot and drive all sorts of traffic to your channels."

"Dude, you're a marketing genius," I say.

"I truly am." Maddy giggles to herself and trains her camera on me. "Okay, gimme your thoughts on your brother and 22 Goats getting to open on a world tour for Red Card Riot. And... action."

I flash the camera my dimples with extra sauce. "Hey, Handsome and Happy Lads," I begin. "And a very special hello to the very beautiful and talented Maddy Behind the Camera. Always a pleasure, sweetheart."

Maddy bats her eyelashes from behind the camera.

For the next two minutes, I do my thing on-camera, spewing a whole bunch of bullshit that amounts to pretty much nothing of any value. But, for some reason, when I'm done talking, Maddy acts like everything I've said is pure genius.

"Perfect, as usual," Maddy says. "I'll post it when the tour is officially announced."

"Cool. Reed says the tour announcement's coming this week."

"Faboosh. I bet you gain fifty percent more followers from this video alone."

"Thanks, baby doll. You da best. That's why I..." I pause, suddenly hyper-aware of my word choice. "That's why I think you're the best," I say, my heart racing.

"You bet," Maddy says. She yawns so big I can see the inside of her underwear.

I laugh. "That's quite a yawn, Scorsese."

She giggles. "You're wearing me out."

I lie back onto the bed and pat my chest. "Come here, baby doll. I'll be your pillow and blanket."

Maddy lies down and snuggles up to me, pressing the full length of her almost-naked body against mine.

"So you've done music videos before?" I ask, stroking her hair. "I wish I'd known that when I was pimping you out to Reed last night."

"You pimped me out to Reed?" She sits upright, her eyes wide.

"Yeah. I told him about *Shoot Like a Girl,* told him you're a genius. He says he's always looking for talented people to shoot music videos and go on tours and whatever."

Maddy throws her palms over her cheeks, her eyes blazing. "Really? Oh my God! Can you imagine if I got hired by *River Records* to shoot a *tour*? Gah!"

I laugh. "Well, don't get too excited yet. You never know. But I told him to watch your movie, so there's no doubt in my mind he'll fall in love with you." I sit up. "Hey, you know what? Reed gave me his card. Why don't I email him links to those music videos you've done before? Couldn't hurt."

Maddy's face pales. "Uh, no," she says quietly. "That's okay."

"Why not? Couldn't hurt, right?"

She waves me off. "I did those videos years ago, when I was just starting out. Reed wouldn't be impressed, trust me."

"Well, can I see 'em? Maybe they're not as bad as you think."

"No, that's okay. Thanks."

"Babe, I'm the guy who watched and loved all your tap-dancing videos, remember? You can do no wrong in my eyes. Lemme see 'em."

Maddy shakes her head.

I'm stumped. Before now, Maddy's happily shown me every single thing I've ever asked to see. Why she's acting so skittish about these particular videos is a mystery—and it's spurring me on even more to want to see them. "Are any of the videos on YouTube?" I ask, grabbing her laptop. "Who are the bands?"

Maddy pauses a long time, biting the inside of her cheek. "It was just one band," she finally says softly. But that's all the information she provides.

"And... that band would be... ?" I ask, my fingers poised over the keyboard.

Maddy exhales. "It was my boyfriend's band." She clears her throat. "Justin's band."

"Ohhhhh," I say, everything making perfect sense to me now. "I didn't realize Justin the Asshole-Douche was in a *band*. Ha! Now I get why you were so gaga over him. That's your 'type,' right? An asshole-douche *musician*?"

Maddy bristles. "Justin wasn't an asshole-douche."

"Sure he was. He broke your fucking heart. And as far as I'm concerned, that makes him an asshole-douche." I hover my fingers over Maddy's keyboard again. "Come on, dude, what's the name of this guy's band? I gotta see this douche."

Maddy shakes her head.

"Your *reticence* is having the opposite effect you desire," I say. "Now you got me crazy curious. Come on, brah. I gotta see this guy. If you won't tell me his band name, at least tell me his last name."

"Why?" She looks stricken.

"Because I wanna check out the guy's Instagram account or whatever. I wanna see what he looks like."

Maddy's staring at me, a deer in headlights.

"Come on," I insist. "I'm totally curious."

Maddy shakes her head, clearly not even tempted to tell me.

"Okay, fine. Well, do you at least have a photo of him on your phone? I just wanna see him."

Maddy's cheeks flush.

I put out my hand. "Come on. Let's see it."

Out of nowhere, Maddy's eyes tear up.

"Aw, shit," I say, my chest tightening. "Fuck. Don't go all wilty-flower-crazy on me. I told you, that guy's not worth your tears."

Maddy wipes her eyes, her lower lip trembling.

I lean into her and hug her to me, nuzzling my nose into her hair. "It's okay, sweet meat." I wipe the tears from her cheeks with my thumbs. "Man, this guy really got to you, didn't he? You want me to break his legs for you?" I smile, hoping to coax a smile out of Maddy in return, but, instead, her entire chin starts trembling.

"Jesus. How long has it been since you saw this guy?"

"Almost three years," she chokes out, wiping her cheeks.

"Three years and you *still* cry over this guy?" I whistle. "Ho-lee shit. He must have really done a number on you."

She bites her lip.

"You loved him, huh?"

She nods, sniffling.

I take Maddy's cheeks in my palms. "You gotta move past this, sweetheart. I'm telling you—it's holding you back." I look into her Tootsie Pop eyes. God, she's so adorable. "Justin didn't know what he had, okay? That's all there is to it. It's no reflection on how awesome you are—how *beautiful* you are. He was just a stupid, young, clueless dumbshit, that's all. Take it from me; I should know—I'm king of the stupid, young, clueless dumbshits." I smile again, but it's no use. Water's streaming down Maddy's cheeks in a torrent. Oh, fuck. She's breaking my heart. "Jesus, Maddy. What the hell did this guy do to you?"

Maddy shakes her head and doesn't speak.

"Did he cheat on you?"

She swallows hard. "No."

"Then, what?"

There's a long beat.

"Did he say something horrible to you? Something that rattled your self-confidence? Because if he did, it wasn't true. You're amazing."

Maddy's gorgeous face is trembling in my palms.

"Maddy, for fuck's sake, what'd he do to you?" I ask, the hairs on the back of my neck rising up. "*Tell me.*"

Maddy lets out a long, shaky breath and blinks hard—sending big, fat tears streaming down her beautiful cheeks. "He died."

Chapter 46
Keane

For the past twenty minutes, Maddy's been quietly telling me the story of the horrific car crash that took Justin's life along with the life of the other driver, and the whole time she's been talking, I've been sitting on the bed, my heart racing and my thumb up my ass.

"I still think about the moment of impact every day," Maddy says softly. "Every time someone drops a glass in a restaurant or slams a car door in a parking lot, I'm right back in that moment." She closes her eyes. "I can hear the sound of metal twisting all around me. Glass exploding. And then eerie silence." She opens her eyes again and sighs. "I still can't make sense of it, to this day. One minute we were driving along, listening to music, chatting about our plans for the weekend, and *literally* in the blink of an eye, without any warning *at all*—without either of us anticipating the impact even for a split-second—the world was suddenly exploding around me like a bomb had gone off in the car."

My heart is panging. I can't stand thinking about Maddy experiencing something like that. Wordlessly, I pull Maddy down from a sitting position to lie with me on the bed, stretching her body alongside mine, until we're lying nose to nose and looking into each other's eyes.

"You know how in movies they always show car crashes in slow motion?" she whispers, her voice barely audible. "Or how people say time slows down when something traumatic happens?"

I nod, nuzzling my nose into hers.

"For me, that's not what happened at all. It was just... *blam*! One second everything was calm and happy and normal and uneventful, and the next second, I was pinned inside this twisted metal coffin, unable to move, unable to think or feel or process. There was no in between—no time during which events unfolded, you know? We were happy and fine and listening to music and then he was dead and I was trapped in the car with his mangled body. I remember I looked over at Justin and..." Her face contorts with pain. "I was gonna ask him if he was okay, but then, when I saw him, there was absolutely no doubt he was already gone."

I hug her to me and she melts into me, crying.

"Were you... ?" I begin, stroking her back. Shit, I don't even know where to begin. "Did it take a while for you to get back in the swing of things?"

"Yeah. The accident happened at the start of my freshman year at U Dub and I wound up taking that entire year off. That's why I'm only a junior now. I should be a senior."

"Do you... think about him a lot?"

"Every day." She looks thoughtful. "I'm not saying he was necessarily gonna be the great love of my life forever and ever, you know? I have no idea about that. Would we still be together to this day if he were alive? I think about that sometimes and the answer is: I have no idea. But I know that I loved him with all my heart and he loved me." Tears flood her eyes and she wipes them. "And I know I haven't been able to feel that same way about anyone since." She takes a shaky breath. "You know how you said Zander unleashed your inner Peen and you never stuffed that fucker back in again?"

I nod, my heart panging, my skin suddenly prickling with goose bumps.

"Well, Justin did that for me—he unleashed my inner Maddy. The only difference is that, when Justin died, I immediately stuffed that fucker back in—way, *way* in." She pauses, her lower lip trembling, her eyes glistening.

There's a long beat.

Maddy takes a deep breath. "Until you," she adds quietly.

Every hair on my body instantly stands on end.

Maddy lets out a shaky breath. "You've unleashed my inner Maddy again."

I don't know what to say in response to that, so I do the only thing that makes sense to me: I grab her and kiss the living hell out of her, pressing my body into hers in a flash of heat and want and near-desperate need.

At the first touch of my lips on hers, Maddy ignites in my arms, her lips and tongue devouring me, her breasts pressed feverishly into my chest, her arms wrapped around my back, clutching me to her.

"Make love to me," Maddy whispers.

In a flash, our underwear is off, a condom is rolled onto my hard-on, and I'm inside her, holding her in my arms and kissing the salty tears off her wet cheeks.

"You're beautiful," I whisper, my body moving on top of hers, my hands exploring her warm skin, my lips covering every inch of her salty face. "You're so beautiful, Maddy. Inside and out."

Oh God, being inside Maddy feels different this time. She doesn't just feel good—or even amazing—it's more like her body was custom-made for mine. I've never felt this way during sex before. I'm not fucking this girl—I'm consoling her, stroking her very soul with mine—willing her to wholeness. I kiss and suck on her lips as her hips move with mine, my fingers greedily stroking her skin as she gyrates beneath me.

When I'm on the cusp of climax, I pull out of her, hungry for the taste of her, aching to make her feel awesome, and I proceed to kiss every single inch of her, from her breasts and belly to her hips and thighs, and finally to the folds between her legs. By the time I get to her clit and lick her ever so gently, she's gripping the sheet and whimpering, arching her back, and shuddering.

I make a guttural sound. She tastes so fucking good. I can't take it anymore. I'm hard as a rock, aching to get inside her and feel the way our bodies fit together again. But I refrain, lapping at her, swirling her tip in my mouth while stroking her wetness firmly with my fingers.

"You're beautiful," I whisper. "Perfect."

Maddy arches her back and screams my name and the muscles gripping my fingers begin clenching and releasing rhythmically.

I crawl back up to her face and kiss her passionately as my cock burrows deep inside her—and the moment I'm nestled all the way in, I feel like I'm home.

A jolt of electricity flashes through my entire body that makes goose bumps erupt on my arms and neck. I cup her cheeks in my palms as I kiss her, my thrusts becoming more passionate.

"Maddy," I whisper, looking into her eyes.

"Thank you," she whispers, though what she's thanking me for I have no idea. I grab her thighs and yank them up around my torso, and she moans at my new angle of entry into her body. With each thrust of my body, each swirl of her tongue with mine, my heart feels like it's reaching out to join with hers. I touch her face again, my passion reaching its boiling point.

Oh, shit. I need to go deeper. I hitch her legs even higher around me, folding her body underneath me, grinding myself into her, splitting her in two, and she shudders with pleasure and yearning. But she's not coming for me a second time.

In one swift movement, I rearrange us, seating myself onto the edge of the bed, positioning her on top of my cock, her legs wrapped around my waist, her arms around my neck, her lips locked with mine.

"You're so beautiful," I murmur, gripping her hips and guiding her pelvis in movement with mine. "Perfect."

Oh, fuck. I can't get enough. I feel like I'm in a frenzy, out of my head with desire. My thrusts are increasing in intensity, my kisses becoming desperate. Her movement on top of me is frenetic. She's fucking the shit out of me, sucking on my lips, snapping her hips forward and back as she rides me. I reach down and touch her clit and she explodes in my arms, twisting and howling and crying with her orgasm.

A few more thrusts and I come inside her, so hard I'm seeing little yellow dots.

After we've both stopped moving, and the room is filled with nothing but our mutual ragged breathing, I kiss her neck and suck on her earlobe and nipples and devour her breasts, swirling my tongue along her jawline, biting her shoulder, not ready for whatever just happened to be over just yet. When my lips finally meet hers, we kiss so passionately, I feel like I'm gonna pass out. Ho-lee shit, my heart's racing, knocking against my chest like it's trying to crack my sternum and leap into her chest cavity.

What *was* that? Nothing in a single instructional video I've ever watched prepared me for sex like this. Everything I've ever watched has shown me where to touch—how much pressure to apply—how fast to move my fingers and tongue and cock to bring a woman to the Promised Land. But nothing's ever prepared me to *feel* this way while

315

fucking a woman—to want to heal and protect her and make her heart stop hurting. *To make her all mine.*

Oh, shit.

I think it's distinctly possible I've *really* fucked up here.

"Maddy," I whisper, my heart lurching into my throat.

Maddy nuzzles her nose into the crook of my neck and presses herself into me, exhaling. "Keane," she purrs into my ear. She skims her lips along my jawline. *"You've unleashed me, baby. I'm brand new."*

Chapter 47
Maddy

Tuesday 10:34 p.m.

For the umpteenth time tonight, I grab my phone from next to me on the bed and check to see if Keane's answered any of my texts. Nope. Still nothing.

I look at my watch. *Where is he*? And why hasn't he at least texted to tell me about today's auditions? I close my laptop and rest my head on my pillow, my eyes weary from the hours of editing I've been doing while awaiting Keane's return from his big day.

I look at my phone again. Nothing. God, I'm actually starting to worry.

All of a sudden, the image of Keane sitting lifeless in the twisted remnants of Fish's car (which Keane borrowed today) flashes across my mind and my stomach clenches violently. Quickly, I force that horrible vision out of my head... but it's immediately supplanted by another horrible image: Keane having sweaty, grunting sex with some boobalicious girl he met at one of his auditions today.

I close my eyes and put my hands over them. Son of a biscuit-eating bulldog, make it stop.

Keane wouldn't do that to you, I think.

Why not? my brain responds to itself. *You've been assuming exclusivity during this fling-thing, but you two never explicitly agreed to that.*

Oh my god, the paranoid side of my brain is right: Keane and I never talked about exclusivity. Which means there's absolutely nothing to keep Keane from running off for a "marathon sesh" with any of the tiny-waisted, big-boobed Southern California hotties he undoubtedly met today, all of whom probably threw themselves at him without shame. Really, what's to stop Keane from banging any girl he meets, anywhere, any time, regardless of our *fling*? Keane's certainly been clear he's *not* looking for a relationship with *anyone*, including me. For the love of God, he's been very, very honest with me: I'm the girl he considers to be nothing more than his *friend*. His friend with benefits. Also known in some circles as a "fuck buddy."

My stomach revolts. Oh my God. I feel sick.

What the hell have I done?

I can't be somebody's "fuck-buddy," not even Keane's! Wait, no, *especially* not Keane's! How can I be Keane's "friend he sometimes fucks" when I feel so deeply for him? Oh, God, wait. I feel *deeply* for Keane?

All of a sudden, the truth is slamming me upside the head. Having sex with Keane without any kind of commitment hasn't made me feel like a man-eater the way I thought it would—it's just made me crave something real with him... which is something he's been clear from the beginning isn't something he's willing to give me.

Oh, God, I'm so screwed.

I swear I had the best of intentions when I suggested this "friends with benefits" arrangement to Keane, I really did. Honestly, I wasn't trying to trick or change him. But that's life for you—it's full of surprises. How was I supposed to know I was gonna unburden my soul on the guy on Sunday night and tell him things I never tell anyone? Or that he'd respond to the unexpected baring of my soul by making love to me in a way I've never experienced with anyone—with the kind of breathtaking tenderness and passion and *beauty* I'd only ever dreamed of experiencing? Talk about a "quiet moment of magic."

I rub my forehead, panic flooding me.

Oh man. This is *so* not good. Keane's definitely not feeling what I am. Keane hasn't told me that, of course, but it's suddenly clear to me Sunday night had the opposite effect on him as it did on me. Yep, in retrospect, it's so damned obvious the guy is freaking out. I guess I just didn't want to believe it before now.

When I woke up on Monday morning and nuzzled into Keane, aching for a repeat performance of the prior night, he pulled away from me and leaped out of bed. "I can't," he said, his massive hard-on contradicting his words. "I've got a meeting with my new agent first thing this morning."

"Wow," I said. "That's exciting."

"Yeah," Keane continued. "I'm gonna meet with him this morning about a bunch of auditions he's got lined up for me, and then I'm gonna hit the gym for a marathon work-out sesh this afternoon." He patted his rock-hard abs. "Gotta keep my moneymaker in top form."

"Oh, sure, no worries," I said. "I've got plenty to do. I've gotta buy my books for all my classes and then I'm attending this transfer-student orientation thing on campus. Plus, I really should start editing Dax's video. It's gonna be a big job."

"Cool. So I'll see you later, baby doll?" Keane said.

"Sure," I replied, my eyes trained on his huge boner. "But, um, you're *sure* you don't have a little time to...?" I asked, motioning to his hard-on.

"Yeah, I'm sure," he replied. And that's when Keane kissed the top of my head with a curt "See you later, sweet meat" and headed into the bathroom, his gorgeous ass teasing me as he went.

Okay, I thought at the time, *so there's not gonna be an immediate sequel to last night's soul connection. No big whoop. This isn't a fairy tale—it's real life. And in real life, people have shit to do.*

So I didn't sweat it.

Of course, not. Because I'm not insane. Shit happens.

But when everyone converged on our two apartments later that evening and our whole group went out to dinner, there was no mistaking Keane's aloofness. He didn't secretly hold my hand under the table or rub my back or rest his hand on my thigh, or do any of the little things I've grown accustomed (and addicted) to him doing. And yet, I shook it off, figuring we'd go back to my apartment and bone the fuck outta each other, Lionel Richie style.

But when we got back from dinner, Keane plopped himself onto Dax's couch to watch *Inception* with the guys, despite the fact that I'd texted him five minutes earlier to say: "Hey, hot stuff, you ready to make me scream?"

But, again, I shook it off. *Keane just hasn't seen my text*, I thought (which isn't a crazy notion when talking about Keane Morgan). So I sat down next to Keane on the couch, snuggled close, and watched the damned movie, figuring we'd go back to my apartment *after* the movie and bone the fuck outta each other, Lionel Richie style.

But we didn't.

Unfortunately, Dax and Keane fell asleep together on the couch like two puppies in a litter before the movie had even ended—and since Dax's head was resting adorably on Keane's shoulder as the two of them snoozed, I couldn't figure out how to wake Keane without waking Dax, too. So I put a blanket over the two of them (after taking several photos of their adorableness) and went to bed alone.

But this morning, when I crept into Dax's apartment intending to wake Keane up and motion for him to sneak into my room for a little bonin' sesh to start the day off right, I was surprised to find him already dressed and sitting at the kitchen table, quietly eating a bowl of granola while Dax and the other guys slept soundly in the bedrooms.

"Hey," I whispered, sitting down next to Keane at the table. "I was hoping you'd come find me this morning. Everything okay?"

"Everything's great," Keane said. "Sorry. I just needed a little quiet time to myself to get my head in the game before all my auditions today. It's gonna be a big day."

"Oh, yeah, of course," I said, suddenly feeling stupid for not appreciating the stress Keane was feeling. "If you need me for anything, just lemme know." I put my hand on his and squeezed, and his face softened.

"Thanks, Maddy," Keane said, his eyes actually focusing on mine for what seemed like the first time since Sunday night. "You're the best. You really are. You're incredible."

Relief flooded me. *I've been imagining the weirdness between us*, I thought. *Keane's just been stressed out about his auditions. His distance hasn't been about me at all.*

"Will you let me know how everything goes today?" I asked, stroking his forearm. "I'm so excited. I want to hear every little detail."

"Of course," Keane replied, flashing me his dimples. But his smile didn't reach his eyes.

"I'll be waiting by the phone all day," I said. "So let me know how things are going the minute you have a chance, okay? I won't be able to breathe until I hear from you—even if it's just a brief text to say things went okay."

"Sure thing," he said. He got up from the table. "Bye, sweet thing."

"Bye, sugar buns," I replied, my heart palpitating wildly. "Knock 'em dead."

"That's always the plan, baby doll."

He winked, kissed me on the cheek, and walked out of the apartment in full swagger-mode... and that was the last I've heard from him all frickin' day.

I look up at the ceiling fan in my bedroom, flapping my lips together in exasperation. Where the hell is he? And why the hell hasn't he texted me even once? Has it truly been *impossible* all day long to text me, even once, to say "First audition done! Went great!" or maybe "One down three to go! Going great!" I just don't understand why he hasn't texted me, even once.

I'm tempted to creep over to Dax's place to see if Keane's back, but I've already done that twice today and I don't think having a restraining order slapped against my ass is the best way to kick off my new life in California.

"Shoot," I say out loud. I grab my phone and tap out a quick text to Keane: "Was hoping to hear from you. Been sitting by the phone all day. Going to sleep now. Left the front door unlocked in case you wanna sneak into my room and maul me when you come back. Hint hint. If for some reason you don't want to have amazing sex with a crazy, ravenous, savage beast tonight, at least come say hi and tell me about your auditions, okay? I'm dying to hear. I know they loved you—but I just can't wait to hear about it from you." I pause, my heart panging. "And if for some reason you're too tired to come to my room at all," I continue writing, my cheeks flushing, "then do me a favor and lock my front door so it doesn't remain unlocked all night. (Hannah's at Henn's.) Hope to see you soon. I miss you. Hope you had a great day. XO M." I attach a heart emoji to the end of my message and place my finger over the "send" button, reading and re-reading the message before pressing down. Damn. This text is coming off as pathetic and lonely and just plain desperate. Which is appropriate, actually, because I *am* pathetic and lonely and just plain desperate. Fuck it. I take a deep breath and press send.

Aw, shoot. The minute the text is gone, panic seizes me. Why'd I send that? Do I have no self-respect at all? That text was the equivalent of baking Keane a basketful of brownies at three in the morning! Shit!

I rub my eyes, a lump rising in my throat.

I'm clearly losing my mind. I'm pulling on my crazy-pants and zipping those bad boys right up.

Damn it!

I just wish I knew what Keane is thinking.

And where he is.

And if he's okay.

I'm ninety-nine percent sure he's perfectly healthy and off somewhere thinking up ways to tell me this thing between us is over, despite the fact that he hasn't left Los Angeles yet, but what if I'm wrong? What if he's hurt? Or what if, by some miracle, he's feeling exactly the way I am, but he's just too afraid to say it first?

I sigh.

No, I'm being naïve. Keane's not feeling what I am. He's been clear from the start he doesn't want a relationship. To the contrary, he wants nothing but exactly what I agreed to give him: friendship and no-strings sex. Two things I've unfortunately just figured out don't actually go together. At least not for me.

So there you go.

I'm about to get my heart broken. It's as simple as that. I'm now officially Lana Del Rey.

With a heavy heart, I swipe into the videos on my phone and look at the short clip I took of Keane during our road trip, when he was fast asleep in the passenger seat of my car. I look at Keane's perfectly symmetrical face. The little indentation in his chin. The long lashes shooting out of his closed eyelids. His stunningly beautiful lips. And I'm suddenly bone-certain I'll never kiss those beautiful lips again, never feel them between my legs, giving me pleasure like I've never experienced before.

I sigh.

Even though I know I'm about to torture my aching heart, I swipe out of the video of Keane sleeping and click on the one of Keane telling his handsome and happy lads what to do in an argument with a woman (the second version where I'd instructed Keane to think the word "Maddy" every time he said "your girl" or "chick").

"Hey guys," Keane says in the video. "Today I'm gonna tell you what to do if you find yourself in an argument with a chick. It's pretty simple actually: concede. Look, let's face it, your girl's a helluva lot smarter than you are, not to mention she's the sweetest girl who ever lived, so you might as well save yourself a ton of time and energy and just admit when you're being a dick. Just say, 'Oops. I'm being a dick. Sorry.' Otherwise, you're gonna miss out on valuable time you could have spent hanging out with her and having a blast." He winks. "You're welcome."

I exhale loudly in my quiet room and put my phone down, forcing down my emotions. Well, it was amazing while it lasted. At least I got to feel like the coolest, sexiest, most beautiful girl in the world for a few magical days of my life.

With a heavy sigh, I reach over to my nightstand, turn out the light, and try my damnedest to drift off to sleep, despite the aching of my heart.

Chapter 48
Keane

Tuesday, 10:48 p.m.

When I enter Dax's apartment, he's on the couch with Fish and Colin, smoking a joint and watching some Tom Hardy movie. I sit down and Fish wordlessly hands me the joint.

"Thanks," I say. I suck on it and pass it to Colin.

"How'd your auditions go?" Dax asks.

"Pretty good, I think. But who knows?"

"So does that mean you're gonna move down here or what?"

"I dunno. We'll see."

"Why not?" Dax says. "You're on the verge of super-stardom, Peen Star, I can feel it in my bones. Take a flying leap, dude."

"Meh, I'm not counting on anything, brah. A guy can't feel disappointment if he has no expectations."

"Yeah, but he can't feel *excitement* that way, either."

I shrug. "I never count on anything 'til it's written in ink. Today went pretty well, I *think*, but everything's still in the callback stage. I never count on anything 'til the money's in the bank."

"Since when? Peen, you're the guy who buys a lottery ticket and starts planning the party celebrating your win before you've even put your ticket in your pocket."

"Not anymore, I'm not."

"Since when?"

"Since I was just about to get called up to the bigs and everything went to shit on me." I rub my elbow absentmindedly.

Dax sighs.

"Nowadays I'm a new man, son. A machine. I count on nothing. Look forward to nothing. Expect nothing. That way, I don't feel like shit when nothing happens."

"Jesus, Keane, that's a shitty way to live."

"Works for me."

"Okay, well, have fun with that. Sounds super awesome. Just know the couch is yours whenever you decide to stop being such a fucking downer and take a leap of faith."

"Thanks."

"Why'd you take so long getting back tonight? I thought you'd be home hours ago."

I lean back onto the couch and spread my legs wide, suddenly feeling exhausted. "The last meeting of the day was with this producer for a reality show about male strippers," I say. "They're looking for six guys with 'dazzling personalities and rock-hard abs.'"

"Oh, *hello*, Ball Peen Hammer," Dax says.

"The producer seems to think so. So, yeah, things were going super well in the meeting and it was starting to get late, so she was like, 'Hey, let's grab some dinner and drinks and keep talking.' So that's where I've been for the past *three* fucking hours." I rub my face, totally spent.

"Female producer?" Dax asks.

"Yeah."

"You think she was hitting on you?"

"Oh, fuck yeah."

"You take her up on it?"

"Of course not. I acted like I didn't realize what she wanted. Just pretended to be a total dumbshit like I always do. Worked like a charm."

"Good thinking," Dax says. "Don't wanna burn that bridge. You never know."

"Yeah, that's what I figured," I say.

"That's so fucking gross, though," Dax says.

"Yeah. I was pretty skeeved out."

"Why?" Fish asks, looking stoned outta his mind. "She wasn't hot?"

"It doesn't matter," I say. "I'm not gonna fuck some producer to get a job, hot or not. She coulda looked like Kate Upton and I woulda turned her down."

"Oh, fuck. She looked like Kate Upton?" Fish asks.

"No," I say. "*Not even the tiniest bit.*"

We all laugh.

"Well, then, you can't know for sure what you would have done if she did," Fish says, his tone indignant.

"Touché, Fish Taco," I say.

"Jeez. Welcome to Hollywood, huh?" Dax says, taking another hit off the joint and handing it to Colin.

"Yeah," I say. "Nice town."

Colin takes a hit and offers me the joint. "Here, Peenie Baby. Numb the pain of the casting couch."

I wave him off. "I'm good. I've got a big audition tomorrow morning before I head to the airport. I gotta be bright-eyed and bushy-tailed when the sun comes up, son."

"What's the audition?" Colin asks.

"Feature film. They're doing a black version of *Magic Mike*—a total rip-off—and they're gonna have one token white guy on the stripper-brigade."

"Is it a speaking part?" Dax asks.

"Yeah, I'd have a couple lines. Plus, I'd be in the background a ton and in some group dance numbers. But my agent said it's the kind of thing if I impress the director enough, he might throw me a couple more lines or give me a little extra screen time. Never know what it might turn into. Either way, I'd get my SAG card out of it. Good opportunity for a first-timer, for sure."

"What's a SAG card?" Colin asks.

"Screen Actors Guild. My agent says it's hard to get. I guess it's a big deal."

"Cool," Dax says. "So what'd everyone think about your blue hair today?"

"They liked it, believe it or not, especially when I told them why I did it."

Dax laughs. "Only you could turn that shit into a positive."

"Just part of my dazzling personality," I say, flashing my dimples. "They think the hair is part of my *steez*."

We all laugh.

"You wanna hear something crazy?" I say. "Those Ball Peen Hammer videos I showed you—the ones Maddy did? That's why all these casting directors wanna see me. They think I'm some sort of quasi-celebrity or whatever."

"Emperor's New Clothes, man," Dax says, taking another hit on the joint. "Maddy totally styled you, bro."

"She sure did," I say. "She's amazing." My chest tightens. *Maddy.*

I've been so focused all day on being Ball Peen Hammer with extra sauce, schmoozing and charming and winning people over, I haven't had a chance to text her even once. No, wait, that's not true. That's just the bullshit story I tell myself so I won't feel like a total prick for ignoring her. The truth is I didn't text Maddy today because I'm a prick and a coward and Sunday night freaked me the fuck out.

"Hey, you guys got any beer?" I ask.

"Yeah," Colin says. He gets up and shuffles to the kitchen.

"Maddy was over here looking for you earlier," Dax says.

My heart squeezes in my chest. "Yeah, I gotta talk to her. We got some unfinished business."

"She looked pretty bummed," Dax says. "She was asking if I'd heard from you about your auditions."

I bite my lip. God, I'm such a prick. Why haven't I been straight with her? I should have let her down easy on Monday morning, straight up, rather than stringing her along for the past two days like a complete asshole.

"You fucked her, didn't you?" Dax says evenly.

Colin hands me a beer.

"Thanks," I say. I look at Dax. "Yeah. Sorry, Baby Brother. I tried to adhere to your ridiculous 'off-limits' designation as long as humanly possible, but it just couldn't be avoided. Can't escape gravity, son."

"You're such an asshole, Keane," Dax says, swigging his beer. "I declared her 'off-limits.' That shit would have meant something to a man of actual *character*."

"Fuck you, I've got character coming out my asshole, douchebag. No sane man woulda heeded your off-limits designation—it was total chicken shit."

"It wasn't chicken shit. The girl lives across the hall from me. Now I gotta sit here and watch her poke stickpins into her blue-haired voodoo doll for the next six months 'til we go on tour. Plus, Hannah's gonna be pissed as hell at me, which means there's gonna be shade from Henn, too."

"You're high," I say.

"Yeah, actually."

"No, I mean, you're on crack. First off, nobody in their right mind would blame you for your brother being a total dick. The fact that you even think that reveals the depth of your egomania to an alarming degree and I think you should get that checked by a psychiatrist. You might have a legit personality disorder, brah. And second off, I know for a fact Hannah doesn't give a shit what Maddy and I do. Why do you think she's been sleeping at Henn's since I got here?"

"Seriously?"

"Doy-burgers, dumbshit. And, third off, Reed himself told me he doesn't give a shit about me fucking Maddy, so quit thinking you're the center of the universe. Nobody gives a shit about you but you, Rock Star. Get over yourself."

"What do you mean Reed told you... Oh my fuck, Keane. *You talked to Reed about Maddy?*"

"Yeah. He said he couldn't give two shits if I fucked her."

"Oh fuck. *Please* tell me you're joking about telling Reed."

"Not joking. I talked to him right before he told you guys about the tour." I swig my beer. "I was like, 'Hey, if I were to fuck the little sister of your best friend's girlfriend—and then if I were to screw things up and make her hate my guts—would you give a shit?' He thought I was insane, I'm pretty sure." I laugh.

Colin chuckles. "You're hilarious, Peenie. I love you, man."

"I love you, too, Colin," I say. "I've always loved you the most of all my brother's friends, you know that, right?"

"*Hey*," Fish says. "Fuck you."

"See? That's exactly why I *don't* love you the most, Fish Head. You're just plain mean."

Fish flips me off.

"Peen's not *hilarious*," Dax says. "He's *penile*. That's why we call him *Peen*. Goddammit, Keane. You're such an idiot, you know that? Why'd you say that shit to Reed? Now he's gonna think I'm a paranoid head case."

"Which you are." I swig my beer. "Whatever, Rock Star. Don't stress it. The guy loves you. Just don't fuck his mom, sister, or girlfriend—or anyone he's even *remotely* thinking about fucking— and you'll be golden all the livelong day."

Dax shakes his head and sips his beer. "I'm too stoned to get pissed at you at the moment, but I'm gonna get super-duper pissed at you tomorrow, I swear to God. Might even pummel your face."

"Fine," I say. "Whatever. Pummel away. Let the whole world pummel my face, I don't give a shit. Life already whacked me across the face with a two-by-four and knocked out half my teeth. Take your best shot."

Colin pats me on the back. "Poor Peenie Baby."

"Fuck Peen," Dax says.

"Aw, be nice to your big brother," Fish says, sipping his beer. "He looks sad."

Dax rolls his eyes. "I don't care. He's a twat."

"I thought he was a *penis*," Colin says. "Make up your mind—is Peen a twat or a penis?"

"Hey, maybe he's a *hermaphrodite*," Fish says, pronouncing that last word with great care, and everyone but me laughs their asses off.

"What's going on, bro?" Dax asks when it's clear I'm not amused.

I don't reply.

"Is it Maddy?" Dax asks.

I nod.

"You really like her, don't you?"

I nod again.

"Well, that's good, right?"

"No. It's terrible."

"How could that possibly be terrible?"

"Because we have this amazing... *connection*. Like, oh my God. Incredible." I roll my eyes. "But I can't handle it. It's too intense. Too much, too soon. She's all-in, brah. She's... really attached. I can't deliver what she wants. I got a life to live and flipping out over some smart girl who lives in L.A. doesn't fit in with the game plan."

Dax scoffs. "You're so fucking predictable. This is *exactly* what I said would happen."

"No, it's not," I say. "You thought I'd fuck her for sport and piss her off and make her hate me. But I'm not fucking her for sport, I swear to God. I *really* like her, Dax." I feel my cheeks blushing crimson. "I'm making her hate me, yeah, but not the way you thought I would."

Dax exhales. "You like her, Peenie. That's a good thing. Maybe it's a sign you're ready to move on from all the doom and gloom and pull your head out of your ass, you know? Maybe it's time for you to stop acting like a total douche now."

"What the fuck are you talking about? I'm handsome and happy all the livelong day. What I'm saying is I'm too happy with my life to change a goddamned thing about it."

Dax shakes his head. "Keane, she's obviously into you. You should have seen her when she came in here asking about you. You're sure you're not feeling it with her?"

"No, I *am*. It's just that I'm Ball Peen Hammer. Don't you understand?"

Dax shakes his head.

I exhale with exasperation. "I can barely stand to be away from her, and when I'm near her, I gotta touch her every second or else I feel like I'm gonna *die*. It's not normal how much I wanna touch her. And I'm not even talking about sex—I just gotta hold her hand or touch her hair or rub her thigh or I else feel like I'm gonna *explode*." I rub my face. "She looks at me with those big brown eyes of hers and I melt. And worst of all, the thing that's the absolute worst, is how guilty I feel if I even *look* at another woman. Shit, Dax! I couldn't even flirt with any of the hot chicks at my auditions today because I felt like I was cheating on her somehow—*and I'm a guy who makes his living making women want to fuck me!* How the fuck can I make the horny pickles wanna hurl themselves outta their jars at me when I'm feeling like this? It doesn't pencil." I'm rambling—I know I am—but I can't stop myself. "I just met her, Dax. I barely know her. She could be planning to chop me up and put my parts into six trash bags, for all I know." My mind is reeling. My chest is heaving. I had no intention of saying all that. I rub my face. "Feelings this intense and fast can't possibly be real. It's just not normal."

There's a long beat.

Fish is wearing a facial expression I'd label as, "*sucks to be you,*" but Colin and Dax are looking at me with nothing but sincere sympathy.

"Colin, hand me one of those beers," I grit out, my jaw muscles pulsing.

Colin hands me a bottle. "Numb the torturous pain of love, Peenie Weenie."

I take a long guzzle of my beer. "I can't make it work," I say, filling the silence. "I'm fucked."

"I guess that depends on your definition of 'fucked,'" Dax says. "Because it sure sounds to me like you're the opposite of fucked."

"What's the opposite of 'fucked'?" Colin asks.

"*Fuuuuucked*," Fish offers suggestively, a smirk on his face, and everyone but me laughs.

I sip my beer, my pulse pounding in my ears, but I don't speak.

"I totally knew you fucked her, by the way," Dax says. "The minute I met Maddy, I knew it."

"Well, that's not exactly a psychic phenomenon," Colin says. "Keane and Maddy haven't been able to keep their hands off each other since they got here. They haven't been what I'd call '*discreet*.'"

"No, I mean, before they got all hands-y. I'm talking about when I very first opened my front door and laid eyes on Maddy, I knew. I was like, 'Oh, boy, he fucked her.'"

"Ha! Well, guess what, Millionaire Matchmaker?" I say. "You were dead wrong about that. When Maddy and I first arrived, we hadn't even fucked yet."

"Semantics. I'm saying I saw her and instantly knew it was a done deal, one way or another."

"And how'd you know that, genius? Just because she's a pickle? Because I'll have you know I'm very *selective*."

"No, dumbshit, because she's *exactly* your type."

I'm flabbergasted. "What are you talking about? Maddy's not my type. She's the complete *opposite* of my type."

"No, I'm not talking about all the Barbies and Bambis you've been 'hunting' lately to numb the pain of your tortured soul. I'm talking about your *real* type of girl—from before you became a complete douche." He snaps his fingers. "Who was that girl who used to live across the street from us? Oh man, that girl *owned* your ass. Remember her? I've never seen you so into a girl before or since—well, until now, that is."

"Kelsey," I say softly, the hairs on my arms standing on end.

"That's right. *Kelsey Kerrington*. Nothing like your first love, right, bro? Maddy reminds me of her. Curvy. Sweet. Girl next door. Kind of snarky but not too edgy. Your type on a silver platter, right down to those little freckles on her nose."

My heart lurches in my throat. *Holy shit.*

"Yup," Fish says, swigging his beer. "We've all got our types, huh? It's like we're all just avatars of ourselves."

"What?" Colin says, chuckling.

"Hey, Keane," Dax says softly.

My eyes train on my baby brother, but I can't speak.

"Go across the hall and talk to her, man," Dax continues. "When Maddy came over earlier, she looked pretty rough. At the very least, give that poor girl some verbal duct tape for her heart, because I'm pretty sure it's shattering right about now."

"Oh, that's a sick lyric," Colin says. "Fish, write that shit down. 'Verbal duct tape for her heart.'"

I exhale. Dax is right. It's time for me to nut up and tell Maddy this friends-with-benefits thing isn't working for me anymore.

"Just tell her the truth," Dax continues. "It's not Maddy's fault she's fallen for a guy with the emotional IQ of a pollywog."

I can't even be offended. Dax is right: I've got the emotional IQ of a pollywog.

I put down my beer bottle and begin shuffling toward the front door of the apartment. "Thanks, Daxy," I say, my heart panging as I open the front door.

"Any time, big bro."

"I can always count on you to give it to me straight."

"That's 'cause I love you the most."

Chapter 49
Maddy

I feel Keane's warm body spooning me in the bed and I let out a low moan of relief and pleasure. "Hi," I whisper, a huge smile overtaking my face. I clutch his arms around me. "I missed you."

"Sorry to wake you," Keane's voice says softly in my ear.

"Are you kidding? I've been horny for two solid days, sweet cheeks."

I turn onto my opposite side to face him and lean in to kiss his soft lips, but Keane pulls back. "Hang on a second, Maddy. We gotta talk."

The hairs on the back of my neck stand up. Oh, shit. I was right. This is it. "How were your auditions?" I ask lamely, wanting to stave off the bad news as long as possible.

Keane pauses.

"I'm dying to hear about your day," I whisper. "We'll talk after that, okay?" I swallow hard. "Please?"

Keane proceeds to give me brief descriptions of his various auditions throughout the day, his face mere inches from mine in the dark, but his voice is stiff and restrained. Clearly, this isn't what he came in here to talk about.

I nuzzle my nose against Keane's and close my eyes as I listen to him talk. Something tells me this is the last time I'm going to feel his body against mine and I want to savor it. "Sounds like everything went great," I say when he's finished giving me the rundown of his day.

"We'll see."

"So do you have any more auditions coming up or was today it?"

"One more," he whispers. "Tomorrow morning before I head to the airport."

My breathing hitches. "You're heading home *tomorrow*?"

"Yeah."

"I didn't know that."

"Yeah, I've been gone a full week. I gotta get home, make some money."

"But aren't there gonna be... I dunno... callbacks and stuff?"

"If I'm lucky, yeah. But maybe not. If so, I'll fly back down. Flights are cheap right now. I really gotta get home."

"Oh." I feel like I'm gonna cry, but I stuff my emotions down. "Do you need a ride to the airport tomorrow?"

"No, Fish said he'd drive me to my audition, and then I'll just Uber it to the airport when I'm done."

I feel like I've been punched in the gut. "Okay," I manage to say.

Keane lets out a long sigh. "Maddy, listen, I—"

"Don't say it," I say abruptly, my body stiffening in the bed.

"No, but, listen, I—"

"*No*," I say emphatically. "*Please, Keane. Don't say it.*"

There's a beat.

"You don't need to say it out loud to me," I say evenly. "There was an expiration date on this thing and I knew it from the start. We agreed it would last only as long as you're in town and now you're leaving so it's over. Nothing else needs to be said."

"You don't wanna talk about it? About what happened Sunday night?"

"No. It's over now so there's no point in talking about anything."

There's silence for a long beat.

Oh my God, I can't stand it. I swore to myself I wouldn't spiral into pathetic desperation during this conversation, but now that it's actually happening, I'm gonna explode if I don't speak my mind. "Except for this one thing I wanna say," I blurt. I take a deep breath. "It turns out I don't do the friends-with-benefits thing all that well, okay? I admit that. I'm sorry, I thought I could do it, but I can't. I'm sorry, I..." I swallow hard, stuffing down tears. "I just totally suck at it."

"Maddy," Keane breathes. He touches my face in the dark, but I pull back and swat him away.

"Don't," I say. "Please. It's too confusing for me. I didn't mean to mislead you. I thought I was capable of *flinging*, but I'm just not wired that way." I don't want them to, but tears flood my eyes. "I'm sorry. I am what I am."

"What you are is amazing," he whispers. "Don't cry. You're perfect."

"Just not for you."

"Maddy, please understand," Keane says, his voice quavering. "I'm not at a place in my life where I can—"

"I know. You've been straightforward about that, all along. This is all on me. I'm not mad at you. I don't feel misled. I truly thought I could be a man-eater, but I can't." I don't know how I'm keeping my tears at bay, but I am. "I don't know how to give my body to someone without giving my heart, too. It's just not in my DNA." I snort to myself. "I guess I'm more like my mother than I realized."

"Maddy," Keane breathes, his voice full of emotion. "I've never felt about anyone the way I feel about you. That's the truth. I love being your friend. I don't want to lose you."

I pause, processing what he's said. "I have no idea what that means," I finally say.

"It means I still want you in my life. I wanna talk to you. Find out how you're doing." He touches my hair. "It means I still wanna be your friend."

I stiffen, all the hurt and anger I've felt all day rising up inside of me. "No, thanks. From what I've seen, you can be a pretty shitty-ass *friend*."

Keane sits up in the dark. "What the fuck does that mean?"

I sit up in the bed, too. "It means you didn't even bother to return my texts today, even though you knew I was sitting here, *dying* to hear from you—even though I've been here every step of the way, cheering you on." I wipe my eyes and jut my chin at him in the dark. "It means my heart is too invested to sit around and let you act like I'm just one of the many *friends* you choose to ignore when it suits you. It means I have feelings and you've hurt them and I'm not gonna pretend otherwise. "

Keane is quiet for a long beat. "You're right. I'm sorry. I was just wrapped up in my shit today. I won't ignore you again. I was a total prick today."

I exhale but don't reply.

335

"So if I promise not to ignore your texts, does that mean we're good—you're willing to be my friend when I leave here?" he asks feebly.

"Honestly, I don't know if I *can*, Keane," I say, my voice brimming with emotion. "I mean, yeah, I'm sure I can be friends with Ball Peen Hammer. That's easy. We'll still do the videos—I'll send you a homework assignment every morning and edit whatever you send me."

"Goddammit, Maddy, I'm not even thinking about that stuff. I'm talking about *us*."

"And will you still be in my movie?" I ask, ignoring his comment.

Keane breathes deeply and I can see the silhouette of his head shaking in the darkened room.

"You won't?" I ask, incredulous.

"Of course, I will. But that's not at all what—"

"Good. We can shoot whenever you're here in L.A. for auditions or whatever, okay? No need for you to make a special trip or give me any special treatment."

"Maddy, stop it. You're going all hardcore friend-zone on my ass. Please, I'm not even thinking about my videos or your movie. I wanna know if you're gonna be my friend after I leave—my *real* friend—you know, answer my calls and texts. Laugh at my jokes. Talk to me the way you always do." He sighs. "You know, not totally hate my guts."

I let out a long exhale. "Keane, I won't hate your guts. I couldn't even if I wanted to—though I'm sure it'd be easier for me if I could." I rub my face. "I'm not saying you're dead to me, okay? This isn't *The Godfather*. I'm just saying I can't handle being 'friends' with you the way we were before. Everything's changed for me and I can't go backward. I can't open my heart to you anymore or hold your hand or cuddle with you while we watch a movie. I can't let you move the hair out of my eyes." I swallow hard, stuffing back my tears. "All that stuff is over, Keane. Because being touched by you like that will just make me want to..." I swallow hard again. "Make love to you," I squeak out. My chest tightens. "And I'm not willing to torture myself that way." Oh, God, my voice is trembling. "Everything's different now and I'm not willing to pretend it's not."

"So what does that mean for us?" Keane asks softly. "We're not even *friends*?" His voice is strained.

I pause for a long time, considering my answer. "I can be 'friends' with Ball Peen Hammer, like I said," I finally reply, my voice strained. "But when it comes to Keane Morgan..." I swallow hard, stuffing down my emotion. "I can't pretend I don't want more."

Keane is quiet for a long time. I can't see his features clearly in the darkened room, but I can make out his silhouette as he lowers his head and runs his fingers through his hair.

The long silence between us is excruciating, but I can't think of anything else to say. I've already said ten thousand times more than I'd sworn to myself I would. The ball's in his court. I've laid myself bare.

"Can I kiss you one last time?" Keane finally asks softly, his voice barely audible.

"No," I say flatly. "My heart won't understand, even if my brain tries its best to explain the situation to it." I take a large gulp of air, trying to keep my emotions from seeping out of my eyes.

Keane makes an anguished sound as he rolls off the bed to standing. "Okay, Maddy. See ya 'round, I guess." His voice breaks. "I'm so sorry, Maddy. I've loved every minute—"

"Please don't," I say. "This was the deal. I knew it from the start. Nothing to apologize for." I take a deep breath. "And no need to say goodbye. We'll be doing the videos. We'll talk or text every day, I'm sure."

"I'm sorry, Maddy."

"Nothing to be sorry for. It was fun while it lasted."

Keane shuffles toward the door of my bedroom in the dark, but he stops before leaving and turns around. "Maddy?" he says softly.

My eyes are stinging. My throat is in danger of closing up. I don't reply.

Keane lets out a long exhale. "I'm really sorry."

"Good luck with your audition tomorrow," I say calmly in reply. "There's no doubt in my mind they're gonna fall head over heels in love with you, Keane." I bite my tongue, forcing myself not to say the words that are practically lurching from its tip: *Exactly the way I have.*

Chapter 50
Keane

Tuesday, 11:42 a.m.

"Peenie," Zander says. "Wake up."

I don't stir.

"Peenie!" Zander barks. "Melissa called. She wants you to call her right away. She's got a job for you."

I don't move a muscle.

"Get up, baby doll!" Zander booms, whacking my shoulder.

I jolt at his assault. "You're Satan," I grumble. "I was having a sex dream. Now I'm totally traumatized."

Zander pushes on my shoulder. "Get the fuck up, sweet meat. Oh, nice woody."

"Thanks."

"Rub that monster out and then call Melissa. She said she's got a huge job for you. Come on, Peenie. We got rent to pay and I'm not gonna pay you alimony after I divorce your ass for being a lazy, self-pitying gold-digger." Zander shoves my phone at me. "The Z-train leaves for the gym in exactly thirty-eight minutes and you best get your miserable ass on it." He claps his hands together loudly, right into my ear, making me jolt again. "No more feeling sorry for yourself, baby doll!"

"Motherfucker!" I shout. "Stop it!"

"I'm gonna get some endorphins pumping into that bloodstream of yours and cheer your mopey ass right up!" He whacks me across the head. "Get the fuck up and stop feeling sorry for yourself, fool. It's been three fucking weeks. She's obviously moved on and so should you."

I put my forearm over my eyes. "Stop *yelling* at me, fucker. Me no likey."

"I'm making eggs and turkey-bacon for you, sweet meat," Zander shouts over his shoulder as he leaves my bedroom. "Get the fuck up."

Jesus. Talk about a rude awakening. No man should be awakened by a dude screaming in his ear when he's in the middle of dreaming about eating a woman's pussy.

Maddy.

Goddammit, I can't stop thinking about that girl night and day, no matter how hard I try. I thought once I got home to Seattle and back in the swing of my awesome life again, all those crazy-intense feelings I'd been having for Maddy would quickly fade—but, man, was I wrong.

I reach down and grab my hard-on underneath my briefs and begin jerking myself off, giving The Talented Mr. Ripley yet *another* dose of the only kind of action he's seen for the past three weeks since I've been home, and, despite my best intentions to not think about Maddy *again* while jacking off, my thoughts immediately drift to her. I swear to God I could *taste* Maddy's pussy in the dream I was just having. And, man, she tasted good.

I jerk my shaft, up and down, letting my mind wander to all things Maddy. Her gorgeous tits. Her tight pussy. Those little freckles on her nose. The look in her eyes when she comes for me—or, rather, when she *used* to come for me.

Fuck.

I thought I'd come home from L.A. and revert right back to the handsome and happy lad I've always been, but since being home, I just can't get my mojo back. Everything I used to do to make myself happy just seems so *pointless*.

Focus, Peenie. This isn't the time to philosophize about the meaning of life. It's time to get yourself off.

I force myself to concentrate on the task at hand (pun intended), imagining I'm inside Maddy, pumping slowly in and out of her and whispering dirty-talk into her ear, and within no time at all, I'm coming all over my hand.

Maddy.

God, I physically *ache* for her. *All the fucking time.* No matter what I do, I can't stop thinking about her. I want to kiss her. Touch her. Fuck her. Just sit and *talk* to her about anything at all.

But it doesn't matter. This ache I'm feeling for this girl is a moot point because Maddy's clearly not feeling the same way about me. Not anymore, she's not. When I was in L.A. the other day for some callbacks, I texted Maddy to see if maybe she wanted to grab some dinner before my late flight home, but she turned me down.

"Sorry," she texted. "I have a huge project due tomorrow and I can't break away."

"No problem," I replied. "Maybe next time."

So I met Dax and the guys for a quick drink and then hauled my aching balls to the airport to catch an earlier flight back home.

Shit.

Maybe Zander's right: it's time for me to move on. Maddy and I live in different cities, after all, and, regardless, even if she lived next door, I'm not in the market for a girlfriend, which is what she wants to be—what she *deserves* to be.

Seriously, I've just gotta turn the page.

But try telling that to my balls.

With a heavy sigh, I roll out of bed and haul my pitiful ass and aching balls into the shower.

Chapter 51
Keane

I'm sitting on the edge of my bed, a towel wrapped around my waist, my phone in my hand.

"Oh my God, you're actually calling me?" my booking agent Melissa says when she picks up my call. "Is it the Apocalypse?"

"Hey, Mel," I say. "What's up?"

"I've got a huge job for you on Saturday night."

"Private gig?"

"Yeah."

"Mel, I told you: I'm only doing club gigs for a while. No privates."

"Yeah, I know. But it's been weeks, Keane, and this is a *huge* job. Five hundred up front, plus you'll kill it on tips. It's some rich cougar who saw you at Hot Spot a few months ago and had to have you for her birthday party."

"Thanks, but not interested."

Melissa exhales with exasperation. "Keane, what's going on? The big money's in the private gigs, not the clubs, you know that."

"I just don't have the stomach for privates these days."

Melissa lets out a long sigh. "It's okay. I get it. You need a break from the scene. It happens. A little time off and you'll be good as new. Just lemme know when you're ready to jump back into the game and I'll book you for a month solid."

"Thanks. I'll let you know."

When we hang up, I check my texts and my heart leaps at the sight of Maddy's name in my inbox. But even a cursory glance at her message and it's clear she's just texting me Ball Peen Hammer's daily homework assignment the same way she's done for the past three weeks.

"Hello, Ball Peen Hammer!" Maddy writes. "Great news! You know that white-cheddar popcorn you love so much? They've agreed to pay you for product placement! All you have to do is eat some of their popcorn (which you'd do anyway, right?) in one video per month, making sure the brand name on the bag is visible. Gotta love the Internet. I'll forward you the email about the pay. It's not much, but, hopefully, this is just the beginning of the gravy train for you, BPH. Congrats!"

I reply immediately: "Thanks, Mad Genius! You da best! But just to be clear: this is just the beginning of the gravy train for BOTH of us, not just me. (We agreed to a 50-50 split on everything, remember?)"

Maddy replies with a smiley face and dollar-bill emoji.

"So what's today's assignment?" I write. "Lemme guess: a shirtless selfie?"

"Wow, you're psychic," Maddy writes. "Just make sure your muscles look extra hawt, BPH. You're gaining a thousand followers a day on Instagram and your shirtless photos get the most likes by far." She attaches a muscle-arm emoji and a dollar bill.

"Roger," I write.

"Rabbit," she replies. "Plus, let's do something for Vine today. Shoot something where you're taking your shirt off and saying something super douche-y like, 'You're welcome!' Just send it to me and I'll edit it down to six seconds and upload it. And then let's have you do a couple minutes for YouTube. I'm thinking something with Zander, the two of you doing something exceedingly stupid (but NOT smoking weed!!). I'm thinking thumb wrestling, a burping contest, beer pong, whatever. Doesn't matter as long as it's something stupid and highly dude-like."

I text back: "Everything Zander and I do is stupid and highly dude-like. Might as well tell me to post a video of us breathing. BTW, I haven't touched weed or alcohol since I got back to Seattle. Been getting ripped for a modeling gig my agent's working on getting me in L.A. Don't know the date I'll be doing it yet, but when I find out, I'll let u know cuz I'm hoping we can hang out???"

Maddy replies quickly. "Sorry. I can't."

"I haven't given u the date yet."

"Yeah, but I'm super busy these days. Can't really hang out with anyone. Nothing personal. Too much to do."

I sigh.

"Hey!" Zander yells from the kitchen. "Z-train leaves for the gym in four minutes!"

I don't reply. I'm too busy thinking about how my balls feel like they're in a vise.

"Yo! Peen!" Zander yells.

"Yeah," I say. "Just a sec."

This is bullshit. I don't care what she said in L.A. There's no reason we can't at least be friends. *Real friends*. Even before the sex thing, Maddy and I could talk for hours about *anything*.

I quickly type out a text to Maddy: "Hey, running to the gym. Will u be around later? Would really like to talk to u. Just wanna catch up."

The reply comes back quickly: "Going to the library to study. Maybe another time? Have fun at the gym. Say hi to Z for me. Gotta go. Bye."

Chapter 52
Keane

My phone rings on my nightstand and I roll on my side to grab
it. When I look at the display screen, expecting it to be my mother or
landlord (because who else would be lame enough to call me?), I'm
surprised to see the call is from my agent in L.A. Oh my God. That
guy doesn't call to chat about the weather—if he's calling me,
something's up.

"Hey, Adam," I say, my heart racing. "What's up?"

"You got the reality show," he says, his voice brimming with
excitement.

"What? Oh my God. Really?"

Adam laughs. "Yup. It's gonna be six guys featured, but they're
gonna build the entire show around you, Keane."

"Oh my God."

"Guaranteed full season. Ten episodes. The money per episode
isn't life changing or anything, but that's reality TV for you. Cheap
bastards." He tells me the amount of money they're offering to pay
me for three months of shooting and, although it's not mind-blowing
or anything, I'm far from disappointed. In three months, I'll earn
what I made in the minor leagues for a full season of baseball. "But
the real game-changer is gonna be parlaying your fame from the TV
show into other gigs—commercials, appearance fees, endorsements,
print ads. I should be able to get you a ton of work from the
notoriety."

"Ho-lee shit," I mutter, my mind racing.

"And if the show gets picked up for a second season, well, that's
when the real money per episode will kick in, especially if you've

344

established yourself as a celebrity by then, which I have no doubt you will."

"Wow. So... did they tell you the game plan for the show?"

"Pretty standard reality-TV fare. Half the time they'll follow you around and film you as you live your exciting and sexy life as a male stripper. You'll do your usual gigs—bachelorette parties, clubs, birthday parties, whatever, just like you already do—and you'll also pick up women right and left the way you describe in your Ball Peen Hammer videos. They really want you to play up the manwhore thing to the hilt—really go over the top with it." He laughs. "I take it that won't be a problem for you?"

"Um," I say, my stomach clenching.

"And the other half of the time," my agent continues, "they'll film you and the other five guys as you live together in the stripper-mansion. Oh, yeah, I should mention: you and the other guys will live together in a mansion in the Hollywood Hills during the whole shoot. "

Again, my stomach churns. "Oh," I say.

"Of course, they want you and the other guys to have all sorts of crazy drama—you know, fights over women, maybe you can accuse some guy of 'disrespecting you' and almost come to blows. That sort of thing, you know. But, of course, they also want to see you having a bromance, too. They *love* the videos you've been putting up lately with you and your roommate. What's his name again?"

"Zander."

"That's right. They love you guys together, so they want you to have a friendship just like that with one of the guys in the house. They're actually thinking about casting a black guy for the role."

I physically shudder. "Hey, maybe I won't even notice the difference," I say coldly.

Adam laughs. "Funny. But, mostly, they just want lots and lots of drama."

"Hmm," I say, feeling at a loss for words. My stomach is churning so violently, I feel like I'm gonna barf.

"It's an amazing opportunity, Keane. Congratulations. There's only one thing they wanted to confirm before they ink the deal—but I already told 'em it shouldn't be a problem: they want you to take down all your Ball Peen Hammer videos and sign over ownership of the name to them."

I can't think straight. I'm physically nauseated. "Why?" I choke out.

"Because they're gonna duplicate all those videos on the show. They absolutely *love* them, Keane. They think they're genius. They went on and on about what a fresh and original voice you have—how there's no one else like you. So there's gonna be a big thing every episode—'Ball Peen Hammer Says'—where you talk straight to the camera and give your one-of-a-kind advice on how to live a handsome and happy life and they don't want any of the content you've already posted to steal their thunder. But you don't care about that, right? I mean, a rinky-dink YouTube channel is chump change compared to the exposure you'll get on national television, especially if we can parlay this thing into multiple seasons. Shit, they squeezed four seasons out of *Jersey Shore* and those kids were getting a couple mill per season by the end. He laughs with glee. "If we can get this thing picked up for a second season, you'll be on the gravy train, big-time."

"But I can't be Ball Peen Hammer anymore?" I ask lamely. I feel like a deer in headlights.

"Well, I mean, your character on the show will be known as 'Ball Peen Hammer,' and you can still call yourself that in relation to the show and your live performances, but they'll own that character for media purposes." He chuckles like I'm a silly toddler who's trying to stick a bobby pin into a light socket. "Trust me, Keane, this is standard procedure. Don't stress it."

I don't reply.

"Oh, and they want you to keep your blue hair," he continues. "You're cool with that, right? I told them you wouldn't have a problem with that. They think it makes you 'instantly recognizable,' which is great for branding. Although they're thinking you'd start out season one with your natural hair color and then dye it blue in episode one to help another guy in the house get laid. You know, they just want you to recreate the story you told them in the audition." He chuckles. "They *love* that story."

"Wow," I say, incapable of saying anything else. I run my hand through my blue hair.

Adam chuckles again. "Speechless, huh?"

"Pretty much."

"You should be. This is an amazing opportunity for anyone, but especially a newbie like you. Some people spend years dreaming of getting a shot like this, and you swooped into town with your blue hair and eight-pack and sparkling personality and turned everyone's head. It's amazing how much buzz there is about you right now, Keane. We've got lightning in a bottle with you, I'm telling you. Once I seal this deal for you, I'm gonna use it to get you booked solid for commercials and print ads. Fasten your seatbelt, baby, because you're about to get whiplash."

"When do I have to give them an answer?" I ask, my pulse pounding in my ears.

"What do you mean?" Adam asks slowly. "What's there to think about?"

"It's a big decision. I just need to mull it over for a bit."

"What?" Adam says, clearly floored. "Is this about the money?"

"No, the money's fine."

"Because for a newbie with no credits to your name, they're paying you pretty well. Like I say, you're not gonna get rich off the actual contract, but the real game isn't the per-episode fee, it's all the stuff I can book for you based on your newfound celebrity status. And, by the way, the deal they were originally offering was twenty percent less than what I negotiated for you."

"Yeah, the money's great. Thanks."

There's a pause. "Okay, well. As your agent, I highly advise you to take this opportunity and run with it like hell."

"I understand. Thanks. When do you need an answer?"

Adam pauses again. "Monday at the very latest."

"Okay. Thanks. I'll let you know by Monday."

"What's the hiccup for you, Keane? I thought you'd be jumping for joy."

"Just wanna think it over, that's all. Big decision. Not sure it's for me."

"Not for you? It's perfect for you."

How the fuck does this guy know what's "perfect" for me? He's talked to me for a grand total of two hours. He doesn't know shit about me. "I'll let you know," I say evenly.

Adam lets out a long exhale. "Well, that didn't go as expected."

I don't reply.

"Okay, um, so, in other news—when it rains it pours, I guess." He pauses for effect. "You won't believe this but right before I got the call about the reality show, I got a call from the casting director for that black *Magic Mike* movie. They offered you the token white guy role."

"Oh my God. Seriously?" My skin explodes with electricity. "*Oh my God.*"

"Wow. Now *that's* the reaction I was expecting for the reality show."

"What'd they say?" I ask, barely able to breathe.

"Okay, hang on. Don't get too excited. It's not nearly as much money as the TV show, since it's a small role for scale plus ten and they only need you for a few weeks of shooting. This movie isn't gonna make you a celebrity like the TV show—I mean, it might get you in the door of your next audition, introduce you to some well-connected people, which is always good, but this part alone isn't gonna be a game-changer."

"Holy fuck," I say, standing up from my bed and pacing around my bedroom. "This is fantastic."

"Yeah, if you didn't get offered the TV show the same day, I'd probably be jumping up and down, popping champagne for you about the movie. But the TV show is a much better opportunity in the big picture—I'm positive I can get things going for you much faster if you're the star of a reality show than a bit player with a couple lines in a *Magic Mike* rip-off."

"But, still, the *Magic Mike* rip-off is a feature film, right? From a major studio? That's pretty huge. And if I do a good job and make friends with everyone, and the casting director winds up really liking me, who knows what other movies they might think of putting me in at some point. Right?"

"Yeah, sure. Don't get me wrong. It's fantastic they want you, especially since you've got no prior experience. That speaks volumes about how much they believe in you. In fact, they already like you so much, they told me they're planning to expand your role a bit from what's in the original script. They're gonna throw you a few more lines, make you more featured. They're even gonna give you a name—you'd no longer be 'Stripper Number Six.'" He laughs.

"Are you serious? I've got an actual *name*?" I blurt. "Awesome! What is it?"

"*Brad.*"

I laugh. "That's most definitely a white-guy name."

"Yeah, the casting director was laughing her ass off about it when she called me."

"Wow, thanks, man," I say. "I can't wipe the smile off my face. Offers for a speaking part in a major Hollywood movie *and* a TV show on the same day. Holy fuck, I feel like I just got called up to the big leagues."

"Slow down, high-speed. Don't get too excited," Adam says. "Unfortunately, you can't have your cake and eat it, too. It's gotta be one or the other—the TV show or the movie. The shooting schedules conflict."

"Oh." I pause for a long beat, considering the situation. "Would the movie require me to stop doing my Ball Peen Hammer videos?"

"No. Actually, it was the videos that tipped them in your favor," Adam says. "They loved you in your auditions, of course—you charmed their pants off—but those Ball Peen Hammer videos convinced them you're not just a dancing monkey. In fact, just 'cause you're so pretty, they might even throw you on the press junket when the movie releases, depending how things go." He laughs. "They called you a 'marketing genius.'"

I laugh. "It's not me who's the genius," I say. "It's Maddy Behind the Camera. Remember Maddy from that night at Giselle's? I introduced you right after I performed."

"Oh, yeah. That's right—your cheerleader, right?" He laughs. "Well, you definitely owe her one. Those videos helped you get both offers. But, like I say, it's a moot point about the movie. It's a great boost for your confidence to get the offer, and it tells me you're a slam dunk in auditions, so that's great, but like I say I recommend you take the reality show. Without a doubt, especially based on who you are, the TV show's the perfect fit for you."

I bristle. "Based on who I am? Who am I, in your view?"

"Ball Peen Hammer, baby," he says brightly. "You're not trying to be some kind of serious actor or anything. You're just a 'handsome and happy lad,' livin' it up. And this reality show will play to that. Think about how *Jersey Shore* launched those kids and made 'em household names. That's what I'm gonna do for you. But that's all down the line, once we've gotten things rolling. First things first, let's call the producer and tell her you're in and that you can't wait, okay?"

"No. Like I said, I gotta think about it before I make my decision."

Adam audibly sighs. "Fine. I'll tell them you're traveling today on a family emergency or something and I can't reach you 'til Monday. That way they won't think you're pulling some sort of diva crap. But I gotta know by Monday, Keane, okay? Or else we're gonna piss them off."

I clench my jaw. "Tell them whatever you want. I'll let you know as soon as I make up my mind."

"Okay. Call me as soon as you can."

"I will. Talk to you later."

We hang up and I sit and stare blankly at the wall for a long minute, my mind racing. Ho-lee shit. I've got a huge decision to make here.

I definitely need some expert counsel from someone who knows me inside and out. Someone who won't bullshit me, no matter what. Someone who loves me the most.

Chapter 53
Keane

"What's wrong?" my mother blurts when she answers my call.

"Why do you think something's wrong?" I ask.

"Because you're calling me."

"I just wanted to hear your voice."

"Oh, thank God," Mom says. "I thought you were calling me from the hospital or jail." She breathes a sigh of relief. "So to what do I owe this rare pleasure, honey? You need money?"

"Nope. Just wanted to say hi."

"Mmm hmm. Are you perhaps calling to charm me into making you a big pan of lasagna, my darling Keaney?"

"No, actually, I *wasn't*, but if you're offering, then hell yeah, dude, I'd totally mack the hell outta some Momma Lou lasagna."

Mom giggles. "All right, honey. Just don't tell the others. They always hate it when I coddle you."

"You're not *coddling* me, Momma Bear, you're *mothering* me—and doing a mighty fine job of it, I must say."

"Yeah, yeah. You can stop charming me now, Keaney—I've already said I'll make you the lasagna."

"Thanks, Mom-a-tron. You da best. But, hey, would you mind making me some chili instead of lasagna? I've got a big photo shoot next week so I'm laying off the carbs. Gotta make my abs pop; you know how it goes."

"Yes, I do. It's a constant battle for me to make sure my abs are popping."

I laugh.

"So what's the photo shoot, Keaney Baby?"

"Remember that modeling agency I told you guys about in our

351

group text? They want me to shoot a bunch of different stuff for a portfolio so they can start booking modeling jobs and commercials for me."

"Ooooh. That's exciting. What kinds of modeling jobs?"

"Fitness stuff, mostly. Some fashion. They said I'm already in the running for a big Calvin Klein campaign even without having the portfolio, just based on some shots I posted on Instagram."

"*Calvin Klein*? Omigosh. Is it an ad for jeans?"

I smile to myself, anticipating my mom's reaction to what I'm about to say. "No, Mom. Underwear."

"*Underwear*?" Mom blurts. "Oh, Keaney." She sighs. "So you're gonna make an entire *career* out of wearing nothing but your underwear?"

I laugh. "Apparently."

"Oh, Keane. For goodness sake." My mother's words are scolding, but her tone tells me she's smiling from ear to ear on the other end of the phone line. "Well, good luck with that. Speaking of you wearing nothing but your underwear," Mom continues, her voice full of warmth, "are you still prancing around half naked for hordes of screaming women these days?"

"Yeah, but not as much. I've decided to try to make a go of the modeling and acting thing."

"Oh, modeling *and* acting? I thought it was just modeling. That's great, honey. I think acting will be right up your alley. I always say you're a ham and cheese sandwich, don't I?"

"Yup."

"I really think you'll have lots of success with acting if you put your mind to it, honey."

"That's actually what I wanted to talk to you about, Mom. I've been going to auditions the past few weeks and I just got offered my first two acting jobs—one on TV and another in a movie."

"Oh my gosh! *Two* acting jobs? Congratulations, honey!" She begins squealing and shrieking in celebration.

"Mom, stop screaming with unbridled glee for a minute. *Mom.* Hey, Mom. Hello?"

"What?"

"There's a glitch. Because of scheduling, I can only take one of the jobs. I gotta pick."

Mom giggles. "Oh, well. That's still worth shrieking about. Either way, you've landed your first job in Hollywood, right? This is so exciting!" She squeals again. "We'll have to have everyone over for dinner to celebrate. When can you come?" She squeals yet again. "I'll make whatever you want for dinner. Gah! I'm so proud of you."

"Mom, listen. Stop squealing like Little G for a second, woman."

We both laugh.

"Dude, I gotta make a huge decision here. I'm stressed out."

"Oh, honey, there's no reason to be stressed. This is a good problem to have. Just tell me about each offer and I'll help you figure it out."

I proceed to tell my momma every single thing I know about the two jobs, including telling her briefly about the videos I've been doing with Maddy (and how the reality show would require me to stop making them), and she listens intently, interrupting only occasionally to ask a few pointed questions.

"So what do you think I should do, Motherboard?" I ask when I'm finished telling her the scoop. "The way I see it, the reality show is the more immediately lucrative pick: more money, more exposure, and a bigger chance of getting other jobs from it, right off the bat. On the other hand, the movie is a small part—really just a glorified extra unless I can somehow razzle-dazzle everyone on-set and make it into something or *maybe* impress the casting director or director so they think of me for their next movie. And, hell, with the movie, there's no guarantee I'd even make it past the cutting room floor. In the TV show, on the other hand, I'd be the star." I sigh heavily, the weight of the world suddenly pressing down on me. "I'd be an idiot to pass up the reality show, right? It's a bird in the hand. A sure thing."

Mom audibly shrugs across the phone line.

"Mom, come on. Just tell me what you think. I need your expert counsel."

"Okay. Here's what I think: in my expert opinion as a mother and a wise old woman, I think you should listen to your gut."

"Come on, Mom. Don't go all Yoda on my ass. Tell me your opinion. It's a huge decision and I don't wanna blow it. I want to make a mature and reasoned decision, not based on emotion."

"Honey, there's nothing immature about following your heart. In fact, having the self-awareness and confidence to bet on yourself and listen to your inner voice demonstrates more maturity and character than anything else. Life is rarely about what you *think*—it's almost always about what you *feel*."

I wait for her to continue, but she doesn't. "So you're telling me to take the movie?" I finally ask.

"I'm telling you that, after hearing you talk about the two offers, it's clear to me which job offer made you feel like a million bucks and which one made you feel like that little poop-emoji with eyes—you know, the one Kat always tacks onto her texts when she's changing a diaper?"

We both laugh.

"Screw your agent, sweetheart," Mom says. "It's his job to get you job offers and provide information to help you make your decision. But it's *your* decision to make because it's *your* life. In my opinion, you should take the offer that makes you feel like a million bucks every time, no matter how the potential money or fame stacks up. I don't know anything about the entertainment industry, but I know a lot about life. And from my experience, in the long run, consistently making choices aligned with your true heart's desire will lead you to your rightful destiny in the end. Life is a marathon, my love, not a sprint. Trust yourself. You'll get to the finish line eventually. We all do. And when you get there, if you've been true to yourself, you'll be able to look yourself in the mirror with pride and a sense of accomplishment—and, most importantly, no regrets."

"Damn," I breathe after a moment. "You *rock*, Mom."

"Thanks. A little bit of brains combined with a lot of experience is a wicked combination."

"Thanks, Mom."

She sighs deeply. "Sweetie, baseball was *one* chapter of your life, but your story has so many unwritten chapters to come. Don't look back and long for what could have been—look ahead and *aspire*. You want to be a handsome and happy lad, like you always say? Then be true to yourself and dream big. You're gonna do wonderful things, sweetheart—exciting things—some of them maybe even with your clothes on."

I laugh. "Thanks, Mom."

"So now that you're gonna be Brad the Token White Guy

Stripper in a Hollywood movie does this mean you'll be moving to L.A.?"

"Yeah. I'm gonna crash at Daxy's 'til Zander can get his ass down there at some point."

"Good. And you'll still do the videos, I presume? You sure look like you're having fun doing them. I especially love watching you interact with that 'Maddy Behind the Camera.' The two of you are adorable together."

My heart lurches into my throat. "You've *seen* my videos? Oh my God, Mom. I didn't even know you knew about them before I mentioned them just now."

"Kitty Kat showed them to me the other day. But don't worry, she warned me you talk about raunchy stuff in some of them, so I only watched the ones she said wouldn't traumatize me. And from what I saw, you're wonderful in them. You light up the screen."

"That's what Maddy always says. She says I come alive on camera."

"You do. Especially when you're talking to Maddy. And, man, does she giggle at everything you say from behind the camera. She's absolutely adorable."

"Zander says she's adorbsicles."

Mom laughs. "I'd love to meet her. Can you bring her to dinner when we celebrate?"

"She lives in L.A."

"Oh. That's too bad. I was hoping to meet her."

"She's awesome, Mom—the smartest girl I've ever met (besides you, of course). She's going to UCLA film school—she wants to make documentaries—so I hitched a ride with her from Seattle to L.A., and the whole drive we just had this incredible *connection*. It was amazing. I felt like I'd known her my whole life. She's the best girl ever, Mom. Sweet. Funny. So smart. Doesn't take any of my shit."

"So she's your girlfriend, then? Or do you kids call it something different these days?"

My chest tightens. "No. Maddy's not my girlfriend. We're just friends."

"*Oh.* Really? Wow. The way you were talking about her, I assumed you two were having a romance."

"Actually, Maddy and I *were* dating for a bit, sort of, but then she made it clear she wanted to get serious and I... freaked out." I sigh deeply.

"Why'd you freak out? You just told me she's the best girl ever. What's there to freak out about?"

"Oh, you know, I was just..." I trail off, not sure of the ending to that sentence.

"Being an idiot?" Mom offers.

I exhale. "Yeah."

"Ah." Mom pauses. "So that's an easy fix: tell her you've come to your senses and now you want to be with her. I'm sure she'll be thrilled. That kind of giggle doesn't happen very often to a girl, trust me."

I run my hand through my hair. "Mom, I know you're just trying to be helpful and all, but you don't understand. It's not that simple."

"Why not? She likes you and you like her. Sounds simple to me."

"Mom."

"What?"

"You don't understand."

"Explain it."

I sigh. "Maddy totally put herself out there—which is something that's really hard for her to do—and I smashed her in the teeth. And now she doesn't wanna have anything to do with me beyond making our videos."

"Aw, honey. She's just protecting herself from getting hurt. You can't expect the poor girl to slam her head into a brick wall *twice*, can you?"

"Mom, I screwed up. I hurt her. Our connection was *amazing*— once in a lifetime—and I acted like it was business as usual. She told me stuff she doesn't normally tell people. And now I can't just pick up the phone and say, 'Hey, Maddy, I'm an idiot. I've realized I'm in love with you. Please forgive me,' and expect everything to be magically amazing like it was before."

There's a long beat.

"Sweetheart, do you realize what you just said?"

My chest tightens. "What?"

"Think about what you just said, Keaney."

I think. "Oh. Wow."

"Yeah. *Wow*. Did you mean it?"

I swallow hard. "Yeah."

"Well, then, for the love of God, stop living up to your penile nickname and call that girl. Trust me, women have a tremendous capacity to forgive the idiots they love."

My face flushes. "Holy shit, Mom."

Mom laughs. "Holy shit, honey."

I'm suddenly completely electrified. "Bye, Mom. Good talkin' with you, babesicles. You know I love you the most, right?"

"Yes, I do. Isn't it amazing what can happen when you actually *call* your mother instead of text her on occasion?"

I laugh. "Yeah, Mom. Point well taken."

"I love you, Keaney Baby. Now go get that adorable girl."

Chapter 54
Keane

I press my phone against my ear, my heart racing, waiting for Maddy to pick up my call. Oh my God, I can't wait to tell Maddy how I feel about her. That I've been miserable without her since I left her. That I was an idiot. That I want to touch her. Kiss her. Fuck her. Hold her close while we watch a movie. And then lick her. Suck on her nipples. Make her come. *Talk to her*. Oh my God! I've got to tell Maddy I'm moving to L.A.!

But my call goes straight into Maddy's voicemail.

"Hey, Maddy," I say at the sound of the beep, my pulse pounding in my ears. "Call me as soon as you get this message, okay? I've got something important to tell you." I pause. "Okay. Well. Bye. Talk to you soon."

I hang up the phone and, for ten minutes, sit on the edge of my bed, staring at my phone, willing it to buzz with an incoming call from Maddy.

But it doesn't.

So I wait another five minutes, feeling the whole time like my balls are gonna explode.

Finally, when I can't take it anymore, I shoot Maddy a text: "Hey, Maddy," I write. "I left u a vm. Gimme a call. There's something I gotta tell u. It's important. Please get back to me ASAP. Thanks. Can't wait to talk to u!!"

I sit and stare at my phone for another five minutes, waiting for a reply, but she doesn't respond.

Fuck.

I can't stand it. I gotta take matters into my own hands.

358

I pull my laptop off my dresser and five minutes later, I've got myself booked on a two-hour flight to LAX, departing Seattle in a few hours.

I check my phone. Still nothing from Maddy.

Shit. My balls hurt.

I get dressed, pack a duffel bag, and sprint out of my bedroom. When I get into the living room, I find Zander entangled on the couch with Daphne, watching a movie. "Hey D," I say to Daphne, my heart racing.

"Hey P," Daphne replies.

I clear my throat, trying to keep myself from sounding like a madman. "Z, can I tear you away from D for just a minute? It's rather important." Oh my God, I'm about to explode.

"Sure thing," Zander says. He lays a soft kiss on Daphne's lips, touches her cheek, languidly disentangles himself from her long limbs like he's got all the time in the world, and rises slowly from the couch. "What's up, baby doll?" He looks at my duffel bag. "Where you going?"

"On safari, son—I'm going big-game hunting in L.A."

Zander flashes a huge smile. "You're finally gonna bag yourself a Maddy?"

I return Zander's broad smile. "Boo-fucking-yah."

"It's about fucking time, Steve Sanders."

"You've got an electric razor, right?"

"Yeah, in my bathroom. Left drawer."

"Actually, I need your help with something. Come on." Without waiting for Zander's reply, I turn around and march toward Zander's bathroom.

"Hang on," Zander says behind my back. "I use that razor to shave my balls."

I stop and weigh that nugget of information for a short beat. "Doesn't matter," I quickly decide, shaking my head with sudden determination. I motion to my blue hair. "Even if I have to rub this shit off using your balls as a scouring pad, it time for this shit to go."

Chapter 55
Keane

Friday, 5:48 p.m.

I rap on the front door of Maddy's apartment, my pulse racing. Why hasn't she answered any of my calls or texts all day long? Since this morning, I've left Maddy a total of five messages—two voicemails and three texts—all of them asking her to please give me a call because I have something important to tell her. I thought for sure when my plane landed in L.A. and I turned my phone back on, there'd be a text or voicemail waiting for me from Maddy—but, no.

And now, honestly, I'm freaking the fuck out, imagining Maddy lying in a ditch in her car or huddled in some far corner of campus after having been assaulted by some sicko. Oh my God, if a single hair on Maddy's beautiful head has been harmed in any way, I'll never recover. Just the thought of something happening to Maddy is turning me into a psychopath.

I knock on Maddy's apartment door again, panic threatening to overwhelm me.

Now that everything's clicked inside me, I'm a man possessed. If I don't talk to Maddy right away and tell her how I feel, I'm gonna explode.

I raise my fist to knock a third time, but the door abruptly opens and Hannah's bespectacled face greets me.

"Keane?" she says. "What are you doing here?" Her tone makes it clear she's less than thrilled to see me.

"Is Maddy okay?" I blurt.

"Yeah. She's fine." Hannah's face flashes concern. "Why? Did something happen?"

"No, I've tried calling and texting her all day, but she hasn't replied."

"Oh," Hannah says, her face relaxing.

"Is she here?"

"She's out."

"I've texted and called her all day and she hasn't replied," I repeat.

The faintest hint of a smirk dances on Hannah's lips. "Gosh, that must feel pretty shitty to be ignored like that, huh?"

My face flushes. "Will you please just tell me where she is?" I ask evenly, choosing to ignore Hannah's obvious barb.

"Why don't you hang out at Dax's for a while?" She motions across the hall. "I think Dax and the guys are at the studio all day, but I've got the key to their apartment if you need it. Just hang out there and I'll text you when Maddy gets home."

"No, I need to talk to Maddy."

Hannah makes a "suit yourself" face at me and begins closing her door.

I stick my arm out to stop the movement of the door. "You think maybe Maddy's at school? At the library?"

Hannah leans against the doorjamb, cool as a cucumber. "Maddy's not at school."

Holy fuck, Hannah sounds like a cold-blooded killer right now. I've never seen her like this. "Well, then, where is she?" I ask, suddenly certain Hannah knows exactly where her sister is.

"I'm not at liberty to divulge that information," Hannah replies primly, staring me down.

I clench my jaw. "Hannah, please. Just tell me where she is. I hopped a flight just to talk to her. I've got something important to tell her."

Hannah's face softens. "You flew down here just to talk to her?"

"Yeah. I've got no other reason to be here. Dax doesn't even know I'm here. She didn't answer my calls or texts so I booked a flight and hopped on a plane and here I am."

Hannah twists her mouth. "Well, that's kind of awesome." She looks at me sideways. "Will Maddy like what you came here to tell her?"

"If she still has feelings for me, then most definitely. And if not, then at least she'll enjoy the satisfaction of watching me grovel." Hannah's clearly on the cusp of helping me—it's written all over her

361

face—so I go in for the kill. "Please, Hannah," I say earnestly. "I know you're pissed at me for hurting Maddy's feelings, but I—"

Anger flashes across Hannah's face. "You didn't 'hurt Maddy's feelings.' You broke her heart." She lets out an angry puff of air. "Maddy's sensitive, okay? More sensitive than the average bear. Maybe what happened would have been no big deal to another girl, but Maddy's not like everyone else. She's not used to being used and thrown away. I know it's par for the course for you, Ball Peen Hammer, but for Maddy, feeling so special like that and then being tossed aside like it was nothing was a crushing blow. She thought you two had something really special." She glares at me. "And now she feels stupid—*pathetic*—like she made the whole thing up in her head."

A huge lump has risen in my throat. "She didn't make it up," I say. "Everything she felt, I felt it, too. I was just too big a chicken shit to admit it."

Hannah crosses her arms over her chest. "Maddy's been the saddest little puppy dog you ever saw since you left. This should be the time of her life—she's at her dream school, studying the thing she loves more than life itself, meeting new people every day who share her greatest passion—and yet all she does is mope around here, missing you and then feeling like a moron for missing you."

My heart is squeezing painfully inside my chest. My eyes are stinging. "I get it," I breathe. I run my hand over my newly cropped hair. "That's why I came down here. To tell her I fucked up."

"I love your hair, by the way," Hannah says, her attention obviously drawn by my hand movement. "It makes your eyes pop. Jeez, your eyes look like they're photoshopped."

"Thanks." I drop my hand from my head. "Hannah, please. Just tell me where she is. I got some incredible news today—game changing, amazing news. And the minute I got it, the only person in the whole world I wanted to share it with was Maddy." I look into Hannah's eyes. "Please, Hannah. I hopped a flight to tell Maddy I'm an idiot. Please let me throw myself at her mercy before I combust. At the very least, give your sister the satisfaction of hearing me say I'm sorry and turning me down. *Please.*"

Hannah visibly softens. But then she does something I'm not expecting whatsoever: she rolls her eyes. "Jesus, Keane. Great timing, you idiot."

The hairs on my arms stand on end. "Why? What's happened?"

Hannah looks up at the ceiling, shaking her head with disdain. "After weeks of wallowing in misery, Maddy *finally* decided to move on *today*. She said pining for you was too hard and she had to face the fact it wasn't gonna happen. This morning, she said she was gonna turn the page and move on."

"What the fuck does 'turn the page and move on' mean? How the hell is she planning to do that?"

"She's on a date, Keane."

"A *date*?" I blurt. "With who?"

"Some guy she met on the drive from Seattle. She said he's here visiting his brother."

"Oh motherfucker. Hell no. The dude from the mini-mart?" I grit my teeth. "Hannah, you gotta tell me where she is right fucking now. *Please*, Hannah. If you don't, I'm gonna go DEFCON-one here."

There's a beat as Hannah makes up her mind. "Okay. Come on, Ball Peen Hammer," she finally says, rolling her eyes. She opens her front door wide. "Maddy didn't say where the guy was taking her tonight, but I'll track her iPhone on my laptop."

Chapter 56
Maddy

"What'd I tell ya?" Brian says as I bite into my hamburger. "Legendary, right?"

I nod, still chewing.

"Best burger ever," Brian says.

"Pretty good," I say. I take a long sip of my water. "It's got a surprising kick to it."

"Yeah, it's the kick that keeps you coming back for more." He smiles wickedly.

I return Brian's smile, but mine is merely polite. Was that Brian's attempt at sexual innuendo? I resist the urge to sigh loudly. "It's funny you should say that," I say, doing my best to keep our stilted conversation humming along. "Because I was just reading an article in *UCLA Magazine* about the top ten places to get a burger in L.A. and it said the—"

"*Maddy.*"

I look to my right and instantly have a seizure. "Keane?" I blurt, blood rushing into my face. "What...?" Oh my God, he looks insanely hot. His spikey blue mop has been shaved down into a dirty-blonde buzz cut—and now that Keane's face doesn't have to compete with his hair for attention, his gorgeous eyes are glowing like two blue coals.

"Sorry to keep you waiting, baby doll," Keane says smoothly, a smile dancing on his beautiful lips. "I was outside, parking my white horse.'"

I open my mouth to speak, but nothing comes out. What the fuckity is Keane doing here? And *now* of all times, when I'm sitting here with frickin' Brian on a freakin' *date*?

"The guy from the *mini-mart*?" Brian blurts. "*Seriously?*"

364

"Hey, Brian," Keane says, smirking. "Sorry to cock-block you *again*, brah, but I gotta talk to my girl." He looks at me. "Hey, babe, you didn't send me my homework assignment this morning. How am I supposed to be Ball Peen Hammer without my partner in crime, Maddy Behind the Camera?"

I'm speechless. *That's* why Keane's here, out of the blue—when I'm on a date with frickin' *Brian*—because I didn't send him a text instructing him what freaking *video* to record this morning?

"I... was..." I stammer. Oh good lord. My tongue feels thick and useless inside my mouth. "I... um. Didn't. Gah."

Keane seems unfazed by my inability to string two words together. "So, seeing as how you left me to my own devices, I was forced to use my pea-brain to come up with my *own* idea for today's video," Keane says, his eyes twinkling. "And, actually, if I do say so myself, I totally nailed it."

I can't fathom what's happening. Why is Keane here out of the blue—and looking so goddamned gorgeous? Is he *trying* to torture me?

"And then, lo and behold, after I'd finished recording my totally *awesome* video," Keane says, his voice cutting through the firestorm of my racing thoughts, "I thought it was so fucking *kewl*—and, yes, I'm spelling that k-e-w-l—I had to show it to you right away or I felt like I was gonna explode."

I look at Brian, my cheeks burning, and find him looking completely annoyed.

"But, gosh darn it, Maddy, you didn't return *any* of my calls or texts *all day long*," Keane continues. "Which serves me right, by the way—I know I totally deserved that shit—so, of course, that left me no choice but to fly down here to show you the video in person." He flashes a huge smile, showcasing his dimples.

I can't smile back at Keane—my mouth muscles don't seem to be under my control at the moment. "You flew all the way down to Los Angeles to show me a *video*?" I sputter. My brain feels like it's short-circuiting. All I want to do is leap out of my chair, throw my arms around Keane's neck, kiss his beautiful lips, and sob to him pathetically about how much I've missed him. But I can't do it. Keane has very clearly informed me he wants to be my friend and nothing more, and I'll be damned if I'm gonna beg a man to want me, no matter who he is or how much I want him. "I can't do this right now," I manage to say, my calm tone surprising myself. "Maybe tomorrow?" I glance at Brian and try to smile reassuringly, though I'm quite certain I'm not succeeding.

Keane holds his phone out to me. "Sorry, man-eater. It's gotta be now."

I feel like I'm gonna pass out from the stress of this horribly awkward situation. Nothing even remotely like this has ever happened to me before.

"Keane," I say imploringly, my eyes beseeching him to leave and stop torturing me. "*Please*."

"Watch the video, Maddy," Keane says evenly, his jaw set. "I'm not leaving 'til you watch it."

Oh jeez. This situation is literally painful. I glance at Brian again. His face is red and his jaw is clenched—and that's all I need to come to my senses. I absolutely can't watch this video, not in front of Brian. The right thing to do is tell Keane he'll just have to wait for me to watch his *kewl* video until tomorrow (*if* I happen to find time in my busy schedule because, news flash, I've got a very busy and exciting life that doesn't involve sitting around pining for a guy who's already told me he doesn't want me after I shamelessly threw myself at him).

Yep, that's most definitely the right thing to do.

And exactly what I'm going to do.

Hell yes.

Starting now.

I open my mouth and then shut it again.

Damn.

I hastily grab Keane's phone from his open palm, blood whooshing into my ears in a torrent, but before I've pressed "play" on the video, Brian's voice commands my attention.

"Hey, Maddy," Brian says abruptly, his tone making it clear he's extremely irritated. "I'm gonna cut out, okay? Seems like you two have a *thing* and I don't wanna—"

"No," I say forcefully, interrupting Brian. I lower Keane's phone to my lap, ashamed of myself. "Keane and I are just—"

Keane cuts me off. "Thanks, man," he says to Brian. "You're absolutely right—Maddy and I do have a *thing*—an awesome and amazing *thing*." Keane looks at me, his eyes smoldering. "A *thing* I'm not gonna fuck up ever again."

I clutch my chest, completely overwhelmed. Holy crap. What the heck on a Ritz cracker does that mean?

"You cool catching a ride home with him?" Brian asks me, but he's already rising from his chair.

I nod.

"I'll get her home safe and sound," Keane says. "Thanks."

"I'm sorry," I manage to say to Brian's back as he strides away.

But he's already gone.

I look at Keane, my breathing shallow, my cheeks hot. "You and I have a *thing*?" I whisper, barely able to get the words out.

"A fucking awesome *thing*," Keane replies.

"And you're not gonna... fuck it up ever again?"

Keane grins. "Watch the video, Maddy. I don't wanna steal my own thunder."

I take a deep breath, look down at the phone in my trembling hand, and cue the video—and, immediately, I'm met with the vision of Keane, shirtless and blue-haired, his muscles more ripped than ever, standing in a bathroom with Zander. Zander's holding an electric razor in one hand and his phone in the other, and he's recording both guys' reflections in the bathroom mirror.

"Hey everyone," Keane says, waving. "Welcome to another edition of 'Ball Peen Hammer's Guide to a Handsome and Happy Life.' You all know my best friend Zander? Say hi, Zander."

"Hi, Zander."

Keane runs his hand through his tousled blue hair and his bicep bulges with the effort. "Hey, lads-in-training, I get asked all kinds of questions in the comments to my videos, so today I thought I'd answer one of the most frequently asked: 'Hey, Ball Peen Hammer, why the fuck is your hair blue?'" Keane smiles at the camera like he's got a secret. "Well, guys, it's funny. Before today, I thought the full and complete answer to that question was this: I dyed it to help Zander bag the girl of his dreams. Basically, Z saw this girl in a bar and fell instantly in love with her ('cause, unlike me, Z has absolutely no problem with love at first sight), and, since Z's dream girl was thinking about dying *her* hair blue, Zander volunteered me to be her guinea pig." Keane shrugs. "At the time, I figured it was a no-brainer—anyone would dye their hair blue for their best friend to have a chance at love, right? Well, I've since learned, based on people's reactions to my hair, that 'normal' people apparently would *not* permanently dye their hair blue to help their best friend bag his dream girl. I know, crazy, right? What's wrong with these purportedly 'normal' people?"

I look up at Keane, confused about where this thing is headed.

"Keep watching," Keane says, motioning to the phone in my hand.

I look down again.

"So I've come to realize something: I'm not normal, guys. And that *epiphany* about myself, along with a well-timed conversation with my momma—thanks, Momma Lou—made me realize the bigger reason why I dyed my hair blue: because I believe in every man's pursuit of happiness. So if my best friend thinks he's found the girl of his dreams, the girl that's gonna make him handsome and happy all the livelong day, then I'm sure as hell gonna do whatever I can to help him bag that girl. He wants to hit a homerun in life, then I'm right there with him, cheering him on. Because I believe in swinging for the fences, guys. I admit I lost sight of that for a while, but I've figured it out again and I'm not gonna forget it. Guys, if you wanna be a handsome and happy lad, you gotta keep shooting for the major leagues, no matter what curve balls life throws at you. If you swing and miss or fall on your face, at least you can say you went out swinging, right? At least you'll have no regrets." Keane takes a deep breath in the video. "Which brings me to the reason Zander's holding that razor: it's time for me to swing for the fences, lads. That's right, I'm gonna take my shot at bagging the girl of *my* dreams this time."

Zander holds up the razor in the video.

"Oh man, guys, this dream girl of mine is smart, funny, sweet. She's *loyal*. Feisty. Creative. Talented. Easy to talk to. And, on top of all that, she's sexy as hell, too. Best I ever had, not even exaggerating, and I've had a lot." He winks. "I mean, seriously, what more could a guy want?"

I feel my cheeks burst with color.

"Don't forget she's adorbsicles, too," Zander says.

"She is," Keane confirms, pointing at Zander emphatically. "A cutie patootie, I'd even say."

"I called it," Zander says proudly. "She called you a 'jerksauce' and 'dickweed' and I knew she was adorbsicles."

"You totally called it, baby doll, right after you sent her an unsolicited dick-pic."

They high-five.

Keane looks at the camera again. "So now I'm sure you're wondering, 'Who the fuck is this amazing girl, Ball Peen Hammer? I wanna take a look-see to satisfy my curiosi-tay.' Well, sorry, guys, you can't see her. Because the funny thing about my girl and me is that, as much as I love being in front of the camera, my girl hates it. All my girl wants to do is be *behind* it and run the show, which is something she does like a boss, bee tee dubs."

"Ooooooh, did you just drop a *hint* about your girl's identity?" Zander asks.

"Whoa. I do believe I did," Keane says, smiling broadly. "I didn't even mean to do that. Ha! Just can't help myself, I guess." Keane's entire face lights up. "Okay, now that I've unintentionally let the cat outta the bag, I might as well tell you: my dream girl is none other than the beautiful, smart, funny, and sexy-as-hell Maddy Behind the Camera."

I lower the phone in my hand into my lap, my entire body trembling, and look at Keane.

Keane touches my hand and raises the phone back up, nonverbally instructing me to keep watching.

I look back down at the video, as instructed, but I can barely focus.

"Now, sadly, Maddy Behind the Camera doesn't know how I feel about her," Keane continues in the video. "She thinks I wanna be 'just friends' because that's what I stupidly told her when I last saw her—*because I'm a fucking idiot*."

Zander laughs. "And a dick."

"*And a dick.* That's right. But I've come to my senses. So, in just a bit, I'm gonna hop a flight to L.A. and do whatever I have to do to make my dream girl agree to be mine-all-mine-'til-the-end-o'-time." He motions to his hair in the bathroom mirror. "Which, of course, means this shit's got to go, son. Because a guy can't gallop into town on his white horse and try to swoop the girl of his dreams off her feet with hair he dyed to impress another man's woman."

I can't watch anymore—my heart's about to burst. I lower the phone to my lap and look into Keane's blazing eyes. "Keane," I breathe, my heart racing.

"I'm sorry, Maddy," Keane says, his face mere inches from

369

mine, his eyes burning. He slides his palms onto my cheeks, making me shudder at his touch. "I'm sorry I made you feel like you're anything less than my dream girl. You're amazing. Perfect. Incredible. *Beautiful*. And I'm a total and complete dick."

"You got the razor fired up, Z?" Keane's voice says in my lap. But I'm not paying attention to the video anymore.

"My heart's been aching without you," Keane says. "*Even worse than my balls.*"

I laugh.

Keane leans in as if to kiss me, but just before his lips press against mine, he stops short, his thumbs rubbing gently against my cheekbones. "I'm in love with you, Maddy Milliken," he whispers, his voice barely audible, his eyes on fire.

Emotion surges up inside me. "I'm in love with you, too, Keane Morgan," I whisper, barely able to choke out the unbelievable words.

Keane plants his soft, warm lips against mine, sending my body into a state of near-euphoria, just as the sound of a buzzing razor wafts out of the phone in my lap.

After a moment, Keane pulls away from our kiss, looking drunk. "I knew you wouldn't be able to resist my *ebullient* charm." He beams a smile at me.

I giggle. "Well, gosh. I'm only human, Keane."

"Let's get out of here, Honey Bunches of O's." He throws a bill onto the table, grabs my hand, and leads me out of the restaurant into the night. For a full block, we walk in silence, our hands clasped tightly, our chests heaving, making our way with purposeful strides toward my apartment five long and tortuous blocks away. "Oh my God," Keane breathes, his hand firmly intertwined with mine. "I do believe this right here is the granddaddy of all 'quiet moments of magic.'"

I feel like I'm floating down the sidewalk next to Keane, being propelled by wings on my back and a jet engine between my legs. "Best 'quiet moment of magic' *ever*," I reply.

Keane squeezes my hand. "You do realize I'm totally obsessed with you now, right?" he says. "You totally shoulda made me sign a waiver, brah. You're not gonna be able to get rid of me now."

I giggle and nuzzle my nose into Keane's shoulder as we walk, breathing in his delicious scent. "How long are you in town? Do we have time for a marathon sesh tonight?"

"Hell yeah. My return flight is tomorrow at noon." Keane grins. "But I'm only going home to pack up all my shit for the move next week." He abruptly stops walking, forcing me to do the same. "I'm moving to L.A., Maddy—I got offered the role of the token-white-guy in that all-black *Magic Mike* rip-off."

"Oh my God!" I throw my arms around Keane's neck, squealing and peppering his face with ecstatic kisses. "This is just the beginning for you, Keane. I *know* it is."

"I couldn't have done it without you, baby. The casting director said our videos were a huge part of why I got the job."

I'm panting with excitement. "Oh my God. I've got so many more ideas for videos I've been dying to tell you about. This is gonna be so fun. And I've got another product placement offer to tell you about, too."

Keane squeezes my hand. "Thank you for believing in me."

"Oh, I do. So, so much." I squeal again. "Where are you gonna live?"

"I'm gonna crash on my brother's couch 'til Zander can get down here."

I bite my lip. "No need to sleep on Dax's couch," I say coyly. "I'll give you a key. Sneak in to see me any time you like, hot stuff."

Keane grins. "I'll come see you every night, sweet cheeks."

"Please do, sugar lips."

We stare at each other, both of us grinning, the heat between us palpable, until Keane grabs my face and lays another kiss on me, this one full of heat. "We're peanut butter and chocolate, babe," he whispers, his eyes blazing. He lets out a long, tortured exhale. "Oh my fuck. My balls are *killing* me, woman. Come on." He takes my hand and pulls me down the sidewalk again, this time practically dragging me. "Is the sidewalk actually *lengthening* as we walk?" he asks, his voice strained.

"Just two more blocks. Tell your balls to stay strong and fight the good fight."

"Longest two blocks of my life. Oh my God, I'm gonna bone the fuck outta you Lionel Richie style while bonin' ya Justin Bieber style." He grunts loudly.

"Justin Bieber style?" I ask, practically jogging to keep up with Keane's loping strides.

371

"Yeah, now that we're official, I'm gonna throw the big guns at you."

"*Justin Bieber* is the 'big guns'?" I say, snorting with laughter. "Well, that's unexpected, I must say."

"Laugh all you want, baby doll, but you won't be laughing the minute I start bonin' the fuck outta ya Justin Bieber style."

I'm at a complete loss. My brain is scrolling through my limited knowledge of Justin Bieber song titles but nothing is making any sense. "Love Yourself?" I finally ask lamely. "That's his big hit right now, right?"

"Hell no, dude. That's all I've been doing exclusively for the past three weeks—'loving myself.' Fuck that shit."

I laugh. "Well, jeez, I don't know. I'm not a fan of The Biebs. The only other song of his I know is 'Baby'—and God help me if you mean that literally." I shudder.

"Oh, Jesus, no. Don't even joke about that." Keane stops walking and grins at me. "You really don't know?"

"Dude, I told you—I'm not a fan of The Biebs. You're just gonna have to tell me."

Keane flashes me his killer dimples. " '*Boyfriend*,'" he says, his eyes sparkling. "Doy-burgers, Mad Dog. I'm gonna bone ya boyfriend-style, Lionel Richie style."

"Ooooh," I say, returning Keane's huge smile. I can feel myself blushing. "Wow. I think Justin Bieber just became my all-time favorite artist."

Keane laughs and pulls me down the sidewalk again. "Come on, sweet meat. I'm *dying*. I'm a horse racing to the barn—a horse following the intoxicating scent of *cherries*."

"Oooh, are we gonna pop some more *cherries* tonight?"

"Hell yeah. His-and-hers cherries. I'm gonna pop my 'making love to my beautiful and smart girlfriend' cherry while you pop your 'getting boned to within an inch of your life by your handsome and happy boyfriend' cherry."

"Ooooh la la," I say, elation flooding me. "Oh, how I love cherries."

We walk for another long moment without speaking, our hands clasped tightly, our bodies warming each other in the cool night. When we reach the front of my apartment building, Keane squares himself in front of me on the sidewalk and levels me with his startling blue eyes.

"I got offered the reality show," he says matter-of-factly. "And I turned it down."

"What? Why? I thought you were really excited about that one."

Keane shrugs. "Turns out it just wasn't for me."

"Are you sure?"

Keane touches my hair and sighs. "I'm one hundred percent positive."

"Oh. Well, then, good for you. As long as you're happy."

"I am. *Elated*, I'd even say." His beautiful smile lights up the dark night.

"So am I," I say softly. "All the livelong day."

"You're awesome, Maddy. You know that?"

"Yeah, actually, I do."

Keane chuckles. "Good. Never forget it—and don't ever let some idiot-douche make you doubt it." He strokes my hair again. "I'm sorry I hurt you. I won't do it again, I promise."

"Oh, Keane," I say. I touch his cheek. "You can't promise that—no one can. We're only human, after all. Sometimes, we hurt each other. Just do your best and that's all anyone can do."

"God-*damn*, Maddy Milliken," Keane says, shaking his head. He lets out a long exhale, wraps his arms around me, and nuzzles his nose into my hair. "And that right there is why I love you the most."

Music Playlist for *Ball Peen Hammer*

"Love Don't Cost a Thing"— Jennifer Lopez
"Candy Shop" — 50 Cent
"Smack That" —Akon
"Pony" — Ginuwine
"Stressed Out" — twenty one pilots
"Trip Switch" — Nothing But Thieves
"Like Real People Do" — Hozier
"Blue Jeans" — Lana Del Rey
"Itch" — Nothing But Thieves
"Ain't No Sunshine" — Bill Withers
"Are You Gonna Be My Girl" — Jet
"Come As You Are" — Nirvana
"All Night Long" — Lionel Richie
"Boyfriend" — Justin Bieber

Acknowledgments

This book is dedicated to The Love Monkeys, my devoted and wonderful readers. Thank you for loving my characters as much as I do. Thank you to my Cuz and Baby Cuz for inspiring Keane-speak and for showing me every day that extremely cool dudes can also be affectionate and loving. What would I do without you boys in my life? I love you. Thank you to my entire family for all your support, love, and encouragement. You're all supes kewl. I love you. Thank you to my team. I couldn't do this without you. Thank you for believing in me and working so hard for me. And, finally, a special thank you to the talented and articulate male stripper in Los Angeles who spoke to me at length during my research. Your insights inspired me greatly in writing this book. Keep shaking that ass, son.

Author Biography

USA Today and internationally bestselling author Lauren Rowe lives in San Diego, California, where, in addition to writing books, she performs with her dance/party band at events all over Southern California, writes songs, takes embarrassing snapshots of her ever-patient Boston terrier, Buster, spends time with her family, and narrates audiobooks. Much to Lauren's thrill, her books have been translated all over the world in multiple languages and hit multiple domestic and international bestseller lists. To find out about Lauren's upcoming releases and giveaways, sign up for Lauren's emails at www.LaurenRoweBooks.com. Lauren loves to hear from readers! Send Lauren an email from her website, say hi on Twitter or Instagram @laurenrowebooks, and/or come by her Facebook page by searching Facebook for "Lauren Rowe Author."

Additional Books by Lauren Rowe

All books by Lauren Rowe are available in ebook, paperback, and audiobook formats.

The Morgan Brothers Books:

Enjoy the Morgan Brothers books in any order:

1. *Hero*. Coming March 12, 2018! This is the epic love story of heroic firefighter, **Colby Morgan,** Kat Morgan's oldest brother**.** After the worst catastrophe of Colby Morgan's life, will physical therapist Lydia save him ... or will he save her? This story takes place alongside Josh and Kat's love story from books 5 to 7 of *The Club Series* and also parallel to Ryan Morgan's love story in *Captain.*

2. *Captain.* A steamy, funny, heartfelt, heart-palpitating insta-love-to-enemies-to-lovers romance. This is the love story of tattooed sex god, **Ryan Morgan**, and the woman he'd move heaven and earth to claim. Note this story takes place alongside *Hero* and The Josh and Kat books from *The Club Series* (Books 5-7). For fans of *The Club Series,* this book brings back not only Josh Faraday and Kat Morgan and the entire Morgan family, but we also get to see in detail Jonas Faraday and Sarah Cruz, Henn and Hannah, and Josh's friend, the music mogul, Reed Rivers, too.

3. *Ball Peen Hammer.* A steamy, hilarious enemies-to-friends-to-lovers romantic comedy. This is the story of cocky as hell male stripper, **Keane Morgan**, and the sassy, smart young woman who brings him to his knees on a road trip. The story begins after *Hero* and *Captain* in time but is intended to be read as a true standalone in *any* order.

377

4. *Rock Star.* Do you love rock star romances? Then you'll want to read the love story of the youngest Morgan brother, **Dax Morgan,** and the woman who rocked his world, coming in 2018 (TBA)! Note Dax's story is set in time after *Ball Peen Hammer*. Please sign up for Lauren's newsletter at www.laurenrowebooks.com to make sure you don't miss any news about this release and all other upcoming releases and giveaways and behind the scenes scoops!

5. If you've started Lauren's books with The Morgan Brothers Books and you're intrigued about the Morgan brothers' feisty and fabulous sister, **Kat Morgan** (aka The Party Girl) and the sexy billionaire who falls head over heels for her, then it's time to enter the addicting world of the internationally bestselling series, *The Club Series.* Seven books about two brothers (**Jonas Faraday** and **Josh Faraday**) and the witty, sassy women who bring them to their knees (**Sarah Cruz** and **Kat Morgan**), *The Club Series* has been translated all over the world and hit multiple bestseller lists. Find out why readers call it one of their favorite series of all time, addicting, and unforgettable! The series begins with the story of Jonas and Sarah and ends with the story of Josh and Kat.

The Club Series (The Faraday Brothers Books)

If you've started Lauren's books with The Morgan Brothers books, then it's now time to enter the world of The Faradays. *The Club Series* is seven books about two brothers, Jonas and Josh Faraday, and the feisty, fierce, smart, funny women who eventually take complete ownership of their hearts: Sarah Cruz and Kat Morgan. *The Club Series* books are to be read in order*, as follows:

-*The Club* #1 (Jonas and Sarah)

-*The Reclamation* #2 (Jonas and Sarah)

-*The Redemption* #3 (Jonas and Sarah)

-*The Culmination* #4 (Jonas and Sarah with Josh and Kat)*

*Note Lauren intended *The Club Series* to be read in order, 1-7. However, some readers have preferred skipping over book four and heading straight to Josh and Kat's story in *The Infatuation* (Book #5) and then looping back around after Book 7 to read Book 4. This is perfectly fine because *The Culmination* is set three years after the end of the series. It's up to individual preference if you prefer chronological storytelling, go for it. If you wish to read the books as Lauren intended, then read in order 1-4.

-*The Infatuation* #5 (Josh and Kat, Part I)

-*The Revelation* #6 (Josh and Kat, Part II)

-*The Consummation* #7 (Josh and Kat, Part III)

In *The Consummation* (The Club #7), we meet Kat Morgan's family, including her four brothers, Colby, Ryan, Keane, and Dax. If you wish to read more about the Morgans, check out The Morgan Brothers Books. A series of complete standalones, they are set in the same universe as *The Club Series* with numerous cross-over scenes and characters. You do *not* need to read *The Club Series* first to enjoy The Morgan Brothers Books. **And all Morgan Brothers books are standalones to be read in *any* order.**

Does Lauren have standalone books outside the Faraday-Morgan universe? Yes! They are:

1. *Countdown to Killing Kurtis*—This is a sexy psychological thriller with twists and turns, dark humor, and an unconventional love story (not a traditional romance). When a seemingly naive Marilyn-Monroe-wanna-be from Texas discovers her porno-king husband has thwarted her lifelong Hollywood dreams, she hatches a surefire plan to kill him in exactly one year, in order to fulfill what she swears is her sacred destiny.

2. *Misadventures on the Night Shift*—a sexy, funny, scorching bad-boy-rock-star romance with a hint of angst. This is a quick read

and Lauren's steamiest book by far, but filled with Lauren's trademark heart, wit, and depth of emotion and character development. Part of Waterhouse Press's Misadventures series featuring standalone works by a roster of kick-ass authors. Look for the first round of Misadventures books, including Lauren's, in fall 2017. For more, visit misadventures.com.

3. *Misadventures of a College Girl*-a sexy, funny romance with tons of heart, wit, steam, and truly unforgettable characters. Part of Waterhouse Press's Misadventures series featuring standalone works by a roster of kick-ass authors. Look for the first second of Misadventures books, including Lauren's, in spring 2018. For more visit misadventures.com.

4. Look for Lauren's third *Misadventures* title, coming in 2018.

Be sure to sign up for Lauren's newsletter at www.laurenrowe books.com to make sure you don't miss any news about releases and giveaways. Also, join Lauren on Facebook on her page and in her group, Lauren Rowe Books! And if you're an audiobook lover, all of Lauren's books are available in that format, too, narrated or co-narrated by Lauren Rowe, so check them out!

87077950R00228

Made in the USA
Lexington, KY
20 April 2018